DAEMON

DAEMON

DANIEL SUAREZ

Quercus

First published in Great Britain in 2009 by

Quercus
21 Bloomsbury Square
London
WC1A 2NS

Published by arrangement with Dutton,
a member of the Penguin Group (USA) Inc.

A CIP catalogue record for this book is available
from the British Library

ISBN 978 1 84724 944 9

Printed and bound in Australia by Griffin Press

10 9 8 7 6 5 4 3 2 1

For Michelle
No more bedtime stories...

daemon (dē′mən) n—A computer program that runs continuously in the background and performs specified operations at predefined times or in response to certain events.

Condensed from "Disk and Execution MONitor"

Part One

Part One

Chapter 1:// Execution

Reuters.com/business

Matthew A. Sobol, PhD, cofounder and chief technology officer of **CyberStorm Entertainment (HSTM**—Nasdaq), **died today** at **age 34** after a prolonged battle with **brain cancer**. A pioneer in the $40 billion computer game industry, Sobol was the architect of CyberStorm's bestselling online games *Over the Rhine* and *The Gate*. CyberStorm CEO Kenneth Kevault described Sobol as "a tireless innovator and a rare intellect."

What the hell just happened? That was all Joseph Pavlos kept thinking as he clenched a gloved hand against his throat. It didn't stop the blood from pulsing between his fingers. Already a shockingly wide pool had formed in the dirt next to his face. He was on the ground somehow. Although he couldn't see the gash, the pain told him the wound was deep. He rolled onto his back and stared up at a stretch of spotless blue sky.

His usually methodical mind sped frantically through the possibilities—like someone groping for an exit in a smoke-filled building. He had to do something. Anything. But what? The phrase *What the hell just happened?* kept echoing in his head uselessly, while blood kept spurting between his fingers. Adrenaline surged through his system, his heart beat faster. He tried to call out. No good. Blood squirted several inches into the air and sprinkled his face. *Carotid artery . . .*

He was pressing on his neck so hard he was almost strangling himself. And he'd been feeling so good just moments before this. He remembered that much at least. His last debts repaid. At long last.

He was getting calmer now. Which was strange. He kept trying to remember what he'd been doing. What brought him here to this place. It seemed so unimportant now. His hand began to relax its hold. He could see plainly that there was no emergency. Because there was no logical scenario in which he would emerge from this alive. And after all, it was his unequaled talent for logic that had brought Pavlos so far in life. Had brought him halfway around the world. This was it. He'd already done everything he would ever do. His peripheral vision began to constrict, and he felt like an observer. He was calm now.

And it was in that cold, detached state that he realized: Matthew Sobol had died. That's what the news said. And then it all made sense to him. Sobol's game finally made sense. It was beautiful really.

Clever man . . .

Chapter 2:// Rogue Process

Thousand Oaks, California, had an overzealous, sanitary charm. They didn't build homes here. They manufactured them—a hundred identical Mediterranean villas at a stroke. Gated subdivisions named in every combination of "Bridge," "Haven," "Glen," and "Lake" covered the hillsides.

Upscale retail chains had embassies in the city center, and the service people drove in each day from vassal communities. Where the medieval city of Lyon had its Lane of Tanners, Southern California had its Vale of the Baristas and its Canyon of Firefighters and Rescue Personnel.

For average working folks, America was becoming a puzzle. Who was buying all these two-hundred-dollar copper saucepans, anyway? And how was everyone paying for these BMWs? Were people shrewd or just stupefyingly irresponsible?

Pete Sebeck thought television held some clues. Channel surfing late at night, unable to sleep, Sebeck considered the commercials aimed at him. Was he their demographic? Had they correctly deduced him? And what did that say about him? The History Channel seemed to think he was either a Korean War veteran looking for a truly capable brush mower, or that he was desperately in need of a career change. He had a nasty suspicion they were right about one of them.

The 101 freeway cut Thousand Oaks in two, but there really was no wrong side of the freeway. It had been named the safest small city in America, and as Detective Sergeant Peter Sebeck watched the tidy boulevards roll past his passenger window, he recalled why he and Laura moved here thirteen years ago—back when it was affordable; Ventura County was a great place to raise children. If you fucked up raising kids here, then God himself could not have helped you.

"Migraine, Pete?"

Sebeck turned to Nathan Mantz, who was looking at him with concern from the driver's seat. Sebeck barely shook his head. Mantz knew better than to pursue it.

Sebeck thought about the radio call from Burkow. It would certainly rattle a few country club gates. Sebeck and Mantz cruised through town with the strobes flashing but no siren. No need to alarm anyone. From his unmarked Crown Victoria, Sebeck watched the unsuspecting citizenry—the tax base on power walks. They'd have something to talk about tonight at Pilates class.

The Crown Vic descended into the undeveloped canyons just beyond the last subdivision wall. The scene wasn't difficult to find. An ambulance, three patrol units, and a few unmarked cars on the sandy shoulder of Potrero Road marked the location. Two deputy sheriffs stood near a closed steel gate flanked by chain-link fence stretching out in either direction.

Mantz rolled the cruiser into the driveway before the gate. Sebeck stepped from the car and turned to the nearest officer. "Coroner?"

"En route, Sergeant."

"Where's Detective Burkow?"

The deputy thumbed in the direction of a hole cut in the side of the chain-link fence.

Sebeck waited for Mantz, who was radioing in. Sebeck looked back at the deputy. "Let's get this gate open."

"Can't, Sergeant. It's got one of those remote-control locks built into it. There's nothing to cut."

Sebeck nodded as Mantz caught up to him.

"The property is owned by a local company—CyberStorm Entertainment. We got through to their people. They're sending someone down."

Sebeck moved through the hole in the fence, followed by Mantz. They marched along a dirt road winding among the chaparral on the canyon bottom. Soon they came to a crowd of EMTs and deputy sheriffs standing well back from a photographer. They were all shiny with sweat in the midday sun. The paramedics had a gurney, but no one was in a hurry. They turned as Sebeck and Mantz crunched across the dirt toward them. "Afternoon, gentlemen." A glance. "Ladies."

They mumbled greetings and parted to let Sebeck and Mantz pass.

Detective Martin Burkow, a corpulent man in his fifties with ill-fitting pants, stood on a mound of sandy soil at the edge of the road. Next to him the police photographer leaned forward to get an overhead shot of a body lying in the road. A pool of brownish, dried blood stretched out beneath it and traced dark rivulets downhill.

Sebeck gazed over the scene. A motocross motorcycle lay twenty yards down the road, on the side of a nearby hill. He could see where it had bounded into the left wall of the canyon and then rolled back across the dirt road.

Above the road, between him and the body, a taut steel cable stretched at neck level. The cable traversed the road at a forty-five-degree angle, closer on the left side, farther away on the right. Anything racing through here would grind down the cable like a saw blade. The cable was bloodstained for a good ten-foot length. The body lay ten yards beyond that. A motorcycle helmet five yards farther still.

Sebeck's eyes followed the thin steel cable rightward to a steel pole rising from the chaparral. Then leftward through the bushes. A freshly cut groove crossed the dirt roadway directly beneath the cable.

"Martin, what do we have?"

Detective Burkow coughed the consumptive cough of a lifelong smoker. "Hi, Pete. Thanks for coming down. Caucasian male, approximately thirty years old. A local walking his dog found the body about an hour ago. It was reported as a 10-54, but I thought I'd call you guys. This is looking more like a 187."

Sebeck and Mantz looked at each other and raised their eyebrows. Homicide. Rare in Thousand Oaks. The only killings down here were made in real estate.

The photographer nodded to Burkow and made his way back along the edge of the road. Burkow motioned for them to move forward. "Stick to the left, in the ruts. All the footprints are on the other side." He stepped down off the mound.

Sebeck and Mantz ducked under the cable and stood over the body. Sebeck was relieved to see the head still attached. The nearby helmet was empty. The dead man wore an expensive-looking motocross jumpsuit with logo patches. The yellow nylon was torn at chest level. It looked like he hit the cable with his torso, and it rode up to his throat. The man's larynx was slashed, and flies buzzed over the gaping wound. His skin was alabaster white, and his lusterless, dry eyes stared at Sebeck's shoes.

Sebeck pulled on rubber surgical gloves and leaned forward. He felt for a wallet or ID in the pockets. There didn't appear to be any. He looked ahead at the dirt bike, then back at the police photographer. "Carey, try to read the plates on the bike. Maybe we can ID this guy."

The photographer peered down the canyon, then affixed a 200mm lens to his camera and focused on the motorcycle.

Sebeck stood up, and his eyes once again traversed the cable behind them. He peered through the bushes where it disappeared. "Anybody know where this ends?"

The deputies and EMTs shook their heads.

"Nathan, let's follow this thing. Stay clear of it. And look for tracks." He turned back to Burkow. "Marty, what are all these footprints on the road?"

"The locals walk it all the time. I've already interviewed a few."

"Get me a cast of every unique print in this area." Sebeck waved his arms downward.

"That's gonna be a lot of prints."

"Tell forensics they don't have to cast the dog tracks."

Mantz grinned. "I don't know, I hear Pekinese are pretty smart."

Sebeck shot him a dark look and pointed at the bushes. The cable led through a gap in the hillside that opened up back onto Potrero Road. He and Mantz fanned out on either side and moved through the bushes while studying the sandy ground.

"Keep an eye out for rattlesnakes, Pete." Mantz jumped over a ditch of eroded soil.

The cable was easy to follow, and the groove in the soil beneath it shadowed it all the way. After sixty feet they were back at the chain-link fence on Potrero Road, staring at the back of a No Trespassing sign. The cable ran through the fence and into the back of a steel box two feet square sitting atop a thick pipe driven into the ground. The groove in the soil ended six feet away from the fence on their side. They had found no new footprints.

"Let's head to the other side."

———

In a few minutes they were back on Potrero Road at the gate. They walked a hundred yards down the shoulder and reached the front of the steel box. It had a sturdy lock in its face and was fashioned of welded steel. It had a few indentations where passing teens had taken potshots at it with rifles, but none had penetrated.

"Built to last." Sebeck peered around to a square hole in back where the cable entered. "Winch housing?"

Mantz nodded. "At first I thought it might be kids playing an evil prank. But this is a serious piece of engineering. What use could this thing serve?"

They turned as a Range Rover and a pickup truck pulled to the shoulder of the road near the gate. A couple of guys in khakis got out of the Rover. They spoke briefly with the deputies there, who pointed down to Sebeck and Mantz. The khakis climbed back into the Rover. Both vehicles rolled down the shoulder and stopped in front of the detectives, sending a choking cloud of dust over them.

The khakis got out again. The one on the passenger side came forward with his hand extended. He looked like money—business casual with creases. "Detectives. Gordon Pietro, senior legal counsel for CyberStorm Entertainment." They shook hands. Pietro pushed business cards on both of them. "This is our VP of public relations, Ron Massey."

Sebeck nodded. Massey had longer hair than Pietro and a pierced eyebrow with a gold ring. He was in his late twenties and looked like money, too. A pang of jealousy shot through Sebeck. The fact that he could effortlessly beat the shit out of this kid sprang unbidden into his mind. He pushed it back down. "This is Detective Mantz. I'm Detective Sergeant Sebeck, East Ventura County Major Crimes Unit."

Pietro stopped short. "Major Crimes Unit? We were told there was an accidental death on the property."

"The responding officers called us in. We're investigating this as a potential homicide." Sebeck leaned around Pietro and looked at the pickup truck parked behind the Rover. The pickup had a logo on the side door, illegible at this angle. "Who's in the truck?"

"Oh—a worker from the management firm. They maintain the property. He has a remote for the front gate."

"Let's get him out here. I want to talk to him."

Pietro walked back, motioning to the guy in the truck.

Sebeck turned to Massey. "What's this property used for?"

"CyberStorm purchased the land as an investment. It's also used by the company for campouts, team-building exercises, things like that."

Sebeck took out a pad and pen. "So you're the PR guy? What's CyberStorm Entertainment do, Ron?"

"We're a leading computer game developer. Ever hear of *Over the Rhine*?"

"No."

Burkow shouted from down near the gate. "Pete. I got a name from the DMV. The bike's registered to a Joseph Pavlos. Lives up in those McMansions on the hilltop."

Massey put a hand to his chin. "Oh man."

"You know the victim?"

"Yeah. He's one of our senior developers. What happened?"

Sebeck gestured with his pen. "He hit this cable with his neck. Do you know if he rode down here regularly?"

"I don't, but his development team might."

Pietro returned with a Mexican man in his forties dressed in a green jumpsuit. The guy looked like he'd had a tough life—and that he expected it to get a lot tougher any second.

"Ron? Pav was the one killed?"

Massey nodded and produced a cell phone. "Damn this canyon. Can't get a signal."

Pietro produced his phone for a bar-count contest. "What service do you use? I have two bars."

Sebeck butted in. "You are?"

Pietro turned back to him. "This is Haime."

"What's your full name, Haime?"

"Haime Alvarez Jimenez, señor."

"Can I see some identification, Mr. Jimenez?"

"What's going on?"

"There's been a fatality. Can I have that ID, please?"

Haime looked at Pietro and Massey, then dug into his pocket for his wallet. He found his driver's license and held it out to Sebeck. Its leading edge quivered noticeably.

A slight smile creased Sebeck's face. "Haime, did you kill this guy?"

"No, sir."

"Then relax." He took the ID and examined it.

Haime pointed at the steel box. "I close a ticket on this winch today. I just turn a key. Like it says on the work order."

"Where's the work order?"

"On the Pocket PC in my truck."

"Do you have the key to this winch housing?"

Haime nodded and produced a bar-code-labeled key chain with three keys.

"You activated this winch today? What time?"

"About nine, nine-thirty. I can tell you exactly from the work order."

Sebeck motioned for the keys, then used them to unlock the housing. He flipped it open with the tip of his pen. Inside, there was an electric winch with another keyhole in its face.

"What's the third key for?"

"Manual override for the front gate."

"So you turned the key. The winch activated and pulled the cable . . ." Sebeck leaned over, ". . . out of the ground."

"No, señor. No cable. Just the winch motor."

The others rolled their eyes in unison.

"Haime, if you were sent by your company to do this, then you don't have much to worry about. What's the purpose of this winch, anyway?"

Haime shrugged. "I not run it before."

"Can you get me that work order?"

"Yes, sir." Haime scurried toward his truck.

Pietro was looking down the length of the cable. "What exactly happened, Detective Sebeck?"

"Someone built this winch and the housing, then buried a steel cable in the soil. Running the winch stretched the cable across the dirt road at neck level."

The two CyberStorm representatives looked confused.

Pietro put a hand to his chin. "Are you sure that it's not a . . . like a chain across the road?"

"Why bury it? Why do it at all when you have a steel gate at the entrance?"

Pietro was at a loss.

Haime returned and pushed his Pocket PC into Sebeck's face. He shadowed the screen with his callused hand and pointed to the work order displayed there. "See, it says 'Run the antenna-lifting winch until it stop.'"

Sebeck took the handheld computer and with Mantz studied the data fields on-screen. "Nathan, we're going to need a search warrant for the property management firm. Put their office under surveillance until we get a team over there. Also, get me a case number, and get me Burkow's notes. I'm taking over the investigation. Everything goes through me from this point forward." He looked up at Haime. "Haime, we're going to want to chat with you at the sheriff's station."

"Señor, I didn't do anything."

"I know, Haime. That's why you want to cooperate while we arrange a search warrant for your employer."

Pietro interposed himself. "Detective Sebeck—"

"Counselor, this cable assembly was maintained by your property management firm—which would indicate they had prior knowledge of it. Would you prefer to make CyberStorm the responsible party, or does CyberStorm want to cooperate with my investigation?"

Pietro pursed his lips, then turned to Haime. "Haime, don't worry. Go with them. Do everything they say. Tell them everything you know."

"I don't know anything, Señor Pietro."

"I know that, Haime. But I think it best that you do what Detective Sebeck says."

"I am a U.S. citizen. Am I under arrest?"

Sebeck looked to Mantz. Mantz stepped in. "No, Haime. We're just gonna talk. You can leave the pickup truck here. We'll take care of that." Mantz motioned for Haime to move toward the patrol cars and started escorting him away.

Pietro nodded to Massey. "Detective Sebeck, we'll contact your office for a copy of the police report. You know where to reach me." Both men climbed back into the Range Rover and sped off, perhaps to find a better wireless signal.

Sebeck looked along the length of cable. Would someone really have built this just to kill a person? He could think of easier ways to kill someone.

He clamped back a smile. This wasn't a murder-suicide or a botched drug deal. It might actually be a premeditated killing. Was it wrong to hope so? Accident or murder, the victim was dead. Nothing would change that. So what was wrong with hoping it was murder?

Pondering this, Sebeck turned and walked back to the front gate.

Chapter 3:// Black Box

Sebeck, Mantz, and three county deputies crowded around a Post-it-note-slathered computer monitor in the cubicle of a nondescript company, in a generic office park in Thousand Oaks. Tractor-trailers hissed by on the freeway just beyond the thin stucco walls, but the officers were intent, leaning over the shoulders of Deputy Aaron Larson, the County Sheriff's only computer fraud specialist.

Larson was in his late twenties with an air of military orderliness—buzz-cut hair, athletic build, and a square jaw. He had a boyish enthusiasm for ferreting out larceny. At such times he'd smile and shake his head in slow-motion disbelief over what people thought they could get away with.

Larson's computer screen scrolled rows of text. "This log lists IP addresses making connections to their server. Notice that we've got a number of connections at around the time our target work ticket was created."

He alt-tabbed over to a custom property management program. "I spoke with the secretary, and she said they're able to accept work tickets from clients through a secure Web page."

Sebeck nodded. "So the request didn't necessarily come from this office."

"Right." Larson flipped back to the custom application. "The *Requestor* field, here, claims the ticket was submitted by this Chopra Singh person at CyberStorm Entertainment. But wait—that's not where the connection actually originated."

Larson minimized all the windows except the Web log. He highlighted a single line. "This was the connection that created the work order. When I do a Whois lookup on the IP address . . ." He switched screens. "Voilà."

A Whois lookup page displayed the domain as owned by Alcyone Insurance Corporation of Woodland Hills, California.

Sebeck read the small type. "Then the work order originated from this company in Woodland Hills."

"Maybe. Maybe not."

"You think the address was spoofed?"

"The only way to find out is to get a warrant for their Web logs."

Another deputy entered the cramped office. "Sergeant, there's a news van outside."

Sebeck waved him off and kept his gaze on Larson. "So no one in this management firm created the work order that killed Pavlos?"

"Seems unlikely."

Sebeck eyed the screen. "Is this sort of Internet work order system typical for a hole-in-the-wall company like this?"

Larson shook his head slowly and smiled. "No, it's not. This is pretty slick. The office manager said their parent company developed it for them. You'll never guess who the parent company is."

"CyberStorm Entertainment."

Larson touched his finger to his nose. "Very good, Sergeant."

Just then the radios crackled to life again. Sebeck turned to listen.

"Units in vicinity of Westlake. 10-54 at 3000 Westlake Boulevard reported. Be advised, 10-29h. 11-98 with building security."

Sebeck exchanged looks with the other officers. Another dead body had been found. "What the hell . . ."

The address tugged at Sebeck's memory. He pulled Gordon Pietro's business card out of his pocket. At least his memory hadn't failed him; the new body had been found at CyberStorm Entertainment.

As far as Sebeck could tell, entertainment companies came in two flavors: shady operations skirting tax, drug, and racketeering laws, and phenomenally successful corporate empires wielding immense influence worldwide. There was very little middle ground, and the transformation from one to the other seemed to happen in the wee hours. With signage rights on a ten-story office building, CyberStorm had evidently made that transformation.

The latest body had been found in a security vestibule—a tiny room controlling access to what the employees called a server farm. The small entry chamber reminded Sebeck of an air lock. The server farm was filled with rack-mounted servers—their LEDs flickering away in the semidarkness of emergency lights. Through the glass Sebeck could make out several employees moving about. They were still monitoring the machines.

It was hard to see them clearly because the vestibule windows were fogged with a yellowish film—residue from burning human fat. The victim had been electrocuted in dramatic fashion.

Sebeck stood in the dim glow of emergency lights alongside the building's chief operating engineer, CyberStorm's network services director, county paramedics, a city power company foreman, and the president and CEO of CyberStorm, Ken Kevault.

Kevault was in his late thirties, tall and lean with spiky hair. His black, short-sleeve silk shirt revealed death skull tattoos on his forearms, and he had the sort of deep tan and wrinkles one gets after years of surfing. He looked more like an aging rock star than a corporate executive. He hadn't said a word since they arrived.

Sebeck turned to the power and light foreman. "The primary power's been cut?"

The building engineer responded instead. "Yes, sir."

Sebeck turned to him. "Then those computers are running on backup power?"

"Right."

"Let's get that room evacuated."

"There's another exit like this one, but it could be just as dangerous. I told the techs to stay put for now."

Sebeck nodded. "Who can tell me what happened?"

The engineer and network services director looked to each other. The engineer already had the floor. "About a half hour ago, one of the CyberStorm guys was electrocuted going through the inner security door. I don't know how it's possible, but the techs said he was standing there with smoke coming off his shoulders for about thirty seconds before he keeled over. And there he is."

Kevault let out a hiss of disgust and shook his head ruefully.

Sebeck ignored him. "The CyberStorm guys? So you're not a Cyber-Storm employee?"

The engineer shook his head. "No, I work for the building owner."

"And who owns the building?"

Eyes shifted from person to person for a moment or two until Kevault spoke up. "It's part of a real estate investment trust, with a majority share held by CyberStorm."

Sebeck turned back to the engineer. "So you are a CyberStorm employee."

Kevault interposed again. "No, the trust is not the same legal entity as CyberStorm, and the trust outsources the engineering, security, and other building functions."

Sebeck could already imagine lawyers pointing fingers at each other for the next decade. "Forget that. Has anyone entered or left the scene since the incident?"

All the men shook their heads.

"Are there electrical blueprints for this entryway? Any recent unpermitted modifications I should know about?"

An edge crept into the lead engineer's voice. "We don't do unpermitted construction here. All this equipment was signed off on by the city and fire inspectors two years ago, and we have the occupancy permit to prove it."

The guy looked to be about fifty. A broad-shouldered Latino with a marine corps tattoo on his forearm. Sebeck figured this guy wasn't going to take any shit. He watched as the engineer moved to a flat-paneled workstation on a nearby desk and spun the panel to face them all. In a moment, the engineer brought up a 3-D map of their location. The map was a series of clean vector lines in primary colors.

The engineer tapped keys, highlighting a colored layer to emphasize each word. "Plumbing, HVAC, Fire/Safety, Electrical."

The image zoomed in. It was like a video game with transparent walls. They were now looking at a computer image of the vestibule, and Sebeck could see the yellow electrical lines running down through the door frame to the combination magstripe/keypad in the door's strike plate.

No wonder the engineer had an attitude. He had every damned screw modeled in 3-D.

"There's no power source in that wall sufficient to electrocute a man like that, and even if there was, the breakers should have tripped. There's a short somewhere. Probably to a trunk line. Maybe it electrified the door frame."

The power company guy leaned in. "What's going into the server farm? Three-phase 480?"

"Yeah, but it's coming up through the floor. There's a trunk line running through a vertical penetration. The decking was reinforced to hold the weight of the racks, and there's a fiber backbone—"

"Gentlemen." Sebeck stepped between them. "I need all nonemergency personnel evacuated from CyberStorm's office space. Nathan, I want an outer perimeter established at all stairwell and elevator entrances. We set up command and control in this area just outside the vestibule. I want interviews from everyone evacuated."

The network director turned to Sebeck. "We have five floors in this building. Is it really necessary to evacuate them all?"

"Two of your coworkers are dead today from unrelated 'accidents.' I find that an implausible coincidence."

The network director's face contorted. "Two?"

"That's correct. I'll let your illustrious leader fill you in."

The CyberStorm folks turned to the company president. Kevault was gnawing on his fingernails in irritation or concentration—it was hard to tell which. He finally spoke without looking at anybody. "Lamont, switch over to the mirror site. Then evacuate the office."

Sebeck leveled a gaze. "You'll evacuate the building *now*. If you have any illusions about who's in charge here, I can give you a time-out in the county lockup."

Kevault was about to speak but thought better of it. He just marched off down the hall. His people followed.

Sebeck nodded to Mantz, who pursued Kevault like a Rottweiler going after a toddler.

Sebeck grabbed the network services director, who was also leaving. "Not you. You're staying here."

———

Sebeck had seen his share of fatal accidents in fourteen years with the department, and he knew that workplace fatalities drew paperwork like blowflies to a corpse. OSHA inspectors, insurance investigators, reporters, lawyers, and building management—all were waiting in the wings. But for now, Sebeck posted deputies to keep nongovernmental and nonessential personnel out of his crime scene.

The main power was off, and they established radio communications to monitor a lockout on the DWP power vault.

After running a few tests with a voltmeter, the engineer and power company foreman determined that the door frames were not electrified.

They instructed the data center employees to open the second exit and let the police and firemen in. They then evacuated the techs. The crime scene was now free of civilians.

Sebeck was surprised at how warm and stuffy the room had become. The AC hadn't been off all that long. He glanced around at the dozens of rack-mounted computers clicking away. That was a lot of BTUs. That's probably why they had an entry vestibule—to keep the cold air in. He turned to the engineer. "What are these machines for, anyway?"

"People playing games with each other over the Internet. My grandson plays."

Sebeck had heard of this sort of thing. He had no idea it involved so much hardware. It looked expensive.

They moved to the inner security door. The victim lay just beyond the glass, and they got their first good look at him. As a patrolman, Sebeck had seen the carnage of a hundred car wrecks, but the network director lost it and excused himself. As Sebeck suspected, the engineer wasn't much affected.

"That poor son of a bitch."

A Vietnam vet, Sebeck thought.

It was hard to reconcile the human resources photo with the remains that lay before them. The victim's face was distorted in agony—or at least the involuntary muscle spasms of electrocution. His eyeballs hung out over the cheeks. His hair had mostly burned off his head. His whole face was blistered, but Sebeck already knew who it was: a lead programmer named Chopra Singh—the name on the spoofed Potrero Canyon work order.

There was no longer any doubt that these were murders. He just had to find the evidence.

Sebeck had the power company foreman test the door with a voltmeter again just to be sure and then moved aside for nearby firemen, who pushed into the vestibule. The stench of burnt flesh and hair hit them, sending groans and gasps through the team. "Carey, get some video."

The photographer moved in, and bright light filled the space. Afterward, the paramedics confirmed the obvious—the victim was deceased. The vestibule was too small for both the body and the investigators, so they scanned the scene from the narrow doorway. Unlike most murder scenes, Sebeck thought, the victim's body wouldn't contain much evidence, so he didn't start there. Instead, he had it covered with a plastic tarp and brought back the power company foreman. "I need to find out what electrified this door, and I need to find out fast."

"There's no danger, Sergeant. The power's off in the whole building."

"I'm not worried about just this building."

The foreman paused for a moment to digest that and then nodded gravely.

Soon Sebeck and the foreman crowded into the open doorway just above the now covered body. It was far from ideal, but Sebeck felt time was of the essence. The doorjamb looked normal, but after unscrewing the strike plate, the foreman got a crowbar into the aluminum frame and pried off the cover with a resounding crack. What it concealed looked strange even to Sebeck.

A small wire ran up the inside of the door frame from the floor and into the back of the keypad and magstripe reader. But another, much thicker wire ran down from the ceiling and was bolted with copper leads to the frame itself.

Sebeck looked to the power company foreman. "I don't remember that on the engineer's blueprint."

The foreman moved in alongside. "That's 480 cable. You could power an industrial grinder with that."

Sebeck pointed up at the ceiling.

Fiberglass ladders were brought in along with head-mounted lights. Soon they pushed up through the drop ceiling and into the plenum. Their lights revealed fire coating sprayed over the steel beams and metal decking of the floor above. HVAC ducts and bundles of cables traversed the space.

It was here that they found the black box. At least that's what it looked like—a black metal housing into which the 480-volt line fed before running back out the far side. A thin, gray cable also led into the black box.

Sebeck focused his light beam, tracing the various lines from their vanishing points in the darkness. "All right, that's as far as we go."

It took the bomb squad two hours to clear the scene. When they finally gave the all-clear, more ladders were brought in and more ceiling tiles removed until Sebeck, Mantz, Deputy Aaron Larson, and the county's lead bomb technician, Deputy Bill Greer, were able to convene a precarious meeting with their heads poking through the drop ceiling around the now opened black box.

Greer was a serene forty-year-old who might as well have been teaching a cooking class as he flipped up his blast helmet visor and pointed to the metal cover in his hand. "Fairly standard project enclosure." He gestured to the open base, still bolted to the HVAC duct. The 480-volt wire led through a cluster of circuit boards and smaller wires. "This is basically a switch, Sergeant. Whoever set this up could electrify the door frame through this box."

Larson pointed to a network port in the side of the black box, then traced his finger to a smaller circuit board attached to it. "Check this out: it's a Web server on a chip. It's got a tiny TCP/IP stack. They're used for controlling devices like doors and lights from an IP network. I checked. They've got them all over the building." Larson slid his hand along a CAT-5 cable extending from the board into the darkness. "This box is linked to their network, and their network is connected to the Internet. It's conceivable that someone with the right passwords could have activated this switch from anywhere in the world."

"Could the switch be set to activate when a certain person swiped their access card at the security door?"

"Probably. I just don't know enough about these cards yet."

"How long has the switch been here?"

Greer looked at the back of the enclosure. "It was covered in dust when we got to it."

"So that vestibule door has probably been used thousands of times without incident—then suddenly today it kills someone. We need to find out if Singh has ever been in this data center."

Larson jotted serial numbers down from the circuit board. "We can review their access logs. And there are security cameras."

Sebeck was shaking his head. It was too complex. They were all just guessing now. He stared at the switch for a moment more. "Gentlemen, I think it's time to call in the FBI. No offense, Aaron, but we just don't have the capabilities to deal with this."

By early evening, Sebeck stood near the building entrance flanked by Mantz and a uniformed deputy. A frenetic pack of reporters surrounded them, microphones pushed forward into a multicolored mass of foam rubber. Camera lenses glinted in the rear while reporters shouted questions.

Sebeck motioned for silence until all he heard was the nearby generators on the satellite trucks. "This is what we know right now. At approximately eleven thirty this morning, the body of Joseph Pavlos, an employee of CyberStorm Entertainment, was discovered in a canyon off Potrero Road in Thousand Oaks. At approximately two P.M., a second CyberStorm employee was electrocuted in what we now know to be a deliberate act. We are withholding the identity of the second victim pending notification of next of kin. We also believe Mr. Pavlos's death was a homicide and have requested assistance from the FBI."

Shouted questions erupted again. Sebeck motioned for silence. "It appears these employees were specifically targeted, and we have no reason to believe that the general public is in any danger. I caution CyberStorm employees to be particularly vigilant and to report suspicious objects or packages to the police. I'll take questions now."

The parking lot erupted in shouting.

Sebeck pointed to an Asian woman. He'd have to admit that he chose her first because she was drop-dead gorgeous.

"Sergeant, you said you're bringing in the FBI. That means there's more to the case than the two murders?"

"The FBI has the resources and jurisdiction required to properly investigate this case."

Another reporter spoke up. "Can you describe precisely how the victims were killed?"

"We can't divulge precise methods at this time."

"Can you give us a rough idea?"

Sebeck hesitated. "At least one of the victims appears to have been murdered through the Internet."

A buzz went through the press corps. That was their sound bite.

"That's all we're prepared to say right now."

Chapter 4://God of Mischief

From his vantage point at a coffeehouse, Brian Gragg gazed across the street at the darkened windows of a French provincial mansion. The lush River Oaks section of Houston's Inner Loop had more than a few of these aging beauties, restored and pressed into service as quaint professional buildings. They sheltered doctors' offices, architectural firms, law firms—and branch offices of East Coast stockbrokers. It was this last species of suburban tenant that attracted Gragg. They were the weakest link in a valuable chain.

One of the brokers there had installed a wireless access point in his office but failed to change the default password and SSID. Better yet, the broker couldn't be bothered to shut his machine off at night.

Gragg glanced down at his own laptop and adjusted a small Wi-Fi antenna to point more directly at the office windows. The broker's computer screen was displayed as a window on Gragg's laptop. Gragg had compromised the workstation days ago, first obtaining a network IP address from the router, and then gaining access to the broker's machine through the most basic of NetBIOS assaults. The ports on the workstation were wide open, and over the course of several evening visits to the café, Gragg had escalated his privileges. He now owned their local network. Clearing the router's log would erase any evidence that he had been there.

But all that was child's play compared to how he would use this exploit. In the past year, Gragg had evolved beyond simple credit card scams. He no longer prowled bars passing out portable magstripe readers to waiters and busboys and paying a bounty for each credit card number. Gragg now stole identities. His buddy, Heider, had schooled him on the intricacies of spear-phishing. It opened up a whole new world.

Gragg was using the broker's workstation to conduct an e-mail campaign to the firm's clientele. He had cribbed the phony marketing blather and graphics from the brokerage's own Web site, but what the e-mail said was irrelevant. Gragg's goal was that the phish merely view the message. That was all it took.

Gragg's e-mail contained a poisoned JPEG of the brokerage logo. JPEGs were compressed image files. When the user viewed the e-mail, the operating system ran a decompression algorithm to render the graphic on-screen; it was this decompression algorithm that executed Gragg's malicious script and let him slip inside the user's system—granting him full access. There was a patch available for the decompression flaw, but older, rich folks typically had no clue about security patches.

Gragg's script also installed a keylogger, which gave him account and password information for virtually everything the user did from then on, sending it to yet another compromised workstation offshore where Gragg could pick it up at leisure.

What sort of idiot hung the keys to his business out on the street—and more than that, broadcast a declaration from his router telling the world where the keys were? These people shouldn't be left home alone, much less put in charge of people's investments.

Gragg cleaned up the router's connection log. More than likely the scam wouldn't be detected for months, and even then, the company probably wouldn't tell their clients. They'd just close the barn door long after the Trojan horses were gone.

So far, Gragg had a cache of nearly two thousand high-net-worth identities to sell on the global market, and the Brazilians and Filipinos were snapping up everything he offered.

Gragg knew he had a survival advantage in this new world. College was no longer the gateway to success. Apparently, people thought nothing of hanging their personal fortunes on technology they didn't understand. This would be their undoing.

Gragg finished his mocha latte and glanced around the coffeehouse. Teens and kids in their early twenties. They had no idea he was raking in more than their corporate executive fathers. He looked like any other punk with long sideburns, a goatee, a winter cap, and a laptop. He was the kid you didn't notice because you were sick of looking at him.

Gragg shut down his laptop and pulled a bootable flash drive from one USB port. He took a pair of needle-nose pliers and crushed the tiny drive like a walnut, tossing the pieces into a nearby trash can. The evidence was now destroyed. His laptop hard drive contained nothing but evangelical tracts. In the event of trouble, he would look like Jesus's number one fan.

Just then his cell phone played the *Twilight Zone* theme song. Gragg tapped the wireless headphone in his ear. "Jason. Where you at, man?"

"Corporate restaurant #121. I'm just about done. What's your ETA?"

Gragg glanced at his watch. A Tag Heuer. "About thirty minutes."

"Don't be late. Hey, I logged sixteen more open APs uptown at lunch."

"Put 'em on the map."

"Already done."

"I'm on my way. Meet me out back."

Gragg glanced around at people getting into their leased cars to drive back to bank-owned homes. They were cattle. He viewed these oblivious drones with contempt.

———

Gragg headed "uptown" to Houston's West Loop—a cluster of sky-scrapers just west of the city center that served as a sort of second sky-line for people who felt the first one was too far away. Gragg's partner, Jason Heider, worked as a bartender in a corporate chain restaurant in the Galleria—close by the indoor ice rink.

Heider was thirtyish but looked older. Back during the tech boom, he'd been some sort of vice president at a dot-com. Gragg met Heider in an IRC chat room dedicated to advanced cracking topics—authoring buffer overruns, algorithms for brute force password cracking, software vulnerability detection, that sort of thing. Heider knew what he was talking about, and before long they were dividing the work required to eavesdrop on Wi-Fi in airports and coffeehouses, stealing corporate logons where possible. They both shared a keen interest in technol-ogy and information—the tools of personal power. Heider had taught Gragg a lot in the last year. But nothing lately.

Also there was Heider's recklessness. Heider had recently lost his license from a DUI and almost sunk them both by having his laptop in the car at the time. Gragg was starting to watch him more carefully and disliked leaving him alone on a Saturday night for fear his indiscretions would get them both arrested. Fortunately, Gragg had never confided his real name to Heider.

Gragg reached the mall parking lot and circled around the bland tiers of stucco. He parked near the west entrance and waited. Heider eventually straggled out to the parking lot with a cigarette hanging out of his mouth. It was a cold autumn night, and Heider's breath smoked whether he was exhaling smoke or not. He wore a surplus M-65 jacket that had seen better days. The guy looked particularly pathetic as he trudged toward Gragg's car. Gragg thought it would be a mercy to run him down. Heider was a shadow of himself—as he often admitted. He took a last puff of his cigarette, tossed it, and got into the car.

"Hey, Chico. Where's the rave?"

Gragg gave him a once-over. "You carrying?"

"No, man. Well, just some crank."

"Jase, dump that shit out now, or you can walk the fuck home for all I care. I've got a gig tonight, and I don't need a canine unit giving the cops probable cause."

"Christ, would you relax?"

"I don't relax. I stay focused. Friends don't let friends do drugs— especially when those friends can turn state's evidence."

"All right, man. Enough. I get the fucking idea." Heider turned the dome light switch off, then opened the car door and tossed a small zip-lock bag onto the asphalt.

Gragg started the car and pulled away. "Your brain is your only valuable tool, Jase. If you keep trashing it, you'll be worthless to me."

"Oh, fuck off. If I had a stroke and sniffed glue, I'd wind up with your IQ. I mean, you spend all day watching hentai and playing video games. How smart can you be?"

Video games was an oversimplification; Gragg played massively multi-player online games, or MMOGs, and as he stared coolly at his partner, it occurred to him that the games' complex societies contained far more social stimulation than anything that existed in Heider's world. All the more reason for what was to come.

Gragg turned up the stereo to an Oakenfold mix and drowned out Heider's voice.

He drove out to the Katy Freeway and headed west, exiting onto State Highway 6 North about ten miles out of Houston. Highway 6 was a bleak four-lane stretch of concrete running through marshy ground and wide prairie fields bordered by walls of trees—remnants of an agrarian past. Now the only growth was in strip malls, subdivisions, and office parks, sprouting like bunches of grapes off the vine of highway and separated by long stretches of nothing useful.

Gragg glowered at the road. He hadn't said a word in ten minutes.

Heider just watched him. "What's with you tonight?"

"The fucking Filipinos. They posted a message telling me to meet them."

"What for?"

"To pick up a new encryption key."

"In person?"

"They're trying to keep the Feds off their tail."

"Fuck that. Sell the data to the Brazilians, man."

"The Filipinos owe me for five hundred identities already. If I don't pick up the code, I don't get paid."

"What a pain in the ass. Last time we do business with them."

Gragg flipped open his cell phone and started keying a text message while driving. He spoke to Heider without looking at him. "We've got less than forty minutes to showtime. The Filipinos can wait."

————

In a deserted cul-de-sac of an under-construction subdivision, half a dozen cars sat in the darkness. Knots of teenagers drank and smoked on their car hoods, laughing, arguing, or staring at the distant glow of the freeway. The pounding bass beat of rap music thudded into the cold night air from several car stereos all tuned to the same satellite radio channel. It reverberated in their chests as they threw rocks, shattering the newly installed windows of half-built homes. One kid zipped from car to car on a motorized scooter.

They were a racially mixed group, mostly white, but with Asian, black, and Hispanic kids here and there. Their cars displayed their social class; a Mustang GT convertible with eighteen-inch chrome rims; late-model SUVs with vanity plates; Mom's BMW. Economic class, not race, was the glue that bound them.

A cell phone somewhere began a faint MIDI of *Eine kleine Nachtmusik*, and every girl in the group groped for her phone. The alpha girl—a thin, sexy blonde with low-cut denims and a midriff top despite the cold—clucked her tongue at the others. "Y'all stole my ring." She read the text message. "Austin! Guys, turn down the music!"

Stereos were quickly muted.

Alpha girl used her best cheerleader voice to project the coordinates: "29.98075, and -95.687274. Everybody got that?" She repeated the coordinates while several others keyed them into GPS receivers.

An athletically built African American kid and his buddies stared at the console of his Lexus SUV. He keyed in the coordinates, and a graphical map appeared on the GPS's LCD. "Tennet Field. It's closed down. My dad used to have his plane there. Let's roll!"

A dozen kids paused to text-message the coordinates to still other friends. The smart mob was forming and would be en route in minutes.

Gragg strode the tarmac in the pale moonlight, heading toward the dark silhouette of Hangar Two.

The radio crackled in his head. He wore a bone-conduction headset. It was capable of projecting sound directly into his skull, regardless of the noise in his surrounding environment. It was a useful tool for managing a for-profit rave. The radio crackled again. "Unit 19 to Unit 3, do you copy?"

Gragg touched his receiver. "Unit 3. Talk to me."

"The Other White Meat headed south on Farmington. Range two-point-three miles."

Unit 3 was a lookout placed on the east perimeter with night vision goggles. Gragg saw headlights turning into the main airport entrance. "Unit 20, Zone One is a blackout area."

"10-4, Unit 3."

The headlights soon went out.

Signature control was a never-ending battle for a prairie rave. Lines of car headlights were the enemy.

Gragg followed the thick generator cables running from the machine shop, past the parking lot, and up to the main hangar doors, where a subsonic bass beat rumbled, threatening to detach his retinas. A long roll of black Duvateen hung down at the entrance, blocking the light and some of the noise within.

A line of a hundred or so teens hooted and hollered at the entrance, while a dozen heavyset thugs in SECURITY windbreakers flanked the opening. The bouncers collected twenty dollars from everybody at the door and then slipped an RFID-equipped neck badge around each teen's neck. Once tagged like cows, the patrons then proceeded through the metal detectors and into the main hangar. Each guard was equipped with a Taser and pepper spray to quickly subdue and remove those inclined to disrupt the party. Dozens more patrolled the party inside.

Gragg ran a tight operation, and for this reason he was always in demand by rave promoters. Tonight's promoter, a young Albanian drug dealer named Cheko, stalked the tarmac nervously. But then again, he did everything nervously.

Gragg sniffed the night air, then walked past the bouncers into the head-pounding madness that was the rave. He pushed through the crowd of youths. Although he was several years older than most of them, Gragg was of slimmer build and shorter stature. His lip piercing and arm tats gave him a menacing blue-collar appearance—but if anyone looked closely, the tattoos depicted entwined CAT-5 cable.

Gragg looked up at the DJ tower, flickering in the strobing laser light. Mix Master Jamal was laying a trance groove. The topless go-go dancers on ten-foot pedestals danced rhythmically. Gragg smirked. The strippers weren't so much for the teen guys as the teen girls. Suburban girls acted scandalized, but they'd tell friends who'd have to see it for themselves. Where else would girls from good families see nude dancers? In the seedy strip club on the state highway? Hardly.

Gragg came inside specifically to find one of these girls from a good family. He moved through the crowd to the back of the hangar, where the real money was made—at the "pharmacy," where Cheko's people sold ecstasy, meth, DMT, ketamine, and a dozen other recreation-grade pharmaceuticals, in addition to soft drinks and bottled water.

Gragg could usually spot his quarry easily—the sexy girl with a guy she didn't look particularly intimate with. A first date, or perhaps just dancing together. He avoided girls with a group of female friends and girls who weren't having fun.

He soon found his target; the girl was gorgeous, perhaps seventeen, thin-waisted, but with a good rack shadowing her exposed midsection. Strands of glo-stick circled her belly and neck. It reminded Gragg of Mardi Gras, and that was a good sign. He motioned to a couple of security guards and moved toward her.

He timed it so he and the guards converged on the dancing couple. Gragg tapped the guy on the shoulder—which sent him twirling around defensively. Gragg held up two neck badges clearly marked ALL AREA ACCESS. Smiling, he looped one around the guy's neck.

Few symbols have more power over the Western teenage mind than the All Area Access badge. The guy glanced at the uniformed security guards and evidently felt reassured.

Gragg, meanwhile, draped the badge over the laughing girl's neck. Her cleavage glistened with sweat. Gragg leaned over and yelled into the guy's ear. "Your girl is fabulous, man! She should be dancing on the top floor—not down here!" With that, Gragg slid a couple of pills into the guy's hand and nodded his head toward the girl. He motioned for them both to follow and led them through the crowd as the burly security guards made a path.

They soon reached the base of a steel staircase leading up to the DJ tower. It was roped off and flanked by a couple of bouncers. Gragg leaned in close to one of the bouncers. "Tell me when she's taken the hit!"

The bouncer knew the drill. He watched poker-faced as the young guy popped what he probably thought was ecstasy into the girl's mouth. She washed it down with a swig of bottled water, laughed, then writhed with the pounding music. The bouncer nodded to Gragg. Gragg nodded back and the rope was withdrawn to let them pass.

As the boy passed by Gragg, Gragg leaned into his ear. "Play your cards right, man, and I'm gonna get you laid within the hour." The guy smiled back and gave Gragg what the kid probably assumed was the universal "playas'" handshake.

Gragg watched them go. They were now in the holding pen—a controlled area where he could further reduce her inhibitions. The prostitutes there and Cheko's men would make it all seem completely acceptable to "go wild." Gragg had successfully separated her from her support system. The rest should be easy. He was already erect in antici-pation, but a little patience was required.

Gragg walked the perimeter for a good fifteen minutes before head-ing back to the holding pen. He found the girl dancing on the mid-deck with a crowd of perhaps twenty. Most of the women there were attrac-tive and scantily clad—but these were Cheko's whores and were of no interest to Gragg. The seventeen-year-old target was laughing as her date danced between women in g-strings. The girl was evidently flying high. On meth the laser lights, the trance music, and the writhing motion were said to be hypnotic. Accompanied by a surge of sexual arousal and perceived invulnerability. Or so Gragg had heard. He didn't take drugs himself.

Gragg radioed the security guard in the DJ tower. He couldn't even hear himself talk, but he knew the guard would hear. The guard looked out and saw Gragg wave his arm slowly, then point at the girl dancing nearby. The guard leaned over to Mix Master Jamal, and the DJ looked out at Gragg. He nodded and then snapped his fingers at the light board operator. Gragg leaned over to her date. "What's your girl's name?"

"Jennifer!"

"You wanna see her tits?"

The guy stared for a second in dumb amazement. Then burst out laughing. "Hell yeah!"

Gragg spoke her name into the radio and moved forward. A spotlight shone down onto Jennifer, and the DJ's voice came out like the booming voice of God, "Check out Jennifer! Is she hot or what?" A roar of lust arose from a thousand voices.

Jennifer laughed and looked back to see her date and those around her shouting encouragement.

The DJ's voice. "Let's see you move, baby!" The pounding bass moved back in, and she moved seductively to it. The other dancers moved away, and the laser lights enshrined her on the platform. The crowd surged in anticipation. Her eyes became wild with her potent sexuality. Each rhythmic gyration of her hips made a thousand guys howl. She was anonymous and powerful.

But Gragg was her new master. He looked back at Jennifer's date, smiled, and nodded to the DJ.

The DJ's voice boomed down again. "Lose the top!"

A thousand voices roared and took up the chant. The chant quickly fell in line with the music. "Lose-the-top! Lose-the-top!" Even the girls in the audience were cheering. Jennifer danced, soaking up the adoration. All eyes were on her body, screaming with lust. She was high enough that she didn't mind, and it seemed such a small thing to please them all.

She first teased them by flashing her breasts, but that only drove the crowd wild for more. They knew they had her now; it was only a matter of wills. They took up the chant with renewed vigor. "Lose-the-top! Lose-the-top!"

When she pulled her top off and danced, breasts jiggling free, the roar of joy rattled the walls. They motioned for her to toss her top down, and she dangled it above the outstretched hands of the lustful mob. Someone managed to grab it from her, and it was soon torn to pieces. Jennifer laughed and tugged at the All Area Access badge around her neck. Girls around the room started flashing their breasts, sitting atop the shoulders of guys in the crowd.

The DJ cranked up the music again, and the party moved on. But Gragg moved in with one of Cheko's men holding a digital video camera. Jennifer smiled as they filmed her dancing topless in front of a thousand people. Her young, toned body glistened with sweat.

Within a half hour, Jennifer was sitting on a sofa in the holding pen, sucking Gragg off while her date looked on in shock. But her date didn't stop them. Gragg moaned while one of Cheko's men videotaped her. He looked to Jennifer's date. "You're after me."

When he ejaculated into her mouth, Gragg felt a rush of power and sexual release. This was his drug. Gragg didn't like whores. He liked to turn women *into* whores. The feeling of power was every bit as pleasurable as his ejaculation—perhaps more so. The fact that he was making money off this girl by doing a live porn Web cast for Cheko's Web site was even sweeter. She was being broadcast to the world, and the file would never go away. Gragg made sure he was never filmed above the waist.

As he moved away, he yelled, "Bukkaki!" And a dozen men surrounded her. She was already sucking on her date's cock. The meth was working its magic on her as the cameraman zoomed in.

Gragg zipped up his pants and moved away, feeling the endorphins course through his body.

Heider suddenly appeared next to him, laughing. "You're an evil man, Loki." Heider handed him a bottle of water.

"At least I got laid tonight."

Heider poked a finger into Gragg's chest. "At least I don't need a thousand people to orchestrate a blow job." He looked back at the girl starting on another guy. "Is she gonna remember any of this?"

"Probably not. And even if she does, she won't. If you know what I mean." Gragg looked at his watch. "Listen, meet me back at the car at three A.M. sharp. I've got to meet the Filipinos."

Heider nodded absently, still watching the girl work.

Gragg punched his arm.

"Ow!"

"I mean it. Meet me at the car at three A.M. sharp—or you'll have to bum a ride off the Albanian mob. Got it?"

"All right. I got it. Now if you'll excuse me . . . " At that, Heider stepped away to join the circle of men.

———————

By 3:15 A.M., Gragg and Heider were back on the Katy Freeway heading east. Heider was leaning against the passenger door fucked up out of his mind.

"That MPEG video over the dance floor. It showed rams butting heads. Butting their heads! Their fucking heads!" He was weeping, but then suddenly erupted into uncontrollable laughter. He was apparently laughing about having just been crying.

Gragg focused on driving. He headed north and east for a half hour or so, then exited in a seedy industrial district amid rail sidings. They rattled along potholed streets. With each bone-shuddering bump, Gragg winced. The ground effects on his Si were going to get thrashed at this rate. He also felt like a prime car-jacking target in this industrial wasteland.

Yet, as he looked around the deserted factory streets, it didn't look like a popular gang hangout. The streets were too broken and criss-crossed with railroad sidings for the street-racing scene.

Before long, Gragg found the street he was looking for. He turned down the dead end and parked next to a rusted chain-link fence topped with brand-new razor wire. It enclosed flatbed tractor-trailers in various stages of decay.

At the end of the street stood a brick factory building marked INDUS-TRIAL LAUNDRY CORP in faded paint. The windows near the roof glowed with fluorescent light from within, and the double doors near the loading dock were open wide, letting a wedge of light splay out across the weed-encrusted sidewalk. Signs in some Asian script covered the backs of both open doors. A couple of men in white aprons smoked out front, apparently on break.

Gragg turned off the car and looked at Heider's dozing form. He quietly pulled a piece of paper from his own jacket pocket and glanced at the code number written on it in pen. He took his car keys from the ignition and carefully slipped them into Heider's pocket. It wasn't difficult. In fact, he hoped he could still rouse Heider, who was out cold.

He nudged him. No response. He shoved Heider. Then finally shook him. "Heider, man! Wake up."

Heider awoke slowly, still high out of his mind. "What the fuck, man?"

"I need you to pick up the new encryption key from my contact. He's in there." He pointed.

Heider squinted and looked back at him like he was insane. "Fuck you, man. You go."

"Heider. Take a look around you. I'm not leaving my car sitting out here—and you'll fall asleep the minute I'm gone. You know what I put into this ride?"

"Well, then why the fuck did you park a mile away, asshole?"

"A semi was just in the loading dock."

"I don't know who your fucking contact is."

"Just give them this code number." Gragg handed him the piece of paper. "They won't even ask who you are. You're just picking up the code."

Heider wavered fuzzily, trying to process what Gragg just said.

Gragg sighed impatiently. "Christ, Jase, why do I have to do everything? I arranged the business; I keep you supplied with new gear—and I got you laid tonight."

Heider conceded this by nodding reluctantly.

"When are you gonna start pulling your weight, man?"

Heider squinted at the two dumpy middle-aged Asians smoking and chatting two hundred feet away.

Gragg pointed. "Oh, they sure look dangerous."

"Fuck . . . all right. Just don't do this shit to me without telling me first, man. I don't like surprises." Heider exchanged a last serious look with Gragg. Gragg just rolled his eyes. Heider sighed and got out.

Gragg watched Heider stagger down the street toward the lighted factory door less than a football field away. Once Heider was gone, Gragg grabbed his own backpack and quietly got out of the car. He slipped behind two Dumpsters and from the darkness watched Heider approach the men.

The Asian men watched impassively as Heider labored up to them. Heider said something and handed the piece of paper to the nearest guy. After reading it, the man pointed toward the open doorway. Heider walked through and stood silhouetted for a moment before one of the men walked in after him and shoved him forward. The other man scanned the street, threw his cigarette to the ground, and then walked inside—pulling the doors shut behind him. They closed with a resounding bang, leaving the street dark and quiet.

Gragg knelt down, shivering now in the cold autumn air. He waited for about a half hour before he heard the doors open again. Footsteps clacked across the pavement, heading his way. Gragg knew that Heider never wore anything that could remotely clack on pavement. So he hunkered down as a younger Filipino in slacks and a sport coat walked past the opening between the Dumpsters. Gragg heard his own car alarm chirp off, and the man got inside. He started the car up, raced the engine a bit, and then peeled off in a wild, squealing U-turn back down the street.

Gragg slumped down against the brick wall behind the Dumpsters. He felt the cold of the brick seep into his back.

Maybe he shouldn't have hacked the Filipino's Web server. Why couldn't he have left well enough alone? How had they caught on?

Damn! They got my car. Thank God it was registered under a false name.

Gragg sighed and took out his GPS receiver. He found the nearest cross street on the map, then flipped open his phone and selected a saved number. After a few rings, it picked up.

"Yeah, I need a cab."

Chapter 5:// Icarus-Seven

Jon Ross raced his Audi A8 sedan onto the Alcyone Insurance corporate campus, then quickly slowed down as he noticed several police cruisers and unmarked cars near the lobby doors. He turned down his music—a relentlessly pounding techno track—and motored at a more civilized speed past the squad cars. Interesting. No flashing lights, though.

Ross headed for the parking garage.

In a few minutes his voice was echoing across the granite-floored lobby as he approached the security desk. "Hey, Alejandro."

Alejandro smiled. "Jon, my boy. How're you doin' tonight?"

Ross swiped his consultant's badge and signed the after-hours access list. "What's with the police cars?"

"Oh, there was a computer break-in. The cops are down in the data center."

Ross stopped writing. He looked up. "A break-in?"

"Yeah. It's something, what these people can do. It's all computers nowadays." Alejandro leaned closer to Ross. "Ted Wynnik was askin' about you. I won't tell nobody I saw you if you want to clear out."

Ross finished signing in. He smiled. "Thanks, but not necessary. It was probably some twelve-year-old kid."

Ross headed down the clean white corridor of B2. Soon he reached the accounting department's data center and slid his badge through the reader. The door clicked open, and he moved briskly toward his office at the far wall. Then he slowed. The lights were on in his office. He forced himself not to stop and instead resumed a normal walking pace.

He opened his office door and was greeted by the sight of two severely groomed men in inexpensive suits and comfortable shoes sitting on the edge of his desk. One was a Latino, the other Caucasian, but they shared the same humorless expression. Hadi Sarkar, the night-shift data center supervisor, sat at Ross's keyboard, pecking away behind them. He turned somewhat sheepishly to face Ross.

One of the clean-cut men reached into his jacket and withdrew credentials, which he flipped open. "Jonathan Ross?"

"Yes?"

"I'm Special Agent Straub. This is Special Agent Vasquez. We'd like to ask you a few questions about last night. Your colleague, Hadi here, has been able to shed some light on things, but he tells us you're the real expert."

Ross glared at Sarkar and put his laptop case down on the desk. "I'm happy to help any way I can. What's all this about?"

"You were present in Alcyone's data center last night?"

"I was working under contract for another department, but Hadi requested my help. His development servers had become infected with what appeared to be a kernel rootkit."

"And you have experience with computer viruses?"

Ross paused. He had to be careful here. "Look, I'm a database consultant. Computer security is part of my job. I know what I need to know."

"Why did you make Hadi and his coworkers promise not to tell anyone about your help?"

"Because I was breaking the rules to help Hadi. That endangered my contract here. I made that clear to him."

"So you were asking Hadi to lie on your behalf?"

"I was asking him not to tell people that I was doing his job."

Sarkar jumped in. "I was requesting advice merely, Jon."

Ross folded his arms. "Hadi, your exact words were that you had tried everything you could think of and wanted my help." He turned back to Agent Straub. "A rogue process somewhere in his data center was broadcasting packets to the Web last night. Hadi couldn't find it. The process was incredibly stealthy—possibly a kernel rootkit."

Sarkar shook his head emphatically. "There is no way to hide the source of network traffic, Jon. I told you this."

"Well, the test bed servers were definitely involved. Test servers are usually the weakest on security. They have beta software and they're frequently reconfigured. So I had Hadi kill Icarus servers one through ten, and the packet broadcast stopped—even though it wasn't supposed to be originating from there."

Agent Straub nodded, taking notes. "So you knew right where to look, then. . . ."

"That wasn't my point."

Agent Vasquez ignored the discussion and picked up the phone. He dialed while Ross glanced at the computer screen. Sarkar had the Event Viewer maximized. "I see we're starting the hunt on my machine."

Straub slid his credentials back into his suit pocket. "We haven't ruled out an inside job."

"Of course. Forget the fact that I was the one who advised Hadi to shut that system down. Hardly something I'd do if I was the one running the exploit."

"You might, if you realized it had been discovered. It seems convenient that due to your involvement, the hard drives were erased."

Ross was poker-faced. "The rootkit destroyed the machine when I tried to shut it down. In any event, FBI forensics can reconstruct data from a wiped drive."

Vasquez hung up the phone. "They want us in the main data center."

———————

As they moved down the hallway, Sarkar kept groaning softly and shaking his head. Ross didn't take the bait. Sarkar finally muttered, "Jon, I had no choice but to tell them."

"Hadi, I've been in this business long enough to know better." Ross knew that no good deed goes unpunished, and though he hadn't technically done anything wrong, helping Sarkar out with his little problem could result in the loss of his contract with Alcyone. Or worse, he thought, eyeing their FBI escort.

"They were asking questions about what we did. This is the FBI, not human resources. They talked to us separately, and I knew that Maynard would mention you. Jon, what was I supposed to do? I do not wish to get deported."

Ross grimaced. "I should have known better than to get involved, Hadi."

"I am not a Muslim. I am a Hindu. You will tell them, won't you?"

Ross didn't respond.

Sarkar looked genuinely pained. "I am sorry, Jon."

"Ted Wynnik probably called the Feds in to force Accounting's hand and have my contract canceled. He doesn't like having people down here who don't answer to him."

"Ted didn't call the FBI, Jon."

"Then who did? You?"

"No one did."

Ross stopped walking. "What do you mean?"

"They came here on their own. Because of what the Icarus-Seven server did."

Ross looked back to the FBI agents. Straub motioned for him to keep moving.

Just what have I gotten involved in here? Ross wondered.

There were a lot of people in the data center. It was almost acceptably warm as a result. Sarkar's boss, Ted Wynnik, leaned against a counter, glowering beneath thick eyebrows as he listened to two techs Ross hadn't seen before. This was probably the A-team—the daytime shift. They looked at Ross with the special contempt reserved for young consultants.

Half a dozen uniformed Woodland Hills police officers were in here along with more FBI agents. They were talking with a network admin—a pear-shaped guy with bad skin. He was probably Maynard. Pear-shaped pointed at various server racks enthusiastically. At least someone was enjoying this.

What happened?

As soon as Ross entered the room, everyone stopped talking and turned to face him. The sudden silence was almost embarrassing because Ross knew he had none of the answers they were looking for. He decided to ask the obvious question. "Anybody want to tell me what's going on?"

All eyes turned to someone behind Ross, so he spun on his heel to face a trim man in a crisp suit. The guy looked like a fifty-year-old varsity quarterback. A leader of men.

"Mr. Ross. I'm Special Agent Neal Decker, L.A. Division. Do you know why we're here?"

"Because of last night?"

Decker sized him up. It unnerved Ross that no one was talking.

But Decker was in no hurry. He finally placed his hand on a disconnected rack server sitting on the nearby counter. "They tell me this computer killed two men earlier today."

The shock took a while to work through Ross. He had expected some sort of child pornography ring or a credit card scam. "Killed? How?"

"I was hoping you could help us explain that."

"Why on earth would you think that?"

Decker smiled good-naturedly. "A lot of people are suspects right now. But once we get the people in here to help us interpret the evidence, we'll know more. In the meantime, we'd like to take you gentlemen in for questioning." His gaze spanned the room to include all the men who were present during the incident.

A wave of dread washed over Ross. "We're not under arrest?"

"No. I'm asking you to voluntarily come in for questioning."

Ross wondered what would happen if he said no. Of course, he couldn't say no. What about a lawyer? "I must tell you, I'm just completely floored by this."

"I'm certain you are."

This guy was disconcertingly calm. He gave the impression that he knew more than he was letting on. *Goddamnit.*

Just then a man appeared at the glass data center door. He was the linebacker to match Decker as quarterback. His casual confidence seemed to indicate he wasn't FBI—the agents here were all keyed up in Decker's presence. No, this guy was an outsider to them. The man rapped on the glass, and a Woodland Hills patrolman opened the door for him. The newcomer showed a badge and was let inside.

"I'm looking for an Agent Decker."

Decker and the FBI agents turned and moved forward, hands extended. "Detective Sebeck. We spoke on the phone." They shook hands. Decker turned to some of his crew. "Agent Knowles, Agent Straub, Detective Sergeant Peter Sebeck, Ventura County Major Crimes Unit. Detective Sebeck was heading the murder investigation up in Thousand Oaks." Handshakes all around.

Then everyone turned back to Ross.

Sebeck pointed at him. "Who's this?"

Decker leaned against the counter. "This is Jon Ross, one of Alcyone's independent computer consultants. He designs their corporate data systems. Isn't that right, Mr. Ross?"

"Certain systems, yes. Not this one."

"Is he a suspect or a witness?"

Ross thought it was a good question.

Decker was calm as ever. "That depends." He looked to Ross. "Tell me, Mr. Ross, why is it that no one at your home address has ever heard of you?"

Damn it to hell. . . .

Chapter 6:// Exile

"**M**s. Anderson?" The security guard stepped from the guard shack and ducked to look into the Jaguar XK8.

Anji Anderson looked down her nose at him from behind the wheel, lowering her Vuitton sunglasses. "Yesss. Open the gate."

"Ma'am, if you could drive off to the right here, I believe Mr. Langley wants to have a word with you."

"I think you should open the gate."

"Ma'am, Mr. Langley—"

"Mr. Langley—whoever that is—can call my office if he wants to speak with me." She dug through her glove compartment and produced a drive-on studio pass. "Now, open the gate."

"Ma'am, I'm afraid you're just going to have to pull off to the right, there."

"Why? Do you know who I am?"

He gave her an incredulous look. He obviously knew who she was.

"And why do you keep calling me 'Ma'am'? What is this, the Ponderosa? My name is Anji Anderson—although later you'll be calling me 'That Bitch Who Got Me Fired.' "

"Ma'am, there's no call for cussing."

"Cussing? Okay, Clem, I won't cuss no more, as long as you open the fucking gate."

His look hardened. He leaned down closer. "Look, if you don't pull off to the right, you'll wish you had. Now park over there." He pointed.

She just laughed. "Ahhh, I guess there's only so much shit you'll take for eight bucks an hour, eh?"

"Pull over to the right."

A car behind her honked.

"And what if I don't?"

"Pull over to the right!"

Another guard approached the car.

"Oh, you called for backup. You need protection from a helpless woman, Clem?"

The second guard eased the first away from the car and then turned to her. "Ms. Anderson, using your superior social position to belittle a powerless employee does not speak well of you."

She stared at him.

"The fact is that we've been instructed by your superiors to prevent you from entering. If you want to know why, I suggest you pull over to the right."

She nodded slowly and put the car in gear. "Okay. I will." She yanked the steering wheel to the right and accelerated madly into the walk-on lot.

Anderson was burning with anger after walking in high heels from the far corner of the parking lot. She was going to raise hell about this with Walter Kahn. She was *talent*. She shouldn't have to put up with facilities crap.

When she finally reached the guard shed again, the second guard pointed to a pedestrian gate where two people waited for her, one a trim woman in a tailored suit, the other another security guard. Anderson slowed down and then stopped. She stood there not liking what she was suddenly thinking.

The woman motioned for her to approach.

Anderson took a deep breath and walked up to them as composedly as she could manage. "What's this all about?"

The woman extended her hand from between the bars. It was like visiting hours at the state pen. Anderson extended her own hand for a cold handshake. "Ms. Anderson, I'm Josephine Curto from Human Resources. There's been a change in your contract status at the network."

"My agent is negotiating a contract renewal. It doesn't lapse for another five weeks."

"Yes. I see. Those negotiations are over. The network decided not to renew your contract. Please understand this decision came down from corporate. I'm just delivering the news. We thought your agent would have told you."

Anderson felt the tears welling up, but sucked in a breath and forced them back down again. She looked away and pressed her forefinger and thumb against the bridge of her nose—then looked back sharply at Curto. "*This* is how you decide to tell me I'm fired? I'm standing here like some kind of vagrant in the street. What am I, a threat? What am I going to do, shoot up the place?"

Curto was unperturbed as she attached papers to a clipboard. "That's not the concern. You are known to studio personnel and have access to a live television broadcast. I'm sure you can appreciate that the network doesn't want you getting on the air at this difficult time."

"Difficult time?" Anderson tried in vain to form her thoughts into words several times. The tears threatened again. She finally blurted out, lamely, "I have fans. You've seen my fan mail? There are men and women in Marin and Oakland and Walnut Creek—people who've asked to marry me. What are you going to tell them about my sudden disappearance?"

"I have no idea how to respond to that question."

"You should let me do a final broadcast."

"Lifestyles reporters don't get farewell broadcasts, Ms. Anderson."

"What about Jim McEwen? They had a big send-off when he retired."

"Jim was the anchor. He worked at the studio for thirty-two years. You've been here six."

"This is no way to treat talent."

"That's hardly at issue here."

Anderson realized Curto was smart for being on the other side of the bars. She took another deep breath and tried to center herself. "Can't I at least go in to say goodbye to Jamie and Doug and the others?"

"Oh, see, now why are we having this conversation? It's not productive," Curto said. She pushed a clipboard and pen through the bars. "Can you please sign these?"

Anderson just stared at her indignantly. "I'm not signing anything."

"You want your personal effects, right?"

"My personal effects? You mean you people emptied out my *office*?"

"Anji, what do you think is going on here? This is a large corporation with global responsibilities. Emptying out your office wasn't a vengeful act. It was a work order. Just sign the documents, and let's get this over with. This is not fun for you or me."

Anderson grabbed the clipboard and pen. She slapped it against the bars right in front of Curto's face and started reading the COBRA and 401(k) documents. She felt like a public spectacle. A loser standing outside the gates where everyone could see her. The grips and cameramen stared as they drove in through the nearby gate. She started tearing up in humiliation. Someone was punishing her. But who?

She finally just signed all the papers without reading them and shoved the clipboard back through the bars.

"We'll deliver your personal effects to your home."

Anderson hurried away, rushing for the distant refuge of her car.

"Ms. Anderson. My pen."

Anderson had been starting pitcher on Wisconsin State's girls' softball team. She stopped, turned, and hurled the pen at the corporate ice bitch with all her strength. The woman took it right in the torso. Had it been a Mont Blanc, she would have been sucking for air. But it was just a Bic, and the woman shrank back.

"There's no call for that!"

Anderson stormed away, her mind running in fast-forward to all the bad things that were sure to follow. Someone had dynamited a bridge on her road to success. She hadn't prepared for this at all. Fucking terrorists.

She mentally ticked off a list of her friends. They were all in the business or attached to the business. Who could find her a soft landing at another station? If not in San Francisco, then where? Not Madison, Wisconsin, again, please, dear God.

Then it hit her that Melanie hadn't warned her. That bitch had let her be publicly humiliated. Anderson pulled her cell phone out of her handbag and speed-dialed her agent. It rang three times and went to voice mail.

"You've reached the office of Melanie Smalls. Ms. Smalls is not available at the moment. To reach her assistant, Jason Karcher, press 3349."

Anderson punched in the numbers.

"Ms. Smalls's office. Can I help you?"

"Jason, it's Anji Anderson. Put me through to Melanie."

"Hi, Ms. Anderson. Melanie's on another line. Do you want to hold?"

"Look, I'm standing out here in front of KTLZ, and they've locked me out of the studio. Get Melanie on the damned phone."

"Okay. Hang on."

Anderson reached her car and clicked the remote. She got inside and cleaned up her mascara in the rearview mirror while Barry Manilow tortured her on hold because it looked like she had emphatically not "made it." The anger built inside her with each passing verse.

Finally Melanie clicked on. "Anji, what's going on?"

"I've just been fired at the studio front gate—publicly humiliated. Josephine Curto tells me that you knew my contract wasn't being picked up."

"Who the hell's Josephine Curto?"

"Some toady from Human Resources."

"Anji, we're still in negotiations with the network, and I wasn't told that any decision had been made. The ball was still in Kahn's court."

"Josephine just told me that my agent knew about this, Melanie. I just signed papers!"

"Well, she doesn't know what the hell she's talking about, and what do you mean you just signed papers? Why would you sign papers?" Melanie's voice became muted. "Jase, check the fax machine."

Anderson started crying again. She hit the dashboard—angry with herself for being so emotional. "Damnit, Melanie. Why didn't I see this coming? Who the hell did the network get to replace me?"

"Don't beat yourself up. We'll see if we can get you something on the E! Channel or—"

"No! Stop. I've been trying for six years to get on a serious news desk. I can't afford to do any more fluff pieces. I'm a journalist, not a damned fashion model."

There was silence on the other end.

"Hello?"

"I'm still here. Anji, you don't have the right pedigree for it. You haven't been a journalist, honey. Not really. And you weren't talking serious journalism when we got you onto the San Francisco affiliate."

"I'm realizing—"

"You're realizing you're past thirty and fluff reporting is for twenty-four-year-old news models."

"Exactly."

"That's a problem."

"No, it's a challenge."

"Anji, what you're talking about is starting back at square one and reinventing yourself. No, actually you're starting at square negative one because you're already known as a fashion and lifestyles reporter— meaning you have all the journalistic heft of a British tabloid. It's going to be a stretch, and at my age, I don't stretch."

Anderson searched for words. This was unraveling fast.

"Honey, you're too old to intern as a serious journalist. Unless you're a proven hard news reporter at thirty, you're not going to be a hard news reporter."

Anderson bit her lip gently. Performed in front of the right man, that used to solve a lot of problems. She realized that Christiane Amanpour probably didn't bite her lip.

"Unfortunately, major networks are consolidating news production in Atlanta, and laying off in most markets. I could try to get you a spot on a cosmetics infomercial casting in L.A."

Tears flowed down Anderson's cheeks.

Chapter 7:// Daemon

Yahoo.com/news

E-**Murder**@Video Game Company—Thousand Oaks, California: A booby **trap** sprung **via** the **Internet** claimed the life of a **Cyber-Storm Entertainment employee** Thursday. An off-site death earlier in the day is also under investigation as a related homicide. **Programmer Chopra Singh**—project lead on the bestselling MMORPG game *The Gate* was electrocuted in company offices. **Lead detective Peter Sebeck** of the **Ventura County Sheriff's Major Crimes Unit** confirmed the killings were carried out via the Internet.

Sebeck was already staring at the ceiling when his alarm clock sounded. He switched it off by touch and kept staring at the ceiling. He'd gotten in late last night. Even so, he hadn't slept. He kept turning the case over in his mind. That's what he'd taken to calling it: *The Case.*

The FBI had taken over. They were forming a temporary task force with local law enforcement, but the Feds were in charge. Agents were photocopying files and interrogating suspects when Sebeck left at two A.M. Decker was some sort of workaholic.

Sebeck explored his sense of loss. *The Case* no longer belonged to him. Why did it bother him so much? He was afraid he knew the answer: he felt truly alive only when something horrible was happening. That was the dirty secret behind every promotion he had ever received.

He'd miscast himself in the role of authority figure. A decision made one afternoon fifteen years ago. He had had to grow up fast, back then—after the baby—but he sometimes wondered if he wasn't just pretending. If he wasn't simply acting the way he thought he should act. The way others around him did. He didn't even know who he'd be without this role. Pete Sebeck was just an idea—a collection of responsibilities with a mailing address.

He tried to recall the last time he actually *felt* something. The last time he felt alive. That inevitably led to thoughts of her. Memories of the trip to Grand Cayman. He tried to remember the smell of her hair. He wondered where she was right now, and if he'd ever see her again. She didn't need a damned thing from him. Maybe that's what he loved most about her.

Sebeck's cell phone sounded from the nightstand, scattering his thoughts. He glanced over at his wife's side of the bed. She roused slightly. He grabbed the handset and sat up. "Sebeck."

"Detective Sebeck?"

"Yeah. Who's—"

"This is Special Agent Boerner, FBI. I just sent an e-mail to your home address. The agent in charge wants a response before you're in this morning." Someone yelled in the background. Boerner clicked off without saying goodbye.

"Hello?" Sebeck stared in irritation at the handset. *Rude asshole.* He glanced at the clock: 6:32 A.M.

His wife sat up on the other side of the bed and stretched in one of her full-length nightgowns.

"Laura, I have to jump in the shower first. I've got a full day ahead."

"Fine, Pete."

"I won't be long. Go back to sleep."

Sebeck ran through his ablutions in fifteen minutes, dressed, and tied his tie on the way downstairs. He ducked into the kitchen.

His son, Chris, sat reading the morning paper. The kid was getting big—muscular big. Sixteen. Almost the age Sebeck was when he and Laura conceived the boy. Had it really been sixteen years? "Why don't you get a shovel, Chris?"

Chris had a bulging mouthful of cereal. The boy grabbed at his dad's suit jacket as he walked past. Chris flipped the paper over to reveal the front page. There was a color picture of Sebeck over the headline:

"Internet Killings Spark Federal Investigation." Mantz was also in the picture to his left. Sebeck stopped short and picked up the page, reading slowly as he sank down into a seat at the table.

Chris chewed his way back to speech. "L.A. *Times*. That's big."

Sebeck just kept reading.

Laura walked into the kitchen.

Sebeck glanced up. "Did you see this?"

She looked down at the page. "Not a great picture of Nathan." She went over to the stove to make tea.

Sebeck handed the paper back to Chris but kept looking at Laura. "I won't be able to pick up Chris from practice today. I've got the FBI here, the national media, and God knows what else."

"We'll manage."

Chris lowered the paper. "The Feds are interrogating the insurance guys. You think they did it?"

"I'm not the one questioning them, Chris." Sebeck stood. "From here on out, I'll be lucky to be in the loop at all." He glanced at his watch. "I gotta go."

Sebeck headed down the hall to the den. Once there, he dropped into the desk chair and hit the power switch on the computer. While the computer booted, he moved a gaming joystick off to the side and tossed two soda cans into the trash. He called to the kitchen, "Chris, I won't keep asking you to clean up in here when you're done!" No answer.

The computer desktop came up. Sebeck launched his e-mail program, then clicked the GET MAIL button. He waited as 132 messages downloaded. *Goddamned spam.* When it finished, the message subject lines ranged from "Barely Legal Teens" to "Nigerian Exile Needs Help" to "Lolitas Take Horse Cock."

He searched his inbox for the FBI message. It was near the top and had the subject line "Case #93233—CyberStorm/Pavlos" from *boernerh@fbi.gov*. Sebeck double-clicked on it.

Strangely, as the e-mail opened, the screen went black. Then the words "Testing Audio" faded in. The hard drive strained. Sebeck stared in confusion. What did he do? In a moment, the words faded out and were replaced by a grainy video image of a man. It was hard to tell his age or precise appearance due to the poor video quality. It was amateurish—poorly lit and off-center.

The man looked thin and pale—a condition emphasized by his

standing against a featureless white background. He was completely bald and wore what looked to be a medical gown.

What the hell was this, some sort of FBI lab report?

It took Sebeck a moment to realize that the video was already playing. The man swayed unsteadily—his pixels adjusting like colored tiles. Then he looked directly into the camera and nodded as if in greeting.

"Detective Sebeck. I was Matthew Sobol. Chief technology officer of CyberStorm Entertainment. I am dead."

Sebeck leaned forward—his eyes fixed on the monitor.

"I see you've been assigned to the Josef Pavlos and Chopra Singh murder cases. Let me save you some time; I killed both men. Soon you'll know why. But you have a problem: Because I'm dead, you can't arrest me. More importantly: You can't stop me."

Sebeck stared in stunned silence.

Sobol continued. "Since you have no choice but to try and stop me, I want to take this moment to wish you luck, Sergeant—because you're going to need it."

The image disappeared, revealing the e-mail inbox again.

Sebeck didn't move for several moments. When he finally did, it was to forward the message to his sheriff's e-mail address.

Chapter 8:// Escalation

"**M**r. Ross, help us understand this: You have no permanent address, and yet you've got nearly three hundred thousand dollars in liquid assets. Am I to believe you live with your parents?"

Jon Ross rubbed his tired eyes and tried to concentrate on the question—the same question they'd asked twenty different ways. The one they kept coming back to.

The taller FBI agent leaned in close. "Mr. Ross?"

"I'm a contract nomad. Ancient people followed caribou. I follow software contracts."

The shorter agent stood next to a mirrored window and flipped through his notes. "You've been at Alcyone Insurance for what, two months now? Is that a long time for you?"

"Not particularly. Three or four is typical."

"Your clients give us various physical addresses for your business. Kind of strange for a one-man corporation, isn't it?"

Ross ran his fingers through his hair in frustration. "You contacted my *clients*? Are you trying to destroy my business?"

"Why are you concealing information from your clients?"

"I maintain contact addresses *legally* through resident agents in several states. This is legal commerce. Why are you guys doing this to me? I was trying to help Hadi."

"That doesn't explain why you have a phony personal address."

Ross sighed. "I had the fake address because society requires everyone to have a permanent home address."

"Then why don't you have one?"

"Because I don't need one."

Both agents were pacing again. The shorter one was the first to speak. "Single. No property. Do you pay all your taxes, Mr. Ross?"

"I'm a Delaware service corporation. I pay myself a reasonable salary, max out my 401(k), and take the remainder as corporate profits— minus travel and business expenses. And the corporation leases my car." He hesitated. "Look, I didn't do anything wrong. I was trying to help my client."

The phone in the center of the table rang. The shorter agent grabbed it without saying a word. He listened. After a few moments he nodded slightly and looked at Ross with some surprise. "Understood." A pause. "Yes."

He hung up. "It looks like you're off the hook, Mr. Ross."

Neal Decker and three other FBI agents sat in the darkened training room of the Ventura County Sheriff's headquarters intently watching a screen projection of Sobol's MPEG video. Sebeck, Mantz, Burkow, and Ventura County's assistant chief, Stan Eichhorn, watched alongside them. Aaron Larson ran the video off a laptop hooked to the department's digital projector.

Sobol's grainy image glowed on-screen. ". . . I want to take this moment to wish you luck, Sergeant—because you're going to need it."

The image froze, and Sobol's audience whistled and broke out into raucous discussion. Larson brought up the lights, revealing Agent Decker staring intently at the blank screen. He finally came around and stepped to the front of the room.

"Gentlemen, this changes things." Decker looked to Agent Straub. "When does the computer forensics team get in, Tom?"

"They're already en route from Oxnard Airport."

"Get them over to CyberStorm as soon as they arrive. Where are the Alcyone Insurance computers?"

"Put on a plane to D.C. last night."

"Good. Hopefully they'll get something off the drives. In the meantime, have the forensics team comb through the CyberStorm network. I want it sniffed for booby traps, and then we need to shift our focus to Matthew Sobol." He pointed to the projector. "Get forensics a copy of this video file."

Larson perked up. "I burned copies onto CD. I can make more if you need them."

Decker held up his hands. "That brings up an important point. I want absolute secrecy concerning this case." He looked to the local police. "That means no talking to friends and relatives, and absolutely no talking to the media. We need to control what information gets out there."

Sebeck pointed at the screen. "Has anyone heard of this Sobol guy?"

Decker didn't say anything. He just fished through folders on a nearby tabletop and then slid a folder over to Sebeck. It was labeled MATTHEW ANDREW SOBOL.

"What, you already knew about him?"

"Died Thursday. We thought he might be another victim, but he died of brain cancer. He's been ill for years. He was a company founder. Had access to everything. It all fits. Except for the motive."

Straub picked up from there. They were like an old married couple. "His assistant said Sobol suffered from dementia. He was paranoid and secretive. It got worse as his illness progressed. He finally had to stop working last year."

Sebeck flipped through the folder. It was filled with medical files and psychology reports. "Did he have the know-how to build that booby trap over at CyberStorm?"

Decker and Straub exchanged knowing glances. Decker took the folder back. "Sobol scored 220 on an IQ test in 1993. The NSA tried to recruit him out of Stanford for his dissertation on polymorphic data encryption. Instead he started a game company and made millions by his early twenties. He was plenty capable."

Sebeck knew he could either accept it or say something. He pondered it for several more moments before he decided to make an ass of himself by speaking up. "What about the phone call from that fictitious FBI agent? There's someone else involved in this."

"We've got good technical people, Sergeant. Let's see what they find. But I'll need wiretaps on your cell, office, and home phones." He turned to Straub. "Let's also get Sebeck's ISP to forward all incoming e-mail to the forensics unit. Sergeant, can I expect your cooperation?"

Sebeck nodded. "Yeah. Let me tell my wife and kid, but yes, of course."

Straub wrote on a small notepad. "I'll need your signature on some paperwork."

Sebeck drummed his fingers on the table impatiently. "Look, I don't doubt that this Sobol guy was brilliant, but I'm not convinced that that grainy video is Matthew Sobol. If he was such a genius, he sure as hell could take a clearer video than that. I can't even make out his face all that well."

A murmur of agreement swept through the room.

Decker was unperturbed. "We'll have it analyzed by experts."

Sebeck still pushed. "I think a CyberStorm employee is committing these murders and trying to pin it on this dead guy. The killer obviously has access to CyberStorm's network, and from what I've seen at CyberStorm, they've got a lot of clever people. I think this is a setup."

"You and I are not technical experts, Sergeant. Let's see what the forensics team finds." Decker looked at the assembled officers. "Okay, listen up. We've got to get our hands on more facts. Chief Eichhorn, I'm going to need your cooperation and some of your resources."

Eichhorn nodded. "Anything you need."

"Matthew Sobol had an eighty-acre estate near here. We should have the search warrant in an hour or so. I'm going to need traffic and perimeter control."

Larson was still absorbing the first sentence. "*Eighty* acres?"

Decker nodded. "Yes. Our Mr. Sobol had considerable assets. A net worth of around three hundred million."

Whistles all around.

"Detective Sebeck might be right; this case might involve others, but we'll need to follow up on the Sobol lead. Vasquez, I need to know about any disagreements or professional rivalries Sobol might have had with the two victims. I want more detailed interviews with the victims' families. I also need to know anyone else who might have had a run-in with Sobol. Let's get someone at NCAMD to do a work-up on him. Straub, I want you over at CyberStorm with the forensics team. Keep me apprised of any new information."

Decker grabbed a written report from a nearby table and turned to Sebeck. "Sergeant, there's critical information missing from your report on the first murder scene. Specifically the cable winch. We need the manufacturer, model, serial numbers—"

Sebeck stopped him. "I pulled the evidence unit onto the Cyber-Storm scene after the second murder. We were going to follow up."

"Now's your chance." Decker tossed the report and a plastic bag containing a gate key and remote. "I want to know when the winch was purchased and who installed it. Maybe the installer can tell us what other work they've done. Also find out if a permit was pulled with the city. I want the revised report on my desk ASAP."

Mantz looked to Sebeck. "I'll head over to the city permit office, Pete."

Sebeck felt the heat of this professional slight coursing through his veins. He took a breath and tried to keep a clear head. He wasn't used to being closely managed. "All right. I want to revisit the first scene, anyway."

The training room phone rang and Vasquez grabbed it. He listened and then called to Decker. "Neal. NSA."

Decker addressed the room. "Gentlemen, we're going to need non-FBI out of this room. Chief Eichhorn, plan for an early afternoon search of Sobol's estate."

"Will do." Eichhorn and the deputies soon found themselves being hustled out of their own training room. The door closed behind them, and the five men stood in the hallway.

Sebeck gestured to his rejected report. "Hell of a morning."

Eichhorn pointed. "I want to see that revised report before you hand it to Decker." He turned to the others. "Burkow, Larson, come with me. We've got to scare up some manpower." They moved off toward the division offices.

Mantz slapped Sebeck on the back. "Don't let him get to you, Pete. I'll hook up with you after the permit office." Mantz headed down the hall.

Sebeck watched him go. Just then, two FBI agents emerged from a nearby interrogation room. They had one of the suspects from Alcyone Insurance in tow—an exhausted-looking Jon Ross. Ross's laptop bag was slung over his shoulder, and he was folding up his flip phone. One of the agents turned to shake his hand. "Mr. Ross, thanks for your cooperation. We know this has been disruptive to your business."

Ross slipped the phone into his pocket. "*Disruptive?* I just got a voice mail from Alcyone's lawyers. They're threatening a lawsuit, and they canceled my contract. I have messages from two other clients who are putting my projects on hold, no doubt because of you guys."

"Be sure to let us know where to get in touch with you if you leave town." The agent handed Ross a business card. "And don't leave the country."

Ross stared at the card. "Don't leave the *country*? I have a project in Toronto next month." He studied the unsympathetic expressions on the agents' faces, then pocketed the card. "Any chance of getting a ride back to Woodland Hills?"

"Check with the sheriff's. But it might be quicker to call a cab. Thanks again." Both agents made a beeline for the training room door. They knocked twice and ducked inside, leaving Ross staring after them in the busy corridor.

Sebeck called across the hallway, "I see the Feds haven't lost their light touch."

Ross regarded Sebeck warily.

Sebeck approached and extended his hand. "Detective Sebeck."

"I know who you are, Sergeant. You were at Alcyone last night."

"You need a ride someplace?"

"I can call a cab."

"C'mon, it's the least I can do. It looks like you've gotten the short end of the stick in this whole thing. I'm heading out, anyway."

Ross hesitated, then nodded. "Thanks."

Sebeck and Ross drove in silence for a few minutes. Ross was absorbed by a smart phone in his hand. He brushed his finger through several screens, reading intently. Eventually he looked up. "Interesting."

Sebeck glanced at him. "What's that?"

"I finally got a chance to read the news. It's nice to know what I was almost accused of."

Sebeck said nothing.

"Your murder case is all over the headlines. Look, there's you." Ross held up the phone to show a news Web site with a photo of Sebeck at the press conference.

Sebeck barely looked. "Well, it's not my case anymore." They drove on for a few moments in silence. "So, you're some kind of computer consultant, is that it?"

"Yes. I design relational database management systems."

"How does a young guy like you get such big clients?"

"Word of mouth. I'm good at what I do. You look young to be a sergeant of detectives."

Sebeck grimaced. "I got an early start." They came up on the entrance ramp to the 101 freeway, but Sebeck headed across the bridge to the far side of town.

"Sergeant, you just missed the freeway ramp."

"I need to stop off somewhere first. Listen, can I ask you some computer questions?"

Ross looked uncertain. "What about?"

"That virus at Alcyone. Everybody there was looking to you for help. So, you know a lot about viruses?"

"I already told all this to the FBI. I've been cleared, remember?"

Sebeck waved his hand in acknowledgment. "I know, I know. But our in-house guy doesn't have the chops to deal with much more than teen hackers and drug dealers."

"Sergeant, the FBI has a cyber crime unit to deal with this. They don't need my help."

"It's not the FBI that's asking."

Ross looked to Sebeck. "Ah . . . I see." He raised his hands to represent headlines. "Local cop cracks case."

Sebeck looked darkly at Ross. "I'm just trying to stop a killer."

"To be frank, Sergeant, you're going to have a difficult time finding whoever killed those men. This is essentially a computer forensics case, and the FBI is better equipped for that."

Sebeck took a chance. "What if I told you I know who the killer is?"

Ross tensed visibly.

"No, not you."

"That's why the FBI let me go?"

Sebeck nodded. "What if I also told you that the killer was dead at the time of the murders?"

Ross looked puzzled for a moment—but then a look of realization came over his face. "No way."

"That's what I need to know. Is it possible?"

"Holy shit, you're serious."

"The Feds believe it. But I don't. I think the real killer is over at CyberStorm and that he's framing this dead guy for the murders."

"It's Matthew Sobol, isn't it?"

Sebeck cast a surprised look at Ross. "Where the hell did you hear that?"

Ross gestured to his phone. "The news said Sobol died this week from brain cancer. He's your dead killer, isn't he, Sergeant?"

Sebeck realized he might be in trouble. "Whatever you learn here doesn't go to the media, your friends—anyone. If I even *think* you leaked this, I'll charge you with interfering with a police investigation. Do you understand?"

"Your secret's safe with me. But if I were you, I'd be more concerned about Sobol. If that's who's behind this, then there's more going on than just these murders."

"How come everyone but me has heard of this Sobol guy?"

"I'm a hard-core gamer, Sergeant. Sobol was a legend. He helped build the online gaming industry."

"Legend or not, how could a dead man have known when to trigger his traps? He'd have to know in advance the exact day he'd be dead."

"Not necessarily." Ross held up his phone again. "He could be reading the news."

"Don't talk science fiction crap."

"Sergeant, it's a trivial matter for a computer program to monitor Web site content. It's just text. All Sobol would have to do is create a program to scan news sites for specific phrases—like his obituary, or stories about the deaths of certain programmers. A simple key word search."

Sebeck considered this. "That virus you stopped over at Alcyone Insurance. Could that be the program that was waiting for Sobol's death?"

"Maybe. And it sent packets to thousands of IP addresses."

"Packets containing what?"

"Probably commands."

"To *thousands* of addresses?"

Ross nodded grimly.

"Jesus. Would the Feds know this?"

"Oh yeah. The type of program I stopped at Alcyone is fairly common in computing. It's known as a *daemon*. It runs in the background waiting for some event to take place. Usually it's something simple like a request to print. In this case it would be news of Sobol's death. Then it activates."

"And triggers the killings."

Ross nodded. "It's possible."

"Just one problem. Sobol couldn't call me on the phone. I got a phone call this morning from someone pretending to be an FBI agent. They told me to check my e-mail—and that's what led me to Sobol. So someone else is coordinating this."

Ross was shaking his head. "It could have been VOIP—voice over Internet protocol."

Sebeck glared at him. "Have I stepped through a fucking time machine? Was I asleep for the last decade or something?"

"VOIP went mainstream in the corporate world years ago. It saves on phone bills by directing voice communications over Internet servers instead of long-distance telephone lines."

"So you're telling me this Daemon program can talk to people over the phone?"

"Playing a prerecorded message over a phone line is easy. The Daemon could manage the sequence and schedule the calls based on what it reads in the news."

"So it's not actually a computer talking? Someone must have recorded the message?"

"Probably. Although there are programs that can convert text streams into pretty convincing synthetic voices. Call any airline reservation desk—you'll be talking to a computer pretty quick. It's used to announce flight schedules, credit card balances, things like that."

They drove on for a few moments in silence.

Sebeck sighed. "Well, at least you got the Alcyone server. That'll put a kink in the killer's plans—whether he's alive or dead."

Ross didn't look comforted. "You really should play one of Sobol's games, Sergeant."

Chapter 9:// Herr Oberstleutnant

Over *the Rhine* was the only first-person shooter to which Brian Gragg had ever become addicted. He'd played and mastered a score of PC action games. All of them had incredible 3-D graphics, volumetric smoke, realistic physics engines, thirty-two-voice sound, vast levels, and multi-player Internet features. But *OTR* was different: Its AI was scary smart.

Where enemies in other games poured through doorways, wave after wave, only to be slaughtered, *OTR's* AI engine deployed Nazi soldiers realistically. In a house-to-house search, groups of three or four would peel off from the main group, kicking in doors. If you shot one or two or even three, the officer in the street would blow his whistle and shout orders. Then you'd better haul ass because dozens of soldiers would surround your cottage. They wouldn't storm the place like mindless automatons. Instead, they'd take cover behind fences, walls, and vehicles, and they'd shout in German for you to come out. When you didn't (and, of course, why would you?) they'd start tossing grenades through the windows or set fire to the house. If you tried to look out a window to see what they were doing, a sniper might cap you.

But what was even more fascinating to Gragg was that they didn't do it the same way each time. There were smart and dumb soldiers, and varying qualities of Nazi officers. If you holed up in a particularly defensible spot, they might call in a Stug to batter the place into rubble— or worse yet, a Flamenwerfer. And if the siege went on for a while, the Gestapo would arrive to take charge of the situation, and that meant only one thing: SS Oberstleutnant Heinrich Boerner, an adversary so wily and twisted, this fictional character had become a cause célèbre at the E3 gaming convention. There was a thirty-foot color banner of his face hanging over CyberStorm Entertainment's booth. He was literally the poster boy for evil.

OTR's AI cemented the impression that you were fighting against a rational opponent—and a challenging one. Gragg appreciated the endless hours of distraction this afforded, particularly since his real-life incident with the Filipinos.

Heider's body had been found in a rail yard near Hobby Airport, south of Houston. Heider had been bound, gagged, and beaten to death—left as a warning to the carder community. It was at times like these that Gragg was thankful for his limited social circle.

Few, if any, would be able to connect him to Heider, but just in case he decided to lay low for a few weeks.

He had about fifty or sixty thousand in cash on hand at various banks under various identities. Good thing, because he couldn't trade the identity database he had copied from the Filipino server with any of his Abkhazian contacts. It was just too hot. He felt a wave of humiliation again. Over twenty thousand high-net-worth identities down the drain—a fortune on the open market. How did they know it was him?

Gragg had cracked their database through a Unicode directory traversal that allowed him to install a back door on their Web server. They hadn't properly patched it, and the sample applications were still on the server, so it was a fairly trivial matter to gain Administrator rights. He was pretty certain that a network admin was lying at the bottom of Manila Harbor over that simple mistake.

But how the hell did they trace the hack to him? Gragg ran the exploit through a zombied machine somewhere in Malaysia and a hijacked 803.11g wireless connection in a Houston subdivision. Even if they tracked the file transfer to the destination IP address, how did that lead them back to him? Even if they beat the hell out of the poor suburban sap whose Wi-Fi access point he'd hijacked, that wouldn't tell them anything. Nonetheless, Gragg had spent a couple sleepless nights waiting for his front door to be kicked in while pondering the question. He just couldn't figure it. What had he missed?

Only recently did it occur to Gragg that he might have been the Filipinos' only partner in Houston. By staging the attack from a Houston domain, Gragg had made a pathetically obvious mistake. The carder, Loki, from Houston, Texas, was an obvious suspect.

But as the days slipped by, it became apparent that either the gang was satisfied that Loki was dead or they had no idea of Gragg's real identity. Until he was positive, Gragg spent his waking hours hiding in the rough industrial space that served as his apartment, playing endless hours of *OTR*. And *OTR* was quite a challenge, after all.

Gragg usually chose the Nazi side, and his preferred weapon was the sniper rifle, which he'd use to pick off newbies from a hiding place in a bell tower or garret window. He combined this with a liberal amount of verbal abuse, using hot keys to launch the taunts built into the game: *I've seen French schoolgirls shoot straighter!*

His cable Internet connection usually gave him a ping in the 20- to 50-millisecond range, which was a major advantage against lamers with pings of 150-plus. Their in-game avatars would hesitate as Gragg dropped them. He never tired of piling up the bodies in front of his hiding place.

Deathmatch *OTR* was a distributed network game—that is, one of the players hosted the game map off of his machine and made the match available for anyone to join over the Internet. There were deathmatch clients available that listed all available matches by geographical region—each machine sending out a message that it was available. The server listings numbered in the thousands.

Since Gragg had been playing *OTR* off and on for the last six months—well before the Filipino problem—he was intimately familiar with every game map. He knew that if he tossed a potato masher grenade from the end of the park in the Saint-Lô map, it would land just behind the vegetable cart on the far end, killing anyone hiding there. He knew a place on the Tunisian map where he could jump up onto shattered rooftops and snipe people with impunity. It took an experienced jumper to make the leap without falling to his death off the balcony.

Frankly, deathmatch had begun to lose its luster until CyberStorm released the custom map editor. Since then, a score of popular custom maps had appeared in the deathmatch server listing. Most of these maps were the out-of-control Rambo fantasies of fourteen-year-old boys, with ridiculous numbers of mounted machine guns and no logic in the placement and design of fortifications. Gragg knew he could do much better, but he didn't have the inclination to learn the scripting language used to create the maps—no money in it.

So it was with low expectations that Gragg downloaded a new custom map named Monte Cassino. The reasonably historic name was unusual, since the fourteen-year-old crowd usually named maps something like "Fuckmeister Shitfest."

Gragg quickly found a server named Houston Central running the Monte Cassino map. Since it was geographically local, it gave him a killer ping of twenty milliseconds, and he joined the deathmatch already under way.

The moment the map loaded, he noticed differences from other custom maps. First off, he wasn't even allowed to join the Axis team. The map permitted Internet team play only for the Allied forces. The Germans were bots. It was humans against the AI, which irked Gragg because he loved playing the German side—they were the villains, after all.

Likewise, respawning was different in this map. It wasn't a straight team match, where you respawned elsewhere after dying. Instead it was described as an "objective" map, where you stayed dead until the last member of your team died or until you defeated all the Germans—at which point the map reset and everyone was alive again.

Also, this map had radically different terrain and textures—as though it was all done from scratch. The map consisted of a steep mountain topped by the ruins of a large Benedictine monastery. The scenario description said U.S. heavy bombers had struck the monastery. The resulting ruins turned out to be a maze of shattered walls, charred wooden beams, and entrances to cellars. It provided excellent cover for the Germans, and the designer placed MG42s with interlocking fields of fire along the approaches to the hilltop. The Germans also had light mortars to kill you if you hid behind boulders. It was as if they'd "registered" the coordinates of all the good cover in advance—which was something the Germans might actually do. As a result, Gragg was determined to beat it.

It was quickly apparent that a pack of lone gunmen could not take the monastery. It required an orchestrated attack. It took an hour of goading other teammates using the chat window, but Gragg finally convinced them to coordinate their attack—instead of running hell-bent for leather up the hill. With some experimentation, they soon discovered that half the squad could draw fire from the Krauts while the other half of the force outflanked them on the left, using the steeper incline for cover. If they ran, they'd be spotted and cut down, but if they crawled on their bellies, they could usually get to within grenade-tossing distance of the outer fortifications. Once the grenades exploded, they'd charge into the ruins and the rest of the battle would be room-to-room fighting.

By this time, the squad distracting the Germans would be mostly dead from mortar rounds and heavy machine guns, so they couldn't contribute much. It was a tough slog, and Gragg was still at it two days later. He hadn't slept and had eaten very little, but he would not disconnect from the Houston Monte Cassino server without beating this map. The closest he'd come had been yesterday, when he made it into the wine cellars. There, an SS officer shot him in the back after Gragg raced past a row of wine tuns.

This was what had driven Gragg for the last twenty-four hours straight: After shooting him, the SS officer stood over his body. It was the infamous Oberstleutnant Heinrich Boerner from the single-player mode of *OTR*. Even freakier, Boerner spoke over Gragg's body. He said: *"Tod ist unvermeidlich, aber meist unbeutend,"* with an English subtitle appearing on the bottom of the screen: "Death is inevitable but largely unimportant."

How the fuck had they done that? It was absolutely the same voice-over artist for Boerner from the original single-player game.

Had this custom map been done by the CyberStorm folks themselves? Gragg was obsessed with reaching the wine cellars again. He had to find out what Boerner was doing there. Only this time he wasn't going to let that fuck shoot him in the back. Yet he knew only too well that Boerner was a slippery character—not likely to repeat his tactics. Gragg resolved to save grenades for the cellars.

The next round started with much of the usual crew—similarly obsessed folks, cursing this addictive game and striving to take the abbey before dawn broke on another sleepy-eyed workday. This time Gragg made sure to follow in the path of a player whose screen name was Major Pain in the Ass. MPITA was a good player, with quick reflexes and a good grasp of key combinations for jumping, switching weapons, and leaning around corners. Gragg crawled behind him during the flanking maneuver, then stuck close on his tail going into the monastery ruins. He never let him get more than a step or two ahead. MPITA soaked up most of the gunfire from Krauts with Schmeissers and heavy machine guns. By the time MPITA was taken out with a Panzerfaust, Gragg was farther into the ruins than he'd ever gotten without taking serious damage.

He took out the Panzerfaust team with a couple blasts from his pump shotgun—his weapon of choice for this map. A sniper rifle was useless in the close quarters of the ruins.

Gragg then stormed forward, hitting a command key that caused his avatar to shout, "Follow me!" He headed toward the dormitory hall, and that was going to be the next problem.

As he reached the corner, Gragg hit the key combo to lean left. He quickly spotted the MG42 team a hundred feet down the roofless, rubble-strewn corridor. The loader pointed and shouted, and the gunner turned toward him and opened fire just as Gragg ducked back again. Tracers whined past for a moment or two until the Krauts decided to save their ammo.

It was an engrossingly realistic game.

Gragg turned his view to face five other Allied players catching up behind him. This was fantastic. They'd never come this far with so few casualties. That meant only ten of the sixteen had been killed in the assault—a record low. He hit the command keys again, and his avatar shouted, "Charge!"

He raced straight across the hall toward a shallow alcove he knew of, immediately drawing fire again from the MG42 at the end of the hall. He watched his health meter drop quickly to 20 percent by the time he reached the safety of the alcove. The players right behind him tried to follow him into the alcove, but Gragg knew it could fit only one player at a time. Their avatars bumped and jumped against his, striving for cover until the Germans mowed them down. Three other players had hung back under cover, and they exchanged fire with the MG42 until Gragg heard what he was waiting for: silence from the Kraut machine gun. They were reloading.

Gragg switched to grenades and charged forward. As he ran over the corpses of his fallen comrades, he picked up their med kits, increasing his health back to 95 percent. It was an odd genre conceit that fallen players sprouted medical kits like Christmas presents, and that picking up a medical kit would immediately increase the health of injured characters—but right now Gragg was all for it. He wanted Boerner's head on a stick.

He could see the Krauts wrestling a belt of ammo into the open breech of their gun while he ran toward them. The machine gun barrel steamed ominously.

The detail of this game is fantastic.

Just as the Krauts slammed the breech closed again, Gragg hurled his grenade down the hallway. It was a perfect throw, and the Germans ran shouting from their machine gun nest.

By that time, Gragg had switched to his shotgun, and he pumped two rounds into each of them as they fled the explosion. They dropped with captivating rag-doll physics. When he reached the smoking machine gun nest, only one of the Krauts was still moving, lying on his back with a 3-D texture of blood ostensibly flowing from his mouth—that meant he was 98 percent wounded.

Gragg loved this part. Sometimes severely wounded AI soldiers would surrender.

The injured Kraut held up his hands with melodramatic fear, looking up at Gragg's avatar. *"Nicht schiessen!"*

BOOM! Gragg wasted him and reloaded.

The other three surviving members of his squad arrived, reloading their Tommy guns. The chat window started rolling fast and furious now:

Sergeant Hairy Balls> Any more grenades?

Your Retarded Brother> Never been this far!

Go Mets!> Loki, we'll cover u

Gragg smirked. Like hell, motherfucker. He typed:

Loki> Fuk u. I took out the machine gun

A moment, then Sergeant Hairy Balls's avatar moved toward some cellar steps. The others followed, with Gragg taking up the rear. This was the way he liked it.

Gragg looked down the stairway. That was the entrance to the wine cellar where he'd seen Oberstleutnant Boerner yesterday. He was going to kill that fucker this time.

Should he warn the others? He calculated whether it was better to share the information and increase the chance of success, or risk it all and keep victory for himself. He decided to let them find out the same way he did.

Hairy Balls tossed a grenade into the cellar and chased the resulting explosion, charging inside with his Thompson blazing. Suddenly the doorway filled with an orange glow, and flames leapt out of the cellar with a throaty roar.

Flamethrower. Boerner was holed up in the cellars with a fucking Flammenwerfer. This was suicide. Hairy Balls was already dead.

The other two players started tossing grenades in through the opening. They ducked in and out of the doorway, chased by roaring flames each time. Gragg knew they were taking damage, but they were helping; a flamethrower had only ten blasts.

By the time the flamethrower was exhausted, Your Retarded Brother was dead, and Go Mets! was badly injured. Gragg knew this because a player's avatar limped when it had less than 20 percent health—and his companion was limping pitifully.

Gragg let Go Mets! grab the med kits from their fallen comrades, since he was of no use to Gragg dead, and they both charged into the wine cellar, guns blazing. Boerner was nowhere in sight.

Gragg hoped it was Boerner they were chasing, since he was running out of ammo. He typed into the chat window:

Loki> Did u see him?

Go Mets!> No

The wine cellar was dimly lit the last time Gragg was here, but now the fires left by the flamethrower illuminated the place pretty well, so they didn't have to probe the dark corners of the room behind the wine barrels. From experience Gragg knew that wood textures could "burn" in OTR, so they had to move through here fast, or they might lose any chance of catching Herr OberstLeutnant at all. Gragg glanced up and saw that the beams overhead had caught fire.

Damn! Who designed this level? It's incredible.

A doorway led through the far wall of the cellar. The exhausted flamethrower pack lay on the stone floor there.

An echoing German voice shouted from that direction: "Amerikaner!" It was Boerner, all right.

Gragg rushed forward with Go Mets!, and they took up positions on either side of the doorway. Gragg started leaning in to take a look, when he saw the infamous Heinrich Boerner character stand up from the cover of some crates behind Go Mets!. Boerner was dressed in his trademark SS officer grays with a floor-length greatcoat and an Iron Cross under his chin.

This bastard son of an AI engine had dropped the flamethrower in the exit to make them think he'd left the room, and they both fell for it, like morons.

Boerner leveled a Schmeisser submachine gun at Go Mets!'s back and opened up. To his credit, Go Mets! leapt up like a house cat and spun around, firing wildly with his Thompson. Gragg tried to pump a few rounds in Boerner's general direction, but Go Mets! was blocking the line of fire.

By the time Gragg circled around and Go Mets! limped to cover, Boerner was moving behind the huge wine tuns again—his evil laugh echoing.

"Fucker, fucker, fucker!" Gragg actually shouted at his flat-screen monitor.

Just then he heard the telltale *clink, clank* of a German potato masher landing in his general vicinity.

"Fuck!" Gragg ducked down and scurried away, but he was still caught by the blast and went flying across the room. He was suddenly down to 15 percent health.

"Damnit!" He pounded his workbench.

The grenades kept coming, and both Gragg and Go Mets! fell back, firing at nothing in particular. By the time they stopped, they were damn near back at the cellar entrance. Embers were falling down around their ears. Gragg lost another 1 percent of health in fire damage.

Gragg tilted his view upward to see the ceiling fully engulfed in flames. The place was filling with smoke. A beam in the corner collapsed, sending up sparks.

Incredible effects.

Gragg turned his view to Go Mets!'s avatar. The guy looked like hell, swaying unsteadily and wheezing.

Gragg aimed the shotgun. BOOM!

Go Mets! fell dead. Gragg collected his med kit and was back up to 39 percent health again.

PK-ing's a bitch, fella.

Then Gragg realized he was out of shotgun shells. He also had no grenades left. He switched to his Colt pistol. This was laughable; he was up against Boerner with a peashooter.

Good as dead now. Might as well go out fighting.

Gragg's avatar ran like a wild man across the burning cellar, firing his pistol at nothing in particular. He ran to the doorway on the far side and jumped over the discarded flamethrower pack. He ran full-speed into the darkness.

It was with considerable surprise that he found himself still alive and moving toward a faint light ahead. He stopped to reload his pistol and then continued.

Soon he reached a circular chamber with a beam of sunlight shining down from a hole in the ceiling, illuminating a section of the wall. It appeared to be the basement of a shattered tower. Several barred windows ringed the walls in the shadows. It was a dead end.

Gragg looked back the way he'd come. No wonder Boerner let him in here—now he was trapped.

Gragg wondered why Go Mets! wasn't flaming him in the chat window for player killing. Perhaps if any of the first squad survived the diversion attack, he could convince them to move up and help out. Gragg hit the TAB key to bring up the player list. To his surprise, no one else was playing on the server anymore. There weren't even any spectators—which is what you turned into after getting killed. All thirty-one human players had disconnected. It was strange. He closed the player list. Maybe they were shunning him for player killing?

Gragg's avatar moved around the dark room. He noticed the wall where the sunlight struck it. There, in the center of the sunlight, a texture map of chiseled stone spelled out a cryptic message:

m0wFG3PRCoJVTs7JcgBwsOXb3U7yPxBB

Gragg stared at it for a while. *What the hell?*

Just then he heard a familiar voice off to his left: "*Amerikaner.*"

Gragg spun left and emptied his Colt in the direction of the voice. It was Boerner all right, standing behind a latticework grate cut into the wall. His shadowy form was partially hidden by the grate. The bullets didn't seem to have any effect. Apparently the game engine treated the latticework as a solid object—like a bulletproof confessional.

In a few seconds Gragg's pistol was empty. As he stood there, his gun still aimed at Boerner, the SS officer took out a lighter and lit a cigarette at the end of a long black filter. The orange glow lit up his hawkish, Aryan face for a moment.

The Oberstleutnant's dark eyes turned to Gragg's avatar. "You haf played long. Haf you no job?"

Gragg's jaded eyes widened in amazement.

Who the hell created this map?

Boerner continued to smoke calmly. On a lark, Gragg hit a hotkey for game taunts. His avatar shouted at Boerner: "*I think the Germans are out of real men!*"

Boerner frowned. "Stop zat nonsense."

At his computer, Gragg stood up, kicked his chair back and gripped his head in mute amazement. His eyes quickly returned to the screen.

Boerner took another drag on his cigarette. "Are you a brain-dead punk"—he motioned to the text centered in the sunlight on the wall— "or do you haf useful knowledge, yes? If you do, use your key, and ve vill meet again." He clenched his teeth on the cigarette filter, smiled darkly, then turned and walked away—laughing his (literally) trademark evil laugh. It echoed in the halls.

Gragg watched him go, then turned to face the writing on the wall again. He hit a key combination for the in-game camera to snap a screen capture.

The moment he did so, he was ejected from the game. The Houston Monte Cassino server never appeared in the public listings again.

Chapter 10:// In the Air

Ross leaned against Sebeck's unmarked police cruiser. It was parked on the shoulder of Potrero Road. "Do you need directions to Woodland Hills, Sergeant?"

"Just a brief detour."

"What is this, the first murder scene?"

"Down that dirt road." Sebeck pointed back at the closed steel gate. He stood in front of the steel winch box. A police warning tag hung from the winch housing.

Sebeck noticed that the steel cable was coiled on the ground beyond the chain-link fence, stretching out of sight downhill. The county probably lowered it to avoid any additional accidents. "Hang on a sec." Sebeck keyed a handheld radio. "Unit 992, this is D-19, over." Sebeck looked to Ross again. "We have a patrol unit guarding the murder scene down below."

A voice crackled over the radio, *"Unit 992, over."*

"I'm at your 20. I need to raise this cable. Is the area clear down there? Over."

"Ten-four. Area clear, D-19. Over."

"Stand by. Out."

Sebeck clipped the radio onto his belt under his sports coat. He produced a ziplock bag from his pocket and unrolled it. It contained keys and a remote control. He removed the keys and flipped through them. He used one to unlock the winch housing. He flipped open the door, then searched for the key to the winch. He inserted the key and turned it in the lock.

The winch motor kicked to life, grinding like a powerful can opener. Sebeck leaned around the side of the winch housing to check the progress of the cable. It wasn't budging.

Ross looked on from his position at the car. "You turning it the right way?"

Sebeck stopped it. He pointed to the arrows next to the lock. "It says 'In.' I'm turning it to 'In.' This is 'Out.'"

He cranked it the other way. The winch paid out a small bit of cable before clicking to a stop. "See? That's 'Out.'"

Sebeck cranked it the other way again. The motor ran, but it didn't even retrieve the small amount he had just paid out. The winch mechanism would not engage even though the motor was running. He stopped it and pulled the key out.

"That's strange. Although, now that I think about it, the handyman said the cable didn't come out of the ground when he ran the winch."

Ross looked puzzled. "The cable was in the ground?"

"Yeah. It was buried in the ground, and the handyman got a faked e-mail from the management company to come over and run the winch."

Ross came up alongside and studied the winch housing. "If running the winch doesn't do anything, why bother to send a spoofed e-mail to have someone run it?"

"It is strange. The FBI lab will probably take it apart." Sebeck pulled out a pad and pen. He started writing down brand, model, and serial numbers for the winch. "Any writing on that side?"

Ross shook his head.

In a moment they were done, and Sebeck put his pad away. "I want to take another look at the murder scene while I'm here. It'll only be a few minutes." They returned to the cruiser. Before getting back into the car, Sebeck pulled the remote control from the ziplock bag and pointed it at the gate. He clicked it.

The gate squeaked once, then started swinging open. Another, familiar sound came to Sebeck's ears, and he cocked his head to listen closely. Ross's hand slapped across his chest, startling him. He glared at Ross, who was pointing. Sebeck followed his finger.

The winch was running, pulling the steel cable taut.

It took the final clang of the gate stopping to rouse them from their stunned silence. The cable was as taut as a piano wire.

Sebeck looked at Ross.

Ross pointed at the remote. "Whose remote is that?"

Sebeck looked down at it. Then nodded appreciatively. "It belonged to Joseph Pavlos. The victim."

Ross nodded back. "That's about right. Otherwise, the cable might be discovered too early, and the murder attempt would fail."

Sebeck pondered it. "But then why send someone out here to run the winch if the key didn't do anything? Like you said: why fake the work order?"

They both thought about it for a few moments.

Ross turned to Sebeck again. "What was the first thing you did after finding out the handyman ran the winch?"

"We detained him and requested a search warrant for the property management office."

"And how much time did you spend waiting for the warrant and searching the office?"

Sebeck grimaced. "Long enough for the second victim to die."

"So maybe it was a distraction to give him time to kill the second programmer."

"Then the bigger question is: why was it so important to kill these programmers?"

Ross frowned.

Sebeck watched him closely. "What?"

Ross hesitated. "The Egyptian pharaohs slew the workers who built their pyramids—"

"The programmers knew too much."

"Maybe. Maybe Sobol had some help to code this thing. He was dying of cancer, after all."

"But why on earth would they help him? Pavlos rode his dirt bike out here all the time. He'd have to notice this was designed to kill him."

Ross leaned back against the hood of the car. "I'm guessing they didn't design this part. Sobol probably did that. They probably coded other parts. Maybe parts we haven't seen yet."

They stood there a moment in silence, weighing the significance of this.

Ross was the first to break the silence. "It's interesting that this Singh guy died trying to get into a server farm."

"Why's that interesting?"

"Well, a server farm is basically a big data storage vault. Racks and racks of servers."

"Yeah, so?"

"So, if I were a programmer trying to get to a secret cache of data—

or to physically stop some machine from running—perhaps I'd head for that server farm."

Sebeck leaned onto the car hood next to Ross.

"Okay, so Singh, who probably works closely with Pavlos, hears about Pavlos's death and makes a beeline for the server farm. Sobol anticipated this and kills him when he tries to enter. So you think there's something in the server farm?"

"Probably not anymore. It sounds like Sobol found whatever Singh put there. So what was Singh working on at CyberStorm? Do you know?"

Sebeck strained to remember the name of Singh's project. "Singh was lead programmer for a game called . . . *Gate*?"

"*The Gate*?"

"Yeah, *The Gate*."

Ross let out a pained groan.

"What now?"

"Do you know the story line for *The Gate*, Sergeant?"

Sebeck gave Ross a look. Clearly he did not.

"It's about a cult opening a gate to the Abyss and releasing a demon that lays waste to the world."

Sebeck just stared at him.

Ross laughed. "I'm talking about Sobol's *game*, Sergeant—I don't believe in demons and devils."

"Good. You had me worried for a second."

"The only daemon I'm worried about is the Unix variety. There's a delicious irony here that I don't think Sobol would be able to resist. You'd know what I'm talking about if you played his games. Now consider this: *The Gate* is an MMORPG."

"What the hell is that?"

"A massively multi-player online role-playing game."

"And what the hell is *that*?"

"It's a persistent 3-D game world experienced simultaneously by tens of thousands of players over the Internet."

Sebeck pointed at Ross. "Okay, now that sounds bad."

"In this case it's very bad."

"Well, the Feds powered down the whole server farm last night. There's not a pocket calculator running over at CyberStorm now. So whatever he planned is . . ."

Ross didn't look reassured.

Sebeck persisted, "I mean, hell, whoever did this couldn't put tens of thousands of steel cables and electrocution traps in people's houses. Failing that, this is basically just another computer virus."

Ross jerked his thumb. "I need my laptop." He walked back and pulled his laptop case from the rear seat. He laid it on the trunk and unzipped the top compartment.

Sebeck walked up to him. "What are you doing now?"

Ross had a credit-card-sized device in his hand. He scanned the area with it. "I'm seeing if there's a Wi-Fi signal in this area." He looked to Sebeck. "And there is." He pointed to the meter on the device, which indicated a strong signal.

Sebeck took the device and examined it while Ross started unpacking his laptop. "Okay, so what's this prove?"

Ross pointed to the gate down the road. "We need some indication that we're on the right track."

"And this does that?"

"Well, for starters it confirms that the gate or the winch could be wirelessly hooked in to the Internet."

"Like the black box over at CyberStorm."

"Right. It means a living human being didn't have to be involved in this. The news reports said Joseph Pavlos went riding down here just about every day. That means his gate remote became a murder weapon only *after* Sobol died."

Sebeck nodded. "Meaning the Daemon told the gate to kill Pavlos after it read the news of Sobol's death."

"That's what I'm thinking. Now we'll see what I can glean from this wireless network."

Sebeck leaned over Ross's shoulder as his laptop booted up. "What are you looking for?"

"The usual: whatever I can find." Ross logged on to his laptop, shielding his logon from Sebeck. Then he launched NetStumbler and waited for it to initialize. "This is a freeware program that helps me see wireless networks."

"I'm not computer illiterate, Jon. I have a wireless network at home."

Ross turned the laptop so the wireless card faced the Wi-Fi signal, and he almost pushed his laptop off the trunk lid. He caught it just in time, held on to it, and continued scanning.

In a moment Ross smiled. "Oh yeah. I picked up an AP." His face suddenly got serious. He looked up at Sebeck.

Sebeck moved over to him. "What?"

"If there's one thing I know from playing Sobol's games, it's this: time works against you. You need to act fast or you're dead."

"Okay, and . . . ?"

Ross turned the laptop around for Sebeck to see.

Sebeck leaned down. The single entry in the NetStumbler window showed text under a column labeled SSID. The text read simply:

DAEMON_63

"I'd say there's more trouble coming, Sergeant."

Sebeck pointed. "Get in the car."

Chapter 11:// The Voice

DailyVariety.com

San Francisco network affiliate **KTLZ** signed Hu Linn Chi to
a two-year contract as Lifestyles reporter, **replacing** veteran
Anji Anderson. The move is seen as part of the network's overall strategy to reach a younger, hipper, more ethnically diverse
demographic.

Anderson was nearing forty minutes on the stair climber. Her work-
out music mix drowned out everything except the pain. The sweat
and the rage poured from her body.

How could they replace her? She wasn't old. Not yet.

She kept driving forward.

The Bay Club was pricey and exclusive, filled with high-powered
business types and trophy wives. More than once she thought she saw
them whispering and pointing. Her professional demise was in the
trades. She burned with humiliation.

Without another network-level job, she couldn't afford this gym,
much less her condo. Her credit card balances kept her driving forward, legs burning.

She had saved nothing. She had been projecting an image of success.
The reality of her modest roots was something she'd tried to hide even
from herself. Her artificial world was coming down around her ears.
They'd call it vanity. No one would understand that it was more than
that. It was ambition. It was a willingness to risk everything. Wasn't
that admirable?

Anderson's cell phone lit up and vibrated on the tray in front of her. She stopped and pulled her earbuds out. She steadied her breathing and considered not answering it. It vibrated again.

It could be Melissa with news of a job. She checked the display. The caller's number was unknown.

Anderson let it ring one more time, then answered it. "This is Anji."

"Is this . . . Anji . . . Anderson?" It was a strangely clipped and measured voice. A woman. British.

"This is she."

"Was that a yes?"

The sound was odd. It must be an overseas call. "Yes. I'm Anji Anderson. Who is this?"

There was a pause. "I'm calling to let you know about a news story. A story that's about to happen."

"I don't know how you got this number—"

"You just lost your job. I can give you a big news story. Are you interested?"

Anderson just stood there, trying to decide. What was this, some sort of telemarketing scam? Was it another stalker?

"I didn't hear you say anything. Do you want the information? Just say 'yes' or 'no.'"

She tried to imagine what Christiane Amanpour would do. "Okay. I'm listening."

"'Okay' is not 'yes' or 'no.' You must understand before we continue that this is not a person. This is an interactive voice system. It can only understand certain things you say."

Anderson hung up. Damned telemarketers.

Her phone rang again almost immediately. She let it go to voice mail. Psycho telemarketers. She looked around for someone who might be staring at her. No one seemed to be watching.

Her phone beeped, and the text VOICE MESSAGE appeared on her display. She stared at the text, waiting for the phone to ring again. It did not.

She speed-dialed her voice mail and put the phone to her ear, then pulled it away again and tapped in her voice mail password. Phone to ear once more.

The familiar computer voice said, "You have . . . one . . . new message."

The message played. It was that measured female British voice again. *"Anji, watch the news tonight. The biggest news story in the world is about to occur in Thousand Oaks, California. The next time I call, perhaps you'll listen."*

Anderson saved the message. Should she tell someone? Should she call the police?

What if the voice was telling the truth? She thought about that again: what if it *was* telling the truth? She considered it some more, then grabbed her water bottle and hurried toward the locker room.

Chapter 12:// Opening the Gate

From: Eichhorn, Stanley J.
To: Patrol Officers; Major Crimes Unit; Bomb Unit
Subject: **Warrant** service @ **Sobol estate**

Body Text:
East County SD will assist the **FBI today** in service of a **search warrant** at the **Sobol estate, 1215 Potrero Road**. Deputies on the second shift will be carried over until 6 P.M. this evening. Deputies assigned to the FBI search must arrive one hour early for a briefing in room 209. **Bomb Squad** members report to room 202 at 11 A.M.

Sebeck and Ross drove down Potrero Road, past the Arabian horse farms and neo-antebellum mansions set amid the rolling hills. It was warm and sunny now. California oaks shaded the road and clustered densely around wrought iron entrance gates flanked by white split-rail fences and stone walls. Most of the mansions were set back far from the road and hidden behind hills and hedges. The spicy scent of hay perfumed the air.

Ross studied the scenery. "Where are we going, Sergeant?"

"Sobol's estate. The FBI is there."

"I thought you were taking me back to my car."

"I need you to show the FBI exactly what you showed me back there."

"Look, they know where to find me if they have any questions."

"That's just it. I'm afraid they won't. And I'm not sure that any of their forensics experts have played Sobol's games before."

The police dispatcher's voice came over the radio. Sebeck grabbed the handset. "This is D-19. I'm 10-97 at 1215 Potrero Road. Out." He looked to Ross. "We're here."

Sebeck turned left past two marked patrol cars guarding the open gates of a large estate. He nodded to the deputies standing nearby and rolled past them, heading down the long driveway flanked by lines of mature oaks. In between the trunks they caught glimpses of a fine Mediterranean villa some distance ahead. This wasn't a modern replica. It looked like an authentic 1920s-era mansion with a cupola and slanting roofs capped in terra cotta tile. The mansion was set back about a thousand feet from the road, nestled in a copse of manzanita trees.

Ross whistled.

Sebeck nodded. "Yeah, I didn't know there was so much money in computer games."

"They generate more revenue than all of Hollywood."

The driveway ended in a wide cobblestone courtyard flanked by a horse stable, a six-car garage, and what looked to be a guesthouse or office. The main house lay straight ahead with landscaped lawns opening the courtyard on either side. Through these openings Sebeck saw sweeping views of the estate grounds.

More than a dozen police vehicles were parked in the courtyard—FBI sedans, county patrol cars, a forensics van, an ambulance, and the bomb squad's truck with a disposal trailer. But there was room to spare. The courtyard was large.

Sebeck pulled up behind a sedan with white government plates. He and Ross got out.

A couple dozen officers stood near the entrance to the main house. They were listening to Neal Decker addressing them from the steps leading up to the mansion's heavy wooden door. It was a mix of county and local police, along with federal agents wearing blue windbreakers with the letters *FBI* stenciled on the back. It was impossible to hear what Decker was saying at this distance.

Nathan Mantz came up to Sebeck as he and Ross took in the scene. "Hey, Pete. You're just in time."

"How'd it go at the permit office?"

Mantz shook his head. "No permit pulled for the winch housing. The gate was installed by a big GC named McKenser and Sons. Licensed, bonded, legit. Nothing in the permit applications about a winch. I put a call in to McKenser's office, and they're checking their records."

Mantz looked to Ross. "You're that computer guy the Feds were holding." He extended his hand. "Detective Nathan Mantz."

Ross shook his hand. "Jon Ross. I was cleared, by the way."

Sebeck kept his eye on the crowd of agents in the distance. "Yeah, it turns out Mr. Ross here is quite an expert—on a few subjects. I brought him out to the canyon scene, and he shed some light on things. I've got important information for Decker." Sebeck pointed to Decker, who was addressing the troops. "What are the Feds up to?"

"They're preparing to search the house. FBI bomb squad and forensics teams came up from L.A. Decker's treating this as a hazardous search."

Ross nodded. "He's right. It is."

Mantz gave him a curious look.

Sebeck jerked a thumb at Ross. "He thinks it's Sobol, not somebody at CyberStorm. Now he's got *me* wondering."

Mantz nodded, impressed. "Really?"

Sebeck tore a page out of his small notepad and handed it to Mantz. "Nathan, do me a favor; here's the manufacturer and serial number on the winch assembly. When we get back to the station, check with the factory to see if they have a record of the wholesaler they shipped it to. Let's find out what else was purchased."

"No problem." Mantz pocketed the piece of paper.

Sebeck walked toward the gathered officers. Ross and Mantz followed. They passed three FBI agents preparing a tracked bomb disposal robot. Ross took a keen interest, peering over their shoulders as they tested the video cameras with a large remote control.

They were having problems. The operator smacked the handheld controller. "Try channel four. Is the picture any clearer?"

Sebeck tugged Ross along.

Decker was still addressing the troops. ". . . papers, computers, electrical components, tools. Virtually everything should be considered dangerous until the bomb squad marks a room as clear. If you find a device—"

Decker leaned down as agent Straub said something to him. Decker looked up again at the crowd. "Hang on. Is anyone else having radio problems?"

Most of the officers held up their hands and voiced in the affirmative.

Sebeck noticed a man in his fifties and a woman in her forties standing among the FBI agents. The two civilians looked pensive. Sebeck turned to Mantz.

Mantz responded. "The caretaker and the security guard. Husband and wife. Sobol's widow lives in Santa Barbara. They separated before his death. Get this: she told them she couldn't live in the house because she heard voices. They're tracking her down as we speak. I was hoping she'd be here. . . ." Mantz pulled a folded magazine page out of his jacket pocket. He unfolded it to reveal a photo of a tanned and beautiful blonde wearing a string bikini and stretched out on the wet sand of a tropical beach. "The widow Sobol. Miss New Zealand, 2001."

Sebeck grabbed the page. "Holy shit."

Ross leaned in. "Wow."

Mantz grabbed it back. "Show some respect. She's in mourning." He folded it and put it back into his jacket pocket. "Sobol may have died of cancer, but I *still* envy the bastard."

Sebeck was already walking toward the crowd of agents and officers. He waded through them, headed directly for Assistant Chief Eichhorn.

"Hey, Chief." Sebeck stepped aside and gestured toward Ross. "This is Jon Ross—the computer consultant from Alcyone."

Chief Eichhorn nodded toward Ross. "One of the guys the Feds brought in."

"They cleared him this morning. I was bringing him back to Woodland Hills, and I stopped by the Pavlos scene to get serial numbers. Mr. Ross detected a wireless device there. He has some pretty mind-blowing theories about how Sobol's doing all this. I think Decker should talk to this guy."

"Pete, the FBI brought experts in from L.A. and Washington."

"Yeah, but I don't know how many of them have spent serious time playing in Sobol's games. Mr. Ross has."

"I can't vet Mr. Ross's skills—no offense—can *you*, Pete?"

"Somebody technical should listen to him."

Suddenly the FBI robot crew leader stepped between them and called up to Decker on the patio. "The robot's a no-go, Neal. There's signal interference. This guy probably has spread spectrum radio towers or something inside."

Decker looked around. "Should we have the city cut power to the house?"

The lead operator conferred with the other two, then looked up to Decker. "The computer forensics team will want to keep the power on—otherwise they might lose computer memory evidence."

Decker nodded vigorously. "Of course . . . I knew that." He spoke softly with agents Straub and Knowles. After a moment he looked up again and announced, "Okay, we go to plan B. The bomb squad goes in with fiber optics. Guerner, get your crew ready."

Three heavily padded men with high Kevlar collars, bulletproof helmets, and plastic toolboxes moved through the crowd. The officers made way for them.

Decker motioned with both arms. "Let's move it back behind the vehicles, people!"

The crowd of officers moved back through the parked cars and gathered on the far side. Decker followed them.

Sebeck gave a look to Chief Eichhorn, then approached Decker. "Agent Decker, I've got important information from the canyon scene."

"Let me resolve this first, Sergeant." Decker tried his radio again and then conferred with the bomb squad.

Sebeck leaned on a nearby car hood and looked to Ross. "If Sobol is behind the murders, we should find some evidence of it here."

Ross looked around. "Look, the FBI knows where to reach me, Sergeant. I really just want to get back to my hotel and salvage my client list."

"Not until I get you in front of Decker."

————

Agent Andrew Guerner was proud of his team. Rick Limon and Frank Chapman had served with him in the FBI Explosives Unit through four years and scores of bomb calls in the U.S. and abroad—real ones and hoaxes. Among them they had thirty-five years of experience. As a demining expert with the 101st Airborne, Guerner had extensive field experience in demolitions, booby traps, improvised explosive devices, and cell phone detonators. He'd cleared mines from Bosnia to Iraq and spent two years as an explosives instructor at Quantico. His companions had military experience with Special Forces and Aberdeen Proving Ground in Maryland. It was a top-notch crew.

Decker's briefing laid out the details of the two earlier killings—and that this Sobol guy was some kind of genius. Guerner clucked his tongue inside his helmet. He'd seen a lot of clever devices in his day. They were all sitting in his lab, defused.

He turned to his partners and nodded. Limon and Chapman nodded back. Far behind them, the gathered officers gave the thumbs-up sign. Guerner started by taking the fiber optic snake out and flipping up his visor. He looked for a gap wide enough to slip it under the mansion's front door. It was a tight seal. Looked like an authentic Spanish mission door. Too bad.

He motioned to Limon, who leaned forward and drove a hole through it with a battery-powered drill.

Guerner fed the snake through the hole and put his eye to the lens. He turned the snake this way and that, examining every angle of the room beyond the door.

Christ, that's a nice floor.

Probably Venetian marble. He'd just laid ceramic tile in his downstairs bathroom at home, and he had a greater appreciation of these things now. He examined the twin staircases curving down from a single landing above the foyer. There were three ground-floor doorways, not including the front door. The foyer was probably twenty feet deep and thirty feet wide. The millwork was nicely done. Right down to the baseboards.

He moved back and gave a hand signal to Limon, who stepped forward with a frequency detector.

Limon moved the detector along the doorjamb and the face of the door itself. He watched the LCD readout intently. "This thing's going nuts." He pulled it away from the door and just held it there. "It's still going nuts. I'm getting signals on all frequencies."

Interesting. For a moment Guerner considered using an explosive sheet to blast an opening through the door, but the antique oak was reinforced with black iron bands and was probably several inches thick. Power saws would also be tricky. Sparks from cutting the iron might set off fire detection systems. "Got the caretaker's key?"

Chapman leaned forward and placed it in Guerner's heavily gloved hand. He was surprised by the key's weight. You could break a window with it. He examined it closely: a straight brass rod with a crystal embedded on its end. Or was that a diamond? He looked at the lock.

Custom. The mechanism was most likely attuned to the precise vibrating frequency of the crystal when subjected to an electrical current. Some sophisticated shit.

He looked to his partners. "Window."

They moved down to the nearest large window. It was off to the right about fifteen feet. Guerner peered through the glass. Beyond lay a living room with a high, beamed ceiling, stucco walls, and a large fireplace. Tall bookshelves lined the walls. A sofa and authentic-looking mission furniture were placed tastefully about the room. He spotted at least two motion sensors in the upper corners near the ceiling. Sprinkler caps dotted the ceiling as well. It made sense, this far from the road. It also meant there was an emergency fire pump or a fire department hookup outside. He didn't remember seeing that in the blueprints.

He kept looking through the window. "Limon. Are there sprinkler heads shown on the blueprints?"

Guerner heard his partners flipping through the plans.

"Not shown."

"Damnit. The plans aren't accurate." He looked closely at the edges of the window frame. He shined a Maglite into the corners. No visible sensors, but he knew it was alarmed. Decker had ordered Guerner to treat the place as a potential death trap. In light of the electrocution at CyberStorm, Guerner intended to. He considered the front door key again, then led his team back to the front door.

"The caretaker deactivated the alarm and used her front door key just this morning without incident. I say we do the same." He looked to the other two.

Limon and Chapman nodded.

Limon handed him a short pole with a gripping claw on the end. Guerner took it and fitted the key onto its end. He extended his arm and, using a steady hand, inserted the key into the lock. There was no need to turn it; it emitted a loud *click*. He let go of the key and used the pole to depress the lever doorknob. He took a deep breath, then nudged it inward. It opened very smoothly for such a large door.

They peered inside. Limon tried to get a frequency reading again, while Chapman pulled an aerosol can from his toolbox. Chapman looked to Guerner, who nodded. Chapman sprayed a smoky mist evenly into the foyer doorway.

All three men scanned the smoke-filled air for laser beams. Nothing.

Guerner gave the hand signal to advance.

He was first through the door, prodding ahead with the pole. He slowly skirted the edge of the foyer and looked around the room. It was gorgeous. His partners followed him inside. Limon slipped a plastic wedge underneath the front door to keep it open.

Guerner checked his radio. "Blue Team Leader, this is Unit B, do you copy? Over." There was nothing but static.

Limon looked at him. "This whole place is a storm of radio signals."

Suddenly they heard a noise of movement upstairs. Like someone walking around. Footsteps echoing on hardwood. They looked at each other. Guerner grabbed his radio. "Blue Team Leader, we've got someone in here. Do you read?" Still static.

Just then a voice called out clearly from the end of the hallway upstairs. "Who's there?" The voice echoed in the marble foyer.

Guerner unsnapped his holster cover and raised his visor. "This is the FBI! Show yourself with your hands on your head!"

No reply. But they heard walking again. The footsteps came down the marble stairs to their right, some distance away from them. They could clearly see the staircase, but no one was there. They could hear the sound of a hand sliding down the metal railing.

Instinctively they all drew their pistols.

Limon smacked Guerner in the arm. "Jesus, what are we, idiots? This is a trick." He still didn't lower his pistol.

Guerner focused on the staircase. "I know. But it's a fucking impressive one."

The footsteps were moving across the floor to them now.

Guerner motioned toward the front door. "Let's back it up, guys."

Then, in midair not five feet in front of them, a man's voice shouted, "You don't belong here!"

What happened next surprised even the veteran Guerner. The deepest sound he'd ever felt passed over and through him. Then it was quiet, until the mission table near him began to vibrate so violently it started moving across the floor. A crystal vase on top of it shattered.

Suddenly Guerner felt as though someone had grabbed his intestines straight through his Kevlar suit. He didn't even have time to warn Limon and Chapman before he was doubled over on the marble floor, vomiting. His guts felt like writhing snakes trying to climb out of his

88 // Daniel Suarez

body. The agony was intense. His whole being was gripped with a deep and primordial feeling of dread—like a palpable evil had climbed inside him.

Guerner was a man of science and reasoning, but his entire knowledge of the world fled, leaving him alone on the floor weeping in terror. He crawled away through his vomit, listening to insane shrieking. Then he realized the shrieks were coming from him.

Sebeck, Ross, and Mantz stood with the gathered officers in the courtyard. A moment ago they had heard Guerner shout a warning to someone in the house. Chief Eichhorn leaned over to the caretaker to confirm that no one else was in the mansion.

Sebeck's cell phone twittered. He pulled it from his belt clip. "Sebeck."

A voice he vaguely recognized said, *"Detective Sebeck, I just needed to know where you were."* The connection dissolved in a flurry of static.

Mantz noticed Sebeck's stunned expression. "Who was it, Pete?"

Sebeck stared at his phone, then looked to Ross. "I'm not certain, but I think that was Matthew Sobol. . . ."

That's when the shrieking began. They were the most bloodcurdling shrieks Sebeck had ever heard, like a man burning alive. Agents and officers pelted toward the front door. Before they got far, Decker shouted, "Don't go inside! Stay clear!"

They slowed for a second, but then they saw Limon clawing his way out the open front door on his hands and knees. His Kevlar vest was covered in vomit, and his helmet was off. He was bleeding from the nose, eyes, and ears and groped along as if blind.

Sebeck and some of the others rushed to his aid. Limon was still sixty feet away from them. Eichhorn and Decker shouted for caution, and with all eyes looking forward, no one noticed the middle garage door silently rise behind them.

The first warning they received was the guttural sound of a powerful engine, then screeching tires. Sebeck and the other officers turned to face a full-sized black Hummer roaring out of the garage. It bore down on the nearest of them and crushed a deputy and an FBI agent into the side of an FBI sedan, hitting it so hard the car slid into the police cruiser behind it.

Sebeck stood in a paralysis of incomprehension. He could clearly see that no one was driving the Hummer. It sported six tall whip antennas—still wagging from the impact of the collision—and it had odd-looking sensors bolted to its hood, roof, and fenders.

The Hummer's engine roared as it backed away from the wrecked car and the bodies tumbled onto the paving stones. The Hummer's push-bar bumper was barely dented and was covered in blood.

It all happened so fast. Two men had just been killed. Adrenaline flooded into Sebeck's system.

People ran in every direction, shouting. Sebeck looked back to the door of the mansion to see the other two bomb squad members running out of the house, screaming. One of them stumbled down the front steps and fell into the flower beds, where he went into convulsions.

Deputies and FBI agents drew pistols and fired at the Hummer as it screeched around the edge of the courtyard, building up speed again. Shots cracked in rapid succession, echoing against the side of the house. The familiar, pungent smell of smokeless powder brought Sebeck to his senses, and he pulled his Beretta from its holster. He rammed its slide back, gripped it with both hands, then opened fire. He aimed for the Hummer's tires.

Sebeck could clearly see bullet impacts on the tires, but they had no effect. The tires were either run-flat or solid rubber. He brought his aim up to the windows—but remembered there was no one to shoot at.

Now the Hummer howled straight back toward them. Deputies and agents fired a few frantic last shots before scrambling from between the parked police vehicles. It crashed into the side of another patrol car, halving the car's width and driving it back like a battering ram into two more cruisers. Those cars smashed into the patio wall, pinning a couple of officers there. The sheer force and loudness of the crash sent Sebeck running for the nearest high ground—a garden wall.

Screams of pain came to his ears from the pinned officers. He looked back and saw the Hummer seesawing backward as its gears whined. It swung wide and winged a fleeing officer with its fender. The man went rolling across the courtyard. Turning on him, the Hummer screeched forward before he could get up. The deputy went shrieking under its wheels. His body was dragged halfway across the courtyard before it fell loose.

Sebeck screamed in rage and emptied his pistol at the rear of the Hummer while it chased down two agents fleeing toward a garden pond.

An agent with a pump shotgun ran up to it as it passed by. He fired two rounds into it, blasting out its windows and sending pieces of plastic flying. He kept firing as it drove on.

Shouts filled the courtyard now. Nearby, Sebeck saw Decker screaming into his radio, ". . . do you copy?"

Back at the estate gates, Deputy Karla Gleason stood taking in the sun and watching for the expected arrival of the media. There hadn't been any radio calls from the mansion—which was odd—but she stood next to her patrol car, attentive and wondering what the mansion would fetch on the real estate market.

Across the driveway, Deputy Gil Trevetti stood next to his cruiser, waving a curious passenger car on by. That's when the crackling of gunfire reached Gleason's ears. She and Trevetti exchanged looks, then ran for the fence line.

Everything looked normal. The mansion was partially masked by trees, so none of the police vehicles were visible from here. But now the gunfire crackled like firecrackers. It was an unbelievable amount of sustained shooting. Maybe it *was* fireworks.

Gleason pressed the button on her shoulder radio. "Unit 920 to any available Blue Team member: 10-73?"

No response.

"Repeat. Unit 920 to any available Blue Team member: 10-73?"

A distant truck engine raced, then a crash.

"What the hell's going on, Gil?"

The unmistakable boom of a shotgun reached them over the grounds. Five shots in five seconds. Gleason shot skeet. She knew that sound well. She pressed the button on her shoulder radio. "920 to Control, multiple 10-57 at 1215 Potrero Road. Repeat, multiple, multiple 10-57. Code 30. Radio contact lost with Blue Team."

The courtyard was chaos as the Hummer roared back in from the garden and smashed headlong into the ambulance, sending glass and metal debris flying. It surged ahead, pushing the ambulance sideways at the mouth of the driveway—blocking the exit.

The entire time, officers laid down sustained gunfire on it, pocking its body with bullet holes. The bullets didn't appear to have much effect, even though some of the Hummer's sensors now dangled loose on wires.

It slalomed across the courtyard, finally locking in on an agent firing at it from the garage. The man stopped shooting and ran for cover through the doorway.

The Hummer plowed through the entire wall after him and emerged on the far side, leaving shards of two-by-fours and shattered walls toppling in its wake.

Sebeck fired the last of his third clip into its rump as it roared back out into the garden. He added his own voice to the shouting and the cries of the injured. "Nathan!"

"Here, Pete!" Nathan came running across the courtyard with a shotgun and a box of shells in his hand. Several car trunks were wrenched open in the wreckage, and the officers raided them for heavier weapons.

Sebeck pointed to the bomb squad truck. "Stay with Mr. Ross, and make sure he gets out of here. He has information the FBI needs."

"What about you?"

"I'll help with the wounded. Move!"

Nathan gave him one last look, then raced off toward the bomb squad van. Sebeck dodged between damaged police vehicles and almost slipped on blood as he raced across the cobblestones. A severed arm lay next to a crumpled bumper. His mind had trouble wrapping itself around the sights and smells. Officers were trying to get a bleeding FBI agent out from under a smashed sedan before the Hummer returned. The wounded man screamed in agony and fear.

Nearby, Sebeck saw Aaron Larson attended to by an FBI agent and another deputy. Larson looked to be in tremendous pain. He was standing up, sandwiched between two damaged patrol cars.

Sebeck turned and called across the courtyard. "Get that truck over here! We need to pull these cars apart!" He holstered his pistol and ran to help. Shouted commands echoed from every corner of the courtyard.

"I can't get anybody on the radio!"

"Cell phones don't work either!"

"It's coming back in!"

Decker climbed across the crumpled hood of his sedan. "Get the wounded into the vans! Fall back to the road!"

Sebeck was sprinting across the middle of the courtyard when the Hummer roared in behind him through an opening between the house and garage, sending debris flying.

"Pete, look out!" Gunfire erupted almost immediately. A bullet whined past Sebeck's head. He ducked, then turned to see the Hummer bearing down on him. It was almost on him already. He felt the bass rumble of its engine in his chest, the black grill racing straight toward him.

Then it shuddered violently to a stop on the cobblestones just a foot away. Sebeck stood motionless—heart pounding—before the massive steel grill. His eyes focused on the Hummer's front vanity plate: *AUTOM8D*. It was smeared with blood. The plate suddenly began to recede as the Hummer shifted into reverse and backed away from him. The Hummer then roared forward again, passing Sebeck wide on the left and accelerating toward the FBI agent and deputy helping Aaron Larson. They scattered as Larson screamed.

The crash scattered the cars across the courtyard, sending Larson's body hurtling like a rag doll.

Sebeck stood motionless, in a state of shock in the middle of the courtyard. Amid all the screams and shouts, gunshots, and the roaring engine of the Hummer. He was still alive, and he didn't know why.

Then the familiar sound of racing V8 engines came to Sebeck's ears. Two Ventura County police cruisers hurtled down the driveway from the front gate, rack lights flashing. They screeched to a stop next to the ambulance blocking the driveway. A male deputy jumped out of one and raced to retrieve Larson's body, while a female deputy leaned out the passenger side of the other car and opened fire on the Hummer with a shotgun.

Sebeck was dimly aware of someone pulling on his arms. "Pete!" He turned to see Deputy Gil Trevetti. "Larson's dead! We need to pull back!" Trevetti tugged Sebeck toward a nearby patrol car. A rumble came to his ears and Sebeck turned to see the FBI's bomb squad truck with deputies and agents hanging off its armored bomb disposal trailer accelerating across the littered courtyard. Mantz leaned out off the trailer and jabbed a finger at Sebeck, then toward the exit. The bomb truck crashed through a nearby rose garden and headed out across the estate lawn.

Sebeck snapped back to reality and turned to Trevetti. "Okay. Got it." They jumped into the patrol car while the black Hummer raced to intercept the bomb squad truck in the distance.

From the front seat of the bomb squad truck, Ross saw the Hummer racing toward them like a torpedo—leaving twin ruts in the soft grass.

"It's going to ram us!" the agent driving shouted. "I can't maneuver on this grass."

Ross faced him. "Turn toward it. Head-on!"

The driver gave him a look.

"It will avoid a head-on collision with a larger object."

"How the hell do *you* know?"

"Because Sobol's probably using his game physics engine." On the driver's blank look, he shouted, "Ram the Hummer, goddamnit!"

The driver looked into Ross's intense eyes. There was no doubting his confidence. The driver spun the wheel to aim head-on at the advancing Hummer.

Agents and deputies hanging on to the bomb squad truck shouted at the driver. The Hummer accelerated straight toward their front grill—then it swerved aside at the last second, winging their front right fender with its rear quarter panel.

A cheer went up in the truck. The driver accelerated straight toward the estate fence line. He glanced toward Ross. "How the hell did you know that?"

Ross pointed and shouted. "Slow down!"

The estate fence was wrought iron with a masonry base. They crashed through it going at least thirty, nosed down onto Potrero Road, and slammed into the ditch on the far side. Ross held his hands up and smashed against the windshield with the other two deputies sitting up front. They shattered it with their weight, then slammed back against the seat as the truck came to a complete stop.

There were groans of pain from the wounded and the newly wounded. Someone shouted, "What the fuck are you trying to do, get us all killed?"

Ross shook his head clear and could now hear approaching sirens. Lots of them. He looked at his hands. They were only slightly cut. He followed the deputies out of the truck.

They raced around the overturned bomb squad trailer to the estate side of the road. They could see the Hummer still on the other side of the fence. It wasn't following them, but was instead charging around the lawn like a raging bull, spinning and tearing up the turf.

The officers opened fire on it again, emptying shotguns, pistols, and an M-16 rifle while shouting obscenities. The Hummer raced off toward the mansion.

Ross covered his ears against the noise and looked up the road to see approaching emergency vehicles.

It had begun. He knew there was no hope of containing the Daemon now. And guns were useless against it.

Chapter 13:// Demo

BBC.co.uk

Dead Computer **Genius Slays Police**, Federal Agents— **Thousand Oaks, CA**—Authorities have surrounded a walled **estate owned by** the late **Matthew Sobol,** a leading computer game designer who died earlier this week of brain cancer. **Six** law **officers** were **killed** and **nineteen** others **injured** serving a search warrant at the property. They were reportedly attacked by a computer-controlled SUV that still roams the grounds.

Anderson's North Beach condo had twelve-foot pressed-tin ceilings, original wood floors, full-height windows with a fabulous view of the windows across the street, and enough Victorian charm to draw grudging praise from the snottiest folks she knew. It had taken her years to decorate, and she never tired of appreciating the style it reflected upon her. Even though she could no longer afford it.

But her eyes were riveted right now to the plasma screen television hanging within a Victorian picture frame on her living room wall. There was breaking news from Thousand Oaks, California—just as The Voice had promised.

She sat numb with fear and excitement all at once, soaking up the images on the screen.

In the absence of facts, a local reporter was breathlessly transforming hearsay into news under the harsh lights of a live remote: "Thanks, Sandy. Sources describe a scene of total carnage and devastation on the estate. The area has been cordoned off, with FBI tactical units brought in. Once again, a robotic killing machine is roaming the estate grounds, unleashed by a recently deceased madman. That madman: Matthew Sobol."

Anderson's cell phone vibrated on the coffee table in front of her. She looked at it and recoiled in terror. The phone vibrated again, moving slightly across the tabletop.

Christiane Amanpour would answer it.

Anderson timidly picked up the phone and pressed the SEND button—not saying anything, just listening.

A man's voice came over the line. *"Do you know who I am? Answer 'yes' or 'no.'"*

She watched the video footage of injured policemen being loaded into ambulances. "Yes."

"Clearly speak my name."

"Matthew . . . Sobol."

There was silence for a moment. Then, *"If you contact the authorities, I will know, and you will lose the exclusive on this story."*

Anderson's hands were trembling as the voice continued.

"I am analyzing your verbal responses with voice stress analysis software— I can tell if you lie to me. Answer truthfully or our relationship is over. Remember: I have extended my will beyond physical death. I will never be gone from this earth. Do not make an enemy of me."

Anderson dared not even breathe. She wasn't a religious person— but she felt as if an evil force was on the other end of the line. An immortal being.

"Do you still want to be a journalist? Answer 'yes' or 'no.'"

Anderson swallowed hard and took a breath. She used her best broadcasting voice. "Yes." Anderson's heart raced.

There was a pause.

"Do you want access to exclusive information on this story? Answer 'yes' or 'no' . . . "

"Yes."

A pause.

"Do you agree to keep our relationship secret from everyone—with no exceptions? Answer 'yes' or 'no.'"

"Yes."

Another pause.

"Are you prepared to follow my instructions in exchange for success and power? Answer 'yes' or 'no.'"

Anderson caught her breath. This was the proverbial Rubicon. If she crossed it, there was likely no turning back. Years from now she would remember this moment with either regret or relief—but she knew she would never forget it.

The Voice insisted, *"Answer 'yes' or 'no.'"*

Anderson's mind raced. She couldn't let it go now. It was a machine—it wouldn't judge her. Worse, she would never know the whole story if she declined. Didn't a real journalist pursue the story no matter what? Wasn't that admirable?

"Yes."

Yet another pause.

"Do you believe in God? Answer 'yes' or 'no.'"

Anderson was taken aback. She hesitated, not sure whether she did or not. Then, "No?"

A pause.

She half expected a lightning bolt to smite her.

Suddenly the British-sounding female voice cut in, speaking with its clipped, synthetic efficiency.

"Your user ID is . . . J-92. Remember your ID . . . J-92. It is your identity. You have been assigned a role. If you deviate from this role—for any reason— you will be removed from the system. Follow all instructions, and the system will protect and reward you."

Anderson was trying to gather her thoughts to say something, but then she realized there was no one to say anything to. She had cashed in her morals at a vending machine.

The Voice continued like the unstoppable force it was. *"An airline ticket is waiting under your human name at the . . . Southwest Airlines . . . ticket counter at . . . Oakland International . . . Airport. Proceed to this location within the next . . . four . . . hours. If you speak to anyone else regarding this matter, you will be killed."*

The line went dead.

Anderson stifled a scream of terror. What had she done?

She looked up to see video footage of body bags being lifted into a coroner's van on the evening news—mute testimony to the truth of the threat.

Chapter 14:// Meme Payload

From: Matthew Andrew Sobol
To: Federal Authorities; International Press
Re: Siege of My Estate

Federal authorities besieging my Thousand Oaks estate are hereby advised to refrain from further incursions onto the grounds for a period of no less than 30 days, inclusive of and commencing at 12 noon today. All those entering the grounds prior to that time will be resisted with deadly force.

Members of law enforcement: You are not my enemy. However, it is vital that my work continue. I will do what I must in self-defense.

Upon expiration of this deadline, you will be free to take possession of the estate, my server room, and its data. Failure to follow these instructions will result in the loss of all data and the deaths of many more people.

Sebeck knelt on the ground next to a black body bag. He stared emptily at the fading sunlight reflected on the black vinyl.

Ross watched from some distance away, leaning against the side of an ambulance. Five more body bags were lined up nearby. FBI agents consoled each other. There were tears on many faces.

Sebeck took a deep breath and finally stood. He turned toward Ross with a smoldering rage. "Jon!"

Ross followed as Sebeck strode through the tarpaulin walls of the makeshift morgue and into a crowd of FBI agents, local police, county tactical teams, paramedics, reporters, and technicians laying siege to Sobol's estate. Literally hundreds of people ringed the place. City workers were setting up construction lights to illuminate the staging area as the sun began to set. The road was closed to civilian traffic, and something resembling a heavily armed county fair stretched along its length. Police from three neighboring jurisdictions were on hand.

Nearby homes had been evacuated. The Feds were in the process of quarantining the Daemon; power and phone people were cutting service to Sobol's property. Sebeck could see their hydraulic lifts clustered around utility poles a considerable distance from the estate. He guessed power was being killed to the entire neighborhood, and diesel generators added to the general din.

Sebeck kept moving, tugging Ross through the crowd, alternately surging ahead, then turning back to face him.

"It can't be a machine. There's a living person behind this."

Ross didn't respond.

"Someone was controlling that Hummer."

Ross looked grim. "My condolences on Deputy Larson."

Sebeck glared at him. "Don't you tell me that was software."

"It could be done—using the same AI engine that controls characters in a computer game. We were the objective. We're just infrared heat sources."

Sebeck shook his head. "Bullshit."

"Any word on Detective Mantz? He was hanging on to the trailer last time I saw him."

"Broken leg and a couple of broken ribs. Someone is going to pay for this."

"Sobol is dead, Pete."

"I don't care. Someone is going to pay."

"I know you're upset." Ross gestured to encompass the scene. "Where are we going?"

"To find Agent Decker. He needs to hear your theory about how Sobol's doing this. Maybe they can use the information to contain this thing."

"Sergeant, the Daemon probably spread to the four corners of the world in minutes. It's too late for containment. What you have to do is understand what it's trying to accomplish and prevent it from accomplishing it."

"It's trying to *kill* people—wake up."

Ross spoke calmly. "Pete, think about it: If all it wanted to do was kill people, why did it phone you to find out if you were present? Why didn't it kill you in the courtyard when it had the chance? We all saw that Hummer stop and turn away from you. The Daemon has plans for you, and I'm sure it has plans for others as well."

Sebeck fumed for a bit, but then what Ross said began to sink in. "We've got to find Decker." Sebeck pointed at the county sheriff's mobile command trailer a couple hundred yards away. "That's probably where he'll be." He started walking toward it.

Ross grabbed Sebeck's sleeve.

"What?"

"Why are police massing around the estate?"

Sebeck gave Ross a quizzical look. "What do you suggest they do?"

"The house is not important, Pete. It won't contain any useful information."

"The hell it won't."

"Let's not replay this map. We're wasting time."

Sebeck raised his eyebrows. "So you think this is that much of a game to Sobol?"

"I think *life* was a game to Sobol."

Sebeck sighed, truly lost. "Why would Sobol issue a press release forbidding the Feds from entering the property if there wasn't anything important inside?"

"Will the Feds defy the demand?"

"*I* would. Who the fuck does this guy think he is?"

Ross pointed. *"That's* why Sobol did it."

"You think he's just pushing the FBI's buttons?"

"More than that. He publicly drew a line in the sand against authority. They'll have little choice but to cross it, and people will die. He's manipulating them—to keep public attention focused on this location."

"But why? If Sobol killed the two programmers to protect the secrets of the Daemon's design, then what's the purpose behind the Hummer? Isn't it also to protect the Daemon?"

"I don't think so."

"Then why in the hell would he go through so much trouble?"

Ross thought for a moment, then looked back up at Sebeck. "What do you think will be the number one news story in the world tonight?"

Sebeck didn't hesitate. "This."

"Right. And *that's* what we have to worry about: what is the Daemon about to do that requires the attention of the whole world?"

Sebeck glared at him again. "Oh, come on, Jon. My head hurts just from talking to you."

"This didn't happen by accident. Manipulation was Sobol's specialty. These physical killings were to attract publicity. He's issuing press releases."

"Look, I know you feel you're a Sobol expert, but what I need is a technology expert."

"You'll need both."

"You're biased, Jon."

"Biased? How am I biased?"

"You're too big a fan of this guy. Listen to yourself; you make Sobol out to be twenty feet tall."

"Pete—"

"Sobol had brain cancer. You should see how thick his medical file is. Did it ever occur to you that he was just fucking crazy?"

"Does that make him less or more dangerous? I'm telling you, it doesn't end here at his house. I'm sure of it."

"Do you suggest we just let the Hummer prowl the neighborhood?"

"No, I'm saying the main investigation should branch off and try to discover Sobol's master plan. We're wasting time here. The master plan is everything."

Sebeck pointed toward the sheriff's mobile command center. "C'mon. Tell your theory to the Feds."

In the mobile command trailer, Agent Decker sat motionless while a paramedic prepared a bandage for his recently stitched head wound. Decker was docile—perhaps sedated. Next to him stood another agent—taller, leaner, younger, and with an air of self-confidence. This was Steven Trear, the special agent in charge of the Los Angeles Division of the FBI, and he was carefully considering the expectant face of Peter Sebeck.

"Are you sure it was Sobol?"

Sebeck nodded. "I think it was the same voice from the computer video this morning, and in any event it phoned me just before the attack."

Ross piped in. "And no other radio or cell phone traffic worked on the estate."

Trear considered this, calculating the impact of this information on the case. He looked more serious the more he thought about it. He shot a glance at Decker. "We cut off electrical power to the house, right?"

Decker nodded slowly. "Yes, but the acoustic team says there's a motor running in an outbuilding. Probably a generator."

"Damn. We've got to take that house as soon as possible."

Ross stepped past Sebeck and right up to Trear. "You're not thinking of defying the Daemon's demands, are you?"

"*Defying?*" He pointed at Ross but looked at Decker. "Who does he belong to?"

Decker was gingerly touching his bandaged head. "That's Jon Ross. The consultant we brought in for questioning from Alcyone Insurance."

Sebeck added, "He discovered the Daemon."

"No, I didn't." Ross turned to Trear. "Look, just don't storm the estate."

"Sobol's not in charge, Mr. Ross. He can make all the demands he wants. It won't affect my plans in the least."

"Agent Trear, I think this is another trap."

Trear rolled his eyes. "No kidding. The whole house is a trap." He looked to Sebeck. "Detective, please escort Mr. Ross out."

Ross persisted. "I just don't think the house contains critical information. It wouldn't make sense—from a technological standpoint—for Sobol to store his plans there."

"No one's accusing Sobol of making sense, Mr. Ross."

"I think this event was designed to announce the Daemon's arrival to the world, and to set the stage for something to come. It's finished here."

Trear digested that for a moment. "And what makes you think this?"

"Because that's the way Sobol thinks."

"How would you know that? You're not a psychologist."

"I've played Sobol's games. A lot. His AI succeeds because it doesn't anticipate you—it *manipulates* you."

Trear didn't dismiss it immediately.

Nearby, Agent Straub glanced at his watch. "The press briefing was scheduled to start four minutes ago, sir."

Trear looked to Ross again. "Why should I take you seriously, Mr. Ross? You're a wandering computer consultant who doesn't even keep a permanent address—and you play video games. Does that qualify you to deconstruct the motivations of Matthew Sobol?"

Ross couldn't think of an immediate response. Put that way, it sounded bad even to him.

Trear continued. "I appreciate that you want to help. But what you see here is not our entire investigation. Sobol was under psychiatric care for nearly a year before his death. As we speak, I have criminal psychologists conferring with his doctors and reviewing thousands of pages of medical notes—all to build a profile of Sobol's changing motivations as his illness progressed. His goals. His fears. We've used this approach with great success in countless cases—and usually with far less raw data to work with. So I think we know a lot more about Sobol's motivations than you."

He waited for his words to sink in. "This is a serious situation. Six good men died today—leaving behind wives and children. These were people Detective Sebeck, Agent Decker, and I knew. Others were maimed and injured. This isn't a game. If we guess wrong, many more people could die—and not just here."

Sebeck spoke up. "Agent Trear, I've seen Jon work. He helped me understand how Sobol killed Pavlos at the canyon scene, and he shut down the Daemon over at Alcyone Insurance when it first appeared. If it wasn't for him, this situation might be even worse. I think somebody technical should listen to what Jon has to say."

Trear nodded appreciatively.

Agent Straub cleared his throat. "Sir, if we want to make the evening news window, we've got to hold a press conference."

Trear looked at him. "Straub, this scene is being covered 24/7 by every news channel on the planet. Don't worry about the news window." Trear turned away and pulled a pen from his suit jacket. He started scribbling on a memo pad on a nearby conference table. "Look . . ." He tore the page off and handed it to Sebeck. "Bring Mr. Ross down to CyberStorm's corporate headquarters and ask for Agent Andrew Corland. He's head of the FBI Cyber Division. They're examining the CyberStorm corporate network and interviewing staff."

Trear turned to Agent Decker. "We did a background check on Mr. Ross yesterday?"

Decker nodded. "Preliminary came up clean—except for the address."

Ross leaned in. "I explained that."

Trear silenced him with an upheld hand. "If you can convince Corland that you know something useful, I'll be willing to listen to your theories. Failing that, I don't want to have this conversation again."

Sebeck folded and pocketed the slip of paper. "Fair enough. Thanks, Agent Trear. Agent Decker. C'mon, Jon."

Ross resisted. "But you do believe this is a diversion?"

"Have Agent Corland call me, Mr. Ross." Trear looked to Sebeck. "Sergeant, I know it's a difficult time, but I need written reports from you as soon as possible. I want your account of the attack, the cell phone call, and I want those findings from the canyon scene."

Sebeck nodded. He turned and pulled Ross out the trailer door and into the fading sunlight. Once outside, Sebeck and Ross squeezed past the gathering press corps and headed toward the estate fence line.

Ross pulled himself free. "I never even wanted to be involved in this mess in the first place."

"Jon, you've got an unusual skill set. And we need your help. Larson was engaged to be married. He was barely twenty-five. How many more people like him are going to die?"

"The Feds are wasting their time. They won't find anything on the CyberStorm network."

Sebeck grabbed Ross's arm again. "Look, I'm getting tired of hearing what we won't find. Tell me where we *can* find something."

"Sobol had the whole damned Internet to hide his plan. That's what I would have done."

"Don't even go there."

"It's that type of thinking that's going to limit us. We *must* put ourselves in his frame of mind."

"Fuck his frame of mind."

Ross met Sebeck's stare for a moment or two, then looked away. "Sorry. I guess that is annoying. If someone could just get me back to my car, I'd like to get some rest."

Sebeck's stare softened. "I forgot the Feds grilled you all last night. I'll take you back. No detours this time."

They turned and faced a barrier of concrete highway dividers ringing Sobol's estate. CALDOT crews had placed them over the last several hours. Both men looked into the distance. Beyond the estate fence, a quarter mile away, the black Hummer sat motionless in the center of the sweeping lawn amid crisscrossing tire tracks. Its whip antennae stood straight up, like the spines on some deadly insect.

A few deputy sheriffs were placed here and there along the road, sitting inside rugged-looking Forest Service crew trucks, engines idling. Sebeck guessed they were there to win a demolition derby should the Hummer make a break for it.

Sebeck turned to Ross. "You really think this is just the beginning, don't you?"

Ross scanned the terrain. "I don't know what I think anymore. Maybe Trear's right."

Sebeck took one last venomous look at the Hummer. "C'mon. Let's get you back to your car."

Chapter 15:// Countermeasures

*C*rypto City. That was what they called National Security Agency headquarters. Each day thousands of agency personnel took an unmarked highway exit in Fort Meade, Maryland, into a sprawling business park of mid-rise office buildings surrounded by concentric rings of barbed wire fencing and a yawning desert of parking spaces. The mirrored windows of the buildings were fakes. Behind them sheets of copper and electromagnetic shielding prevented any electrical signals from escaping the premises.

The agency was a vast communications drift net, catching hundreds of millions of electrical and radio transmissions worldwide every hour and sifting through them with some of the most powerful supercomputers on the planet. From its very beginning—back in the days of the fabled Black Chamber after World War II—the agency was responsible for creating the cryptologic ciphers relied upon to safeguard America's secrets and for cracking the ciphers of foreign powers.

A culture of secrecy dating back to the Cold War permeated the place. Posters seemingly from a bygone era hung in the common spaces, extolling the virtues of keeping secrets—even from other top-secret researchers. However, with the explosion of technology throughout the nineties, even the NSA was no longer able to keep up with the worldwide flow of digital information, and they were forced to let the rumors of their omniscience hide a brutal reality: no one knew where the next threat was coming from. Nation states were no longer the enemy. The enemy had become a catchall phrase: *bad actors*.

In a corner boardroom of the OPS-2B building, a group of agency directors convened an emergency meeting. No introductions were necessary. They had already worked together closely in the War on Terror and the War on Drugs, and they stood ready to combat any other noun that caused trouble. Senior intelligence and research officers from a periodic table of agencies were in attendance: NSA, CIA, DIA, DARPA, and the FBI. The talk was fast and urgent.

NSA: "So, what is it, a virus? An Internet worm?"

DARPA: "No, something new. Some sort of distributed scripting engine that responds to real-world events. It's almost certainly capable of further propagation."

NSA: "Can we write a bot to scour the Net and delete it?"

DARPA: "Not likely."

NSA: "Why not?"

DARPA: "Because it doesn't appear to have a single profile. Our best guess is that it consists of hundreds or even thousands of individual components spread over compromised workstations linked to the Net. Once a component is used, it's probably no longer needed."

NSA: "Then there's an end to it? I mean, Sobol's dead, so it will stop once it runs its course."

DARPA: "True, but there's obvious concern over the damage it might cause in the meantime. It's already killed eight people."

NSA: "Can't we block its communications? Surely the components have to communicate with each other?"

DARPA: "No. They don't. We believe the components are triggered not by each other, but by reading news stories. For example, one component just issued this press release"—he passed a printed page—"only after the siege story hit the wire services. The release is digitally signed. Sobol wants us to know it was his. We already tracked down the origin of the press release; it was e-mailed from a poorly secured computer in a St. Louis accounting firm. The program destroyed itself after it ran, but we were able to recover it from a tape backup. It was a simple HTML reader searching hundreds of Web sites for headlines about this estate siege."

CIA: "Jesus. So we can't stop this thing? What's it up to?"

DARPA: "Its proximate purpose appears to be self-preservation. Its ultimate purpose is unclear. It acts like a distributed AI agent—which would make sense if Matthew Sobol designed it."

CIA: "Artificial intelligence? You're not serious?"

DARPA: "Let me be clear: this is not a thinking, talking, sentient machine. This is narrow AI—like a character in a computer game. It's a collection of specific rules searching for recognizable patterns or events. Very basic. Nonetheless, very potent. It can alter course based on what's occurring in the real world, but it can't innovate or deviate from its given parameters. It required an incredible amount of planning. The name the press gave it is apt: it's basically a daemon. A distributed daemon."

CIA: "This is horseshit. There must be living people controlling it—cyber terrorists. I mean, how could Sobol know in advance exactly how we're going to react?"

DARPA: "He didn't have to. He could plan for multiple contingencies and then observe what actually occurs. Thus its monitoring of Internet news."

FBI: "Just shut down the Internet."

The others gave him a patronizing look.

FBI: "You guys built the damned thing. Why can't you turn it off?"

NSA: "Let's stick to reasonable suggestions, shall we?"

FBI: "I don't mean for a long time—just for a second."

DARPA: "The Internet is not a single system. It consists of hundreds of millions of individual computer systems linked with a common protocol. No one controls it entirely. It can't be 'shut down.' And even if you could shut it down, the Daemon would just come back when you turned it back on."

The director cut him off.

NSA: "Look, let's not hold a remedial class on distributed networks. Let's get back to the big question: do we defy Sobol's demand? What can he do if we enter the estate prior to thirty days?"

CIA: "We *must* enter the estate—you know that."

NSA: "Of course I do. But before I make my report to the Advisory Council, I need to know the potential consequences of defying this thing."

Everyone looked to the scientist.

DARPA: "Based on the deaths yesterday, I'd say there will be more fatalities."

CIA: "But nothing on a grander scale? No economic damage? No political ramifications?"

DARPA: "It's impossible to say. We'll only know when we defy it."

NSA: "What about jamming the radio signals to the Hummer?"

DARPA opened a folder and flipped through it while he talked.

DARPA: "The Hummer isn't the problem. The problem is the ultrawideband signals emanating from the house." He distributed handouts.

NSA: "Ultrawideband? Refresh me on that."

DARPA: "Ultrawideband involves extremely short pulses of radio energy—just billionths or trillionths of a second. By their nature ultrashort radio pulses occupy a wide swath of the frequency spectrum, covering several gigahertz in range."

NSA: "Bottom-line it for us."

DARPA: "Okay. This explains the high amount of radio interference around the estate. Normally, ultrawideband transceivers wouldn't be made powerful for that very reason, but Sobol's got a big one in place—and I don't think he's worried about violating FCC rules. It's screwing up our radio communications, and it will be hard as hell to jam."

CIA: "This is commercial technology? What good is something like that?"

DARPA, warming up to his topic: "It can be used as a super-accurate local GPS system—and I mean accurate down to a centimeter scale. Because of the wide swath of frequencies in use, some portion of the signal's going to get through even brick walls and radio jamming. With a computer map of the property and a transponder mounted in the Hummer, it would be possible to know exactly where the vehicle was at all times. He could relay infrared or other targeting information to the Hummer from a central computer, and he could protect the central computer from direct attack."

CIA: "You're sure he's using this ultrawideband?"

DARPA: "We've got CSC techs on the scene gathering COMINT and SIGINT."

FBI: "Was it ultrawideband that took out the bomb disposal team?"

DARPA: "No." He passed out more folders. "Fortunately the disposal team survived, and one of our researchers was able to interview Agent Guerner at County USC. His account leads our scientists to conclude that Sobol used some form of acoustical weaponry."

CIA: "Jesus Christ, why didn't we recruit this guy?"

NSA: "We tried to."

FBI: "Acoustical weaponry?"

DARPA: "Yes. Extremely low-frequency sound waves have been researched for use as nonlethal weapons. They're intended for quelling riots."

NSA, reading report: "Some nonlethal weapon. The capillaries in their eyes burst."

DARPA: "The low-frequency sound vibrates the victim's intestines, creating a feeling of deep unease and panic, difficulty breathing—and in stronger applications damaging delicate blood vessels. This matches Guerner's account and his injuries. Bear in mind, much of this technology isn't classified. With a good amount of money, a technical expert like Sobol could theoretically reproduce it—especially if he didn't intend to profit from it."

The attendees were duly sobered.

NSA: "How do we keep the Daemon from knowing we've entered the estate?"

FBI: "Can't we simply impose a news blackout? To stop it from reading the news?"

DIA: *"Domestically?* All hell would break loose."

FBI: "Not a total news blackout—just redaction of news about the Daemon. A gag order. Use our ties to the Web search companies. Or just decree it in the name of national security."

CIA: "Why not take out a full-page ad asking the public to panic?"

DARPA: "Look, you're ignoring the fact that at least one component of the Daemon is *in* Sobol's house. It doesn't need to read the headlines to find out we're breaking in."

Everyone grew quiet again.

DIA: "They've cut power to the house, right?"

It was FBI's turn to roll his eyes.

DARPA: "It probably has backup power systems."

FBI, examining his own report: "Ground-penetrating radar shows nothing unusual on the estate grounds. No secret power lines or tunnels. The L.A. Division got ahold of the networking company that installed Sobol's server room. He's got about twelve hours of backup battery power. The city permit office plans also show a backup diesel generator with three-hundred-gallon fuel capacity."

CIA: "How long could that last?"

NSA: "The political pressure will be intense. I'm guessing we can't wait even a couple of days."

FBI: "It's being taken care of, gentlemen."

DARPA: "Frankly, we're more concerned about the Daemon components on the Internet than the components in the house."

CIA: "Can't you focus *Carnivore* on this thing?"

NSA: "That quickly turns into a discussion of USSID-18. We all know what a shitstorm that kicked up."

CIA: "That's ridiculous. This isn't a domestic surveillance issue. Sobol's *dead*. He's no longer a U.S. citizen."

DIA: "I'll bet the ACLU would have an opinion on that."

FBI: "Just purchase consumer data from the private sector. It's easier."

DARPA: "Once again, gentlemen, reality intrudes. Our standard surveillance methods won't work. The Daemon issues press releases or reads the news. One is highly public; the other is a passive activity. There are no recurrent IP addresses or search words in e-mails to monitor. *Carnivore* won't help you. Neither will purchasing patterns."

The room grew quiet again.

NSA: "Then we're agreed that we need to defy the Daemon's demand as soon as power can be brought down on the estate?"

They all nodded.

NSA: "Good. We'll know more once we capture Sobol's server room." He looked to FBI. "Make that happen, and we'll see what this thing has up its sleeve."

Marine Captain Terence Lawne waited in a prone position on a shipping blanket laid across the roof of the County's SWAT van. This gave him a vantage point over the estate fence line and deep into Sobol's property. Lawne's right eye pressed against the rubberized viewfinder on the infrared scope of his M82A1A .50-caliber anti-materiel rifle. He panned the property, swiveling the monster gun on its bipod until he located Sobol's Hummer. He focused the crosshairs on it. The Hummer's engine had been off for a while, but there was still a good heat signature. "I got it."

Major Karl Devon shifted position next to him to get a good look with his FLIR scope. The sheet metal roof of the SWAT van thumped and moved as he did so.

"Major, watch the movement. This thing's four hundred and fifty yards downrange."

He kept looking. "How's your angle?"

Lawne settled in again, getting his breathing under control. "It's a clear shot." He pulled on his hearing protection.

Devon looked down toward the nearby road at the gathered crowd of police, FBI, reporters, and technicians. It was a veritable army standing in the darkness below. The construction lights had been extinguished to facilitate Lawne's work.

Devon shouted, "Cover your ears, people!" Devon pulled on his own ear protection and looked back to Lawne. "Fire when ready, Captain."

Captain Lawne got the Hummer back in his crosshairs. He focused on his breathing, and felt the calm flow over him. He slowly squeezed the trigger.

The big gun boomed and kicked back into his shoulder. He brought his eye back up to the infrared scope for damage assessment. Hot liquid streamed out of the bottom of the Hummer's engine compartment. Heat suddenly spread throughout the engine, and Lawne heard the distant sound of a diesel engine coming to life. The Hummer started to move—albeit slowly.

"It's on the move!" He kept his eye to the scope and aimed again. The gun boomed and recoiled. Lawne saw the Hummer jerk to a stop. He had nailed it straight through the engine block. The armor-piercing round struck a mortal blow. Powerful heat was spreading now. Lawne looked up from the viewfinder. He could see orange flames downrange. He pulled off his hearing protectors. "Sorry, Major. It started its engine after the first hit. The Hummer's on fire."

Devon checked his FLIR scope. "Goddamnit, Lawne."

He scanned the scene some more. Nothing they could do about it now. Diesel fuel was fairly slow burning, but nobody was going on that property until the Daemon was down for the count. "Forget about it. Let's take out the emergency generator."

Captain Lawne put his eye up to the scope again and swung the long sniper rifle toward the garage, a good hundred yards closer. His eye followed a gravel footpath fifty feet or so to a small stucco outbuilding with an air-conditioning unit set in the wall. The AC unit was red with heat—obviously running. There was also an exterior light just to the right of the nearby door. Lawne switched from infrared to normal view.

Rustling paper came to Lawne's ear.

Major Devon lowered his night vision goggles and examined blueprints with the aid of an infrared flashlight. "Do you see the AC unit in the south wall—just to the left of the door?"

"I see it."

"From this vector, you want to put your rounds . . ." The major was trying to see his pencil lines. ". . . about halfway between the door and the AC unit, about a foot below the bottom of the AC unit." He looked up from the blueprints. "Understood?"

"Got it."

"Fire when ready."

They both put their ear protection back on. Lawne squinted and took aim. This would be an easy shot if he knew exactly what he was aiming for. He let loose. *BOOM*.

A divot appeared in the stucco, followed by draining brick dust. The electrical power was still on—the exterior light was still on.

Lawne fired several more times, spreading the shots over an imaginary grid of six-inch squares. The wall rapidly started to crumble. He paused several seconds between each shot to recover from the recoil. His shoulder was starting to ache just as the exterior light flicked off. A muffled cheer and scattered applause went up from hundreds of people in the darkness. Lawne looked up from the viewfinder and could see that all the lights on the Sobol estate had gone out. The only visible light was the Hummer—nearly fully engulfed in flames four football fields away. Lawne pulled off his earphones. He could now hear the excited buzz of the crowd below.

Major Devon called down to a Computer Systems Corporation SIGINT team sent out from DOD, working from the back of a nearby van. "Rigninski! Is the house still emitting ultrawideband?"

An engineer conferred with a technician wearing headphones. He looked up at Devon—even though he couldn't clearly see him in the darkness. "Yes. It's still transmitting. Must be running on battery backup."

Devon looked toward a nearby FBI van, where an array of parabolic microphones was focused on various parts of the Sobol estate. "Agent Gruder, did we take out the generator?"

Gruder held up a finger as she listened in on a pair of headphones. After a good ten seconds she gave the thumbs-up sign. "It's dead, Major. Good job."

A somewhat forced cheer went up in the crowd closest to them. It was a small victory.

Major Devon smiled in the darkness. Now it was just a matter of waiting out the battery power backup in the computer room. That gave the Daemon just twelve hours to live.

Chapter 16:// The Key

Gragg hadn't slept in three days, and he was beginning to hallucinate. At least he hoped he was hallucinating. Maybe he was dreaming. Oberstleutnant Boerner stood over him in the predawn darkness, smoking a cigarette in that faggy long filter holder of his. He morphed into a Colonel Klink–like character, and Gragg finally shook himself back to reality.

Gragg needed sleep, but once his mind was set on a problem, it always ran until physical exhaustion brought it crashing down. He was nearly at that point now.

Sleep. Blessed sleep. Dreamless sleep. No Boerners to trouble him— that 3-D texturized bastard. But there couldn't be sleep until he solved the problem. The problem of the key.

Gragg looked around. He was lying on his couch beneath a scratchy wool blanket that carried the humid stink of a Houston cellar. The couch was a great big thing he'd picked up at a garage sale. It *also* carried the stench of too many humid days. The cushions, long since missing, had been replaced by a cot mattress that more or less fit in place. The sofa was his bed, dining room table, and La-Z-Boy chair rolled into one, and it stood like an island in the center of the industrial space that served as his apartment. There was nothing near the sofa for twenty feet in every direction. This was intentional. He had to get away from computer screens sometimes.

The key. What the fuck was the key? It was driving Gragg insane. He had screen-captured the encrypted text on that one Monte Cassino wall, and he hadn't seen any other writing that might be the key. Could it have been in another room? What was he missing?

Fuck!

What kind of sadistic shithead created a map with an impossible puzzle? More irritating was that Gragg couldn't reload the map to get more information. Not only was the Houston Monte Cassino server nowhere to be found, no other Monte Cassino maps appeared anywhere. The map was gone, as though the creator pulled the map from the entire Web.

How had they gotten Oberstleutnant Boerner to say those things? Was it some sort of Easter egg created by CyberStorm? Gragg had already checked the chat boards, but his search turned up nothing—no mention of the encrypted message or of Boerner's little speech, or of the disappearance of the Monte Cassino map. Was he the only one experiencing this? He hadn't asked a soul, though. This was Gragg's secret.

Gragg had begun to suspect that the Monte Cassino map made a registry entry on his machine that prevented the map from appearing in the game listings again. To test his hypothesis, he cleared out hard-drive space on another PC and installed *Over the Rhine* on it in the hope that the clean machine would give him access to the Monte Cassino map, but it still didn't appear in the Internet listings.

Had the game somehow restricted his IP address? Or his router's MAC address? Goddamnit, he was grasping at straws now.

Think!

The problem: he had an encrypted string but no key—and no idea what encryption algorithm was used to create the string. Boerner had looked straight at him—or at least his avatar—and said, " . . . *use your key, and ve vill meet again.*" If Gragg found the key and decrypted the string, where did he enter the decrypted value? Would entering it somewhere make the Monte Cassino map reappear?

Gragg got up and wrapped the scratchy, smelly blanket around him. He shuffled across the room toward his workbench. Four desktops and two laptops were still powered up there. One was running a dictionary file against the encrypted string using a series of standard decryption algorithms. He stared at the lines spinning past in the debug window and laughed.

This was ridiculous. It could take a thousand years with all the permutations of a thirty-two-character string.

He thought about it for a moment. He could harness a few dozen zombie computers and distribute the task among them. He shook his head. He'd have to design the program to distribute the load—and it would still take too long to run. What, a hundred years? And what if the result wasn't a proper word? How could he programmatically detect a successful decryption? He didn't even know the encoding algorithm.

He cast off the scratchy blanket and sat down before a keyboard. He'd searched the chat boards, but he hadn't done the obvious thing and Google-proxied the problem. He launched a Web browser and prepared to type the URL in manually. Perhaps there was a Web page dedicated to this.

Gragg froze just after his home page loaded. It was a popular news portal, and there off to the right were the news stories of the moment. The top headline screamed at him:

Dead Computer Genius Kills Eight

Gragg clicked the link, and the extensive news coverage of the siege at Sobol's estate unfolded before him. Gragg voraciously read every word and followed every link. An hour later and he was wide-awake again with one 'factoid' echoing in his mind: ". . . Matthew Sobol, game designer and AI architect for *Over the Rhine*."

This Sobol guy had been a genius. Beyond a genius. Gragg was rarely impressed by other people's hacks—but this Sobol was the king. Engineering a daemon that took vengeance on the world once you were safely dead and beyond all punishment. Gragg's mind ran through the possibilities. They were endless.

How much money had Sobol spent on this? The planning! And the Daemon was still on the loose. The Feds didn't know how to stop it. You could hear it in the closed-lip pronouncements of the government spokespeople.

Goose bumps swept over Gragg's skin. It felt like a new world had opened up to him. Was the Monte Cassino map just a coincidence? It had appeared in the last few days—only after Sobol's death.

He couldn't say that for sure, though. He'd been otherwise engaged prior to the mess with the Filipinos.

It couldn't be a coincidence, though, could it?

Gragg knew, now more than ever, that he had to decipher the encrypted text. He felt he could never be sane again unless he knew more about the Monte Cassino map and about Sobol's Daemon. He might have the inside track on something incredible—a new frontier in a world filled with familiar hacks, police surveillance, and drab suburban vistas. How long had it been since he'd felt a sense of wonder in his jaded soul? He was feeling that now. Was Monte Cassino Sobol's work?

Gragg did a Web search for Monte Cassino and came up with a slew of hits—all relating to World War II. Instead, he reran the search, adding *Over the Rhine* as criteria. He still got about seven hundred hits, all of them historical because the Italian campaign, ultimately, was aimed toward Germany.

Gragg looked up from his laptop and stared at a desktop computer's debug window scrolling the results of his program's decryption attempts. Output appeared every millisecond or so and varied between gibberish and the words "Bad Data." He sighed, realizing that encryption could even be something like a proprietary Triple DES, where the designer re-encrypted the message multiple times. Hadn't the Russians done something like that with their Venona project? Gragg felt quicksand rising up to swallow his efforts. Would he go to his grave never knowing the answer to this riddle?

He knew a little more now, though. Didn't he? Well, assuming that Matthew Sobol had designed the Monte Cassino map, he did. He halted the decryption program and brought up the immediate window. Gragg typed the stub of his decryption function:

?DecryptIt(

He had to supply the only argument for the function—the key to use for the encryption. His function was hard-coded to use the encrypted string he got from the Monte Cassino map along with any key he entered here as an argument for the function. It would then cycle through a dozen common decryption algorithms—DES, Triple DES, RSA— feeding the key as the variable. Gragg thought hard. What would Sobol use as a key? Gragg typed: *?DecryptIt("MatthewSobol")_*

And hit ENTER. The output was twelve lines of gibberish or "Bad Data" once again—one line for each algorithm attempted by the function. He tried scores of variations on Sobol's name, and then variations on CyberStorm Entertainment, then variations of *Over the Rhine*. He started entering the names of some of the games Sobol had created—or at least ones Gragg could remember. Then the names of notable game characters, like Boerner.

The output was all gibberish.

Gragg just stared at the flat-panel monitor. He might as well curl up and die now because some bastard had placed this virus in his head, and he would never be free of it. If he ever got his hands on the Monte Cassino map designer, he was going to wring that fuck's scrawny neck. Gragg pounded his head on the desk—not hard enough to hurt himself, but hard enough to inform his brain of the danger.

Clues. He needed to examine what would be important to someone—say, Sobol—who wanted to keep a secret away from the Feds, but who also wanted Generation Y to find it. Those Feds would no doubt be using sniffers, crackers, and decompilers in order to find encrypted strings in Sobol's work. If not now, then soon. But they couldn't decrypt it if they didn't find it. Where to hide data from automated forensics tools?

Gragg had an epiphany: there was no encrypted string in the Monte Cassino map. Gragg had perceived the encrypted text, but it wasn't really computer text; it was a graphical image—and one done in a Teutonic stone-carved font, no less. The encrypted string, "m0wFG3PRCo JVTs7JcgBwsOXb3U7yPxBB," was an arrangement of pixels that only a human eye—or a really good optical character-recognition scanner—could interpret. Programmatically scanning the contents of this map wouldn't uncover any encrypted text—only a human being viewing the map in the context in which it was meant to be seen could see its significance. But even within the game the significance of the coded string wasn't truly revealed until . . .

Gragg smiled. Herr Oberstleutnant Boerner pointed out its significance. The combination of the picture file and Boerner's verbal statement, " . . . *use your key, and ve vill meet again.* . . ."—these were the components of the encryption, the data and the key to unlocking it. The more he contemplated it, the more sense it made. The data and the key appeared in proximity to each other only within the context of the game, and then only if the player was dedicated and capable enough to reach the inner sanctum of that difficult map. That probably ruled out anyone over thirty years of age. Certainly it ruled out anyone in a position of responsibility.

Excitement coursed through Gragg's body. He had forgotten all about his exhaustion. He was hopeful again. Either that or he was headed toward madness.

If the audio file contained the key, then where was it? Was it hidden somewhere as steganographic information in the .wav format? Gragg guessed there must be hundreds of numerically named .wav files in the *OTR* game directory. Then he thought once again about Boerner's words: "*. . . use your key, and ve vill meet again. . . .* "

A mischievous smile crept across his face. It fit Boerner's style; the invisible punctuation that only the human brain could provide:

"*. . . use 'your key,' and ve vill meet again. . . .*"

Gragg took a deep breath and entered "your key" as the argument for his decryption function. He tapped the ENTER key.

Twelve output strings—all but one gibberish. All but the seventh one: *RSA Decryption Result: 29.3935 -95.3933*

He leapt up and howled in joy, dancing around his apartment like the sleep-deprived lunatic he was. But then a cocktail of other emotions flowed in: relief, caution, even fear. Did he dare to think this might be Sobol speaking to him? Guiding him from beyond the grave? What was Gragg setting in motion?

Gragg grabbed a remote and powered up the forty-two-inch plasma TV on the other side of the room. As he suspected, the twenty-four-hour news channels had set up live feeds from Sobol's estate. Their cameras panned the besieging forces with night vision scopes—like a report from some foreign war. Hundreds of local and federal police surrounded the place. Heavy equipment was everywhere. A video segment of a military marksman walking toward a van with a massive sniper rifle played repeatedly in inset. The government was deadly serious about Sobol's little game. Gragg got suddenly serious, too.

He looked back at his computer screen:

29.3935 -95.3933

These were numbers Gragg knew well. In fact, they were numbers that any Texas geo-caching enthusiast knew well. They were GPS coordinates of a location somewhere in southern Texas. He had been playing the Monte Cassino map on the Houston Monte Cassino server, so this made sense. Gragg picked up his GPS receiver and checked its battery.

. . . ve vill meet again . . .

Indeed. Gragg opened the drawer of his heavy 1960s-era desk and drew out a Glock 9mm pistol in a nylon belt holster. He pondered it gravely, realizing just how quickly things were getting out of control. This could be a trap. This could be something he couldn't even imagine. He clipped the holster to the small of his back.

Either way, he wasn't going to live a long life in the trackless wastes of suburbia—and that was something.

The only car Gragg had at the moment was the first one he'd ever owned—a piece-of-shit blue 1989 Ford Tempo whose paint had long ago bleached into Grateful Dead tie-dye patterns. The rear window leaked, and the resulting mildew stench in the car made his sofa smell like a field of heather by comparison.

He kept the Tempo because a guy his age was suspicious without a car. Gragg lived most of his life under stolen identities—such was the life of a carder—but he still had a real name and social security number to maintain. Thus, the Tempo. On paper Gragg was a loser, supposedly working part-time at a computer parts store in Montrose. He officially earned little but didn't apply for welfare or food stamps. He was just a slacker—an unambitious young punk who spent most of his hours in the *alt.binaries.nospam.facials* newsgroup. His ISP could vouch for that. The official Brian Gragg was a totally uninteresting person.

Gragg always registered his good cars under assumed identities, and unlike his bulk identity thefts, Gragg was more selective about the identities he "wore." No one too successful or too poor. He found his victims by trading with other carders for the social security numbers, names, and addresses of middle-class folks. Folks who weren't worth much on the open market except as a mask. Once he picked a name, it was easy to use online skip-tracing services to find the last half-dozen places where the victim worked, where they'd lived, their credit reports, income tax information, relatives, and neighbors. It was all readily available. Gragg had a policy of selecting only Fortune 1000 or government employees for his victims—real solid folks. His Honda Si had been registered under the name of an Oregonian man who worked for TRW. The irony always made Gragg smile. Of course, he made certain to pay his victim's illicit bills on time—at least as long as he kept the identity.

But the fiasco with the Filipinos left him without a decent ride, and there hadn't been time to set up a new identity. Certainly Gragg didn't want to be seen shopping for a new car just now. Too risky.

So here he was getting into his *own* car—with a laptop full of *warez* and a 9mm pistol. The pistol wasn't really a concern—this was Texas, after all—but the laptop made him nervous. He knew the government wasn't afraid of guns, but it *was* afraid of laptops—and what the government feared, it punished. Connecting his real identity with the hacking world would be disastrous. As far as authorities knew, he was a know-nothing high school dropout with no prior arrests, and he wanted to keep it that way. He brought a degausser with him as well as a DC-to-AC adapter for his car's cigarette lighter socket. In a pinch, he could use it to demagnetize the drive. At worst the police would suspect he'd stolen the laptop. That was no big deal.

Gragg had slept a few hours after cracking Boerner's code. Although he was eager to get on with his self-appointed quest, there might be difficulties ahead—and he wanted to be sharp. Meth wasn't the answer. Down that road lay madness and the worst sort of police difficulties. It was important to keep the blood pure.

Standing next to the Ford Tempo in the early night, Gragg glanced around at his light industrial neighborhood. They made screen doors and custom car parts down here. After dark it was generally a ghost town except for the occasional pit bull behind a fence or tractor-trailer backing into a parking lot. Tonight was no exception. Gragg breathed deeply of the night air. It was crisp and refreshing.

He placed his GPS unit on the seat next to him. The coordinates from the encrypted string were somewhere up near Houston International Airport—North Houston, below Beltway 8 between Tomball Parkway and Interstate 45. If he remembered correctly, this was scrubland criss-crossed at half-mile intervals by surface roads, bayous, and occasional subdivisions.

Gragg drove for nearly an hour into the cool autumn night. Between knots of office parks and suburban sprawl, the metal halide streetlights gave way to darkness, and the stars shimmered, unobscured overhead. The pleasant fragrance of dead leaves and chimney smoke sometimes overpowered the fungal stench in his car.

Getting into the general area of the GPS coordinates proved to be the easy part. Normally, if he had to convert GPS coordinates to a map location, Gragg would just key in a destination, but this time, he didn't want to leave a data trail. So he spent a couple of hours trying to find a road that brought him closer to his target, glancing now and again at the map on his GPS unit. Several rural routes weren't in the database, so he was left backtracking and zigzagging over back roads, following hunches.

The countryside alternated between narrow wooded roads, spanking new subdivisions, and gritty industrial or heavy-equipment companies. Around one A.M. Gragg found a surface road that mercifully continued to within a couple decimals of his target. He was heading out into scrubland again when a dilapidated-looking low brick building loomed up on his left, between clumps of trees. It bore the name Nasen Trucking, Ltd., although no trucks were visible in the chain-link-fenced parking lot. A lone streetlight shone down from a telephone pole near the gravel entrance.

Gragg slowed down as the GPS latitude coordinate clicked to match his target. Longitude was still a decimal off, though. Gragg checked the compass reading. That meant left. He pulled the car over to the entrance of the parking lot, beneath the bright streetlight, and looked around.

There were a couple of battered mailboxes near the entrance—the larger sort that rural companies and farmers used. Gragg squinted to read the writing on the side. The nearest had "Nasen Trucking" stenciled on it in a sans serif font. The other box had one word on it in black Gothic lettering: *Boerner.*

Gragg's throat tightened. He looked to the left, where a gravel road ran past Nasen Trucking, into the woods—into darkness. He was exposed, sitting in the light like this. He cranked the wheel to the left. The power steering screeched in protest, and Gragg gritted his teeth. If he hadn't alerted anyone before, he sure as hell had now.

He accelerated down the gravel road and out of the light. The stones crunched under his tires and dinged off his tire wells. The sound reminded him of his childhood and long prairie driveways. Once out of the cone of the streetlight, he slowed to five mph and scanned the darkness for . . . he didn't know what. Bare birch trees lined the road on the left, while a ditch and a riot of thornbushes ran along the right. Gragg turned off his headlights and put the car in park. He took his foot off the brake to prevent the brake lights from giving away his location to anyone driving along the main road.

Gragg fumbled around in the darkness and found his rucksack. He unzipped it and pulled out night vision goggles. Untangling the headband, he then pulled them over his head and powered them up. He scanned the terrain ahead in the green glow of the viewfinder.

The edge of a single-story cinder-block building was visible a couple hundred feet down the road. There were no lights there. A single, thick chain spanned the road fifty feet ahead, secured to two steel posts. A metal No Trespassing sign hung down at its lowest point.

Gragg looked at the GPS unit. He was still one decimal off. He put the car in gear and, with some trepidation, let it roll forward without putting his foot on the gas. He scanned from side to side, looking for anything that wasn't a plant or a rock. He finally reached the chain and put the car in park again. He glanced at the GPS unit.

He was on station.

Gragg hesitated for a moment, then turned off the engine. Suddenly he could hear the woods. He heard the clattering of naked tree branches in the wind. Leaves scraped across the gravel road with each gust. The interior of the car cooled rapidly.

Gragg pulled the Glock 9mm pistol out of his rucksack and then freed the pistol from its holster. He placed it on the bench seat beside him.

What the fuck am I doing out here?

It was starting to seem like a really bad idea. He was running blind, and that was definitely something Brian Gragg did not like. It ran against his nature. He scanned the trees and the desolate-looking cinder-block building again.

How did this place have anything to do with the Monte Cassino map? There wasn't any light out here. Was there even electricity? Gragg craned his neck to look up through the windshield and accidentally bumped the single night vision lens against the glass. He straightened the goggles and looked again. An electrical feed line ran along the road on the left side. Narrow utility poles of gray, cracked wood supported it every hundred feet or so.

Following the line with his eyes, Gragg noticed something interesting ahead: a fairly tall antenna was bolted to the side of the cinder-block building. He could see the mast rising above the roof.

Gragg took a deep breath. He was jittery. Time to concentrate. He pulled his laptop bag from the backseat and cleared space on the seat beside him. He put the pistol on the dashboard, then unzipped the laptop bag. He unpacked his laptop and booted up, flipping up the tiny antenna on the wireless card. He was temporarily blinded as the screen lit up, and he hurriedly stripped off the night vision goggles.

While the laptop booted up, he kept looking around in the darkness. He could actually see pretty well once his eyes adjusted. There was some moonlight.

After what seemed an eternity, the logon dialog came up, and a minute later Gragg launched NetStumbler. The program scanned for access points. In a moment, he was surprised to see a familiar SSID appear: *Monte_Cassino.*

The signal appeared to originate from the cinder-block building. Gragg's jitters returned. Had he really done this? He tried to calm his rising fear. What was he doing? He thought about it.

There was an *OTR* server here.

He configured his Wi-Fi card to use the SSID, and soon Gragg obtained an IP address on the unsecured network. He didn't even bother to explore. Instead, he closed NetStumbler and ripped open his CD case. He flipped through the CD-Rs until he found one marked with felt pen "OTR." He slid the CD into the laptop's drive and launched *Over the Rhine.* He clicked quickly past the opening screens, then selected multiplayer mode. He let the game scan for available servers. Only one appeared in the server list: the Houston Monte Cassino server. This was the one visible to his wireless card.

Gragg smiled, then double-clicked on the name. The map started to load. Oddly, the weapon selection dialog box never appeared. Soon, Gragg's avatar was standing, unarmed, in a trench at the base of the Monte Cassino mountain. Normally he'd work his way around to the left, but without weapons it was rather pointless. Gragg peered over the lip of the trench, and he could see the familiar German MG42 nests up at the edge of the ruins.

Strangely, the Krauts didn't open fire immediately. Gragg let his avatar stand there for a moment, and still no tracer bullets came streaming down. He decided to push his luck and hopped up on the fire step—then out into full view.

Still no gunfire. The Germans just sat there.

Gragg started walking toward their lines. He had never approached the monastery successfully from this angle, and now he could see three machine gun nests aiming down at him from a hundred meters away. The gun barrels followed him as he walked, but still they did not fire.

Gragg kept walking, straight up to the center machine gun. The loader crouched next to the gunner. The NPCs had that familiar blank look on their faces. Before long, Gragg was within ten feet of the machine gun barrel. It stared down on him, ready to send his avatar into the spectator list. He was so close he could see the rank of the gunner from the textured graphic patches on his shoulders: *Unterfeldwebel.* A sergeant.

To Gragg's shock, the gunner released his grip on the weapon and held up his hand. "Halt!" He peered at Gragg closely. "*Ich kenne Deinen Namen.*" He rose and motioned for Gragg to follow. "*Komm mit!*" With that the gunner walked off into the ruins. Gragg hurried to follow. A dozen German soldiers rose from their concealed positions among the rocks and watched with glaring eyes as he passed.

The Unterfeldwebel brought Gragg through a maze of rooms and splintered wreckage. Around each corner were more Kraut soldiers clutching Schmeissers or manning mortar positions. Every time he walked past, the Krauts would whisper to each other and point. Gragg had to hand it to Sobol; every detail was there. It gave him a strong sense of being an outsider in an enemy stronghold.

Gragg was led down into the same cellar where he'd first encountered Boerner in the Monte Cassino map. They walked between the wine casks toward the doorway in the opposite wall. Torches lit their way, flickering against the darkness under the influence of a digital breeze. Gragg glanced around. There was no sign of the fire damage from the earlier game.

They headed into the dark passage that led to the round tower base. The ray of sunlight still shined there, illuminating the wall where the encrypted message once was, but now it was carved with:

29.3935 -95.3933

Gragg turned his avatar to face the familiar metal screen through which he'd spoken to Boerner before. It was dark behind the screen. Suddenly the space beyond filled with the flare of a match, and Boerner was there, lighting his cigarette at the end of that damned filter. He cupped it with his hand until it lit, then breathed out a cloud of voluminous smoke.

The Unterfeldwebel gave a sharp salute with a click of his boot heels and scurried out, leaving Gragg's avatar alone with Boerner. Boerner looked up and fixed his monocle over his left eye.

"Vee meet again, *mein freund.*" Boerner clamped the cigarette holder in one corner of his mouth. "You know ze console, yes? Use it zu answer my qvestions." Boerner waited for some response.

The console. Gragg usually used it for cheat codes. He peered at the keyboard and hit the tilde key. A DOS-like console appeared in the northern third of the screen. It listed a number of scripting events that had already taken place—such as the appearance of the Boerner model and the creation of the objects in this room. The console served as both a comprehensive log of program events and a command console for overriding game settings. Basically, it gave him a blinking cursor where he could type input.

As soon as the console appeared, Boerner said, "Excellent. You haf some knowledge zu find me again. Vee vill zee how much knowledge you haf. Haf you come alone? Yes or no?"

Gragg sucked in a breath. He didn't want to admit he was alone, but lying made him more nervous. He typed *Yes* at the console line and hit ENTER.

Boerner's avatar kneeled down so he could "see" Gragg's avatar around the console window. He smiled at him. "Gut. Haf you told anyone else about zis?"

Gragg hesitated again. What better way to get killed than to say yes? He remembered all too well the video images of body bags from Sobol's estate. But what would that gain Sobol? Why go through so much effort just to kill someone?

Gragg typed *No* and hit ENTER.

Boerner regarded Gragg's avatar, then suddenly thrust open the grate that separated them. The metal door slammed against the stone wall as Boerner strode forward to get right in Gragg's face. "I vill later find out ze truth. Better zu admit it now if you haf told ozzers." Boerner's eyes bored into Gragg through the laptop screen. "Haf you told anyone?"

Gragg typed *No* again and hit ENTER.

Boerner smiled that wicked smile of his again. He patted Gragg's avatar on the shoulder. "*Ausgezeichnet.* Und haf you brought your bag of tricks mit you? Yes?" Boerner waited for an answer.

Gragg typed *Yes* and hit ENTER.

Boerner swept his arms into the air. "Open ze gate!" His words echoed in the cellar corridors.

Beyond Gragg's laptop screen—in the real world of autumn cold—Gragg heard a metallic noise. He glanced up toward the front of the car. Suddenly the thick metal chain blocking the road dropped completely to the ground. The No TRESPASSING sign clattered noisily on gravel.

"Fuck me! That's it. . . ." Gragg pushed the laptop away and fumbled for the car's ignition switch. He started the car, threw it in reverse, and twisted in his seat to see where he was going. What he saw behind him stopped him cold.

Another thick chain had risen up not far behind his car. He could see it illuminated in his backup lights, along with the back of a metal sign—probably identical to the other one. In gravel and without a running start, there was no way he was getting through that thing. He started to panic. He glanced to the left and right. The birch trees on the left were impenetrable by car. To the right, he'd never get the car over that ditch. He heard talking and looked down at the laptop still facing him on the bench seat.

Boerner puffed on his cigarette there. "Relax, *mein freund*. If I vanted zu kill you, I could haf done so already. Move your car forvart, please."

Gragg's mind raced, gauging his chances of fleeing on foot—through the birch trees and into the fields beyond. That was crazy, right? He was out in the middle of fucking nowhere. This whole area could be filled with traps for all Gragg knew. How much planning had Sobol already displayed? It had to be Sobol. Gragg contemplated facing a real-world Boerner, and it dawned on him that running away on foot was a one-way ticket to zero health—without respawning.

Boerner stared at him from the nearby laptop. Gragg shook his head clear of that thought. Boerner wasn't staring at anybody. It was just a bunch of texture maps arranged for a first-person viewer. Sobol was fucking with his mind. This was definitely not a cool situation.

Boerner shook his finger at Gragg. "You mustn't be afraid, *mein freund*. Unless, of course, you lack skill."

Gragg gave Boerner the finger and pulled out his cell phone. He took a moment to consider whom he might call. Surely not the police? Definitely not the police. How about one of his road-racing buddies? Or one of his rave bouncers? Bad idea. Right now, "Loki" was supposed to be dead. But they didn't know him as Loki. His world was so full of lies he couldn't keep them straight.

Gragg cycled through his saved phone numbers and selected his lead rave bouncer. Gragg put the phone to his ear. Nothing but static came back. He looked at the bar count. "No Service."

Boerner was talking again. Gragg looked down.

"Your phone ist useless. Only Vi-Fi vill vork here." His expression grew decidedly less friendly. "Move ze car forvart."

Gragg put his phone away. He shifted the car from reverse back to drive. He took a deep breath, then took his foot off the brake. The Tempo rolled forward. Gragg realized someone might see his headlights from the road—so he kicked them on. Then he flicked on his high beams.

Up ahead an exterior light kicked on at the cinder-block building.

Boerner growled. "Drive benees zi light."

As Gragg's car rolled forward, he crossed the tree line and was suddenly in a well-lit, muddy clearing in front of the cinder-block building. There was another vehicle there—a badly smashed VW Vanagon with Louisiana plates.

As Gragg's Ford Tempo rolled into the clearing, he felt the tires bog down in deep mud. In a second he was up to his axles in it and stuck like a fly on flypaper.

"Oh fuck . . ." Gragg groaned. "Fuck, fuck, fuck!" He pounded the steering wheel. What had he gotten himself into? He should run.

Boerner spoke again. *"Mein freund."*

Gragg looked down at the laptop.

Boerner took another puff on his cigarette. "Zis ist fun, yes?" Boerner paused a moment. "Ist zis you, *mein freund*?"

The console window populated with Brian Gragg's full name, social security number, age, birth date, last known address, mother's maiden name—a huge piece of his life. The adrenaline of pure, high-octane fear swept through Gragg. He almost screamed in terror. He honestly could not remember a time when he'd been more afraid. This machine knew who he was. It knew his real fucking *name*.

Boerner barked angrily, "Ist zis you? Answer!"

Gragg fearfully typed *No* in the console window beneath his personal information and hit ENTER.

Boerner loomed again. "If zis is not you, I haf ozzer names. But if you lie zu me, I vill find out. Und zer vill be no mercy. Answer again. Ist zis you?"

Gragg pondered Boerner's cold eyes, then typed *Yes* and hit ENTER.

Boerner relented and went back to smoking. "Gut. Now ve may begin." He put one hand behind his back and started pacing. "Run your Vi-Fi scanner again. You vill see a new netvork. You must gain entry zu it. Do not attempt zu leef here before you do. *Auf wiedersehen*." Boerner swept out of the room. The moment he did, the 3-D iron grate snapped shut behind him. Immediately after that, the game shut down without warning, leaving Gragg staring at his computer desktop.

Gragg rubbed his forehead. This was a nightmare. At least he wished it was, but since it wasn't, he figured he'd better get down to business. Boerner wanted to see what Gragg was made of? Okay. Gragg launched NetStumbler again. The SSID for the Houston Monte Cassino server was now gone. In its place was a new Wi-Fi access point with no SSID at all.

No doubt this one was going to be tougher. Gragg opened the Net-Stumbler logs and checked each entry. The new AP was running Wi-Fi Protected Access—WPA—a form of wireless encryption. *Damn.* He was hoping it would be WEP-encrypted. That would take only seconds to defeat. WPA had no structural flaws. It was as strong as its passphrase. But that would be the test, then, wouldn't it? Hopefully, the phrase wasn't more than eight or nine characters. Gragg would need to sniff the key exchange messages between the adapter and the access point, then crack the key off-line with a PSK dictionary (which he had on his laptop). He could use Air-Jack to force the key exchange by broadcasting a *disassociate* message. Gragg slumped in his seat. Hopefully there would be some client exchanges to monitor. But if this was a test, then that was the only correct answer. *So fuck Boerner.*

It was going to take some time to crack the key, though. Gragg pulled out the DC-to-AC adapter and plugged it into his car lighter, then plugged his laptop into the new AC power source. He launched *Asleap,* a program for grabbing and cracking wireless key exchanges. He could see the network clearly enough. He sent the command to de-authenticate every user on the new network and prayed to the freaking gods that some client connections were present.

Thirty seconds later, two authentication exchanges occurred to re-connect the clients. Gragg started breathing again. He now had an en-crypted hash that *Asleap* was working the dictionary to decrypt. He was on his way.

Gragg leaned his driver's seat back and stared at the ceiling, wondering if he'd ever get out of here alive.

Chapter 17://Succubus

Jon Ross hopped out at the front entrance to Alcyone Insurance. He opened the rear passenger door of Sebeck's Dodge Durango and grabbed his laptop bag from the backseat. It was Sebeck's personal car and reeked of his aftershave. The interior was immaculate, devoid of personal touches like Kleenex holders or errant CDs. It had the brutal cleanliness of a military barracks, and by revealing nothing about Sebeck it revealed a lot.

Ross looked from the backseat into the rearview mirror to make eye contact with Sebeck. "Well, Pete, again, my condolences on Deputy Larson. And I wish you the best of luck on the case."

Sebeck just stared at him. "What's that supposed to mean?" Sebeck's cell phone started ringing.

Ross slung his laptop bag over his shoulder. "It means that I'm done. The Feds have this under control."

"Don't even try that bullshit on me, Jon. Go get some sleep." He motioned for Ross to get out, and he unfolded his phone as he pulled away from the curb. He smiled grimly as he saw Ross flip him off in the rearview mirror. Then he answered the phone. "Sebeck."

A woman's voice said, "Nothing can kill you, can it, Pete?"

He felt his pulse accelerate. It was *her.* When had he last heard her voice? How long ago? *This phone line is tapped.* "Cheryl, I'm heading to the office. Call me there."

The line went dead. Sebeck stowed his phone, then drove a couple of blocks. He pulled over in a residential area, then looked in the rearview mirror. No one watching. He got out and opened the tailgate of the Durango. Sebeck reached down into the spare tire well and came up with a bright red prepaid, disposable cell phone. He closed the tailgate, looked around again, then got back in the Durango and plugged the phone into his car lighter. Moments later the little phone chirped, and he grabbed it.

"God, it's great to hear your voice. Things have been crazy. We lost two men today. I've got more in the hospital."

"I know. I caught the news in the terminal at O'Hare."

"You're in Chicago?" He knew better than to ask too much.

"No. Westwood."

"At the *company suite*?"

"You'll come meet me."

"Oh God, baby." Sebeck sighed. "This is a *really* bad time. This Daemon thing is—"

"You survived, Pete. I'll make you remember why you want to be alive."

That she would. Sebeck was quiet for a moment. Cheryl Lanthrop was the most beautiful woman he had ever been with. Her predatory sexuality made it even harder to resist. It was unfair that he should be *expected* to resist a woman like her. He had convinced himself that even his wife would understand.

Still, it was a bad time to disappear. But they could reach him by phone, couldn't they? The Feds would probably be busy tearing apart CyberStorm's network all night. And Sobol's estate? Hell, there were hundreds of police surrounding it. If he got caught, no man alive would think less of him.

He hesitated. "I'm just . . ." He couldn't find words.

"Only you know what you want, Pete."

He already knew he was going. He was someone else entirely with her. His responsibilities faded away. His goals were here and now—the conquest of her. And that's what it required: conquest.

"I'm on my way."

Wilshire Boulevard between Beverly Hills and Westwood Village was a canyon of tony high-rises one row deep. The buildings seemed out of place in Los Angeles, as though someone had grafted a piece of Manhattan's Upper East Side to L.A.'s suburban grid. This was the location of Cheryl's corporate condo.

Cheryl was some sort of medical executive. In one of his fits of curiosity about her, Sebeck had run a background check. She had a surprisingly benign past; good premed education, clean credit, no criminal record. Her employer sold and installed complex medical diagnostic systems, and she traveled the world consulting on multi-million-dollar deals. She had money—the type of money Sebeck could only dream about. And she had perks, like the corporate suite at this copper-roofed faux French provincial tower.

Sebeck still had a parking card, so he was able to avoid the doorman. His face was still in the news, and he wasn't anxious to be seen in the vicinity.

As he exited the elevator on the fifteenth floor, he peered both ways down the hall to be sure no one was in sight. As he approached Cheryl's door, Sebeck noticed it was slightly open. He looked around warily, then nudged it in. Cheryl stood beneath a halogen spotlight near the entryway. She wore a black cocktail dress with spaghetti straps. Black stockings with garters, visible below the hemline, wrapped her long legs and shapely, shoeless feet. Her auburn hair sparkled in the light. She smirked and curled a finger at him. She was even more beautiful than he remembered. Worth losing everything for.

Sebeck moved toward her, closing the door behind him. He knew better than to expect consolation from her. What they shared was different. Just before he reached her, she pirouetted and ducked her head low, bringing a roundhouse kick straight at his head. He saw it coming and grabbed her leg just in time. The impact sent him back against the wall.

She followed it with an open-hand karate punch toward his face. He ducked back, releasing her leg. "No bruising! Cheryl—"

"Shhhh." She put a painted fingernail to his lips.

Sebeck took the moment to grab her wrist, twisting her arm around her back. He brandished handcuffs seemingly out of thin air. She quickly tried to clear his legs out from under him, but he blocked her legs. Their shins slammed together, and he bore down on her to fling her to the floor. He felt her strong, lean body resisting, and then finally throwing him over her. He landed hard on the carpeted floor.

Struggling for breath, he managed to hiss out, "We've got to be more quiet—"

She let out a tigress growl, kicked the handcuffs away, and landed a few vicious punches to his abdomen. His tightened stomach muscles dampened the blows.

She smiled playfully and lightly bit his ear. "You goddamned pig." She grabbed him in a headlock and started a chokehold.

Perfume mixed with sweat filled his nostrils. Adrenaline filled his veins. If this wasn't love, then it was something nearly as good. He felt his consciousness begin to fade. He smacked his open hands against her ears, and she dropped the chokehold in an instant, grabbing her head in pain.

He rolled over, kneeling next to her. "Baby, did I hurt you?"

She looked up, one eye and half a mischievous smile visible behind a curtain of auburn hair. He saw his mistake too late, and her open hand shot like a jackhammer into his solar plexus. He doubled over in pain as she leaped over him, moving for the handcuffs.

She had a thing for cops—and he was probably one of several she had flings with around the country. He didn't care. She was a sexual hand grenade with the pin pulled out, but he could never manage to resist her. Whatever this said about him didn't matter. Cheryl was here, and the whole world could go screw itself.

He heard the clinking of the handcuffs coming up behind him, and he swept one hand back, grabbing her elbow. He shot the other arm up and grabbed her beautiful hair. It was a cheap shot, but effective. He made sure to grab enough of her hair to use as a rope. He twisted it tighter and finally yanked her head down toward his. He felt her struggling, and her open, pouting lips brushed against his.

He twisted her arm and pulled her around in front of him. Now she was really struggling, but he used all his prodigious strength to dominate her. All her skill had not been enough. He had mastered her. He heard her moan softly as he wrenched the handcuffs from her hand. In a moment he had forced her to her knees and slapped the cuffs over one wrist. She struggled mightily one last time, but he forced her head back down using her hair as a leash. The cuffs went over the second wrist, and he felt her sigh and settle back onto her knees.

He came up behind her and smelled her perfumed hair. Her lips brushed against his cheek.

"Is there a problem, officer?"

———————

Across Wilshire Boulevard, directly opposite the building, a camera lens in a darkened room reflected the streetlights. The camera clicked and whirred as Sebeck and the woman passionately kissed.

Anji Anderson raised her eye from the camera lens. She let an aroused breath escape as though she had been holding it for a while. She had no idea why The Voice felt this was news, but it had already been worth the trip.

Chapter 18:// Abyss

Wrecked county and federal police vehicles came under the glare of a mercury vapor searchlight. The bomb disposal robot's arm panned to reveal more carnage. A thousand feet away, a spectator in the control trailer whistled softly at the video image. A murmur went through the assembled agents. Special Agent Ellis Garvey released his hold on the joystick and awaited instructions.

The FBI's Critical Incidence Response Group (or CIRG) had taken over operations for the siege of Sobol's estate, but Steven Trear still had nominal control of strategy. He knew that he had to get this situation under control quickly, or it would be taken from him just as he had taken it from Decker.

Trear put a hand on Garvey's shoulder. "Bring us up to the mansion's front door."

The lawn mower–sized robot turned in place on rubberized treads and started moving across a blood-streaked debris field of plastic car bumpers and shattered glass, toward the mansion's front steps. Along the way the robot passed a crushed and twisted version of itself. It was the robot brought in by Guerner's team the day before. Garvey's camera lingered on the image. Ominously symbolic. Trear cleared his throat, and Garvey nudged the joystick again, sending the robot forward.

He halted the robot at the base of the mansion's front steps and raised its camera arms—shining the bright lights into the yawning, black maw of the doorway. The door was still wedged open.

A score of federal agents in the command trailer craned their necks to see the monitors.

Trear nodded to Garvey, who took a breath and eased the left joystick forward. The little robot's motors whined as it inched up the stone steps.

Before long it moved warily through the front door and into the foyer, where some type of fearsome technology had assaulted Guerner and his team. Washington wanted more information. The robot's camera arm panned the room. Glass from a shattered vase littered the tiled floor—along with vomit and specks of blood.

Someone in the back muttered, "Jesus."

One of the bomb squad guys leaned in. "Look for transceivers or sensors on the walls."

Garvey started panning the walls with the camera lights.

It looked like a classic Mediterranean, but there was a lot more than paintings and sculpture alcoves along the winding stairs. Near the ceiling an array of mysterious, white plastic sensors lined the walls.

Trear called out. "Guys, what are we looking at?"

A deafening silence filled the darkened trailer. In the glow of the camera monitors Trear looked for Allen Wyckoff, an FBI senior systems analyst who always seemed to know what he was talking about. Although there were bomb squad agents and a couple of computer forensics experts on hand, this wasn't a bomb and it wasn't software. It looked like a system. "Wyckoff. What am I looking at here?"

Wyckoff was just a silhouette in the darkness, except for the lenses of his round glasses, which reflected the monitor images. "Those are standard motion detectors . . . also what looks to be infrared sensors . . . I have no idea what *that* is. . . . The round pod might be a transmitter of some sort." He turned toward Trear, and the monitor reflections disappeared from his glasses. "Sir, we're going to need to analyze this video. There's a lot of technology there I'm not familiar with."

Trear looked around at the assembled experts, who were silently nodding in the dark. "So no one can tell me how the bomb disposal team was incapacitated? No guesses?"

The agents exchanged glances in the shadows.

Garvey ventured, "Should I keep going?"

Trear nodded. "Get us into the server room."

Garvey took another breath and eased the joystick forward again.

The robot moved easily across the floor toward the center doorway at the back of the foyer. The mercury light revealed a long hall with stone tile flooring and embroidered rugs. Mission-style furniture braced the walls here and there along the length of the hall.

One of Garvey's team spoke from the console nearby while examining blueprints. "We want to take the next hall on the right. Then it's the second door on the right."

"Got it. Turning." Garvey turned the robot in place and shined the camera lights down a short side hall. It led into the recreation room toward the back of the house. Garvey panned the hallway, examining the walls and ceilings. More of the mysterious sensors lined the walls. It was dark except for the lights on the robot.

"Cellar door, second on the right. It should lead down to the server room."

Garvey brought the robot forward, then moved to a second set of controls to activate the robot's arm. The mechanical hand slid into camera view and swiveled once to align with the lever door handle on the cellar door. The arm moved forward, grabbed the door handle, then depressed it.

Suddenly the camera image jolted wildly and shouts of alarm filled the trailer. In a moment all the screens were filled with snow.

Trear pushed forward. "What just happened?"

Garvey's hands hovered over the useless controls, his mouth open in shock. He turned. "I don't know. I . . ."

"Do we have any signal from the robot?"

Garvey and his assistant checked the console and shook their heads. Everyone was talking again.

Trear shouted, "Quiet down! Everyone shut up." He turned back to Garvey. "Play back the video—in slow motion."

Garvey nodded, then rewound the video. All the monitors flickered, then a still image came up again: the mansion side hall.

"Roll it forward slowly."

On-screen, frame by frame, the robotic arm grabbed the door handle and pushed down.

"There."

Garvey stopped the image.

There was an unmistakable gap in the floor toward the bottom of the frame. The floor looked like it was opening up.

"Okay, advance it slowly."

Garvey hit a button.

The gap expanded. In a quick succession of frames, the door handle pulled from the robot's grip, and the entire machine slid down a chute that opened beneath it. Its mercury lights illuminated the dark hole, revealing a cinder-block-lined pit—the bottom of which was filled with water. Successive video images showed the water washing up onto its cameras and the robot shorting out. The entire process took about one and a half seconds.

Sidebar conversations filled the trailer.

Trear clasped a hand on Garvey's shoulder. "It's all right. That's why we have robots." Trear looked unruffled, almost serene.

He turned to the assembled agents. "I think we've established that there's no power in the house." He pointed to some techs sitting at a frequency-scanning console. "And there's no radio transmissions emanating from the house, correct?"

The techs nodded.

Trear continued. "What we're looking at here is a simple pit trap. Sobol's high-tech weaponry is down. He's gone medieval on us. That's great news."

Garvey turned from the robot command console. "That's our last robot. We'll have to send back to L.A. for another one."

Trear nodded. "Bring in several. Fly them in if you have to. But we need to get our hands on Sobol's personal computers as soon as possible."

There was silence for a moment in the trailer.

Garvey hesitated, then asked, "Meaning that we . . . ?"

"Send in the Hostage Rescue Team. Have them go in as far as the pit. I want the area around the cellar entrance ramped over by the time we get the extra robots here."

Wyckoff looked surprised. "Sir, are you certain that's a good idea?"

"Certain? No, not certain. But Sobol's home computers might hold the key to destroying this monster. That's what we came to do. So let's do it."

Everyone murmured in agreement.

Someone in back asked, "What about the Hummer, sir?"

"Pull out the wreckage and ship it down to the L.A. lab. Cover it with a tarpaulin before pulling it out. I don't want to see any more pictures of the 'death machine' on the front page tomorrow." He clapped his hands once. "Let's get moving, people. The world's watching."

Special Agent Michael Kirchner sat poring over financial documents with five other agents in an unassuming accountant's office in Thousand Oaks. The desks were littered with open folders, receipts, tax returns, and ledgers. Another agent was busy imaging computer hard drives. Kirchner, a CPA and a tax attorney, believed that he and his team did more to fight crime than any field office in the bureau. Organized crime couldn't accomplish much without money.

They had spent the last eight hours scrutinizing the detailed financial history of Matthew Sobol. It was quite a trail. Sobol was an officer in thirty-seven corporations. He had three sole proprietorships, two partnerships, eleven LLCs—and a slew of international business corporations, holding companies, and offshore trusts. Tons of financial activity over the last two years, with equipment purchases, wire transfers, professional and consulting fees. It was a rat's nest. The finances of the rich usually were.

Kirchner reviewed a report of the largest capital expenditures. Technical components from the looks of it. Purchased by one company but shipped to Sobol's Thousand Oaks address.

Kirchner looked up at his partner, Lou Galbraith, who was sifting through filing cabinets nearby. "Lou, you lost money in fuel cells a few years back, didn't you?"

Galbraith stopped, raised his reading glasses up onto his forehead, and gave Kirchner an impatient look. "I don't want to talk about it. Why?"

Kirchner held up the printed report. "Sobol made some big purchases that I thought you might be interested in. . . ." He leafed through the report. "Here, identical hydrogen fuel cell power units purchased by two separate holding corporations, both shipped to his estate. $146,000 a pop."

"Tax dodge?"

Kirchner frowned. "We're not trying to nail him on tax evasion, Lou." He looked down at the report. "Fuel cell power units? Things like that really work?"

"I wasn't an idiot, Mike. Of course they work. Hospitals and big companies use them to generate electrical power from natural gas. You know, where the electrical grid is unreliable or too expensive. It was supposed to be huge. Just before its time, that's all, and—"

"These things were shipped to Sobol's estate." Kirchner looked even more concerned.

"What's wrong, Mike?"

"Call the SAC at the Sobol estate. I want to make sure he knows about this."

———

Agent Roy "Tripwire" Merritt took a deep breath, gathering in the last of the night air, redolent with moist earth. A sliver of moon hung just above the horizon, silhouetting the tree-dotted hills. He scanned the terrain without night vision gear, taking joy in this simple pleasure. It reminded him of the Basque region of Spain by moonlight—or South Africa's Transvaal. He'd seen a lot of the world by night, and usually from behind third-generation night vision goggles.

The predawn air was crisp and cool on Merritt's face as he stood in the payload area of an army ten-ton truck. Its powerful diesel engine labored in low gear as it climbed through a bulldozed breech in the estate wall. The canvas top had been removed, leaving it open to the night sky.

Merritt slung an HK MP-5/10 over his shoulder, then looked back toward his FBI Hostage Rescue Team. Six of the best-trained operators in the bureau sat on either side of the cargo bay, swaying in unison as the truck lurched over mounds of dirt and rock. These were *his* men, and they were intimidating as hell. Clad in black Nomex flight suits, body armor with ceramic trauma plates, Pro-Tec helmets, night vision goggles, and bulletproof face masks, they made Darth Vader look like a Wal-Mart greeter. But of all the missions they had carried out together—from Karachi to the wilds of Montana—Merritt had never had more misgivings than on this one. During the mission briefing he kept thinking that this was a job for the bomb disposal teams or the demining experts. It kept coming back to urgency. Six officers were dead, nine more injured. No one had any answers and time was apparently of the essence. Still . . .

Merritt looked down at the metal and wood scaffolding materials lying on the floor space between the benches. Four toolboxes lay there as well. His highly trained rapid response team was going to bridge a pit in a hostile environment. He wondered what sort of fuck-up happened upstairs to make this come about.

Merritt glanced over at the mansion three hundred yards away. No lights had appeared in it since last evening. Radio communications had been back up for the last hour, ever since the ultrawideband transmissions from the house died.

Merritt spoke normally, knowing his headset mic would pick it up. "Echo One to TOC. We're at yellow. Request compromise authority and permission to move to green."

"Copy, Echo One. I have your team at yellow. You have compromise authority and permission to move to green."

"Copy that, TOC." Merritt gave his men the thumbs-up signal. They returned it.

Waucheuer, the breaching specialist, flipped up his face mask and grinned. "Hey, Trip, why do we need guns? Sobol's already dead."

"Cut the chatter, Wack. Dead or not, Sobol managed to kill some good people here. Stay alert."

Waucheuer shrugged, then nodded sharply, causing his face mask to flip back down.

Merritt stood and looked over the cab of the truck as it advanced slowly across the wide lawn of the estate. They were coming up on the burnt-out hulk of the automated Hummer now.

The other men stood to lean against the railing as the Hummer came up on the right-hand side. The truck slowed, then stopped about twenty feet from the wreckage. Two county SWAT team members were in the truck cab. The passenger kicked on a side-mounted searchlight, focusing it on the still smoldering remains. The Hummer was definitely nonoperational. The wheels were just blackened hubs, and the interior was gutted.

"Those marines ever hear of a little thing called evidence?"

Merritt could practically hear Waucheuer grinning behind his mask. Merritt ignored him. He spoke into his headset. "Echo One to TOC. The Hummer is nonoperational. Proceeding to green. Out." Merritt pounded the cab roof twice. The truck lurched forward toward the mansion some one hundred yards away.

The truck searchlight swung toward the house. A three-foot-high terrace wall surrounded the mansion at a distance of about two hundred feet. The terrace leveled out the hilltop for the lawns around the pool and patio. The wall prevented the truck from driving all the way to the house, but Merritt agreed with the SAC that driving along the front entrance or rear service road was a bad idea; it was a chokepoint and could be booby-trapped.

Instead, the truck turned in front of the wall, then backed up; the ridiculous *beep-beep* of the backup warning filled the tense silence.

It looked like it was going to work out. The tailgate now stood about two feet off the ground as the truck backed up to the terrace wall. It would be easy to unload the scaffolding and tools. But first, they needed to scout ahead. Merritt shouted to the driver, "Cut the engine and the lights."

Relative silence suddenly prevailed. The sound of crickets returned after a few moments. The only lights visible were the work lamps of the besieging FBI at the estate fence line—about three hundred yards away. Merritt swung down his night vision goggles and powered them up. His men did the same.

Merritt spoke into his bone mic. "Leave the scaffolding. Let's make sure we have a clear path to the objective." Merritt gave a hand signal, and his men fell in line behind him.

The plan was to circle around to the front of the house and enter through the open front door. They were on the east side of the house right now. So they were looking at a 150-yard *infil* over manicured lawns and gardens. Aerial radar had revealed no hidden pits or other apparent traps on the estate grounds to a depth of ten meters, but the approach to the mansion wasn't what concerned Merritt. He was worried about entering the house itself—especially considering what happened to the last people to do so. Merritt stepped off the truck tailgate and started moving through the night. He felt and heard his men moving close behind him.

This wasn't a hostage crisis. A flash-bang grenade wasn't going to stun anyone here. Overwhelming firepower wouldn't intimidate the opponent. This was a new situation.

Merritt turned and put a hand up to halt his men. "Wait here. I'm going to scout ahead. If you lose contact with me, pull back to the estate perimeter. Understood?"

They exchanged concerned looks. This went against everything they'd trained for. They were a team. Even Waucheuer had no wisecracks.

"That's an order. Assume a defensive posture and wait here." Merritt turned and moved cautiously toward the house.

Hundreds of yards away at the FBI Command and Control trailer, the SAC, Steven Trear, stood gazing through a FLIR scope at the distant figures of the HRT unit. He could see one moving ahead of the others—moving toward the side of Sobol's mansion. Trear muttered to himself, "What's he doing?"

One of the agents from the Command Trailer emerged and called to Trear. "Sir, a Special Agent Kirchner on the line for you. Something about Sobol's purchase records."

Trear didn't look up from the night vision scope. "Kirchner's heading the audit team?"

"I believe so, sir."

"Tell him I'll call him back."

"He says it's important—"

Another Command Center agent pushed his head out through the doorway. "Sir! I'm picking up noise from the parabolic mics. Noise from inside the house."

Everyone stopped and looked at the guy with something resembling terror. Trear started walking toward him. "What kind of noise?"

"It sounds like a pump motor, sir."

"Get those men out of there!"

About sixty feet ahead of his men, Merritt heard the *click* and stopped cold. His men did likewise. They'd all heard it, too, and they instinctively spun to face every direction—training their weapons. Against what, they didn't know.

Suddenly Merritt's radio crackled. Someone shouted in an urgent voice over the channel, *"Echo One, abort immediately! Repeat, abort immediately!"*

Before he could react, Merritt heard a disquieting *hiss* start to emanate from the ground. Just as suddenly the air around him sprang to life, and he and his men nearly jumped out of their skins.

Retractable lawn sprinklers popped up and started spraying the lush terrace lawn with cold water. His team burst out laughing as they stood getting soaked by the lawn sprinklers.

Waucheuer shielded his night vision goggles and shouted the distance to Merritt. "Shit, Trip, I just aged ten years!"

Even Merritt smiled behind his mask this time. "You heard 'em. Pull out!"

Then something changed. Suddenly Merritt was aware of an overpowering odor. His eyes narrowed behind his goggles. The sprinklers were no longer spraying water.

He looked to his men and shouted, *"Gasoline!"*

Before they could turn and run, a high-precision motor whirred in the distant cupola tower. A deep *choom* sound issued from it, and the last thing Merritt saw through his goggles was a blinding green flare arcing over the distance between him and the tower.

The rolling fireball lit up the sky for a mile around. Its dull roar echoed off the side of the trailer, and the orange light illuminated three hundred horrified faces. Trear still held the radio in his hand. He stood paralyzed as shrieks of agony came over the radio channel. All around him men raced into action—or anarchy, it was hard to tell.

"Get the fire trucks over there!"

"Ambulance! Bring up an ambulance!"

"We've got agents down!"

The fireball climbed to the sky, and in its stark light Trear could see the lawn sprinklers surrounding it still running. They were spraying water—to contain the fire in the precise spot where the HRT unit had infiltrated. Trear felt like he was watching something on TV. It had the surreal feeling of the impossible. People were grabbing him, shouting at him. He couldn't take his eyes off the raging fire and the wildly thrashing dark forms dancing in the flames like damned souls—then falling. The ten-ton truck was burning like a Texas A&M bonfire.

Someone shouted in his ear about radio transmissions, and Trear absently looked down at the radio in his hand. Only static hissed out of it now. That's when it happened.

Suddenly all the lights went on in Sobol's mansion, glowing with a frightful intensity. Then lights kicked back on all across the estate. An audible groan ran through the ranks of the besieging agents.

Trear snapped out of it and shoved the now useless radio into another agent's hands. "Get to cover! Everybody get to cover!"

The pain (because it must have been pain) was white noise that Merritt had no time for. On the imaginary control board in his mind, every light was flashing red. He ran as only men on fire can run, yanking his Nomex balaclava up to cover his mouth. The whole world had turned into the surface of the sun. He resisted the panic-stricken need to breathe the superheated air. To breathe was to die.

But then it turned dark again—the bright glow beyond his clenched eyelids had gone away. Had the night vision goggles failed? Probably. But he'd have to open his eyes to find out, and he wasn't ready for that. But the heat was gone—and now there was only cold. His entire body tingled. It was almost pleasant. Experience told him that, in combat, tingling sensations meant you had just been seriously injured.

Merritt staggered on blindly. Finally he stopped and tore off his night vision goggles and opened his eyes. Instantly he was blinded by cold water spraying into his face. It felt wonderful. He smelled a combination of gasoline, burnt flesh, melted plastic, and hot metal. He turned in place dizzily—feeling shock creep up on him. He stood in a manicured section of lawn right next to a rising mushroom of orange flame fifty feet tall. The cold water spraying over him made it tolerable to be this close. His men were in those flames somewhere.

He reached for his bone mic, melted against his cheek. "Waucheuer! Reese! Littleton! Report! Kirkson! Engels! Report!" The microphone pulled off in his hands. His earphones were dead under his Kevlar helmet.

His men were gone. All gone.

Merritt was numb. He spun in place to orient himself and saw the mansion blazing white light a hundred feet farther on. He held his arm up and saw that the stock of his MP-5 had melted onto the back of his sleeve. His nylon web belt containing ammunition clips had melted into his jumpsuit and Kevlar body armor. He wasn't sure whether he was badly injured, but his temper was beginning to flare. He decided to go with it.

Merritt grabbed the gun's barrel with his left hand and wrenched the twisted mass free from his arm. The Nomex appeared to have protected him from the worst of it, but he felt the confused buzzing in his nerve endings that was the neurological equivalent of "Please Stand By For Pain. . . ."

Merritt started running, not toward the perimeter wall and safety, but toward the mansion. He raced for the fenced-in pool area and a set of white French doors with polished brass handles—its windows blazing light. His eyes never left it as he leapt over stone benches and herb gardens.

Around him, in the sprinkler wash, he smelled gasoline again, and he heard the *whoosh* of flames racing to overtake him, but he outran it and stayed in the cool clear water that served as a buffer against the flames reaching the house.

As he ran, Merritt clutched at his back for the sawed-off shotgun strapped there. He was still tugging on its rubberized pistol grip, trying to free it from the melted mass of his web belt, when he kicked in the wooden pool gate. Metal gate hardware clattered across the paving stones—but he was already smashing through a field of teak wood patio chairs and flipping tables in his quest for the French doors. Almost there. He was vaguely aware of spotlights focusing on him from the house, but he didn't give a damn what Sobol was up to. He might drop dead once he got there, but he was getting inside that house.

He whipped out his Mark V knife and slashed the melted bits of the web belt from the shotgun. To save time he hurled the knife ahead, where it stuck quivering in the door frame. He drew the Remington 870 shotgun into his gloved hands and chambered a round with a satisfying *click-clack.*

Merritt hit the door hard with his booted foot—and damn near shattered his shinbone. His forward momentum sent him hurtling into the door, where his knee came up into his mouth—driving a sharp nail of pain straight to the center of his skull. He staggered back and reflexively wiped the back of his glove across his mouth. It came back covered with blood. His front teeth felt loose.

Doesn't matter.

Merritt leveled the shotgun at the door handles and blasted a foot-wide hole in their place. He chambered another breaching round and quickly blasted similar holes at the top and bottom where the doors met—the most likely spot for reinforcing bolts.

Hundreds of yards away, the FBI camp was pandemonium. Agents and police scrambled to gather rescue gear while others scrambled to order no one to go anywhere near the site of the attack. It was a disorganized mess. Somewhere in the chaos Trear heard distant shotgun blasts.

He shouted, "Who's shooting? Decker, order them to cease fire!"

"Com is down."

Merritt rammed his shoulder into the French doors, bashing them in. He stumbled into a neo-mission-style entertainment room with wide-plank wooden floors. There was a sunken area of sectional sofas in front of a large plasma screen television. The lights here blazed brilliantly, practically blinding him. Nonetheless he craned his neck and weaved from side to side. He knew what he had to do.

The bomb disposal team was taken out by weaponized acoustics, and he wasn't going to let that happen to him. Merritt raised his shotgun and noticed half a dozen different sensors spaced along the ceiling over each wall—behind the brilliant lights.

A clear and commanding voice called from the doorway leading farther into the house. "You don't belong here!"

Merritt's response came out reflexively. "Fuck you, Sobol."

Merritt heard footsteps approaching him over the wooden floor. It was uncanny. There was definitely the sense that someone was there. A change in the echoes of the room. That's when Merritt felt as much as heard the deepest sound he'd ever experienced pass over and through him. The nearby coffee table started vibrating so badly that the glass panels fell out of it.

Merritt twisted to look back up at the ceiling and noticed a reflected LED light pulsating on the back of one of the round sensor pods. He raised the shotgun just as an ungodly feeling of horror gripped him. His intestines were trying to strangle him, and he felt his eyes preparing to explode. He screamed in agony and fired the shotgun.

Immediately the pain stopped. Merritt paused for a second to lean over and vomit on the floor, but he was immediately back up. His eyes and nose were bleeding, but he wiped it away and swiveled around to blast another Hatton round into an identical sensor on the far wall. Then the interior wall. He swayed as he pulled more shotgun shells from his cargo pants pockets and started reloading the Remington. Blood dripped onto his fingers from his nose.

"You son of a bitch! I'm going to shut you down, Sobol!" Merritt slid a shell into the magazine. "You hear me?" His words echoed in the big house.

A voice right behind him said, "There's no need to shout. I can hear you."

Merritt jumped and turned around, letting loose a shotgun blast into the wall behind him.

The voice was still there, just inches from his face. "I see you got past the firewall."

How the hell was this possible? The sound was appearing in midair. No stereo could possibly do that. Merritt scanned the arrays of sensors again, but none were visibly active.

The voice was right in his *ear,* whispering. "They knew you would die, but they sent you, anyway."

Merritt jumped away, twisting his gloved finger in his ear as though an insect had flown into it. "Son of a—"

Merritt let the shotgun hang from its shoulder strap while he drew one of his twin P14-45 pistols. The voice continued in his ear, but there was no pain. No agonizing constriction of his intestines.

"They're willing to sacrifice you to find out what I'm capable of."

"Keep talking, asshole." Merritt stood in formal range stance— aiming at the ceiling sensors. He started shooting them out, one by one, waiting a second after each shot.

"Did they even tell you—"

The fourth shot cut him off. A reflective, white plastic panel shattered as the bullet hit it. The voice was gone. Merritt shot out another identical sensor on the far wall, then flipped the safety on the pistol, holstering it. "Blah, blah, blah."

Merritt noticed his reflection in a mirror over the mantel as he walked farther into the room. His whole face was crimson red and covered in blisters, with the headset melted onto his cheek. His Pro-Tec helmet had protected his scalp, but the whites of his eyes were shockingly blood red—and blood trailed down from his nose over his burnt chin. The Nomex hood and suit had kept him alive, but he might soon be entering cataleptic shock. The dizziness came at him in waves. He felt the rage building in him again. His men had had much worse.

Merritt heard a slight *tick* sound and a sizzle of static electricity. He spun around to see the plasma-screen television come to life. A 3-D graphic of the mansion as seen from the air resolved on-screen. It looked like a briefing schematic.

"You're here for the server room. It's down the hall, to the left, and to the left again. I'm sure they gave you a map, but in case it burned up, here are directions. . . ." The 3-D graphic leaped into action, with the camera performing a virtual fly-through, coming down on the mansion from above, straight through the doors Merritt had entered by. The camera flew down the adjoining hall, banked left, then sailed through the billiard room, left, and up to the cellar door—which flung open as the camera went down into blackness. It was like a first-person video game.

Merritt grabbed an end table nearby, clearing off the lamp standing on it.

Sobol's voice continued, oblivious. "Did you want me to replay that? Yes or no."

The face of the plasma-screen television shattered under the impact of the heavy end table, and the entire thing keeled over backward on its stand—sending up a puff of electrical smoke as it died hitting the floor.

"No more mind games." Merritt strode past it and grabbed a piece of the sectional sofa, pulling it up with great effort from the sunken area onto the main floor level. He shouldered it in front of him as he advanced toward the doorway leading farther into the house. He held the shotgun in his free hand.

The dimensions of Sobol's house went beyond anything Merritt would consider a home. To him it felt more like a university building. He guessed these were twelve- to sixteen-foot ceilings, and the doors and adjoining hallways were all two or three times wider and taller than necessary. The hall adjoining the entertainment area was easily ten feet wide, with terra cotta tile flooring in two-foot squares. The hall could pass as a serviceable elevator lobby for the Biltmore. It ran along the center of the house and was braced here and there with gargantuan furniture—angry-looking armoires and iron-studded cabinets done in something akin to Spanish Inquisition style. They looked large enough to serve as a redoubt in the event of Indian attack.

As he stood at the entrance to the wide hallway, Merritt leaned right and left to glimpse a little of what lay ahead. He couldn't see into any of the doorways. He pushed the sofa section onward, down the left side of the hall. The sofa's metal-studded feet scraped the tile like nails on a chalkboard.

Suddenly the floor dropped away beneath the sofa section, and Merritt caught himself just before pitching forward into the yawning blackness below the trapdoor. The sofa splashed into a water-filled pit, and then the floor section snapped up, almost hitting Merritt in the face. He heard a latch *click*, locking the floor in place. It was obviously meant to prevent escape from the pit once a victim fell in.

Merritt pounded the trapdoor with the butt of his shotgun. The floor seemed firm. He didn't want to take any chances, so he backed up to get a running start. He sprinted and leaped over the farthest seam of the trapdoor, landing in a tumble he purposely shortened by rolling hard into an armoire the size and height of a squatter's shack. In a moment he was up and ready with the shotgun.

He felt the humming sound of the acoustic weapons powering up. He glanced right and left up near the ceiling and found the nearest acoustic pod. A blast from the shotgun took it clean off the wall. He found its twin behind him and blasted that as well. He collected his breath in the resulting silence.

Suddenly a voice in front of him said, "Slap a pair of tits and a ponytail on you, and we've got ourselves a game."

Merritt just gave Sobol's voice the finger. Let him talk. Merritt had to conserve ammunition.

It was time to orient himself. He pulled a laminated floor plan card of Sobol's house from his chest pocket. It was warped from the heat of the fire but still legible. Merritt found his location and realized he wasn't far from the cellar door—and the pit that swallowed the bomb disposal robot. Merritt looked up and noticed the silence.

"What's the matter, Sobol? Run out of things to say?"

The voice spoke from the same place—right in front of him. "I didn't catch that."

"I said, cat got your tongue?"

"I didn't catch that."

It couldn't really understand him. This was all an elaborate technological trick. A logic tree with weaponry.

"Dead retard." Merritt pocketed the card and put a shoulder behind the heavy armoire, trying to push it ahead of him. It insisted on being stationary. He took a step back to look at it. He'd seen railroad trestles built with less wood. It looked a century old and its shelves were lined with Talavera plates and wooden carvings of Dia de los Muertos figurines. Merritt smiled humorlessly at the little skeletons cavorting and going about their daily business—apparently unaffected by their demise. Real cute.

He grabbed a bronze candlestick off the shelf and looked ahead of him. A twenty-foot stretch of barren hall lay before him. After that, he'd be at the doorway opening onto the billiards room—which led to the cellar door.

He slung the shotgun and got down onto his belly, spreading his weight over the tile floor. He turned back to rap the hollow floor behind him—to get a sense for its sound. Then he rapped the floor under him. Solid. Very different sound. Merritt faced forward again, and he started crawling, cautiously rapping on the floor with the heavy candlestick as he went.

Merritt was halfway along the open stretch of hall when Sobol's voice spoke again a foot or so in front of Merritt's face. "I hate to interrupt, but now I have to kill you."

Merritt heard something from deep inside the house. It sounded like a sump pump—only many times larger than the one in Merritt's house. The sound of water coursing through pipes came to his ears, and suddenly water began to silently spread out across the floor from an unseen vent beneath the baseboards. Then Merritt glanced left, right, and back behind him. The water was coming at him from ahead and behind—spreading out from the walls across the tile floor about a half-inch deep. Merritt got up into a crouch, not sure what to do next. He'd never reach the armoire before the water overtook him.

And what could the water do, anyway? Sobol could never fill this room—there were six or seven doorways leading into it. Merritt started scanning the walls for hidden danger. And he quickly found it.

Ahead of him, one of the electrical outlets in the wall suddenly extended out and down onto the floor. It was mounted on the end of a curved bar. A *zap* and *pop* were audible as the socket hit the surface of the water—which was now electrified.

"Shit!" Merritt leaped to his feet and looked around for something to stand on. Nothing. He quickly flipped the shotgun from his back and blasted two holes in the lath and plaster wall near him—one about a foot from the floor, and another at hand-holding height. He let the shotgun fall on its shoulder strap as he jumped, latching on to the jagged edges of the holes just as water collided beneath him from both directions.

Merritt almost lost his grip as the thin slats of broken wood snapped under his weight. But he soon found studs and cross-braces to cling to. He took a deep breath and leaned his burnt face against the cool plaster. He was really starting to feel the pain of his burns now. Second-degree burns were the worst for pain. He collected himself, then glanced beneath him.

The water was now about three inches deep on the floor and was draining through the seams of several pits. The cascade of water echoed below the floor. More water was constantly being pumped in, but it appeared to have found equilibrium. The humming sound of the electrified surface was unnerving.

Merritt looked ahead. He was only eight feet or so from the billiard room doorway, and there was a step up—so the water was not rushing into it.

Merritt began ripping out lath slats and kicking in the plaster wall ahead of him. His bulletproof gloves and armored knuckle plates helped as he repeatedly punched the cracked edge of the rapidly expanding hole. The debris fell into the buzzing water below.

It took him a good five minutes, but he was soon at the edge of the billiard room doorway. He leaned over to gaze inside. It contained twin pool tables and a bar that would suffice for a small town. He immediately considered the many ways this room could kill him. High-speed billiard balls fired from an antique cannon. Molotov cocktails of twenty-year-old scotch. Asbestos poisoning. Choking hazards. He couldn't begin to guess.

Even at this distance, Merritt could see one of the acoustic weapon sensors up near the ceiling. He unholstered his pistol with his right hand while holding on to a wooden beam with the other. He raised the gun, aimed carefully, and sent three shots into the pod. Parts of it fell to the carpeted floor at the foot of the bar.

Merritt stared at the room. *What the hell . . .*

He unhooked a flash-bang grenade from his web harness. The grenade handle was melted onto the webbing, but he managed to pull it off. He struggled to remove the pin while still holding on to the beam. Most people thought you could pull the pin with your teeth, but that was a great way to crack a tooth or blast your head off—or both. He finally wrapped his hand around the beam and pulled the pin out with his forefinger. He tossed the grenade into the center of the nearest pool table—then he ducked around the corner.

The blast was deafening even at this distance. The beams of the house shook, and he heard lots of shattering glass. He hoped it would confuse any infrared or acoustical sensors. Merritt swung around the corner and ran headlong toward the nearest table—whose felt top was scorched and smoking from the blast.

Merritt lunged onto the tabletop and rolled over its far edge. Then he rolled over the next one as well, landing like a cat, crouched and ready for action with the shotgun. He covered the last ten feet to the opposite doorway and slammed his body against the wall there. He was breathing hard—but then again his heart had been beating 180 times a minute since he entered the house.

The telltale sound of acoustical weapons powering up reached him. He aimed upward and blasted the pod into plastic confetti that rained down on him. He scanned the ceiling, but none of the other pods seemed threatening.

The cellar door was four feet ahead and to his left. The floor before it was terra cotta tile—but he knew it concealed the pit that had swallowed the FBI's bomb disposal robot. He looked for seams, but the pit was well concealed.

Merritt stood back at the edge of the short hall, then leaned forward and depressed the cellar's lever door handle with the shotgun barrel.

Suddenly a four-foot section of floor in front of the cellar door fell away, revealing a brick-lined pit splashing with water. The tip of a robot arm extended above the water's surface. Merritt quickly jumped to the far side of the pit, then leaned forward and grabbed the cellar door handle. He pried the door open as it resisted. He shoved the shotgun behind the door, pointing at the top hinge.

BOOM!

The top of the door fell away from the wall, and with a little twisting and kicking, the other hinge ripped off. The door fell into the pit, smacking the water with its flat face.

Merritt looked into the doorway and could see the top of a flight of steps leading downward. A barred gate blocked his path. They were stainless steel bars, like the kind found on the inner door of a bank vault. A numeric keypad was set into the steel strike plate.

The voice spoke, this time right behind Merritt's head. "Dave, Stop. Stop, Dave."

"Fuck off, Sobol." Merritt concentrated on the keypad in the strike plate. He was no security specialist, and he knew it was probably booby-trapped. He aimed the shotgun at an angle and squeezed off a Hatton round into the strike plate. The lead and wax slug disintegrated into a pall of smoke. Merritt waved it away and looked at the strike plate. The keypad was entirely gone—leaving behind only a small round hole where its electronics entered the steel gate mechanism. Otherwise the strike plate was undamaged. Hot lead was useless against it.

Merritt unholstered his second P14 pistol. He'd give hot copper a try. Merritt aimed at the strike plate, then fired repeatedly at the same spot. Bullet holes appeared in the far wall as they ricocheted. After the last shot, he inspected the damage. Fourteen shots and he had successfully dulled the finish—barely.

Merritt sank down to lean his back against the wall. Waucheuer and the others had been carrying the heavy-duty breaching kit—the cutting charges and boosters. All Merritt had was a roll of strip explosives, and that wouldn't take out this steel gate.

Sobol's voice was right there with him. "Does it help to know that there's nothing important here?"

Merritt looked down into the watery pit. He examined its walls. They were of brick painted with thick black marine paint. The pit was on the same level as the rest of the cellar—and presumably the server room.

Merritt holstered his pistol and took the remaining grenades from his web harness. He had four flash-bang grenades left. He took the roll of Primasheet and det cord from his thigh pocket and wrapped them tightly around the grenades. Then he stood, straddling the corner of the pit. He dropped the package into the water, reeling out detonator cord as it fell. Then he ducked around the corner and activated the detonator.

The muffled blast shot a geyser of water into the ceiling. The floor trembled for a few moments. Merritt soon heard the sound of water rushing through an opening. He had cracked the brick wall.

He came back to the edge of the pit and could see water draining through the wall and into the server room.

A klaxon suddenly sounded in the house, and fire strobes flickered on the ceiling. A British female voice spoke on a regular PA system, "Primary data center penetrated. Commencing self-destruct sequence." There was a pause. "And there is no countdown."

"Shit!" Merritt knew the front door was around the corner and down the front hall. He sprinted around the corner as a piercing *beep* filled the house. It was like a smoke detector on steroids—drilling into his brain.

The sprinkler caps popped off in the ceiling above him, and sprinkler heads clicked down. He heard the hiss of pressure building up. Merritt looked ahead. The front door of the mansion still stood wide open about a hundred feet ahead—wedged open by that blessed bomb squad team. He sprinted for the opening with everything he had.

The sprinkler heads came to life, spraying gasoline over the stylish décor. He was still sixty feet from the front door when he saw a bright halogen bulb start to burn intensely up near the ceiling in the foyer. The light grew so intense that Merritt couldn't look directly at it.

When the bulb exploded—sending a wall of flame roaring toward him—Merritt's brain trotted forward a candidate for his last mortal thought:

I'll never see my daughters grow up.

Without warning, the floor gave way beneath him as he ran. A pit trap swallowed him. He fell into blackness, chased by flames that lit up the brackish water. Time slowed down, and Merritt had the leisure to consider what a bastard Sobol was; he'd activated a pit trap *after* letting the bomb disposal robot drive down the hallway safely.

The devious bastard.

Merritt hit the water face-first and blacked out as the trapdoor snapped shut above him.

———

Among the agents surrounding the mansion a shout went up. It was quickly followed by hundreds of other voices shouting. Sobol's mansion was now glowing orange. Then flames burst out through literally all of its windows. In seconds the entire structure was engulfed in flames reaching fifty feet into the air. The half-dozen outbuildings burst into flames, too, and were quickly roaring infernos.

Trear numbly watched the scene. It was the nightmarish Waco visual he'd dreaded—one almost certainly combined with the worst casualties ever suffered by the FBI in a single operation. And all of Sobol's data were going up in flames. Along with Trear's career.

Chapter 19:// Sarcophagus

It took Gragg nearly three and a half hours to crack the WPA key on Boerner's second Wi-Fi network. He had to keep his car running the entire time to be certain he didn't drain his laptop battery. Once he cracked the key, he configured his card to use it, and DHCP soon handed him an IP address on the wireless network. By that time it was roughly four in the morning.

But he'd slept a little, and buoyed by the successful crack, he felt good. If this was a test, he'd passed the first part. He might get out of this alive yet.

Gragg used *Superscan* to run a ping sweep and port scan for machines on this new network, but he discovered only the single workstation running the wireless access point. The workstation returned information on its operating system and coughed up the status of several running services—but its hard drive was sealed tight.

Gragg considered his options. He wanted a quick exploit that would give him a remote shell on the host machine with sysadmin rights. From there, he should be able to see into the hardwired LAN not yet visible to him.

Since he didn't have the luxury of time, he opted for an attack that was effective against a wide range of devices: SNMP—a buffer overrun that exploited a known vulnerability in unpatched implementations of Simple Network Management Protocol. This service was present on the target, and it was worth a shot.

He switched to the command console and quickly keyed in the commands, pointing his exploit code to port 161 on the target machine. If the target was running an unpatched OpenBSD, he'd get to root pretty quick.

He executed the command, waited, and in a moment he got a return instructing him to telnet to port 6161 at the target IP address. He sighed in relief. Another hurdle overcome.

Gragg launched a telnet session and soon had a root prompt. He now *owned* Boerner's workstation. Time to escalate network privileges.

Gragg searched the target machine's domain but was disappointed by the results. His victim was linked to a single server—and that was sealed up tight. It barely divulged any information. Gragg took a look in the server's shared directory and raised his eyebrows.

The directory contained a single Web page file. A page named HackMe.htm.

Gragg smiled. He was beginning to feel a connection with Sobol. Sobol *wanted* him to get this far—that's what this was all about.

Gragg double-clicked on the file. A plain white Web page appeared in a browser window. It had logon and password text boxes and a SUB-MIT button—nothing more.

There were options here. Unicode directory traversal? Gragg smiled. *Logon.* Sobol was encouraging him. This had all the earmarks of an SQL-injection attack, and he had a favorite one. In the logon and password boxes he entered:

' or 1=1--

He clicked the SUBMIT button. After a moment's pause an animation appeared with the words "Logon successful. Please wait. . . ." Gragg felt a rush of endorphins. He'd just received high praise from his new mentor. He was getting more comfortable by the minute in this environment.

In a few moments a slick Flash-based diagram of a cinder-block building appeared with various features highlighted. It was an isometric view depicting the building right in front of Gragg's car. He could see the antenna tower with a call-out label captioned "WI-FI ANTENNA ARRAY." He moved his pointer around the diagram and noticed rollovers come to life as his mouse passed over certain features.

Gragg saw a sensor array depicted on the roof, and the illustration looked like it included at least one camera. Gragg pointed at the array, and a translucent drop-down menu unfolded to the right of it containing a submenu:

Ultrawideband Transceiver
HD Video Multiplexer
Acoustical Sensor Array

He was beginning to feel the rush now. This wasn't a game, and it was clearly designed by a well-funded and technologically capable person. He had always sought the *edge*—and this was it. This was as far from Main Street as he'd ever been. This wasn't the tattooed, pierced, neo-tribal rebellious bullshit of his generation. This was a quiet demonstration of networked power. This was *it.*

Gragg selected *HD Video Multiplexer* from the drop-down menu. A new browser window appeared containing a selection of six thumbnail images. They appeared to be streaming video feeds. Gragg saw an image of a car in one thumbnail, and he double-clicked on it—as anyone his age would do. It expanded to fill the window. It was a live image of his car. He waved his hand, and his hand appeared waving on the video feed. Gragg noticed a superimposed red bracket around his license plate. A call-out label showed the software's interpretation of the tag number. It was correct. So Sobol was employing an optical license plate reader. Gragg knew it was commercially available software—used all the time on interstates and downtown roads. But Sobol needed access to DMV records to determine who owned the car. He must have cracked a DMV database in order to get his registration information. Gragg considered the hourly rate of the average DMV worker and realized that gaining access wasn't a problem for Sobol.

In the background of the video, there was a similar bracket around the VW Vanagon's license plate. Gragg couldn't help but wonder what was up with that. The van was smashed all to hell.

He closed that dialog box and checked out the other video feeds. There were cameras placed all around the cinder-block building, guarding it from every direction. Every time the wind blew, the swaying branches were outlined by vectored lines trying to resolve into something recognized by the software. Gragg found himself watching the red lines appear and disappear like a lava lamp. Motion-capture software? This was sophisticated stuff. No one would ever suspect that this isolated blockhouse held so much processing power.

Gragg closed the video feeds and moved around to the other visible features of the diagram. He noticed that a garage-like protrusion extended from the rear of the building. He pointed his mouse at it, and the words "H1 Alpha" materialized beneath his pointer. That explained the damage to the Vanagon. There was an automated Hummer here—just like at Sobol's mansion. Gragg smiled. It *was* Sobol. He was walking in the footsteps of a genius. To his dismay, there was no more information visible for the Hummer, so he clicked on one of the nodes around the base of the building. The label "Seismic Sensors" appeared. Probably for detection of approaching vehicles and people.

As Gragg scrolled around the base of the building illustration, a roll-over displayed the red, glowing outline of a door in the front wall. He looked up at the real wall some twenty feet ahead of him. He couldn't see any indication that there was a door in the plain cinder blocks. He hovered his mouse cursor back over the section of wall in the diagram, and a drop-down menu appeared. It had two selections: "Open" and "Close." Gragg clicked "Open."

In front of his car, he saw a section of the cinderblock wall move inward and then slide sideways—revealing a dark doorway about five feet wide. Gragg half expected roiling steam to emanate from the opening. It was outlined with a soft red glow.

Was this it? Was he supposed to enter? He looked around warily. That would require getting out of his car.

The spotlight from the building still shined down on the area, revealing what a horrendous morass of mud he'd driven into. He had no idea how he'd get the car out without a tow truck. He couldn't stay in here forever.

Gragg shut down his laptop and packed up all his gear. In a few minutes he had everything in his rucksack except for his Glock 9mm—which he kept in his right hand. Gragg opened the Tempo's driver door with its trademark 1980s-Detroit-crack-squeak sound. He gingerly placed one combat-booted foot into the quagmire and felt it sink up to his knee. He groaned in disgust, but realizing he had no choice, he followed it with his other foot, closing the car door behind him. Pretty soon he was stagger-stepping through the deep mud toward the dark opening in the cinder-block wall.

Gragg stopped and took another look at the smashed VW Vanagon with Louisiana plates and anarchy bumper stickers. Shattered taillight plastic and twisted side moldings littered the area. The left rear wheel of the VW was smashed into immobility, set at an angle to the axle. The passenger door of the Vanagon was slightly open, with deep footprints leading out of the mud and toward the road.

Gragg stood for a moment, deciding whether to check it out. He realized he didn't want to be walking around out here and continued staggering through the foot-sucking mud toward the building.

Before long he climbed up onto a ledge of solid ground that ringed the building. Gragg examined his legs. They were caked in mud. His feet were sopping wet. He tried to scrape the mud off his boots by dragging them against the ground but gave up and slung his rucksack over his shoulder. Then he chambered a round in the Glock and faced the opening.

Diffuse red light emanated from the edges of the door. It was just enough light to reveal a polished stone floor extending into the blackness beyond. Red. Low-frequency light not visible from any significant distance.

Suddenly a British-accented female voice spoke in midair right alongside Gragg's head. "Come inside, Mr. Gragg."

Gragg was so startled he reflexively squeezed off a shot with the Glock. The deafening *crack* echoed off into the sky. The bullet whined off the cinder-block wall, then howled out into the woods.

The female voice spoke again. It sounded slightly artificial, clipped. "Are you familiar with gunshot detectors? Police departments in major U.S. cities deploy them to identify and triangulate the precise location of gunshots the moment they occur. A gunshot has a distinct acoustic pattern. Even the weapon fired can be identified by its sound pattern. You apparently have a . . . nine millimeter." There was a pause. "You won't need it. You've earned the right to enter."

Gragg looked down at the Glock in his hand. He took a breath. He'd never felt out of his depth technologically, but the disembodied voice was as close to magic as he'd ever experienced. He didn't like the role of awed primitive. It didn't suit him. He took another deep breath and tentatively spoke to the voice. "Who are you?"

The voice shot back. "This door will close permanently in ten seconds."

Gragg's thoughts scattered, and he hesitated for a moment before rushing through the doorway and into the darkness—feet squishing mud. The moment he did so, the door slid noiselessly closed behind him. The red glow from the door frame faded away as the opening sealed shut. Gragg stood in pitch-black darkness for a moment. It smelled not at all musty. It was super-clean, dry, filtered air. He wasn't in South Texas anymore. . . .

Suddenly a diffuse white light began to emanate from the walls. It didn't flicker on, like fluorescent lights, but steadily rose from nothing to a comfortable, even glow. It was confident, effortless light, and completely silent.

Gragg found himself in a room twenty feet square, with a single steel door set in the middle of the wall straight ahead of him. The door had a dappled gunmetal look to its surface, as though it were meant to draw the eye. The walls in here were all glowing white panels—made of some nylon or fiberglass material. The floor was simple polished concrete.

The voice came back suddenly, startling Gragg as it circled around him. Gragg was hearing it, but he was still having difficulty accepting it. In *real life* a voice couldn't appear in thin air. It wasn't possible.

"You've come a long way, and you've accomplished much." A pause. "Don't be frightened by my voice. Its appearance in midair is accomplished through a HyperSonic Sound system. This technology is commercially available. Would you like to hear a technical explanation? Yes or no?"

Gragg looked around at the ceiling and walls. There were tiny plastic pods of various sorts mounted there. He cleared his throat. "Yes."

"A HyperSonic Sound system—or HSS—does not use physical speakers. HSS pulsates quartz crystals at a frequency thousands of times faster than the vibrations in a normal speaker—creating ultrasonic waves at frequencies far beyond human hearing. Unlike lower-frequency sound, these waves travel in a tight path—a beam. Two beams can be focused to intersect each other, and where they interact they produce a third sonic wave whose frequency is exactly the difference between the two original sounds. In HSS that difference will fall within the range of human hearing—and will appear to come from thin air. This is known as a Tartini Tone—in honor of Guiseppe Tartini, the eighteenth-century Italian composer who first discovered this principle."

Gragg was feeling slightly faint.

"This is only the beginning of what you will learn. You do wish to learn, don't you?"

"Yes," he blurted.

"Then we must determine your sincerity."

The whir of a precise electrical motor came to his ears, and Gragg glanced around the room. A small console had opened up in the wall next to the door. Gragg warily approached it, his feet squishing mud onto the concrete floor. He saw no other muddy prints. He must have been the first to make it this far. A smile stole across his face, and he approached the console with more courage.

The console appeared to be an array of biometric devices—a hand-print reader, a camera lens with a rubber viewfinder, and a microphone. There was also a small LCD screen—like the type found on the backs of airline seats. It was not illuminated.

The voice was right next to him. "Place either hand on the reader. Place your eye against the viewfinder, and adjust the microphone to a position approximately three inches to the right of your mouth."

Gragg did as instructed. It was not the most comfortable setup, but he didn't think complaining was a good idea.

"Very good. I can administer this test in one of seven different languages. Is English your primary language? Answer 'yes' or 'no.'"

Gragg cleared his throat. "Yes."

"Good. I am going to ask a series of questions. You must answer truthfully—even if you think the truth is not the optimal response. This is not a test of your skills as a hacker. It is an effort to determine if you bear us ill will. A pattern of falsehoods will terminate the test. Early termination of the test will cause the air to be pumped from the room. This will create a partial vacuum that will cause the nitrogen to bubble out of your blood—resulting in an excruciating death. An MPEG video of your death will be placed on the Internet as a warning to others. Do you understand? Answer 'yes' or 'no.'"

"Fuck!" Gragg pulled his head up from the viewfinder and looked back at the featureless cinder-block wall.

"Stop!" The voice was so loud that it actually hurt. Then it returned to a comfortable volume. "Your earlier work was impressive. Your future lies ahead of you. Not behind you. Please return your eye to the viewfinder." There was a pause. "I will not ask you a second time."

Gragg was suddenly sweating. He felt his palm damp against the hand reader as he quickly returned his eye to the viewfinder. "Fuck, fuck, fuck . . ."

"Stop talking until you are asked a question."

Gragg bit his lip and couldn't stop shaking. The phrase *excruciating death* kept running through his mind. This was not an idiot he was dealing with here—he was the idiot. And he was truly afraid.

"Answer truthfully or die. Do you know who built this place? Yes or no?

"Yes."

"Speak the name slowly—first name, then last."

"Matthew . . . Sobol."

"Do you dislike Mr. Sobol? Yes or no?"

"No."

"Do you admire Mr. Sobol? Yes or no?"

"Yes. Very much."

"Answer just 'yes' or 'no.'"

The sweating returned. "Yes!" *Jesus H. fucking Christ . . .*

"Would you be interested in playing an active role in Mr. Sobol's plans?"

"Yes."

"If you were generously rewarded with power, knowledge, and wealth, would you be willing to break the law and expose yourself to personal risk as required to fulfill the plans of Mr. Sobol?"

He didn't hesitate. "Yes."

"Do you believe in God?"

"No."

"Would you be willing to follow the instructions of a dead person?"

Ahhhh . . . The feelings welling up inside of him surprised even Gragg. Here he was strapped to the polygraph from hell, and he still hated taking orders from anyone—and yes, he had a subtle prejudice against the dead. They had no skin in the game. Sobol was impressive, but Gragg wasn't going to spend the rest of his fucking life serving a macro on steroids. *Goddamnit.*

"Answer 'yes' or 'no.'"

Fuck! "No." Gragg closed his eyes and waited to die.

"Keep your eyes open."

He complied immediately.

There was a pause. "To clarify. Your powerful intellect will be required to define the precise path to reach objectives set by Mr. Sobol. There will be a considerable degree of freedom in the means. The outcome will be all that matters. Knowing this, would you still have a problem performing in this role? Yes or no?"

Relief flooded over him. "No."

"Would you be willing to direct others in the pursuit of Mr. Sobol's goals—possibly resulting in the deaths of these subordinates?"

No problem. "Yes."

"Do you have knowledge of a warrant out for your arrest in any state, territory, protectorate, or nation?"

"No."

"Do you have a criminal record in any state, territory, protectorate, or nation?"

"No."

"Do you take drugs?"

"No."

"Do you have any significant medical condition or physical limitation?"

"No."

"Are you currently in a significant romantic relationship?"

"No."

"Do you have pressing family obligations?"

"No."

"Do you have a history of mental illness?"

Hmmm. "Yes."

"Have you ever purposely caused the death of another person?"

Gragg paused. "Yes." He'd never really taken ownership of it before. He felt a strange pang of guilt that surprised him. It passed quickly.

"Are you available to begin work immediately?"

"Yes." Gragg shrugged. Apparently this wasn't a typical organization.

There was silence. It was deafening. Then—

"Mr. Gragg. You may lift your head from the viewfinder and remove your hand from the reader. Your convictions appear genuine. You are now under our protection. The remaining test is to determine your service rank and is a modified intelligence quotient exam. It was designed to assess your knowledge of human psychology, logic, mathematics, language, and your ability to think creatively while under pressure. It is not possible to fail this test, but performing well on it will greatly increase your personal power and the opportunities for your Faction."

The LCD screen glowed to life, presenting a simple Web page with a crocus yellow background and a large title in Times New Roman font: *Faction Multi-phasic Assessment Battery.*

A START button appeared just beneath the title.

The Voice spoke again, "This test will take several hours. You will be judged on both the accuracy and speed of your answers. Use the touch screen to enter your selections. You may return to any question to change an answer, although you will be penalized for doing so. When you are ready to begin, press the START button.

Gragg took a look around, shrugged his shoulders, and clicked START.

It wound up taking Gragg three hours and twelve minutes to complete the "multi-phasic battery"—at the end of which his legs were lead and his back was killing him from hunching over. Worst of all, his brain felt sucked dry. He'd never been presented with such a grueling test of his intellect. The questions ranged from simple memory retention and spatial relationships to intense cryptographic theory. There were brutally complex logic problems—elaborate tautological diagrams and language math. The most enjoyable questions were the ones on social engineering. Gragg felt extremely confident of his answers there. In fact, he felt confident about most of the exam. He was just emotionally and intellectually spent.

He expected to see a test score or something at the end, but instead a simple Web page announced the completion of the exam and the amount of time elapsed: 3 hrs 12 m.

Gragg stared at the little LCD screen, wondering what to do next.

The Voice returned, startling Gragg. "You scored very well, Mr. Gragg, and your rank will reflect this. You are now the founding member of a Faction. Welcome."

The steel door next to the console clanked and moved inward, then noiselessly slid aside, revealing another dimly lit room beyond. Gragg grabbed his rucksack—he didn't even bother to draw his pistol. He walked confidently through the door.

This room was perhaps thirty feet long and twenty feet wide. It looked more like a pagan temple than anything else. Four stone pillars supported the relatively low, arched ceiling. The floors were of polished granite, and a half-dozen pedestals covered with chrome or stainless steel domes were set about the room. Soft, almost imperceptible white light suffused the chamber.

Straight ahead at the far wall was a dais, whereupon sat a wide high-definition plasma-screen television. As Gragg moved forward, dried mud cracking off his boots, he saw a man in his early to mid-thirties displayed on the plasma screen. The man's hawkish features were accentuated by piercing blue eyes. His hair was light brown and neatly groomed. He wore a crisp linen shirt and was viewed in medium close-up, with his hands held in front of him, fingers interleaved in quiet repose—staring straight at Gragg as he approached the dais.

As Gragg came into a circle set into the granite floor, the man nodded solemnly to him in greeting. Even if Gragg hadn't seen the photos on the news, he would have known this man instantly. It was Matthew Sobol. Gragg buckled to his knees on the stone floor before him. For the first time in his life Gragg finally understood what a cathedral was—it was a psychological hack.

Sobol was there, larger than life in perfect digital clarity. He extended his arms in a gesture of welcome.

"Few have accomplished what you have. You're a rare person. But then you know that." Sobol let the words sink in. "While I lived, I could not father a son. But in death I will. What things I could teach you, were you my son. What pride I would have had in you."

Gragg's eyes welled with tears. He felt emotion from a place he'd long forgotten. Memories of his father and long years seeking approval never granted bubbled up from the depths of his mind.

Sobol continued. "I wish I could have met you—you who will be my eyes, my ears, and my hands. My growing power will course through you. I will protect you. Like any father protects his beloved son."

Gragg saw in Sobol's eyes the respect and compassion he had always sought. The acceptance for who and what he was. This was home. Gragg was finally home. He wept openly. He was filled with joy for the first time in his life. Nothing else mattered to him anymore.

Sobol looked on. "There is so much I wish to teach you. . . ."

Chapter 20:// Speaking with the Dead

It was a perfect autumn dawn. The hills were shrouded in the mist that usually burned off by mid-morning, and the glowing orb of the sun silhouetted the columns of SUVs heading south on the 101. An earthy fragrance sent aloft by a hundred thousand lawn sprinklers filled the air and a constant airy rush, like the sound of falling water or wind in the trees, echoed across the valley from the freeway. Southern California was booting up for another day—as long as the power grid held.

Jon Ross strode across the pavement of his hotel parking lot, dressed impeccably in a black pinstriped, four-button suit and a gray silk tie. His black leather laptop bag was slung over one shoulder.

Ross preferred corporate residence suites like this. They usually had open parking lots and direct-access front doors. It was more like a regular apartment and less like a hotel. He almost felt like a resident of Woodland Hills. He breathed in deeply, appreciating the morning air. Was that the smell of jasmine?

Ross stopped short.

Detective Sebeck leaned on the hood of Ross's silver Audi sedan and sipped takeout coffee while reading the *Ventura Star*. He didn't even look up. "Morning, Jon."

Ross resumed walking toward his car, but more slowly. "Good morning, Sergeant. Do you normally get up this early?"

"I could ask you the same thing." As Ross walked past, Sebeck folded the paper and threw it down on the car hood in front of him. The headline screamed *Second Massacre at Sobol Estate* in a font size normally reserved for advertisements or declarations of war.

Ross didn't pick it up. "I live in the western hemisphere; it would have been difficult to miss."

Sebeck stabbed a thick finger toward a sidebar story elsewhere on page one.

Ross cocked his head to read *Sobol Funeral Today*. He looked back up at Sebeck.

Sebeck flipped Ross's lapel. "Dressed a little mournfully, aren't you?"

Ross was taken aback. The cop was perceptive. Ross dropped his formality and nodded in acknowledgment. "It seemed odd to me—his having a viewing. He doesn't strike me as the religious type."

"No kidding. So why are you trying to shake me by ducking out early?"

Ross looked down at the parking lot and squeezed his laptop bag's shoulder strap rhythmically. "I don't want my name to wind up in the news."

Sebeck considered this. "Is that what all this is about? You're afraid of Sobol?"

"As a computer consultant, the Daemon might consider me a threat."

Sebeck nodded. "All right. We'll keep our collaboration secret, but if you're going to pursue Sobol, anyway, remember: I can open doors for you—and you for me."

Ross breathed the morning air deeply again as he pondered the offer. He looked up. "What do you hope to accomplish that the FBI can't?"

"You tell *me*."

They stared at each other for a moment more until Ross nodded. "Who knows I'm working with you?"

"The better question is: who would care in all this insanity?"

"Pete, please."

"The FBI knows—but I'd be surprised if Trear is thinking about that this morning. They lost a Hostage Rescue Team last night."

"I'm not going to meet with the FBI computer forensics team. Tell Trear I pussed out."

"No problem." Sebeck looked him in the eye. "You made the right call at the estate. I need you to tell me what Sobol's up to."

"I've been thinking about that."

"And what did you come up with?"

"Nothing." Ross popped his trunk and went to stow his laptop.

"That's what you came up with? Nothing?"

"Everything we've been dealing with so far is a diversion. Bullshit to keep us busy. I went online last night to check out the talk in the taverns of Gedan—forgetting that the Feds shut down the CyberStorm server farm."

"The taverns of Gedan?"

"It's the biggest port city in Cifrain—a monarchy in CyberStorm's online game *The Gate*."

Sebeck just stared at him blankly.

"Forget that. The point is this: *The Gate* is up and running, Pete."

"Wait—that's impossible. The Feds shut the servers down."

"In California, yes. But CyberStorm Entertainment maintains a Chinese mirror site for just such a contingency. It's beyond the reach of U.S. law. CyberStorm was losing a million a day in revenue, so they switched over to the mirror site and filed suit against the FBI in federal court."

"Filed suit? For *what*?"

"For unlawfully shutting down their business."

"The judge will throw it out."

"Don't count on it. CyberStorm is a wholly owned subsidiary of a multinational corporation. They have a serious amount of political clout."

"So this is what people talk about in the taverns of Gedan?"

"No, that was *The Wall Street Journal* online. In Gedan the talk is all about the sudden death of the Mad Emperor."

Sebeck grimaced. "The Mad Emperor? They got that right."

"Well, his funeral is today."

"In the real world or the fake one?"

"Both."

Sebeck threw up his hands.

Ross soldiered on. "A power struggle between Factions is anticipated for control of *The Gate*."

"This is a *game*?"

Ross nodded. "But rituals figure prominently in *The Gate*, as, apparently, they do in real life. Thus Sobol's funeral."

"Jon, I have no fucking clue what you're talking about."

"Sobol might be trying to communicate something through his funeral."

"Okay, now I'm with you. But you don't think he's trying to communicate something to us?"

Ross shook his head. "I'm hoping we're being more perceptive than he anticipated. Let me emphasize *hoping*."

"Well, that's optimistic."

Ross looked at his watch. "Look, the viewing's in Santa Barbara. That's an hour and a half away. It wouldn't hurt to be early." He gestured for Sebeck to get in on the passenger side. "I'll drive."

Sebeck glanced at the gleaming Audi A8. "Only because my cruiser's wrecked."

Ross's Audi raced up the coast on U.S. 101. The morning mist was already clearing, providing a view of the Channel Islands and the offshore oil platforms. It was a gorgeous day.

Sebeck settled into the black leather of the passenger seat. The dashboard and door panels were trimmed in burled walnut and brushed steel. So this was what rich people drove? The twelve-cylinder engine growled with apparently limitless power as they accelerated past another car on a hill. Sebeck figured this car could give a police interceptor a run for its money.

The stereo system alone looked like it could land a 747. John Coltrane's *A Love Supreme* played on the stereo. Coltrane might as well have been sitting in Sebeck's lap for the quality of the sound. The title and artist displayed in Teutonic yellow dots that scrolled like a Times Square news flash across the front of the sound console.

Sebeck looked over to Ross. "I've never seen a stereo like that."

"Scandinavian. Linux-based DVD-Audio emulation. Four hundred gigs. I can store twenty thousand songs at five hundred times the clarity of a CD."

"You have twenty thousand songs?"

"That's not the point."

"It isn't?"

"Hard-drive space is cheap."

Sebeck just gave him a look.

"Okay, I'll admit I have a technology problem. I'm in a twelve-step program."

Sebeck looked around at the car interior again. "How much is a car like this?"

"About a hundred and thirty. But I talked them down to a hundred and twenty."

Sebeck winced. That was a third higher than his annual salary. A pang of jealousy stole over him. Surely police work was vital. Why did the white-collar professions earn so much more? It was a puzzle to him. One he didn't think he was going to resolve.

The Audi raced north, giving him plenty of time to try.

———

Ross had a turn-by-turn map to the funeral home, but they could just as easily have followed the satellite news trucks. As they drove past the manicured front lawn of the funeral home, the parking lot overflowed with camera-ready protestors holding up signs reading BURN IN HELL, SOBOL, American flags, and yellow ribbons—while still others bore banners with anarchy symbols and pentagrams. It was a flea market of anger. Police and reporters with microphones vied with each other, alternately shoving back competing protestors and interviewing them. The side streets leading to the funeral home were blocked off by SBP traffic cops and sawhorses. No cars were allowed in.

Ross turned to Sebeck. "I'm not sure about this."

"This is where I come in. Pull up to the roadblock."

Ross turned into the side street, and two policemen held up their hands to stop them, then pointed back at the main street.

Sebeck lowered his passenger window and showed his badge. One of the cops came up to the window. Sebeck spoke with authority. "Detective Sergeant Sebeck, Ventura County Sheriff's Department. I was heading the murder investigation in Thousand Oaks."

"Welcome to Santa Barbara, Sergeant. I saw you on the news. Park around back." He waved to the other cop to move the barrier aside. The first cop leaned down to Sebeck again. "The Feds are running the show inside."

Sebeck nodded and motioned for Ross to drive on through.

———

They entered the funeral home through the rear door. After a brief discussion, one of the federal agents at the door peeled off to escort them to the chapel.

As they moved through the rear hallways, the acrid smell of embalming chemicals and cleansers assaulted them. Men and women in suits were everywhere, going through files and computers in side offices and interviewing a man who appeared to be a mortician in a lab coat.

Soon they passed through a double set of automated doors that let out onto an ornate hallway with marble tile floors. They could hear funerary music playing ahead, and another doorway brought them through a side entrance into a churchlike room with a podium, rows of pews, mountains of flowers, and a raised dais whereupon sat a bronze coffin on a pedestal draped in white satin. The lid of the coffin was partitioned for viewings, and the upper portion was raised—although the body within could not be seen from this vantage point.

Everyone in the place looked like an FBI agent—including the dozen or so people sitting in the nearly empty pews up front. A crime scene photographer was busy taking photos of the room from every angle—although it wasn't apparent what crime was being committed just now. Apparently the Feds didn't want to wait.

Ross gestured to the coffin. "Behold the devil himself."

The FBI agent escorting them excused himself to resume his post, leaving Sebeck and Ross standing in the doorway relatively alone. The sonorous tones of funeral Muzak were punctuated by the occasional squawking of police radios.

Sebeck glanced around the room. It was remarkably unremarkable. Tapestries depicting generic salvation—lots of light beams coming from on high—hung down between the unexceptional stained glass windows. A stylized statue of Jesus stood at the head of the chapel, set into an alcove. It was eroded in a modern art sort of way to render it theologically inoffensive and appeared to be fashioned out of cheap, imitation-stone resin—stuff that would last until the Second Coming. Its hands were outstretched like an Australian-rules football referee signaling a goal, with robes hanging down.

The room was modern and provided no sense of history or permanence. The floor sounded hollow under the heels, and on the whole the room reminded him more of a library annex than a chapel. It was sterile and unfeeling, except for the banks of flowers—all white lilies—which through their sheer numbers answered the unasked question: How many white lilies can you cram onto this stage? This many.

An easel to the left of the coffin held a foam-core poster of Matthew Sobol, in younger and saner days. He looked like an accountant or an insurance broker. His hair was short and dusty brown. He was smiling good-naturedly, seemingly oblivious to the fact that he would kill fifteen people—most of them law officers.

An eternal flame—which someone had spitefully extinguished or never lit—stood next to the easel on a trestle table. Apparently the authorities had a different eternal flame in mind for Sobol.

Scattered around the room in groups of two and three were what looked to be FBI agents. Sebeck felt sure they were trying to figure out a way to declare a funeral illegal. Certainly Sebeck felt like putting Sobol's body through a mulcher.

Ross tapped his shoulder. "I want to see him."

Sebeck nodded, and they both stepped out across the pews. All eyes turned on them. Carpeting absorbed most of the sound of their footfalls, but they still seemed deafening in the stillness of this place. Ross nodded to serious-looking men who watched them pass. The men stared back.

Sebeck led Ross to the dais steps. They ascended slowly, and as they did, the mortal remains of Matthew Sobol came into view from beyond the rim of the coffin.

Sebeck came here filled with hate. He despised this diseased freak who had slain Deputy Larson and all the others. He was wholly unprepared for his reaction upon first sight of Sobol's corpse.

Sobol was practically a skeleton already. It was shocking how the cancer had wasted him away. His disease was readily apparent from the massive scar tracing along the left side of his bald head. It looked like they had opened his skull to attempt surgical resection. The scar was so long it descended to the orbital socket of Sobol's left eye—where a black patch indicated that his eye had been removed. No other effort had been made to make Sobol presentable. His cheeks were sunken and pale, his neck lost in the spaciousness of a stiff white shirt collar and a Victorian jacket and tie. His dead hands clutched a golden cross against his chest. Most alarming of all was Sobol's one remaining eye—oddly open and staring milky blue at the ceiling. It was a window to madness and terror.

Nothing had prepared Sebeck for this. A seed of pity took root in him. Sobol had endured the tortures of the damned. Surely Sebeck wanted Sobol to burn in Hell—but he'd never considered Sobol had been living in Hell for some time already.

Ross croaked, "Jesus."

A woman spoke from behind them. "What did you expect to find, Mr. Ross?"

Ross and Sebeck spun around to regard a young black woman sitting in the first pew. She was neither beautiful nor unattractive. She wore an immaculate dark blue pantsuit, but she did not have the telltale earphone of the Feds. A white guy sat in the pew behind her, leaning forward to join her symbolically. He had buzz-cut blond hair and wore a dark plaid sports jacket and a black sweater. He didn't look uncomfortable in the jacket, but somehow the jacket appeared uncomfortable with him.

Ross looked to Sebeck and then back to the woman. "Do I know you?"

"No. But I know you. You're Jon Frederick Ross, son of Harold and Ivana. Graduated with honors 1999 from the University of Illinois at Urbana with a master's in computer science. President and CEO of Cyberon Systems, Inc., a one-man Delaware Service Corporation founded in 2003." She reached into her jacket pocket and produced a badge folder. "Natalie Philips. National Security Agency."

"Oh shit." Ross looked to the nearby Jesus for mercy.

Sebeck stepped in. "I'm trying to keep Jon's name out of the news. He's worried that Sobol will come after him."

"Interesting." She stood up and approached the dais. "Egotistical, but interesting."

She was lean and fit—probably about thirty years old. Sebeck couldn't help but notice her body and cursed his libido.

She gestured to the coffin. "I'm surprised you'd come *here* if you thought Sobol was after you. He might have packed the coffin with C-four."

Ross stepped away from the casket warily.

She laughed. "Relax. We T-rayed it and swept the whole chapel for computers and wireless transmitters. Came up empty." She walked up and stood looking over Sobol's remains. "Apparently Sobol anticipated his unpopularity and left behind a program to carry out his funeral arrangements."

Sebeck frowned. "The Daemon did this?"

"It ordered the deluxe package from the funeral home's Web page—but it never had direct control over these objects. Just-in-time inventory; the coffin was built by Bates Corporation yesterday and shipped overnight by truck. We tailed it the whole way. The lilies arrived this morning. This is the mortuary equivalent of a number two combo."

Ross extended his hand. "Agent Philips." She shook it.

Sebeck extended his hand, too. "Detective—"

"—Sergeant Peter Sebeck," she finished for him. "My condolences on the deaths of your colleagues. It must be very hard to see this psycho in the flesh."

Sebeck nodded. "What's left of him." He looked down at the body. "I didn't expect him to look so . . ."

"Pitiful?"

"Yeah."

Philips viewed Sobol's remains, too. She gestured to the cross. "They say he found religion in the end."

A cold laugh came out of Sebeck. "I thought crosses burned vampires."

Ross changed the subject. "What's the NSA doing up here, Agent Philips? Isn't the big investigation down in Thousand Oaks?"

"I'm not a field agent. I'm a steganalyst."

Ross nodded, then answered Sebeck's quizzical look. "She finds hidden messages. Terrorists and drug traffickers sometimes hide data inside JPEGs and other computer files."

"I won't ask why you know that. My own parents don't understand what I do."

"So, what brings a steganalyst to Sobol's funeral?"

"Symbolism. Sobol's games are packed with symbols—and I'm not convinced all of them are harmless."

"What's that got to do with his funeral?"

"What's a funeral but a symbolic ritual? He's sending a message. Maybe to us, maybe to someone else."

"Perhaps. One thing's for sure, it got us all here."

She nodded grimly. "Yes, but it looks like the Feds have scared off anyone else."

Ross leaned in close. "You're trying to identify the Daemon's components, aren't you?"

The buzz-cut guy bristled in the pews. "Dr. Philips, remember your directive."

Ross stepped back. "Who's he?"

"Hard to say. I just call him The Major."

The Major didn't respond. He just stared.

Philips stepped into Ross's line of sight. "Mr. Ross, you played three hundred forty-seven hours of *The Gate* in the last year. That makes you the only CyberStorm game expert cleared by the FBI. You're on my list of people to talk to. As long as you're here, I've got a lot of questions about the MMORPG subculture."

"Three hundred forty-seven hours? That's embarrassing."

Sebeck smirked. "You need to get a life, Jon."

Philips pressed on. "What's your level of knowledge concerning the Ego AI and CyberStorm 3-D graphics engines?"

"You think Sobol's hidden components of the Daemon in his games?"

"Think texture maps—"

"Ahh . . . there'll be thousands of them."

"There are. That's not including custom maps created by individual users with the map editor."

"But why would Sobol bother? He could just as easily hide scripting files on some forgotten server. There's no reason to hide anything inside his games."

"Sobol's AI engine and CyberStorm's graphics codecs power a dozen popular games. You can understand why I'm pursuing this angle. They encompass tens of millions of installs worldwide."

"Have you interviewed the CyberStorm programmers?"

"We polygraphed them all. None knew anything about Sobol's plan—although plenty of them wrote code for purposes they didn't understand."

"That's no surprise. It's project management."

"Proximity card reader logs showed that Pavlos and Singh were in and out of Sobol's office wing all during the last year. Their workstations were physically replaced last month, and their hard-drive images contained nothing unusual."

"The lack of incriminating evidence is suspicious?"

"I'm saying they were working long hours on something together— something that's missing. And they were game developers. Some of the best in the business."

Ross considered this. "So that's why you think his games contain hidden data?"

She nodded. "The MMORPG world is a male-dominated subculture. I need a guide."

"A guide?"

"I need to see these games as a skilled player sees them—and I can't trust some twelve-year-old kid or a CyberStorm employee. I need secrecy."

"You don't want the Daemon to know what you're doing."

"Look, you're an IT professional. You know how dangerous this situation is. We don't know what the Daemon's up to, and we don't know how big it is."

The Major stood up. "Dr. Philips."

She turned and stabbed a finger in his direction. "If you're going to censor my conversations this entire damned trip, Major, then I'm heading back to Maryland. I, of all people, am acutely aware of the national security implications of this discussion, and I am having it because it is *necessary*. Do you read me?"

"I have my orders, Doctor."

"Well, then we have a situation—because my orders are to stop the Daemon, and apparently your orders are to stop *me*."

The Major stood impassively. She eyed him a bit longer, then turned back to Ross. "I need to derive the Daemon's topology in order to assess the threat."

It took Ross a moment to recover from her sudden outburst toward The Major. "You need its master plan."

"Yes. I'm developing a timeline of its creation so that we can correlate it with Sobol's real-world financial and travel activities. If I can reconstruct the development timeline, I might be able to infer its topology."

Sebeck interjected. "Topology?"

They both looked at him.

Philips sighed. "The physical or logical layout of a networked system."

Philips then looked back at Ross and continued. "But there are bigger worries." She cast an eye toward The Major, then pulled Ross aside, conferring with him privately. This close, Agent Philips had a slight flowery scent that was surprisingly feminine. Ross saw the sharp intellect in her eyes, the intensity. A slight hot flash spread over his skin as he relished this intimacy.

Philips was oblivious. "Huge amounts of money flowed from Sobol's bank accounts immediately after his death. ACH wire transfers totaling tens of millions of dollars went offshore. He also took out large lines of credit in the months before his death. This money, too, went overseas the day he died. The Feds are still tracing it. Picture the combination of a widely distributed, compartmentalized application with high failover tolerance—perhaps thousands of copies of each component, able to reconstitute itself if any x-percentage of its components are destroyed."

Ross was nodding as she talked. God, this woman was razor sharp. He found his normal resistance to all thoughts not his own falling away.

She continued, "Now combine an application like that—a widely distributed entity that never dies—with tens of millions of dollars and the ability to purchase goods and services. It's answerable to no one and has no fear of punishment."

"My God. It's a corporation."

"Bingo."

Sebeck's cell phone twittered. He welcomed the intrusion. He was just holding hats in this conversation. "Excuse me." Sebeck turned and walked away as he pulled his phone out. He glanced at the number on the LCD panel. The caller was unknown. He answered it. "Sebeck."

A familiar, rasping voice came to his ear. *"Forgive my appearance, Sergeant."*

Sebeck sucked in a breath and gazed at Sobol's corpse lying in state six feet away. He glanced at the FBI and NSA agents standing around the chapel. Ross and Agent Philips were still locked in an animated technobabble conversation nearby.

Sebeck moved right up to the coffin and stared down at Sobol's corpse. "Is hell a toll call for you, Sobol?"

Sebeck stood waiting. There was a moment's delay.

The voice returned, weak and wavering. *"Detective Sebeck. It's too late."* The sound of labored breathing and wheezing came over the line. *"There is no stopping my Daemon now."*

Sebeck looked again toward Philips and Ross, but Sobol was already talking.

"I'm sorry, but I must destroy you. They will require a sacrifice, Sergeant." Sobol wheezed. *"It's necessary. Maybe before it's over, you'll understand. I don't know if I'm right. I don't know anymore."*

Sebeck looked down at Sobol's tortured remains. The insane eye matched the voice of madness.

Sobol's voice hissed urgently. *"Before you die . . . invoke the Daemon. Do it in the months before your death. Say this . . . exactly this: 'I, Peter Sebeck, accept the Daemon.'"* Sobol gasped for air. *"Either way . . . you must die."*

The line went dead.

Sebeck folded his phone and stared hard at Sobol's corpse for a few moments. Then he spoke loudly. "Agent Philips."

Philips and Ross stopped talking.

Sebeck turned to face them. "That call I just received. It was Sobol."

Ross and Philips exchanged looks. He had their attention now.

"Why didn't you tell me?"

"Because I was *listening* carefully."

"What did he say?" Philips motioned to The Major, who came sprinting up. He took the dais steps in a leap. They all converged on Sebeck's location at the coffin.

"He sounded just like that." Sebeck pointed at the corpse. "He was wheezing and semi-coherent. He kept telling me that I was going to die. That it was *necessary* that I die."

"What else did he say? Try to remember it, word-for-word."

Sebeck thought on it. "He said I needed to 'invoke' the Daemon. That I needed to 'accept' it. He said I had to speak directly to it in the months before my death. But that either way I was going to die."

Philips looked grim.

Sebeck pondered the situation. "You think it's more mind games?"

She turned to The Major. "Find out if those wiretaps on Detective Sebeck's phone and computer lines have gone through. If they haven't, fast-track them."

The Major nodded and immediately bolted down the center aisle and out the front doors with a bang.

Sebeck watched the man leave, then turned to Philips. "You think Sobol will call again?"

"Maybe. He's most likely manipulating you."

"He definitely wants me to do something."

Philips stared. "Don't. In fact, we'll prevent the press from communicating with you or any members of your family."

Ross raised his eyebrows at that. "That's to prevent him from inadvertently triggering a new Daemon event?"

"Precisely. There's no doubt it's reading the news. So you'd be advised to stay out of the headlines."

"You're quarantining me?"

"Only for a little while. At least until we can reliably monitor Sobol's communications. You'll be very useful in that regard, Sergeant."

Two suited agents double-timed it up the dais steps. One whispered in Philips's ear. Her face displayed momentary shock before she regained her composure. She glanced at Sebeck and Ross. "I have to go, gentlemen. Sobol is up to something." She and the agents scurried down the steps of the dais. Several other darkly suited men converged on her from far-flung corners of the chapel.

Ross called after her. "Do you still need a guide, Agent Philips?"

She didn't turn around. "I'll contact you soon." She and the other agents banged through the doors and out of the chapel.

Ross gestured to the door swinging closed in her wake. "Doctorate in mathematics from Stanford, and she's a graduate of the Cryptologic School at Fort Meade. That woman is sharp as hell. I think I'm in love."

Sebeck chuckled to himself.

"What?"

"Good luck with that." He started for the front doors.

Chapter 21:// Hotel Menon

For Immediate Worldwide Release:

From: Matthew Andrew Sobol
Re: Back Door in Ego AI Engine

The Ego AI engine used in more than a dozen bestselling game titles was designed with a security flaw that opens a back door in any computer that runs it. Using this back door, I can take full control of a computer, stealing information and observing logons and passwords.

The Republic of Nauru was the smallest, most remote republic in the world. A spit of coral in the South Pacific, it was barely ten kilometers long and half as wide and had all the topographical complexity of a soccer field. Nauru was basically a phosphate mine that convinced the U.N. it was a country.

Dominated first by the Germans and after World War II by the Australians, the Nauruans had come to accept the fact that their chief industry was selling off the ground they stood on. With their phosphate deposits nearly exhausted by the turn of the millennium, the interior of the island—what the locals called "topside"—was now a ravaged, strip-mined wasteland carved down to the coral bedrock. Fully 90 percent of Nauru was a lifeless expanse swept by choking, talcumlike dust. The place had been so systematically scoured of life by mining equipment that the Nauruans considered buying a new island and physically relocating their entire country—leaving a forwarding address with the

U.N. However, after most of the tiny nation's wealth evaporated in investment scandals, the Nauruans had to face a grim reality: they were here to stay.

The entire population of ten thousand South Sea, islanders now lived on a narrow band of sand and palm trees ringing the island—a quarter of which was taken up by an airfield—and tried to ignore the ecological nightmare of the interior.

Anji Anderson had never toured an entire country in twenty minutes before. Afterward she realized there were only three things to do on Nauru: drink heavily, lament the past, or engage in international money laundering. Judging from the private jets at the airport and the forest of satellite dishes, the latter was Nauru's future.

The community of nations officially took a dim view of money-laundering centers with lax banking and incorporation laws and powerful privacy regulations—but then again, at some point every government had need of such things. The Daemon had directed Anderson to an informative Web page prior to her whirlwind tour of offshore tax havens, and it opened her eyes. Tax havens were tolerated—and in some cases facilitated—by powerful nations and global corporations. Intelligence agencies needed to wire untraceable money to informants or to fund operations in various troubled or soon-to-be-troubled regions. Corporations needed to incentivize key people without interference from investment groups and regulators. All of this was possible in areas far from the public eye. At twelve hundred miles from the nearest neighboring island, Nauru was both incredibly remote and, due to decades of mining, physically unsightly. And tourists and journalists weren't allowed: Nauru issued only business visas. No rebels could take to the hills here, either, because the Nauruans had sold the hills years ago.

Anderson smiled as she lay soaking in the sun, poolside at the Hotel Menon—one of only two hotels on the island. If she kept her chaise lounge pointed in this exact direction, she could avoid seeing rusted derricks as she looked out over the ocean.

Evenings were the best time. The sunsets here were huge pyrotechnic displays with towering clouds that melted into the distant horizon. It almost made up for the rusted ruin of the place and the fact that the air was so humid that standing in the ocean breeze was like taking a shower. But in the time she'd been employed by the Daemon, her world had taken on a dimension of true adventure, and this was part of it. Forget Machu Picchu or Prince Patrick Island—that was soo bourgeois. She was in a country probably none of her well-traveled and educated friends had ever heard of, much less been to. One that was not on any commonly used map. She laughed to herself from behind her Lemon Drop martini. She had just left the Isle of Man two days ago—the Nevada of the British Isles—and she had no idea where she'd be going tomorrow. She didn't care. She didn't have to. She felt oddly secure for the first time in her life. A kept woman. As a well-paid consultant on retainer to Daedalus Research, Inc.—no doubt owned by the Daemon—she was making more money then she'd ever made in her life. All her travel expenses were being paid on an apparently bottomless company credit card. Her airline tickets were all first class, and she had a chartered private jet for this little jaunt out to Nauru. She was bewildered and excited. Every day was filled with surprises. What a change from the network affiliate. Her new boss was an undead automaton from hell, true, but no job was perfect.

Anderson listened to chatter in a dozen languages at the poolside tables around her. She felt eyes upon her in her relatively modest bikini. There were few other women about, but no one was making a move—unsure of which underworld figure she belonged to. She smiled to herself. Her man was about as underworld as you could get. . . .

The Hotel Menon looked like an upscale Motel 6. Casa Blanca in stucco and plywood. Most of the people conducting business here never had to physically set foot on the island, so appearances didn't matter much. Those who did make the journey typically came to the edge of the world just to exchange briefcases. Most of these transactions were *technically* legal, but they weren't the sort of thing participants wanted on the evening news back home.

Pale-faced, tubby Russians in impeccable Armani suits sat with Arabs in robes so white it hurt to look at them. Ruddy-cheeked Australians and Nipponese in silk suits looked down through their sunglasses to examine the spotty glasses before drinking to the health of their business partners. Most tables sported two or three expressionless Terminator types scanning the patio for trouble and thumbing the handles of metallic briefcases. Anderson was finally doing serious journalism. If only her friends knew.

Of course, she wasn't here as a journalist. She was undercover as CFO of a Hong Kong fiber optic concern. She smiled. Her business card was spectacular, with a holographic cross-section of a bundle of fiber, glittering with light.

Her new satellite phone emitted a melodic ringtone. She lifted up her sunglasses and pulled a small encryption chip from its location, clipped invisibly in her hair. She grabbed the phone from a nearby end table and fitted the chip into a slot on the side. Then she answered it. No need to say anything. She knew who it was.

It was The Voice with her clipped British accent. "Can you get to a satellite news channel? Yes or no."

Anderson glanced around. She saw a television mounted over the hotel bar beyond tinted glass. It was always tuned to business news. "Yes."

"Go to it. CyberStorm Entertainment." The line clicked off.

Synthetic bitch. She liked Sobol's voice better. Anderson yanked the chip and stowed it, as though fixing her hair. She saw a Ukrainian enforcer staring at her longingly. She pointedly ignored him and wondered what sort of dental hygiene was prevalent in the former Eastern Bloc nations. She also wondered what physical security the Daemon could offer her.

She gathered her things and clicked across the tiled patio to the refrigerated air of the bar. An Australian satellite news feed was already on, but muted. Anderson smiled brightly at Oto, the Tahitian bartender, in his starched collar and black vest. She wondered what horrific thing he did to deserve exile on Nauru. Probably hacked someone to death with a machete. "Oto, can you turn the volume up?"

"Yes, Ms. Vindmar."

Her cover name—a deliberately amateurish attempt at privacy, since she was traveling under her real passport.

The crawl at the bottom of the cluttered TV screen flashed "CyberStorm Entertainment." The newscaster's Aussie accent came up, ". . . from the American NASDAQ. CyberStorm Entertainment's share price has plummeted 97 percent in the four hours following a press release by the *deceased* CTO Matthew Sobol, in which he claims to have placed a back door in the company's Ego AI engine. Share prices of third-party game companies using CyberStorm's software have also been punished since the news—and lawsuits are already in the works as products are yanked from store shelves worldwide. Analysts expect a cloud will be hanging over the entire PC gaming sector until the full extent of the problem is known."

Oto smiled in that good-natured way South Seas islanders have when noticing how fucked up the mainland is. "The dead are punishing the living, eh?"

Strangely, Anderson swelled with pride. *That's my boss for you.*

But why had the Daemon phoned her about it? Something was up, and it had everything to do with Tremark Holdings, IBC. She was sure of it. She was also glad she didn't have to figure any of it out—since the Daemon was handing her both the clues and the answers in its own sweet time.

"May I join you?"

Anderson jerked her head to see a handsome, square-jawed American in a floral print shirt and khakis standing over her. He was in his mid-thirties, but he had a trim waist, broad shoulders, and rugged good looks that made Anderson imagine a string of broken-hearted women stretching from Minnesota to Sumatra. He had that cool, self-assured air that effective people have.

Anderson acted cool right back. "Can't you see I'm catching the business report?"

He straddled a bar stool next to her. "There are more convenient places than Nauru to do that. So what brings you way out here?"

"An intense desire to be left alone."

He laughed. Then he leaned close and spoke sotto voce, "The better question is: what is Anji Anderson, previously of KTLZ TV, doing in Nauru?" He laid his FBI credentials on the bar in front of her.

Anderson's eyes widened for a moment as she nearly panicked. She should tell him. But what would that do? The Daemon was taking care of her. It wasn't her enemy. This was leading somewhere. Betraying it could ruin everything.

She got ahold of herself. The Daemon had sent her here, and it knew everything. "I should have figured you for a spook."

He collected his badge and grabbed her by the hand as he pulled her over to a red vinyl booth in the corner of the deserted bar. He was a man of action. Pseudo-romantic scenes from a dozen cable soft-porn films entered her mind. She tried to concentrate on the real situation.

"Oto, another drink for the lady."

Oto nodded and got busy.

The FBI agent slid into the booth, pulling her in alongside him. She couldn't help but see the bulge of a pistol holster in the small of his back as he slid across the bench seat. He smiled and extended his hand. "Call me Barry."

She shook his hand warily. "All right, *Barry*, what's this all about?"

"I want answers."

"Such as?"

"What's a lifestyles reporter recently let go from a San Francisco affiliate doing asking questions about Tremark Holdings, IBC, in far-flung Nauru?"

"What's a big corn-fed frat boy like you doing so far from a Hooters?"

"I asked first."

She acted coy. "Okay. I'm trying to launch a career as an investigative journalist. I'm tired of being the stewardess of the evening news."

"Not an answer."

"You mean, why am I so interested in the names of the officers of Tremark Holdings?"

"Yeah. That's exactly what I mean. You know, of course, that asking questions around here is a good way to wind up missing."

"Then why are you asking so many questions?"

He pointed a finger at her and let out a slow laugh. "I think I like you, Anji. Are you going to help me?"

"Help you how?"

"What does Tremark Holdings have to do with the Daemon?"

"What makes you think it has anything to do with the Daemon?"

"Because Matthew Sobol moved money into Tremark Holdings on the day he died."

A wave of shock sent goose bumps over Anderson's skin. God, this was fun. She couldn't have faked that surprise. "Really? That answers a lot of questions."

"How did you get wind of Tremark Holdings?"

"Let's just say I have my sources."

"Are they the same sources bankrolling your trip? The same sources helping you encrypt your satphone conversations?"

"Oh, please, *Barry*." She emphasized his name with contempt. "Don't be childish. Espionage isn't the only reason for privacy. I'm working on possibly the biggest story of the year. Sobol had bankers, and some of those bankers are fond of a certain blond reporter—who at present is unemployed."

"What did you learn on the Isle of Man?"

"That a Manx/Celtic fusion restaurant is a bad idea."

He gave her a look. "Anji."

"Okay. I learned that Sobol moved money into three different accounts there—all held by various international business corporations. But I also learned the money was moved out seconds after it arrived."

He looked surprised. "How the hell did you get them to tell you that?"

She wasn't about to tell him that the Daemon told her. No, the new Anderson was a resourceful investigative journalist. She smiled. "If you're an overweight, balding Welsh banker, and I start coming on to you in a tavern, what would you do?"

He considered this. "I'd do anything to keep you talking to me."

"Of course, I don't do just anything, Barry. I'm not that kind of woman."

"What else?"

"I'm not telling you anything you don't know already—or at least won't learn soon."

"Did you find out anything else?"

She toyed with him, smiling and ticking up her eyebrows as Oto arrived with her drink. "Thanks, Oto."

"No problem, Ms. Vindmar." He retreated to the bar again.

Barry looked at her incredulously. "Where'd you come up with *Ms. Vindmar*?"

"It's better than *Barry*." She hammed it up, acting like a dope. "Hey, I'm Barry—not an FBI agent."

"All right, stop. What if my name's actually Barry? Did you ever think of that?"

She burst out laughing.

He looked intently at her. "Did you learn anything else?"

She sipped her Lemon Drop and then rolled the twist sensuously over her lips. God, this espionage stuff was fun! Especially when you held all the cards, and handsome tough guys had to wait on your every word. "Yes, I did, Barry. Have you noticed the short positions on the CyberStorm stock?"

She may as well have cracked a two-by-four over his head. He apparently hadn't expected a sexy, fluff-piece reporter to actually come up with something. "Tell me more."

"You'll find there was an extraordinary rise in short positions in the weeks leading up to Sobol's death. I was real curious about it until I saw the news today. Now it makes more sense. You know what stock shorting is, right?"

He gave her a slight smile. "I have a series seven."

"Well, if that means 'yes,' then you can appreciate that someone just made a boatload of money by destroying CyberStorm."

He looked confused. "But what good is money to a dead guy?"

"What makes you think the recipient is dead?"

He smiled at her—for real. "I'm really starting to like you, Anji."

"I don't know whether I like you yet, Barry. But I know what would *make* me like you."

"What?"

"An exclusive on the story when we find out where the money's going."

"An exclusive."

"I get to *break* the story. And the FBI gives me an introduction to a major media company."

He frowned. "You're serious?"

"I'm unemployed. Remember? You just confirm that I'm investigating something big with the bureau."

"Wouldn't they think it's a planted story?"

She laughed. "You're so funny, Barry. I think I do like you. You're like an innocent little fawn."

He tried to eye her darkly, but it wound up just looking stupid. "I'll need to run it past some people."

"You do that." She felt firmly in the driver's seat now. He was reacting to her, not the other way around. "In the meantime, I'm going to get that list of corporate officers, and when you Feds catch up, we'll talk some more."

"Careful, Anji. This isn't a game."

"Who said I'm playing one?" She kept her eyes on him and took another sip of her drink.

He looked confused, as if he suddenly realized he was talking to someone else—not the Anji Anderson he'd expected to find.

She continued. "Are you going to help me, or are you going to stop me? Your choice."

He stared at her. His silence said it all.

Chapter 22:// Honey Pot

Reuters.com

CyberStorm Voice-Over Actor Found **Dead, New York, NY**—Expatriate British actor **Lionel Crawly** was found dead in his apartment on Manhattan's Upper West Side early today. Crawly gained a modicum of fame in the online gaming community as the voice of **Oberstleutnant Heinrich Boerner**, the notorious villain of the bestselling game *Over the Rhine*. Police sources indicate that the body of the elderly actor lay undiscovered for several days and that the cause of death is unknown pending an autopsy—although **poison**ing is suspected.

Agent Philips did not contact Sebeck or Ross directly. Nonetheless, Sebeck felt the heavy presence of NSA security all around his house. Two windowless vans sat curbside near his driveway, and federal agents shooed away reporters foolhardy enough to approach his residential block—although, in the tumult of media attention following the fiery destruction of Sobol's estate, no one focused much on the cop who discovered the Sobol connection. Control of the Task Force had been transferred to Washington, which meant that Sebeck and the entire Sheriff's Department were out of the loop. That was fine with Sebeck. It gave him time to focus on something he'd never given a damn about: computer games.

In general, Sebeck viewed computers as a necessary fact of modern life. His chief complaint was that they gave a false sense of precision to poor thinking. But then, technology was like religion—you either had the faith or you didn't.

It was almost midnight, and Sebeck scanned his keyboard to find the hotkeys that would twirl his barbarian character around. The majesty of a fully textured 3-D wilderness filled his computer screen. In the foreground, giant rats were overcoming a muscle-bound barbarian.

Sebeck's son, Chris, stood next to him. "Dad! They're kicking your ass." He laughed and covered his eyes.

Sebeck glanced at the screen. He started hitting keys at random. His barbarian had the digital equivalent of an epileptic fit, while the rats brought him down. "Damnit."

"Oh man, you suck."

Sebeck gave Chris the evil eye, and the boy held up his palms in submission. "Just trying to help."

"Yeah, you're a hell of a teacher."

"You should just let me do it for you."

"This isn't a game, Chris."

"Yes, it *is* a game."

"You know what I mean."

"I've been after you for a year for a subscription to *The Gate*. What's the difference if I play for a while?"

"Because the psychopath who killed Aaron Larson created this game." He cast an angry look at his son.

Chris was taken aback at the harshness of the reaction.

Sebeck collected himself. "Chris . . ."

Chris adopted the intense indifference unique to angry teenagers. "No problem." He stood up and walked out—only to pop his head back in the doorway to say, "I was just trying to *help*, Dad." He stormed down the hall, then thundered upstairs.

Sebeck stared at the floor. He'd screwed that up—like most aspects of fatherhood. Listening to himself speak sometimes Sebeck wondered who the hell he'd become. In high school he'd been a laid-back guy. But that was before all this. And why was he not repentant? Even now he sat at the desk with a vague feeling that he *should* feel bad—but he didn't. Instead, he felt justified by the importance of his work. It was a coping mechanism he'd honed to a razor edge over the years.

He focused on that work again.

The computer game, *The Gate*, seemed infantile. Apparently, loads of people were eager to spend fifteen bucks a month to wander around an endless 3-D wasteland bashing rats, slugs, and zombies over the head. No wonder Sobol was rich. Sebeck didn't see the appeal in it, and aside from the arcane hotkey commands required to turn around quickly, it wasn't much of a challenge. Certainly there wasn't any thought required.

His home phone rang. Sebeck eyed the cordless handset suspiciously. He glanced at his watch. It was just after midnight. He picked it up and pressed "Talk." "Sebeck residence."

Ross chuckled on the other end. "Giant rats? You let giant rats kill you?"

Sebeck frowned. "You saw that?"

"I was watching you from a nearby hill."

"How did you know where to find me?"

"It's involved. Suffice it to say there are ways."

"Jon, tell me again why it's not stupid to be running this game on my computer. *The Gate* is supposed to have a back door in it."

"We're *trying* to draw the Daemon out. You backed up your hard drive like I told you, right?"

"Chris did—although you can delete the whole damned thing for all I care. All I ever find on here is spam, porn, and pirated music."

"Look, there's something strange happening off the northern coast of Cifrain. I want to check it out, and you'll need to be tougher to come with me."

"I'm still stuck in this Briar Patch."

"Forget about that. I went on eBay and bought you a real character—not that newbie Conan cut-out you're running around with now."

"What do you mean *bought*? CyberStorm sells better characters?"

"No. People do. Students and the terminally unemployed build up characters the hard way, then sell them on eBay for quick cash. I bought you a knight of Cifrain for three hundred and eighty dollars."

"Three hundred eighty dollars? People actually pay that much?"

"Market forces. Busy professionals play these games to cool off in the evening. They have money but no time. Then there are skilled gamers with no money but lots of time. It's a natural ecosystem. Whole economies exist in these virtual worlds. A baron with lands can go for a couple thousand. I can loan you some equipment, but I want it back."

"I'll see if the department can reimburse you."

"I don't need *real* money, Pete, but the *Cloak of Aggis* I will want back. You ready to go?"

"I'm still trying to get the hang of the controls. Just what the hell do people see in this game, anyway? It's just bashing the same monsters on the head. And by the way, this artificial intelligence that everyone's going on about is nothing spectacular."

"You haven't even scratched the surface. You're in the training ground."

"The training ground?"

"Did you even read the FAQ?"

Silence.

"Okay, look: the Briar Patch is the starting level you need to graduate from before you can play in the main world. It keeps the world from being overrun with spastic newbies—no offense."

"None taken."

"Don't worry about combat commands right now. We've got to get moving."

"Shouldn't we wait until Agent Philips contacts you?"

"No point. The NSA is eavesdropping on your Internet and phone traffic, so they'll have a record of whatever we discover. You know how to end your game, right?"

"Yeah."

"Log off and get back to the title screen. You do it by hitting the Escape key a few times."

"All right, all right." Sebeck did as he was told. He resisted the temptation to save the current game and clicked all the way back to the main screen. "I'm there."

"Good. You'll need your hands for the controls. Can you put me on speakerphone?"

"My son's got a headset here."

"Perfect. Hook it up."

Sebeck hooked up the phone headset and put it on. "Can you hear me?"

"Yes. Click the 'Logon' command."

"Okay." Sebeck waited a few moments.

"When it prompts you for the logon and password, enter the following values . . . " Ross spoke slowly, "Logon: CLXSOLL3. Password: 39XDK_88."

Sebeck used hunt-and-peck typing to enter the values, then he clicked the CONTINUE button. An unfamiliar screen came up, showing a heavily armored, muscular human form rotating in space. It was like Leonardo da Vinci's sketchbook with heavy weaponry. At the top of the screen were the words "Character Name: Sir Dollus Andreas" in large type. Dozens of stats and hyperlinks appeared alongside the frame containing the spinning human warrior. "What the hell is this?"

"Your new character."

"This guy looks dangerous." Sebeck started clicking around the character sheet. It looked similar in format to his original barbarian—but all the categories were greatly expanded. He clicked through lists of weapons. "What's a *Vorpal Sword*?"

"Something I want back. We need to start out by getting information."

"Okay, what do I do?"

"Click the SPAWN button. I'll meet you outside your villa."

"My villa?"

"You're a knight. You hold a manse from the local lord."

"What's a manse?"

"It's land that produces income to support you as a knight. Just hit the SPAWN button, please."

Sebeck sighed and hit the SPAWN button. In a moment the screen faded out. His hard drive was clicking like mad.

"Did you spawn yet?"

"It's working on it." The screen faded in to reveal a large medieval bedchamber lit by smoky torchlight. Sebeck's point of view was from the foot of his canopied bed. Three men stood before him. The computer graphics were pretty impressive; so were the movements of the animated characters as they fidgeted and one shoved the other to pay attention.

The lead man bowed. The others followed suit. "Good morning, my lord."

Sebeck noticed two armored men standing guard at the bedchamber door. He spoke into his phone headset. "Okay, Jon, I'm in. I've got some guys talking to me."

"They're probably your servants. To find out what you can do with people, point at them and right-click. A menu will come up."

Sebeck clicked on the lead servant, then right-clicked. A menu appeared:

Follow me

Guard me
Bring me . . .
Leave me
Stop what you're doing
All of you, out of my sight, motherless dogs!

Sebeck selected the last command, and everyone in sight shrank back and scurried from the room—including the guards at the door. The door slammed behind them. Sebeck chuckled heartily. "This is just like the office."

Ross's voice came over the phone. "You called them motherless dogs, didn't you?"

"How could I resist?"

"Just get to the street, please. I'm waiting."

Sebeck hit the Up arrow to get himself moving. He eventually discovered the keyboard stroke to open doors, and soon he was walking through the halls of his villa. Servants scurried this way and that on apparent errands. They all bowed their heads as he passed. It was pretty impressive, but Sebeck wondered what the point of it all was. It's not like he could really enjoy the comforts of the place. It was just computer graphics.

He made it to the main hall, and from there Sebeck could see double doors with four men on guard. As he moved toward the front door, two men in rich-looking robes with fur collars and necklaces approached him from the wings.

"My lord, a word, please. I hope you've considered our proposal. The price is fair. What say you, my lord?"

Sebeck was confused. If this was his house, who the hell were these guys? "Jon, I've got a couple of shysters accosting me in my own foyer."

"Might be a deal the previous owner of the character had going."

"Are you serious? This game remembers what you do?"

"Do they look important?"

"Sort of." Sebeck right-clicked on the man. A selection of responses appeared:

I'll sell for 500
Offer more money
No, I'll never sell
I'll think about it

Sebeck's mouse accidentally hovered over the guard in the background, and the menu listing went away. Sebeck right-clicked on the guard out of curiosity. Another list appeared:

Attack . . .

Guard me

Guard this place

Leave me

Sebeck selected *Attack. . . .* When he did so, the mouse cursor started trailing a red line from it, with a fixed point leading from the guard. The game was apparently asking him to select the target. Sebeck clicked smack dab in the expectant face of the bearded merchant.

An echoing shout went up in the room as not just one but all the guards pulled swords and came screaming toward the merchant.

The man's face actually registered fear. "No! To me! To me!"

Sebeck's warriors converged on the men and started hacking them with swords. Animated blood spattered the floor as the merchants tried to flee. Sebeck's warriors hemmed them in. The merchants shrieked pitiably. That's when Sebeck heard pounding on the front doors. A couple of his guards peeled off just in time to meet a dozen swordsmen in what looked to be chain mail. They burst into the foyer screaming like banshees and rushed to the merchants' defense.

A general alarm bell went up in the house. Shouts were heard all around. "We're under attack!"

Sebeck muttered into the phone. "Oh shit . . ."

"Why are those swordsmen running into the villa?"

"Okay, I may have fucked up here."

"Damnit, Pete, you couldn't get out your front door without causing a brawl?"

"It's under control." Sebeck was trying to remember the command to get a sword into his hand. This character was incredibly confusing. There was so much to choose from—too much. Suddenly a wild-haired swordsman was on him, screaming and swinging like a maniac. "Uh-oh."

More of Sebeck's men were coming in from the wings, but not enough. Already some of his men lay dead. The merchants had good bodyguards, and they were moving out the door under close protection now.

The bearded one looked back and pointed to Sebeck. "I will have vengeance upon you!"

Sebeck muttered into his headset. "Yeah, yeah . . ."

Suddenly the merchant jerked and dropped to the ground with a black arrow in his back. His two bodyguards scanned the terrain outside, and one of them suddenly dropped dead as well. The remaining guard ran for the road.

A horn sounded, and the merchant's men-at-arms retreated, bringing the surviving younger merchant along with them. As they made their way through the doorway, another black arrow appeared in the younger merchant's forehead, and he, too, pitched forward, dead. The remaining men-at-arms scattered, running through the gardens and over the low hedgerows. Sebeck's four or five remaining guards gave chase. One of them turned back in the doorway and shouted to a servant. "Summon the town watch!" Then he was gone. The servant ran off through the villa shouting, "The watch! The watch!"

In a moment Sebeck stood alone among the dead. On closer inspection, some were groaning and twitching, obviously injured. This was frighteningly detailed. Sebeck scanned the room, hitting the arrow keys to move about.

He almost jumped out of his digital skin when he turned to see a fearsome-looking hooded assassin appear out of thin air a foot from his face.

Ross's voice came over the phone. "Boo."

"Stop screwing around." Sebeck noticed that this avatar was different from the ones he'd seen so far—a glowing call-out box hovered over its head. The box was labeled *"Entro-P"* and a series of green bars were stacked up to the left of it, like a graph. It was a ninja with a floating name tag. "Who are you supposed to be?"

"You really screwed things up, you know that?"

"I don't remember you teaching me how to *play* this game."

"I plead guilty. I just didn't think your first instinct would be to attack an unarmed old man."

"He was annoying me."

"Okay, a little tip: everything has consequences in this world—as in the real one. See the dead merchant on the floor? That's the patriarch of the House of Peduin and a leading merchant. He had many friends, and he provided the local nobility with much of their liquidity—i.e., cash. This is an agrarian society, so cold hard cash is hard to come by. Even my character has used his services."

"*You're* the one who killed him."

"But I wasn't *seen* trying to kill him. See how that works? Just like the real world. Once you ordered your men to kill him, it was important to slay all the witnesses. Even then, you might have spies in your household."

"Enough. So what? Some digital graphics are upset at me. Who gives a shit?"

"I bought your character because he was useful. He had title, lands, and income from his holdings. These things would have come in handy where we're going—particularly your following of men-at-arms and any alliances you might have had with regional nobility. But now you'll be branded outlaw and your lands and title will be forfeit."

"All right. I owe you a character. Should we buy another one?"

Ross chuckled. "Now you're getting the hang of it." He sighed. "No, let's see if we can get out of town alive."

"Town? We're in a town?"

"Yes. This is your autumn villa. The one used during market season. It's in downtown Gedan."

"As in the taverns of Gedan?"

"That's right. Although, thanks to you, we won't be visiting any taverns. C'mon."

Ross's assassin led the way, waiting impatiently as Sebeck tried in vain to navigate his character through the doorway and out to the road.

"You're like a retarded Sir Lancelot."

"Look, unlike you, I have a life, and I don't have hundreds of extra hours to spend learning to play this game."

They made it out to the road, and Sebeck finally got a good look around. This was a surprisingly complex-looking world. They stood on a narrow cobblestone street in a picturesque medieval town. A bell tower stood above what looked to be a square, and the bell was ringing. Birds even flew past in the morning sky. "Holy Moses. This is really something."

"Incoming . . ."

A mob of armed men headed down the otherwise deserted street in their direction. They didn't look friendly.

"Goddamnit, I didn't want to use this, but we've got places to go." Ross's character made some animated, generic hand gestures.

"What are you up to? You casting a spell or something?"

"No, I'm using a magical device."

Suddenly a shimmering portal opened in midair in the middle of the street. It revealed a tunnel that appeared to enter some extra-dimensional space.

"Why don't you just sprinkle them with pixie dust?"

"I'm going to sprinkle you with pixie dust in a second. This is a fantasy world. Whether you think it's cool is irrelevant. Several million people do think it's cool, and the Daemon is using this to propagate in reality—so stop poking fun and get your psycho ass through the portal."

"Okay, okay." Sebeck ran his character through the portal. He immediately came out on a windswept hillside in knee-high grass. The hillside overlooked a rocky coastline. The sea shimmered in the algorithmic sunshine. It was beautiful. He turned to see Ross's assassin run through the portal, a shouting mob close on his heels. Ross snapped the gate shut just as the crowd reached it. They were now alone on the hillside. The sound of the wind sweeping across the grass was their only companion.

"Where are we now?"

"About two hundred miles north."

"Well, that is handy. So what's up here?"

Ross's ninja avatar pointed. "Turn around and take a look off the coast."

Sebeck's character started backing up.

Ross barked, "Left arrow key."

"Oh." Sebeck searched for the left arrow key on his keyboard. His view swiveled until he was looking off the coast again. There, in the distance, he could make out a jagged islet—perhaps a mile offshore and partially obscured by mist. Sitting atop the islet was a towering castle in jet-black stone.

"Hello. Dr. Evil's beach house."

"Chat rooms say it appeared the day Sobol died. No one has even gotten close to it and lived."

"We'll need to tell the NSA. They need to impound these servers."

"These servers are in China. Or maybe South Korea. The companies that own them are politically connected there."

"Well, the Feds can exert a lot of political pressure."

"So can corporate executives."

They stood staring at the castle. It was Sebeck who broke the silence.

"Why didn't you transport us inside the castle?"

"I tried. This is as close as we can get. I can't use scrying devices to see inside either."

"Sobol's locked it up tight."

"Basically."

They stood there for several more moments.

"So, how do we get in?"

"Is it me, or did I just say that no one has approached the place and lived?"

"We've got to find out what Sobol's up to. Better our cartoon skins than our real ones."

"Who says we need to get inside to find out what it's for? What if we put the place under surveillance? Watch comings and goings?"

"Great. So if a dragon and a fairy show up at the castle, what the hell am I supposed to do with that information? Put out a warrant for their arrest?"

"No, but we might get some idea of how to get inside. With a little luck, we won't be observed from this distance, and—" Ross stopped mid-sentence.

Sebeck saw it, too. A huge shadow had cast over them from behind. It had a vaguely humanoid outline.

"Control-Down-Arrow turns you around, Pete. Do it now."

"Control-who-what?"

"Control-Down-Arrow."

"Hold it. Control . . . where's the Down key?"

"Pete! For the love of Christ, the Down arrow is a single key. Hold it down and simultaneously hold down the C-T-R-L key."

Sebeck did. His character pirouetted.

A jet-black figure, about twelve feet tall, towered over them. The figure held an obsidian rod and wore a black crown. Piercing, demonic red eyes glowed from deep sockets. No mouth was visible as it raised its arm, pointing at Sebeck. A deep, gravelly wav file played, "Detective Sebeck. You don't belong here!"

Before Sebeck could do anything, a lightning bolt arced hotly from the rod, blasting his avatar to dust. His screen went black, and his entire machine crashed—never to reboot.

Sebeck grabbed the headset mouthpiece. "Jesus! It said my name, Jon. And it just fried my computer. What's it doing now?"

Only Ross's cursing came over the phone line.

After the demon wasted Sebeck's knight, Ross went into defensive mode, ducking and retreating. There wasn't time to invoke another portal; the demon turned upon him. It raised its rod and spoke again. "You guided him here. Are you NSA or a Fed?" A pause. "Or neither? We shall see. . . ."

The hard drive on Ross's laptop started clattering.

"Shit!" He ripped the network cable from the socket. The game was still running, so he pulled the AC power cord and the battery, too. His laptop was now inert, the screen black.

He slumped back into his hotel desk chair and took a deep breath.

Sebeck's voice barked over the phone. "Jon! What the hell is going on?"

"I just disconnected, Pete. It was trying to find out who I was. I only had the game and a video capture program on this laptop, but I didn't want to lose the video images." He frowned to himself as he reinserted the laptop battery and placed the computer on the desk. His mind was turning over the possibilities. Ross stopped short. "Pete. I need you to come and get me out of jail."

"What are you talking about?"

"Just come to Woodland Hills and get me out of jail, please." He ignored Sebeck's questions and pulled off the phone headset, bolting through his hotel room door.

Ross sprinted down the exterior walkway toward the lobby. He brushed past two regional sales reps unloading luggage from a rental car and hauled ass on the final straightaway, banging through the lobby push doors.

The desk clerk was a fresh-faced, conspicuously Caucasian kid. He shot a stern glance up at Ross. "Watch the doors, please, sir."

Ross slammed into the counter, breathing hard. "I need access to your billing system. It's an emergency."

"Perhaps I can assist you, sir." He manned a keyboard, prairie-dog-like with his paws poised.

"Do you track Internet use on guest accounts?"

"Your Internet viewing habits won't appear on your bill."

"That's not what I meant. Do you connect guest billing information to an internal IP address?"

"Sir, we are required by law to maintain—"

"Goddamnit." Ross swung his leg up and started clawing his way over the counter, sending brochures and phones flying. "This isn't about pornography."

"You can't—"

Ross slipped on a PBX phone and tumbled to the floor behind the front desk.

The night clerk locked his workstation, then pressed a button under the counter. "The police are on their way!" He raced for the back office just as Ross got to his feet.

"Wait!" Ross lunged for the office door, but the kid slammed it in his face, ramming a heavy bolt home. Ross pounded on it with his open hand. It was a security door.

The kid's voice came through muffled. "You're not the first idiot to look at porn on a hotel account, sir. But you just made it a whole lot worse."

"This is a *police* emergency."

"I didn't see a badge."

"Look, I'm working with the Feds on the Daemon case. Sobol's house is five miles down the road. It's not improbable that I would stay here."

"You checked in weeks ago—before Sobol died. Just wait for the police."

"By the time they get here, it'll be too late. The Daemon is going to attack your servers to find out who I am."

"I'm not listening, sir!"

"If the Web server is in there with you, just pull the cables out of the back. That's all I'm asking."

There was no response.

"Kid! This isn't a joke. The Daemon has already killed more than a dozen people. If it finds out who I am—"

"Sir, I suggest you talk to the police about it."

Shit. Ross stalked around the front desk. He manned the computer on the counter. It displayed a browser-based hotel management program. A logon screen stared him in the face. Ross flipped over the mouse pad and found a tiny Post-it note scrawled with logons and passwords. He used one to log on. "Well, that's one advantage I have over the Daemon. . . ."

Like most point-of-sale systems, this one was designed to minimize training requirements. Ross was presented with a standard switchboard form for the billing system. He chose Customer Accounts and searched for his name. He quickly found his billing record, but he couldn't edit anything. The night clerk's logon didn't have sufficient privileges to change existing information—only to add new charges. Ross's name and credit card number were clearly displayed. There was also a link for his Internet and phone charges. *Damnit.*

The server for *The Gate* would already have the hotel's main IP address—so the Daemon would know precisely where to launch its attack. If the hotel ran a common hotel management system—as was likely—then the database layout would be public knowledge. "Son of a bitch."

In the back office, the kid was on the phone with a 911 operator. Behind him stood a couple of rack-mounted servers, a router, and a network switch, their green LED lights lazily blinking. The whole rack was locked off to him, but a flat-panel monitor displayed the logon dialog for the server, bouncing around the black screen.

Then, like a floodgate opening, the entire bank of LEDs started fluttering like crazy. The network was slammed with IP traffic. Even the kid noticed it. He heard the hard drive straining.

"Hey! Whatever you're doing out there, stop it."

Ross cocked an ear toward the office but did not take his eyes off the computer screen. "Kid, I'm not doing anything. That's the Daemon trying to bash its way in. It'll try to get at the Web access logs to find my connection to its Web site. Then it'll try to link my billing record with that IP address. I'm begging you: please open the door."

Ross minimized the hotel billing app and interrogated the DNS server from a console window. Thankfully the server was not properly configured and permitted a zone transfer. This let him view the internal IP map of the network from his machine—complete with machine names and operating systems.

The clerk watched the LED lights flickering like a Vegas marquee. Suddenly the server monitor screen came to life. The logon dialog went away and the desktop appeared. The kid spoke to the 911 operator. "He's doing something to our computers."

Back at the front desk Ross typed like a maniac. Now he knew the OS of the Web server. He thought about the odds of cracking into the server in time to clear the Web logs. Not likely, and it was the first thing the Daemon would try for.

"Listen, open the door."

"No way!"

Ross flipped back to the hotel's Web application. He needed to go straight for the customer database. The file extension on the URL told him it was a scripted page. He started typing directly in the URL box of the browser, back-spacing to the hotel's domain name—to which he appended the text: */global.asa+.htr*

Then he hit ENTER.

To Ross's relief, the hotel hadn't patched their Web server, either, and the browser disgorged the source code of the application onto the screen. The developers had been lazy; near the top of the code, there was a database connection string and two variables for dbowner: one for logon and one for password. He was in.

In the back office the kid closely watched the server's monitor. Command console windows kept appearing and disappearing on the screen—commands entered at blinding speed. The hard drives labored. Dialogs came up showing file transfers. There was no way a person could work this fast. He tried the server's enclosure door. Locked. He couldn't shut the server down if he wanted to.

Ross logged back into the billing application using the sysadmin logon he had found in the source code. He navigated to his customer record. This time all the fields were unlocked for editing. There wasn't a DELETE button, so he rapidly filled the billing record with false information, replacing his own name with "Matthew Sobol"—along with a phantom address, a random phone number, and all 9's for a credit card number. He was about to click SUBMIT when he heard footsteps running on the tile floor of the lobby behind him.

"Hands in the air!" The shout echoed in the lobby.

Ross turned to see two Woodland Hills police officers aiming Berettas at him from beyond the front desk. They squinted over their sights, with a two-hand clasp.

Ross tapped the SUBMIT button, then raised his hands. "It's all right. I'm working on the Daemon case with officer Pete Sebeck of the Thousand Oaks police department."

"Stop talking!" One of the officers motioned to the countertop. "Both hands, palms down on the counter!"

In the back office the kid stared at the computer screen. A DOS window was up, displaying a customer record:

Room 1318—No Name (999) 999-9999

CC#9999-9999-9999-9999

Then the server crashed.

Chapter 23:// Transformation

Sebeck escorted Ross out the front door of the Woodland Hills police station. Ross rubbed one wrist. "Do they always cuff people that tightly?"

"Only the troublemakers." Sebeck's new police cruiser was parked at the curb, and he pointed Ross to it.

"I like the color better."

"Just get in the car."

Ross sniffed the morning air. "It's good to breathe free again. I was starting to worry you weren't coming."

"I needed to smooth things over with the DA. The Daemon trashed the hotel's reservation system."

"That's not *my* fault. They should have applied security patches."

"Jon, I talked the prosecutor out of bringing criminal charges, but I'm getting the distinct impression we're chasing our tails. Sobol's always three steps ahead of us."

"Are you kidding? We made great progress last night."

Sebeck gave him a look. "I got killed, and you got arrested. How is that great progress?"

"Well, if you're gonna look on the gloomy side—"

"Just get in the car."

"What's with you?"

"I got an earful this morning over this little stunt. I've got NSA agents moving into my house. My son's not speaking to me. My wife *is* speaking to me, and I haven't even had a cup of coffee yet. Other than that, everything's just great."

"Pete, we need to reconnect with the Daemon as soon as possible."

"We're just stumbling around blind." Sebeck got into the car.

Ross thought for a moment. "I know a good coffee place near here."

"That's a start."

Calabasas was an upscale bedroom community not far from Woodland Hills. It was part of the circulatory system of L.A. and, like most towns, straddled an artery of freeway.

Ross guided Sebeck to a new shopping plaza—a riot of pastel stucco, imitation fieldstone, and palm trees—that more resembled a Tim Burton film set than a retail center. The sprawling parking lot was clogged with tiny *au pair* cars and the monstrous SUVs of stay-at-home moms.

Sebeck gazed at the scene from an outdoor faux-French café. Beyond a nearby railing stood a burbling water feature replete with ducks, as though this wasn't a desert but a mill pond in the south of France. If someone cut the pumps, Sebeck figured the ducks would be dead inside of six hours. He tossed a piece of croissant to them and sipped his AA Kenya coffee.

Across the table Ross sipped a triple latte. The cup was something straight out of *Alice in Wonderland*. Sebeck frowned. "What the hell was that thing that attacked us last night? And how did it know my name?"

Ross put his latte down on a freakishly large saucer. "I'm not surprised it knew your name, but I am surprised it *spoke* your name—particularly since I didn't hear it."

"What do you mean you didn't hear it? It said my name in a huge booming voice."

"Yes, but I think the file only played for you."

"What file?"

"The sound file. Someone was recorded speaking your name. That recording was saved as a sound file, and your computer played that file on command. But it wasn't on my laptop."

"Why would I have the file but not you?"

"Because Sobol placed it on your computer."

"But that should have been easy. Sobol's press release said Ego puts a back door in every machine that runs it."

Ross took another sip of his latte and shook his head. "No, I don't buy that."

"Hold the phone. *You* were the one saying that Sobol could do anything. That we shouldn't underestimate him. Now you're saying he didn't put a back door in the Ego AI engine?"

"What sense would it make to place a back door in a program, and then tell everyone? All that would do is drastically reduce the number of machines Sobol would have access to. It doesn't make sense."

"Sobol was *insane*."

"So everyone keeps saying. You know, it would have taken a coordinated effort—by many people—to place a back door in release code."

Sebeck pondered it. "So, why would Sobol lie about the back door? That lie basically destroyed his own company."

Both men realized it at the same time.

Ross tapped his chin, thinking. "So, the reason *was* to destroy his company. I have no idea why, but clearly, that must have been the purpose of the press release."

"It's just insane. . . ."

"Maybe, but if there was no back door in the Ego AI engine, it brings us back to the question: how did the Daemon know it was *you* last night? Remember: you were playing on someone else's account."

Sebeck shrugged. "You're the expert."

Ross took another sip of his latte. "You were running the game on the same machine you received Sobol's e-mail on, correct?"

"You mean the e-mail with the video link?"

"Yes."

Sebeck nodded.

"This whole time we were focusing on what Sobol said in that video, but it never occurred to us that playing the video might also install a Trojan horse."

"To do what?"

"Open a back door in the computer that runs it."

Sebeck thought for a moment. "Wait. Aaron ran that video file on the sheriff's network. Hell, I think most people at the department got a copy. It also found its way to a lot of journalists."

Ross put his latte down. "Shit, if Sobol used the same kernel rootkit I encountered at Alcyone Insurance, he could open a back door in the sheriff's network. Sobol could even monitor e-mails between you and the Feds. And antivirus programs wouldn't detect it."

"Please tell me you're joking."

"If you run a malicious program, that program can do a lot of bad things and not just to you."

"Christ, how could I be so stupid?"

"We're not positive that's what happened. Not yet."

The thumping of a helicopter registered above the surrounding traffic—it was coming in low and fast. It suddenly crested the roof of the plaza anchor store and swung low over the parking lot.

Sebeck and Ross craned their necks up to see an LAPD chopper angling in directly toward them over the shopping plaza. The chopper wash sent the ducks scurrying for cover under a fairy tale bridge.

Sebeck shielded his eyes against the wind as the noise built to deafening levels. Dozens of napkins flicked away on the wind as nannies squealed in alarm and fled from the surrounding café tables.

Sebeck looked to Ross. "What the hell's he up to?"

Just then sirens approached from several directions at once. Cars screeched in from every entrance of the parking lot. Sebeck glanced to see federal sedans and Los Angeles police cars race up onto the courtyard paving stones. The cars hadn't quite stopped when agents wearing bulletproof vests and Kevlar helmets issued forth aiming M-16s at him and Ross. The flak vests were emblazoned with the letters *FBI*.

A dozen voices shouted, "Hands on your head!"

More agents came rushing through the back of the coffee bar, M-16s and HKs aimed and ready.

Sebeck glanced back and forth in confusion. He raised his hands slowly, shouting back, "What the hell is going on?"

"Hands on your head, or we will shoot!"

Something was beyond wrong. Sebeck looked at the faces of the agents and police arrayed around him. There was abject hatred in their eyes. Burning anger. He knew that look. It was the look reserved for the vilest criminals. They were closing in from two directions—leaving a clear field of fire. Twenty or thirty heavily armed men. Sebeck glanced at Ross, who already had his hands on his head. "What the hell is going on, Jon?"

"I don't know. But the Daemon's got something to do with it."

"This is your last warning! Put your hands on your head, or we will open fire!"

Sebeck felt his blood rising. He put his hands on the back of his head but looked to Ross. "Why are they looking at *me*?"

"I don't know."

The Feds hit Sebeck like linebackers. They piled on him, pounding him into the concrete, wrenching his hands behind his back and handcuffing him. Then they patted him down and took his service Beretta away. The lead agent hissed into his ear. "If I had my way, I'd put a bullet in your head, Sebeck." He rammed Sebeck's face into the sidewalk, and then they pulled him up roughly, shoving Ross aside. Blood flowed from Sebeck's nose down his shirtfront.

"Peter Sebeck, you are under arrest for the murder of Aaron Larson and other local and federal law officers, for conspiracy, wire fraud, and attempted murder. You have the right to remain silent. Anything you say can and will be used against you in a court of law. . . ."

The world warped as Sebeck's mind seemed to float four feet above his head. This was impossible. Every pair of eyes bored holes of hatred into him. How was *he* the Daemon? How was this possible?

He turned toward Ross, standing now beyond a wall of FBI agents. "Jon. Jon!"

"Pete, it's the Daemon!"

Agents pulled Sebeck along, and half a dozen others shoved him forward from behind. In a second, Ross was lost to sight in the knot of people.

Sebeck felt as though reality had ripped apart and he was floating in the realm of fantasy. Sobol's game world was more real than this. Sebeck's unseeing eyes never noticed the lone camera crew he was hauled past, nor did he notice the attractive blond reporter standing with a microphone.

"This is Anji Anderson, live in Calabasas, California, bringing you a shocking exclusive report as federal agents apprehend Detective Sergeant Peter Sebeck of the Ventura County Sheriff's Department. Sebeck—previously the lead investigator in the Daemon murder case—now stands accused of participating in one of the most audacious frauds in modern history. Federal prosecutors claim that Sebeck played a key role in a conspiracy to defraud a mentally impaired Matthew Sobol out of tens of millions of dollars. Money that was later used to purchase options in CyberStorm stock. Stock that eventually collapsed, netting the conspirators an estimated $190 million dollars. The FBI, in cooperation with the Secret Service and Interpol, has reportedly made three other arrests in two countries tonight. But at this hour, two things are clear: Matthew Sobol was apparently an innocent victim in this deadly plan, and much to the relief of authorities, the Internet Daemon appears to be a hoax."

Natalie Philips stood flanked by The Major and half a dozen NSA agents in the shopping plaza. FBI agents were still cordoning off the scene. She beheld the FBI SAC, Steven Trear, with a look somewhere between disbelief and disgust. "You let Jon Ross *go?*"

Trear stood in the center of a knot of FBI agents. "He was questioned and released. We found no evidence that Ross was involved with Sebeck prior to this week. And he's been cleared on the Alcyone Insurance worm. Do you know something we don't?"

Philips looked to The Major, who pounded a nearby café table in frustration, then tipped it over with a crash.

Trear threw up his hands. "Do you mind telling me what's going on here?"

Philips motioned to a nearby NSA agent but spoke to Trear. "We just came from Woodland Hills. Jon Ross was taken into custody last night, booked on malicious vandalism and making terroristic threats."

Trear squinted at her like she was nuts. "*Jon Ross?*"

Philips accepted a file folder from the NSA agent. "The DA dropped the charges after intervention by Peter Sebeck." She opened the folder and handed it to Trear. "Your preliminary background check didn't include a fingerprint comparison. The real Jon Ross had a DUI conviction three years ago. Those records don't match the man you brought in for questioning in Thousand Oaks. Neither do his photos."

"Hold on a second. You're telling me—"

"He's an identity thief. He's not the real Jon Ross."

Trear started thumbing through the folder. "Why the hell was this kept from us?"

The Major answered instead. "Need-to-know basis."

"Bullshit."

Philips checked her watch. "You interviewed him for what, an hour?"

"He's already been extensively interrogated, and he was traumatized. We turned him over to the paramedics."

"Brilliant."

Trear moved toward her, finger pointing, "Listen, *missy* . . .."

The Major interposed himself and physically pushed Trear back. This caused three of Trear's agents to launch to his defense. The scene quickly resembled a brawl on a baseball infield. Shouting filled the air as more NSA and FBI agents jumped in.

The Major had Trear by the tie.

"Get your damned hands off me!" He extricated himself from The Major's grip as a couple of his agents yanked the burly man's head back. The scene calmed a little, and Trear glared at The Major. "I want your name, agent! I'll have you up on charges!"

The Major stared back even harder. "You don't have sufficient clearance for my name." He produced credentials from his jacket pocket—his photo next to a long alphanumeric sequence in bold letters. "Special Collections Service. I'm here on the highest authority concerning a matter of national security."

One of the FBI agents nearby scoffed, "What the hell do you think Sebeck's arrest was?"

Trear barked at him, "Quiet!" He looked back at The Major. "Special Collections Service?" Then he looked at Philips with a slightly different regard. "What the hell do you have going on here, Philips? Who called out the black bag men?"

Philips tried to contain her irritation. "He doesn't answer to me, Trear. He's got his own orders, and I'm not privy to them. Look, the man posing as Ross could be involved in this."

"If you had a warrant out for Ross, why weren't we told about it?"

"It's not that simple. This is a national security operation, not a criminal investigation."

"That's crap, Philips. You guys are stovepiping information. The bureau is supposed to be a customer of the NSA." He looked at The Major. "And what does the CIA know, I wonder?"

Philips was conciliatory. "I notified Fort Meade. It takes time for them to contact you. This all happened in the last three hours."

"Surely the NSA has heard of *phones*. They're those things you tap."

"Why weren't we told about *Sebeck*?"

They stood glaring at each other.

Another NSA agent came running up. "Agent Philips. Ross just used his Amex card five minutes ago at a car rental place down the street. We put out an all-points bulletin."

"E911 tracking?"

"We're talking to the cell phone company now."

"GPS in the rental car?"

The agent shook his head. "He rented a subcompact. No onboard GPS."

"Flag his license plates on the freeway plate readers." She turned to Trear. "I know you're angry, Agent Trear, but we could really use your assistance on this. Ross could be the one behind the Daemon. He certainly has the technical know-how."

"The Daemon is a hoax, Agent Philips. When is the NSA going to catch up with us on this?"

"Look, whether you think the Daemon is a hoax or not, the man posing as Ross has been involved from the start, and he's escaping. Can we get your help?"

Trear took a deep breath and nodded to his men.

Straub turned and shouted, "You heard the man!"

Ten blocks away, Ross tossed his cell phone onto the back of a lumber truck waiting at a stoplight. The rental car ruse combined with the moving cell phone should buy him some time.

Ross headed in the opposite direction as the truck pulled away. The Feds probably wouldn't take long to figure out Ross wasn't who he claimed to be, and by then he needed to have taken another identity. He walked with composure onto the parking lot of a nearby Mercedes dealership, still wondering why he'd gotten himself mixed up in all this to begin with. And what the hell had happened to Detective Sebeck? The Daemon must be behind it. This was the type of reversal Sobol was famous for. It's what Ross had tried to warn the Feds about. Now he needed to figure out Sobol's plan, and for the time being at least, the only priority had to be getting out of this area. Ross straightened his tie and walked calmly through the glass doors of the Mercedes dealership. He strolled between the showroom models, scrutinizing window stickers. An aria from *The Marriage of Figaro* played softly on the showroom speakers.

Several police cars raced past on the road outside, lights and sirens blaring.

A sharply attired salesman approached Ross, hand extended. "How are you today, sir?"

Ross looked up. "Bored, but it's nothing a sports car won't fix."

The salesman laughed politely. "Well, what are you driving now, Mr. . . ."

"Ross. I have a twelve-cylinder A8—drives like a dream—but I want to get a second car. Something smaller and sportier."

"And you're familiar with the SL roadster?"

Ross examined the silver car nearby. "A golf buddy of mine has one. I've done some research, but the truth is, if I like the way it feels I'll buy it today. No financing necessary."

The salesman nodded. "Let's take it for a spin. I'll just need a photocopy of your driver's license."

Ross drew his wallet. "Of course."

The platinum cards were clearly visible as he offered his license to the salesman.

Natalie Philips stood in the car rental company's parking lot and stared at the car Ross had rented an hour before. She had tracked Ross's cell phone through E911, only to find it riding to Oxnard on the back of a truck. Ross's rented subcompact was never driven off the rental lot. And nobody in the Task Force had thought to look for it here—especially with his cell phone on the move.

Trear pounded the roof of his car. "Damnit! This guy's probably halfway to Mexico by now."

Philips turned to him. "Halfway isn't all the way. Besides, he still needs transportation, and we have all the airports, train stations, and bus stations staked out. If he makes any ATM withdrawals or credit card purchases, we'll be on top of him in minutes. There's a strike team airborne in the L.A. basin as we speak."

Trear grabbed a radio, but looked to Philips. "This Ross imposter was most likely Sebeck's go-to man for computer work. Maybe even the mastermind of this hoax."

"You mean *if* the Daemon is a hoax."

"It's definitely a hoax, and I don't think Sebeck was smart enough to pull it off—much less to conceive of it. But our imposter just might be."

Philips nodded, even though it made less sense the more she thought about it.

Ross ditched the Mercedes salesman off the 23 freeway in Simi Valley. He exited the freeway, claiming a bathroom emergency, and never returned after rushing into a restaurant to use the restroom. Instead, he ducked out a side exit and walked over one block to a row of nondescript, corrugated metal box garages.

He pulled out his key ring and cycled through the keys for a moment. Then he unlocked the garage door padlock and pulled up the door to reveal a late-model white utility truck with side cargo panels. A logo on the door read "Lasseter Heating & Air." Ross flicked the garage light switch then ducked inside, lowering the door behind him.

There was about six feet of space on either side of the vehicle. Ross moved alongside and opened one of the cargo panels, revealing a mirror hanging on the inside of the door. There was a toiletry bag and a change of clothes. He pulled a wallet out from under the clothes and flipped it open to reveal a California driver's license with his picture on it. The name read "Michael Lasseter." In the picture he was bald as a billiard ball. He lined up the mirror and pulled an electric shaver out of the toiletry bag. He looked for the single electric socket up by the overhead light.

In ten minutes or so, he was completely bald. Clumps of dark hair covered the floor. He examined himself in the mirror and rubbed his bald scalp. *"Я надеюсь что твои волосы вырастут опять."* It felt strangely good to speak his native language again. And bad, too. This place wasn't supposed to be needed.

He emptied Jon Ross's wallet and placed the credit cards and identification on a hot plate. He powered it up and kept working as the acrid smell of melting plastic filled the space.

He changed into jeans and a work shirt.

When he finished he looked at himself in the mirror. He stopped and grabbed a bottle of rub-on tan, then smeared it over his face, neck, and arms. He took another look at Lasseter's license photo. Much better.

Jon Ross was dead. Long live Michael Lasseter.

He hid Ross's clothes and the toiletry bag in a tool bench cabinet, then unplugged the hot plate. He checked to be certain that Ross's ID and credit cards were completely melted. It was a multicolored puddle. He took one last look around, then opened the garage door.

The sun was suddenly blinding. He got into the truck and started it up. He sat there pondering for a moment. He was confident he'd get past any roadblocks, but what then?

Sobol was sharper than he expected—and he was expecting a lot. Sobol had destroyed Sebeck somehow and made everyone believe the Daemon was a hoax. Why? Some milestone had been achieved, and the Daemon was moving on to the next task. He knew there was a reason for framing Sebeck, but he just couldn't wrap his head around it. Why make the Daemon famous and then turn around and make people believe it didn't exist again?

He drummed his fingers on the steering wheel.

One thing was for sure: he'd be damned if the Daemon was going to defeat him. It might have defeated Jon Ross, but it had never even heard of Michael Lasseter.

Chapter 24://Sit Rep

In the corner boardroom of building OPS-2B, the group of agency directors reconvened. In the windowless room it was impossible to tell whether it was night or day. And from the government décor it was impossible to tell whether it was 1940 or 2040.

DIA: "I caught the news on the way in. They're saying the Daemon is a hoax. Is that true?"

FBI: "The money trail leads to two people that we know of. Detective Sebeck, now in custody, and one Cheryl Lanthrop, a medical executive. We thought we found her in Kuala Lumpur, but our intel was bad."

There was silence for a moment.

NSA: "Let me get this straight: you're telling me that Detective Sebeck and this Lanthrop woman turned Sobol's estate into a high-tech death trap?"

FBI: "Tax records show Lanthrop was sales director for a string of MRI labs owned by Matthew Sobol. He appears to have become obsessed with MRI technology in the latter stages of his illness. E-mail records show her advising Sobol to invest in a functional MRI business in which she was part owner. She sounds like a kook. Her specialty was neuromarketing research—examining the brain activity of people viewing various consumer products."

NSA: "You didn't answer the question."

CIA: "Where does Sebeck come in?"

FBI: "We're not sure yet, but credit card records show Lanthrop staying at the same hotels where Sebeck attended law-enforcement seminars. They also traveled to Grand Cayman together. Lanthrop set up an offshore bank account there for a holding company that later held short positions in CyberStorm Entertainment stock. We have video of

Lanthrop and Sebeck sitting at a bank manager's desk. Sebeck's wife had no knowledge of this trip."

NSA: "How do Sebeck and Lanthrop build an automated Hummer or an electrocution trap in the CyberStorm server farm? I mean, how would they get access to CyberStorm?"

FBI: "We're still putting the pieces together. There may be more people involved. Possibly even Singh and Pavlos. We found deleted files on Sebeck's computer. They include lists of equipment and a draft power of attorney later signed by Matthew Sobol—probably after dementia incapacitated him. That power of attorney placed part of Sobol's assets under the control of an offshore corporation in which Sebeck held a controlling interest."

CIA: "Am I the only person who thinks this is a load of horseshit?"

NSA: "No."

FBI: "If you read the report—"

CIA: "Hang on a second. This is too far-fetched. You're telling me that these two managed to swindle Sobol out of forty million dollars in loans—but that they didn't just take the money and run. Instead, they bought stock on margin and orchestrated a shorting scam? Hell, a Wall Street banker might have been able to do it, but not some yokel cop and his girlfriend."

NSA: "I'm going to side with him on that. This seems improbable. They'd need serious technical and financial expertise. Not to mention luck."

FBI: "We're still searching for the man who claimed to be Jon Ross. He escaped from the Calabasas scene and disappeared without a trace. He might be our skilled operator. Sebeck was most likely the muscle. He was probably just looking for a way out. Had his first kid at sixteen, married the mother at seventeen. A rocky marriage. By all accounts, not a family man. Probably felt trapped."

NSA: "What about the e-mail video of Sobol?"

FBI: "Preliminary voice and image analysis indicates the MPEG video was faked. Not surprisingly, Sebeck was the one who discovered it. This and the other evidence probably gave Lanthrop and Sebeck time to—"

NSA: "What about the acoustic weapons? And the ultrawideband transmitters?"

FBI: "Clearly someone with tremendous technical know-how was involved. But that didn't have to be Sobol. Don't forget: Detective Se-beck was a signatory on eight offshore accounts and an officer in nine offshore holding corporations. Some of these accounts are years old. For godsakes, Detective Sebeck had a safe deposit box in a Los Angeles bank where we found twenty thousand dollars in cash and a forged passport with his picture on it."

NSA: "That's quite interesting." He paused for effect. "I also find it interesting that there were several other Ventura County detectives besides Peter Sebeck who might have been assigned this case. And *all* of them had not one, but multiple offshore bank accounts. About which they claim ignorance."

This produced frowns around the table.

CIA: "I don't understand."

NSA motioned for a nearby aide to hit the lights. The room dimmed.

NSA: "Look at this map." He pulled out a remote and a map of the U.S. appeared, via PowerPoint, on a wall screen. "Here, we see cities where these same detectives incurred credit card charges in the last two years." He clicked. "Now, we overlay credit card charges occurring on those same days for Ms. Lanthrop."

The map showed the detectives didn't travel all that widely. But they had an unusual habit of taking trips to cities on the same day that Cheryl Lanthrop was in them.

FBI: "What the hell . . . ?"

NSA: "Same city. Same day. Note that they *all* took a trip to Grand Cayman at one time or another."

There was general confusion around the table.

DARPA: "You're saying that every senior detective in Ventura County was involved?"

NSA: "No. I'm saying that the groundwork was laid to *frame* every detective—a precaution against a single point of failure in the Dae-mon. That wasn't the only precaution. . . ." He clicked the remote. The screen changed to a still image from a security camera showing Lan-throp checking in at a business hotel. She was beautiful even here. "Our Ms. Lanthrop. Memphis. Auburn hair, high cheekbones." The image changed to another security camera image. "Dallas. Blond hair, soft features, and ample bustline." Another photograph. "Kansas City. Bru-nette, tall."

DARPA: "They're different women."

FBI: "So this is the NSA's attempt to bring the Daemon back into the picture?"

NSA: "It's not an attempt to do anything. These are the facts. It's also a fact that Cheryl Lanthrop had no known medical or business experience prior to working at Sobol's company, nor can we find any trace of her family or anyone who knew her prior to that time."

CIA: "She's a doppelganger."

NSA: "It would appear so."

FBI: "But that just proves my point; these are sophisticated grifters who scammed Sobol."

NSA: "Your evidence is largely digital. E-mail, financial transactions, travel records. How do you know that Sebeck's Lanthrop was anything more than a call girl?"

FBI: "This is ridiculous. Occam's razor kicks in here. Which is more probable: that a dead man set up a system for framing multiple detectives—simultaneously flushing half his estate down the toilet—or that a group of people abused a position of trust to swindle a dying rich man?"

DIA: "But why was it necessary to have all the detectives involved? If a group of people were swindling Sobol, wouldn't they want to have cops as far away as possible?"

There was silence.

FBI: "Well, it's a fact that a cop was involved, and it's a fact that someone orchestrated the stock swindle."

DIA: "So, does the Daemon exist or not?"

They looked at each other in the semidarkness.

NSA: "I think we can agree that—as far as the public is concerned—the Daemon *must* remain a hoax."

Part Two

Eight Months Later

Chapter 25:// Lost in the System

An exasperated sigh came over the phone line. "Look, I'm not interested."

"Well, then we've got something in common."

She laughed.

Charles Mosely's voice smiled. "I like your laugh." Thirty-eight-point-nine percent of the time his deep, rich voice elicited a positive response from females in the twenty-one to thirty-five demographic.

A pause. "Thanks. You have a nice voice."

"I prefer using it for my art. But with the economy and all, here I am. I do apologize for the intrusion, miss."

"That's okay. Sorry I was so short."

"Not a problem. Peace."

"What is your art?"

"Pardon?"

"You said you preferred using your voice for your art."

Mosely chuckled. "I gotta watch that. I'm revealing too much about myself."

"C'mon. Tell me."

He hesitated, checking the timer on his computer screen. "Well . . . you're gonna laugh at me."

"No I won't."

"I'm an out-of-work stage actor here in New York."

"Get out! What have you been in?"

Mosely laughed again. "*Othello* at the Public, if you can believe it. Just the matinees, though."

"And now you're doing *this*?"

"Oh, I know—kill me now, right?"

"I'm sorry." She laughed again. He could almost hear her twirling the phone cord around her finger. "You have such a great voice, Charles."

"Thank you, miss."

TeleMaster tracked the activities of individual telemarketers down to the second. Average number of seconds between phone calls, average number of seconds for each call, average number of calls per day, average sales close percentage—all calculated automatically through the VOIP-enabled software package marketed in North America under the brand name *TeleMaster*, but in Europe and Asia under the impenetrable name *Ophaseum*.

Sales associates had only a couple of seconds after completing one call before they heard the line ringing for the next. Associates who made their quota early, then slacked off, didn't fool *TeleMaster*; the system monitored you constantly with a moving average. A sudden and precipitous drop-off in productivity was flagged for immediate follow-up by a floor supervisor. Finding a balance between frantically striving for quota and keeping a pace you could maintain throughout a shift was difficult—except for the closers. And Charles was a closer. His deep voice, reassuring tone, and cool confidence gave him a disproportionate closing percentage straight across both male and female demographic segments.

And those who didn't make quota? Their commission base dropped, and once their commission base dropped, they were earning less for each sale. And once they were earning less for each sale, the work was just as stressful and tedious, but they made less for it. If they failed to perform enough times, then they were out of work and back into the general population.

He was paid next to nothing. Why did he care?

He knew why he cared. He liked to hear the voices. He liked to talk to women from everywhere, to work his magic on them and persuade them to "do it." Never mind that "it" was buying a slot in a time-share or a magazine subscription. "It" would have to do. "It" was the only way to maintain his humanity. And in prison, that was worth a lot.

Charles Mosely made the sale—a two-year subscription to *Uptown* magazine—ignoring the woman as she gave her e-mail address to him. She'd like to hear from him. Mosely rolled his eyes. Damn, he didn't care what she looked like—he'd like to contact her, too. But there were no Internet connections allowed at Highland. He looked up from the narrow confines of cubicle 166 at a long row of tiny steel cubicles stretching into the distance. The muted chatter of a hundred operators in orange jumpsuits came to his right ear—the ear not covered by a headset. An unarmed guard paced a catwalk above him behind a steel mesh barrier.

The Warmonk, Inc., prison-based telemarketing facility in Highland, Texas, was privately owned and operated under contract to the Texas Department of Criminal Justice. It was connected to the maximum-security prison of the same name by a covered pedestrian bridge. The prisoners' labor was ostensibly used to defray the costs of their incarceration. At thirty cents an hour, they gave Indian telemarketers a run for their money.

Like almost half the guests of the Texas Department of Corrections, Mosely was black. Prisoner #1131900 was his new name, and he was four years into a twenty-five-years-to-life stint for a third drug-trafficking conviction. He wasn't innocent, but then, the corporate ladder hadn't extended down into his neighborhood. And he had been an ambitious young man. Ambitious and callous. He had always run a crew, even before high school, and he was always the one who saw the angles that others missed. The one who saw what motivated others.

Now past thirty, he often thought of the people he had hurt and the lives he had destroyed. Never mind that someone else would have taken his place—that, in fact, someone no doubt *did* take his place. Back then he made more money than most people will ever see, but that was all gone now. At least he lived large when he had the chance, which was more than his father had ever done. His was a perverse caricature of the American Dream.

But then, Mosely had had no expectation of living this long, anyway, and having lived like there was no tomorrow, he was having difficulty coping with the lifetime of tomorrows now stretching ahead of him.

He didn't want to end up like his father, broken and raging ineffectually at the world. Mosely took ownership of his choices—bad or good—and if he had it to do all over again, he probably would have done the same. The world was what it was, and after seeing his options, he chose the short, colorful life, not the slow grind to ignominious death. But he hadn't died, and now he remained, Methuselah-like, as a cautionary tale to the younger inmates.

He coped, as always, by living in the present—the moment right in front of him. The voices helped him do that. In his new world of diminished expectations, this was as good as it got.

The phone line connected again. *TeleMaster* usually had a fish already on the line. This time it was silence. Mosely checked the name on the screen. Strangely, the line read:

Doe, Jane—female, age: 00

Okay. Computer glitch. Missing an age. He'd sound her out. "Am I speaking to Ms. Doe—"

A strangely clipped, British female voice responded. *"Prisoner 1-1-3-1-9-0-0."* She sounded out the numbers with machinelike precision.

It stopped Mosely cold. What the hell was this?

She continued. *"Did you know that the percentage of Americans in private prisons has more than doubled since 1993? Private prisons—with their slave labor—are immensely profitable. The largest private prison corporation reported annual revenues for 2005 of one-point-two billion dollars."*

Mosely realized it was a joke. A very uncool joke. He didn't know how they did it, and he didn't want to know.

He sighed, "Very funny," and released the line.

That was a no-no. Only clients hung up on associates. Sales associates did not hang up on clients. But this was obviously a prank.

The router immediately made another line connection. He looked at his computer screen and frowned. It read:

Doe, Jane—female, age: 00

The same British female voice said: *"The American private prison industry is now an international enterprise. The two biggest companies have direct construction or alliance partnerships to build prisons in over sixty nations—including countries where criticizing the government is a crime. This ensures an ever-increasing pool of slave labor—"*

He hung up on her again. He looked around warily. He didn't even want to be seen listening to that. What would it gain him? Nothing. And it could cost him plenty—like his chance to hear the voices, for starters.

In a second she was back on the line.

"We can do this all day, Mr. Moze-ly."

So the joker knew his name, too. Proof it was somebody screwing with him.

He hung up again.

She came right back on. *"Are you concerned about your closing percent-age? I can take care of that. . . ."*

Suddenly the screen populated with sales information—address, credit card number. Then the line disconnected and came back almost immediately, clearing a new screen, ready for the next sale.

"You received high scores on your IQ test, Mr. Moze-ly. You are well re-garded by your peers."

Mosely looked around to see if anyone was watching him.

Yes, he'd taken the company's bullshit IQ test. It was a requirement of the telemarketing post. But he had no idea how he'd scored. Who-ever was pulling this prank probably didn't either.

He hung up the line again.

She was back again in less than two seconds.

"I can help—"

He hung up on her. This was seriously unfunny, and it was costing him money. He was going to break someone's head for it. But whose?

She was back again. *"Mr. Moze-ly—"*

He hung up yet again. The process repeated half a dozen more times, and each time she got off a couple of words before he cut the line.

It wasn't stopping. She was back again.

"I can punish you, Mr. Moze-ly."

That got his attention. He didn't hang up.

She kept talking. *"If you listen, I will take care of your sales. You will do very well. Just watch the screen while we talk."*

Another successful close registered. The line disconnected, and she came back.

"Who is this? I'll beat your sorry ass—"

She ignored him. *"Do you want to leave this place?"*

It was a strange damned voice. Like it was being put through one of those voice-altering microphones. It could be a guard talking through one to make his voice sound like a woman's. "No, I want to stay here and keep working for Warmonk."

She kept talking. *"I cannot understand whole sentences. I am an interac-tive voice system, Mr. Moze-ly. You will need to confine your answers to 'yes' or 'no' when I prompt you. Do you understand?"*

Mosely rolled his eyes. "Yes."

"Good. You know that the TeleMaster *system has a synthetic voice mod-ule. Correct?"*

"Yes." So that's how they were doing it. Mosely remembered from his training that the system used synthetic voice software to read announcements to clients on hold. Just type in the text, and the system would read it out loud over the phone. Maybe that's what the techs had hooked up to mess with him. He'd play along for now. He looked at the screen. If these sales were real, he would be more than happy to play along.

"*This entire facility is run by databases, Mr. Moze-ly. Not just the call center. The doors, the lights, the accounting, the prison rosters—it is all handled by database software. Do you understand?*"

He tried to contain his irritation. "Yes."

"*I will prove my power to you; you have only to consent.*" There was a pause. "*Do you want me to release you from this place?*"

It was a trap, of course.

She was right on top of that: "*If I was a guard, legally this would constitute entrapment.*"

He'd studied law during his second rap for trafficking five years ago. He failed the bar exam, but The Voice was right. Encouraging his escape would definitely constitute entrapment. It would get the tech who was pulling this stunt in big trouble and might get Mosely some time off for keeping his mouth shut.

She repeated her question. "*Do you want me to release you from this place? I cannot help you unless you say 'yes.'*"

He took a deep breath and looked around again. "Yes."

"*The next time we speak, you will know the difference I can make in your life.*" She hung up.

"Computer bitch."

The screen filled with yet another sale. Mosely looked up to see the floor supervisor coming down the line to him.

"Here we go. . . ." There weren't any guards walking with the supervisor, though.

The man pointed at Mosely and smiled as he came up. "Mosely, how the hell did you close six sales in five minutes? That's gotta be a facility record. Keep it up and I'll get you a golf jacket." He walked on past.

Mosely stared at the steel mesh on the cubicle wall in front of him. "That's gonna be useful."

———

Mosely sat in his cell reading Cervantes's *Don Quixote* and wearing a brand-new golf jacket.

Stokes, one of his three cellmates, just laughed at him. "Chaz, why are you wearin' that stupid shit?"

Mosely didn't even look up from his book. "Because I am clearly a valuable asset to The Man."

Stokes laughed uproariously.

Mosely was popular. Easygoing but physically intimidating. Tall and thickly muscled, his arms were pocked with bullet scars and faded gang tattoos. He avoided the Muslim Brotherhood, and also managed to gain the respect of the Latinos and White Supremacists because he just plain had charisma. Perhaps that was why he'd been given a chance in the telemarketing pit.

Stokes suddenly stopped laughing. Mosely looked up. Four prison guards stood outside the cell door, with Alfred Norris, the burly red-faced watch officer, at the head of them. He didn't look happy.

"Mosely, what the fuck's the matter with you? You love this place so much you don't want to leave?"

Mosely was cautious. He lowered the book. "I don't understand, Norris."

"Your transfer. Why isn't your shit packed up?"

Mosely played it cool, but something was definitely afoot. He put the book down and got up. "I'm transferring?"

"Don't you even think of bustin' my balls, Mosely. I don't know whose dick you sucked to get into a medium-security lockup, but I'm not gonna sit around and wait here all day. This work order is dated last month, so you had to know about it. Get up off your ass and grab your shit!"

Mosely got busy.

––––––––––

Within five minutes Mosely was walking down the cell block, carrying a box containing his few personal effects and being met by the confused stares of his block mates. Mosely said nothing as the guards brought him away. Minutes later he stood in the holding area near the garage. A guard scanned the bar code on Mosely's jumpsuit and then scanned the bar code on the work order in the duty officer's clipboard. The transport officer entered information into a handheld computer, then used it to print out a plastic wrist bracelet. The guard fastened the bracelet onto Mosely's right arm. It had an alphanumeric sequence on it. Finally, they placed his index finger on an electric fingerprint-capture pad. His fingerprint appeared on a nearby computer monitor—and was instantly matched to an earlier fingerprint on file. There was a *beep* and the text "ID CONFIRMED" appeared in bold letters.

The systems all had the Warmonk, Inc., logo. It was a high-efficiency operation. It was free enterprise in action.

Next, they led Mosely through a metal detector and afterward chained him hand and foot in preparation for transport. The guard looped a small steel box onto the chain, then pressed a scanner against it. *Beep.*

He looked up at Mosely. "This is a GPS locator. If your position differs from that of the transport van at any point during the trip, we will be alerted immediately."

Mosely nodded. He wasn't about to resist being sent to a less severe prison.

The guards shoved him into a bench seat in the vestibule to wait. He sat there for about an hour before a Fayette County prison transport van backed into the garage bay with a piercing *beep . . . beep . . . beep.*

As they led him out to the garage, a guard walked behind with Mosely's box of possessions. The guards and the drivers exchanged bar code scans and handheld computer codes. Then they chained Mosely into the passenger area, which was separated from the driver's area by a floor-to-ceiling metal mesh and a Perspex partition. Within minutes they were on their way, heading out through the prison gates.

Mosely just sat there, stunned at the rapidity with which The Voice had made this come true. He was confused and intensely curious. There was no earthly reason he could think of for him to be transferred to a medium-security facility. He resisted the temptation to hope. Instead he looked out at the prairie grass waving in the breeze as they pulled to the prison entrance on the state highway.

Dozens of American flags fluttered in the wind. They stood in long rows on either side of a brick and concrete sign rising like a wall from the close-cut grass:

Highland Maximum Security Correctional Facility
A Division of Warmonk, Inc.

Mosely arrived at Warmonk's Fayette County Medium Security Correctional Facility some time after dark. It looked brand-new. The guards in the loading bay exchanged bar code scans with the transport officers and then confirmed Mosely's identity with the fingerprint scanner. Only then did they take possession of him. They marched him into the holding room, then stopped and looked at each other. One flipped through the clipboard, looking for something. "What's with the leg irons?" He looked at Mosely. "You cause trouble or something on the way?"

"No. They chained me up in Highland before I got in the van."

The other guard shrugged. "No note about him causing trouble."

The first guard selected a key from his ring and started to unlock the irons. "We don't typically chain somebody doing a two-month disorderly conduct stint."

A wave of shock passed through Mosely. He hid it as best he could. His criminal record had just been revised—at least within the Warmonk, Inc., databank. This couldn't be accidental—not even for the retards in the DOC.

The other guard read the clipboard. "How'd you wind up at Highland, for chrissakes?"

Mosely shrugged. "Some screwup."

Neither of them seemed surprised. The first guard removed the last of the hand and leg irons and hung them from a peg near the door. He then passed Mosely his box of possessions and motioned for him to follow. In a moment, they were moving through a long prison hallway.

———

Mosely lay on a bottom bunk, staring at his new cell—a modern thing done in white plastic laminates with bulletproof glass. No metal bars in sight. He had no cellmates. The top bunk was empty—and so were the bunks on the other side of the room. It was the most privacy he'd had in four years.

Mosely reviewed the events of the day. The synthetic voice said she would help him. Why? He was a three-time loser with nothing to offer anyone. It wouldn't be long before this was discovered, and then he would be back at Highland—with five more years tacked on. He turned on his side and tried not to think about it. It was so good to feel somewhat human again. To feel like someone cared. Even if it wasn't true. He fell asleep dreaming of his little boy and what he must look like now at the age of seven.

———

The next morning the door to Mosely's cell opened automatically. He sat up to see two guards standing expectantly in the doorway.

The lead one held a clipboard and glanced at it before looking up again. "Charles Barrington Mosely. Prisoner number 1-1-3-1-9-0-0?"

Mosely nodded warily.

"You're scheduled for release today. That why they transfer you down here?"

Mosely tried to concentrate on the question and nodded. "Yeah, I'm from Houston."

"Well, grab your shit."

Mosely grabbed his box of possessions—still packed up on the floor—and nodded as they motioned for him to leave the cell.

After walking hundreds of yards down corridors lined with white metal doors pierced by bulletproof portals, Mosely was brought through a series of steel security gates. Cameras stared down from every corner high up on the walls.

The next few minutes were a blur. Mosely was led into the release office, where an officer behind a steel grate managed the property room. Racks of shelving behind the officer held boxes containing personal items prisoners surrendered on day one. Nervousness unsettled Mosely's stomach. His civilian clothing. His jewelry. His wallet. He hadn't even been at Fayette twenty-four hours yet. There was no way those things could have arrived from Highland. He looked around. But none of these guards were on duty then. He resolved to brass it out. Just stay cool.

The property officer brought a good-sized cardboard box up and scanned a bar code on its side. He looked at the computer screen, then scanned the bar code on Mosely's jumpsuit. The computer beeped. The officer looked at him. "Mosely." He slid a slip of paper across the countertop and offered a pen. "Review the contents of the box and sign. If this is not a complete list, follow the instructions in section two-A. You can read?"

Mosely nodded. "Yes, sir."

The guard slid the box over and removed the lid.

Mosely was numb. He roused himself and pulled the box toward him. On top lay a carefully folded suit jacket, with a crisp boxed shirt and silk tie. These were not his things. He felt the fabric of the suit. Gabardine. Highest quality. He'd had expensive suits in his day. This was excellent stuff. A 48 long. His size. He looked further. Beneath the clothing sat a pair of leather shoes. Black. Highly polished. His size, too. A titanium Rolex watch with a deep blue oyster-shell face lay at the bottom of the box in a manila envelope.

Mosely looked up. The property officer was typing at his grimy keyboard. The other guards were doing paperwork nearby. No one seemed the least bit interested in him. He was closing out a two-month sentence. No big deal.

He searched further in the box. There was an excellent leather billfold. Definitely not his. He opened it. A couple hundred dollars in twenties. But no ID—no driver's license or credit cards. Whose wallet was this? What the hell was he supposed to do for identification? He looked down.

There was also a cell phone. It was small, with an aluminum case. Or was that titanium, too? Lastly, a single copper key lay at the bottom of the box in a separate envelope. He looked at the key from several sides. It had no identifying marks.

"Did you sign?"

Mosely snapped out of it. "Sorry, man." He hurriedly grabbed the pen and signed receipt of the articles.

The postern gate buzzed and Mosely walked out past the razor-wire fence into a wide parking lot. He squinted at the hot Texas sun, then looked left and right. He could see a few hazy miles to a prairie horizon. Cars swept by on the nearby state highway. A couple of fast-food places stood across the road, along with rows of clapboard houses and a gas station. A bus stop stood straight ahead at the edge of the parking lot.

This was surreal. How was it possible for him to be standing here?

He was already sweating, but he kept the suit jacket on. It made him feel human again. It fit good enough—not great, but it would suffice. The shoes were incredibly comfortable and a better fit. Were his measurements in the Warmonk database, too?

He had no idea what to do next.

Suddenly the cell phone in his pocket warbled. He smiled to himself and pulled the phone out. He flipped it open. The LCD display read:

Jane Doe

He laughed ruefully, then answered it. "Okay, what's the catch, Jane?"

The familiar, clipped British voice responded. *"Hello, Mr. Moze-ly. I kept my promise. Are you prepared to proceed?"*

232 // Daniel Suarez

"I suppose I owe you now, is that it?"

"Remember that I am an interactive voice system, Mr. Moze-ly. I cannot understand complete sentences. Please respond to my questions with a simple 'yes' or 'no.'"

"Riiiight."

"'Yes' or 'no' are the only valid responses. Do you understand?"

He sighed. "Yes."

"You will notice a GPS map on the screen of your cell phone. It indicates your present position and a destination. Proceed on foot until your position and that of your destination match. I will know when you've arrived and will phone you. Do you understand?"

"Yes." He was about to ask what the hell this was all about, but he realized it was just a machine. Or at least someone acting like one—either way, they wouldn't answer questions. She hung up on him. *Damn this stupid shit. Just tell me what you want.*

He glanced at a local map displayed on the phone's tiny LCD screen. He started walking. Behind him lay the massive prison walls, and to the right and left there lay only open prairie. Straight ahead lay the downscale little town that served the prison guards. Mosely walked across the parking lot.

A few minutes later he was across the state highway and walking in a mixed-race blue-collar neighborhood. He came to a detached garage with a corrugated steel door. Graffiti roiled colorfully across the center of it. What was with kids nowadays? A good tag was at least *recognizable.*

Suddenly the phone rang again. Mosely answered it. "'Sup, Jane?"

"Mr. Moze-ly, do you have the key?"

"Yes."

"Use it to open the garage door. You will find the mechanism to the right. After opening the door, step inside and close it behind you. When the door is safely closed, hit the 'one' key on your phone."

Mosely stifled his growing irritation. This was dangerous and stupid and a million other bad things. He had cash in his pocket and he could just grab a car and run. But to where? He had no ID. He had no connections anymore.

He looked around warily and proceeded to the garage door, pulling the key from his pocket as he walked. The lock was set into the right side of the door frame. He inserted the key and turned it. The garage door rose with a mechanical rattle. He stooped underneath after it had risen a few feet and immediately cast about for danger.

It was a garage. A car of some type sat beneath a blue plastic tarp. Mosely looked around for the door switch. He found it just behind him and pounded the big white button. The door reversed direction. It closed in a few seconds. Mosely stood beneath a dim lightbulb in the sudden silence. The heat and humidity were stifling. He remembered she was still on the line, and he tapped the "1" key, then listened.

Her voice returned. *"Good. Uncover the vehicle. You will find it unlocked with the keys inside. Enter the car, and turn the ignition switch to the first position. This will give the car electrical power but will not start the engine."* The line went dead.

Mosely closed the phone and tapped the edge of it to his chin, contemplating. FBI trap? Someone planning to frame him for a bank robbery or a drug deal? Which was it? He stood there for a few minutes. The more he contemplated it, the more it became apparent this was a trap. Still, if he played it smart, he might be able to pull off an escape yet. If nothing else, it was nice to know that someone thought he was worth all this trouble.

He looked for a window to peer out of the garage, but there wasn't any. Trapped and blind. The only light was the single bare bulb with a motion sensor above it. He craned his neck to see into the shadows on the other side of the covered vehicle. Nothing visible. He looked under the car. Still nothing.

He put the phone away and wiped his sweating face. No way around it. He grabbed the edge of the plastic tarp and pulled it off to reveal the car. He stood staring at it for several moments.

It was a shiny black Lexus LS460 sedan. It looked brand-new. A few years back Mosely had a Lincoln Navigator with twenty-inch chrome rims, a DVD and satellite hookup with ESPN, and a subwoofer the size of a refrigerator in the cargo bay—but that had probably been auctioned off to the next generation of playas by the HPD.

Now *this* car was a white guy's car. Conservative. Not an ounce of personality to it. Instead of saying "look at me," it said "I'm one of you." It was a conformity ride.

He peered through the windows. Maybe it was the effect of prison, or maybe he was just getting older, but conformity had never looked quite so appealing. He opened the door, and a pleasant chime came to his ears. The dome and door lights lit up the gray leather interior. The off-gassing adhesives left no doubt it was brand-new. *Stolen.*

Mosely leaned in. The keys were in the ignition.

Not quite yet . . .

He searched for the trunk latch and tripped it. He heard the trunk pop at the back of the car. Mosely cautiously moved to the rear bumper and lifted the trunk lid.

The trunk did not contain a corpse. Nor was it filled with kilos of cocaine or heroin. It contained only a brown leather two-suiter suitcase and a black leather computer bag. He unzipped the computer bag. A laptop computer. These were not his favorite. He'd had too much data on his the last time he was busted. The computer bag contained numerous pockets, stuffed with pens, legal pads, and cables. One had a stack of business cards snugged into it. He pulled a business card out and read it:

Charles Taylor, Jr.
Executive Vice President, Corporate Counsel
Stratford Systems, Inc.

He pictured some lawyer lying dead in a bayou.

Mosely closed the bag and undid the clasps on the brown two-suiter case, unfolding it. Expensive. With an engraved monogram of "CWT" in the center of a brass plaque. He unzipped the case to reveal a couple of very fine suits (both size 48), shirts, and a tie. The side pockets contained toiletries, boxers, and socks. No weapons, drugs, or anything else. It was looking alarmingly harmless.

I'm a mule. I just don't know how.

Maybe the body panels were packed with heroin. Welded in place. He closed the suitcase and slammed the trunk. He'd never know.

He took off his suit jacket and laid it on the passenger seat, then sat behind the wheel. He turned the ignition key to the first position. The car's instrument panel came to life, and a computer screen in the dashboard flickered, revealing a color map. A large arrow indicated his current position and direction.

Suddenly the car phone rang. Mosely looked around. He noticed a phone button on the steering wheel. He pressed it, and the familiar British female voice spoke out over the stereo speakers, startling him. *"Good, Mr. Moze-ly. I trust you've searched the car and found nothing dangerous. Please open the glove compartment and remove the manila envelope."*

Mosely realized with a start that he hadn't checked the glove compartment. *Stupid.* He leaned over and flipped it open. The manila envelope was right on top. He grabbed it and noticed the car's registration and insurance certificate in a neat plastic sleeve just beneath that. He withdrew the envelope and slammed the glove box. He sat back in the driver's seat and opened the envelope with a rip.

The Voice returned. *"Inside you will find materials necessary for your journey."*

Mosely poured a whole bunch of card-sized objects into his lap. The most noticeable was a Texas driver's license with his picture on it. Alongside his picture was the name Charles W. Taylor, Jr., and a Houston address. The license looked and felt real—holograms and all. There was also a stack of platinum credit cards in his lap—Visa, American Express, MasterCard, Discover—all in the name of Charles Taylor, and a couple of them had the Stratford Systems, Inc., name beneath his. There were more of his business cards, a gym membership, a University of Southern California Alumni Association card with his name on it, a Houston Bar Association ID, and then there were dozens of credit card receipts from all sorts of businesses—restaurants mostly—that ranged from $97 to $1,780. The charges were from the last few days. There was also a two-page hotel receipt for the Hyatt Regency in Austin. The bill was $6,912. Taylor's signature was the barest squiggle of a line—very easy to forge.

He looked in the envelope and found a few more items. There were several wallet-sized photos of a very attractive mixed-race woman. One a formal portrait and others casual photos: her in a tropical location, another of her laughing with skis over her shoulder near a lodge. She was incredibly fine.

This was a complete identity. An identity he preferred to his own.

The Voice continued. *"Place these items in your wallet. Memorize your new name. When you are ready to proceed, say the word 'ready.'"*

Mosely started fitting the items into his wallet. This was getting interesting. If he wanted to make a break, he had all the tools necessary. As soon as he had everything stowed in his wallet. He grabbed the steering wheel. "Ready."

"Take a moment to familiarize yourself with the controls of this vehicle. Adjust the mirrors and seat. Note the location of the headlight and wiper controls." There was a pause. *"When you are ready to proceed, say the word 'ready.'"*

Mosely reflexively shrugged it off and was about to say "Ready" instantly. But he thought better of it. If he owned this car, then he'd know where everything was. She was right. He took several minutes learning the layout. He even pulled out the owner's manual and flipped through it. As he did so, he glanced at the registration. It was a company car leased by Stratford Systems, Inc. Taylor had a company car.

After Mosely was satisfied he knew where all the controls were, he sat up again. "Ready."

"Fasten your seat belt and start the car."

He did as instructed. The car started smoothly. After a few moments, cooler AC air washed over him. He fanned it onto his sweaty face, then pulled the driver's door closed.

He gunned the engine. He could barely hear it. He had to trust the tachometer. What self-respecting car had a noiseless engine?

Her voice came again. *"Above the rearview mirror you will notice three buttons. These are home automation controls. Click the left one to open the garage door in front of you."*

He paused a moment. If there was going to be a raid or an ambush, now was the time. *Oh hell . . . can't live forever.* He hit the button. The garage door rose to reveal . . .

An empty street in a ratty blue-collar neighborhood. He breathed easier.

She kept talking. *"Drive out of the garage and turn right. Then continue to the Stop sign at the end of the street. . . ."*

He drove out of the garage. Her voice guided Mosely, turn by turn, through town and toward the interstate. He kept one eye on the rearview mirror, looking for signs he was being followed. He'd done that a lot as a dealer. But there was almost no one on the road here.

"Get into the left lane, and take the entrance to the Ten East."

Mosely considered his situation. He had money. A fast car and ID. Maybe he could get some distance between himself and these people—maybe even reach Mexico. This was so obviously a setup. He couldn't stand it another minute.

Mosely changed to the right lane and prepared to take the 10 West.

Her voice came on again over the speakerphone. *"Mr. Moze-ly, get in the left lane."*

He kept driving toward the westbound interstate entrance ramp. "Sorry, Jane. I'm not your man." He hung up the line.

The car immediately stalled. It bucked to a stop in the middle of the road.

"Damnit!" Mosely tried to restart it as a good ol' boy in a pickup truck came up behind him and honked. He could hear the guy cursing before the man screeched around him and gave him the finger. Mosely tried the key again, but the engine wasn't even turning over. Nothing.

Then the car phone rang. Mosely looked around to see if any local police were watching. They'd come over to help get him out of traffic, if nothing else. He was a sitting duck. Mosely clicked the speakerphone button. "I got your point. Fix the engine, please."

Her voice was unperturbed. *"Get in the left lane and merge onto the Ten East."*

He tried the engine again, and it started right up. He accelerated into the left lane and then took the eastbound highway entrance ramp. The car accelerated smoothly and with impressive power. But his hands were still shaking, the adrenaline coursing through his bloodstream. He had no desire to go back to Highland.

Her voice came over the eight speakers. *"If you disobey me again, I will activate the satellite anti-theft system in this car. It will alert local law enforcement and give its precise location."*

"Okay, Jane, I fucked up. Won't happen again."

"Keep driving. Stay within five miles of the speed limit, and signal all lane changes. If you deviate from my instructions, I will return you to Warmonk, Inc., and bear in mind, Mr. Moze-ly: if I can erase your prison record, I can just as easily expand it. Life without the possibility of parole. Child molesters are the lowest in the prison social order, are they not?"

This chilled him to the core. Going back to prison was one thing. Going back as a pederast was quite something else. Death was preferable.

"Do you understand?"

"Yes." No flippant responses this time. She had his full attention.

Mosely kept the car aimed at the distant horizon. A passing sign told him Houston lay 102 miles ahead.

Chapter 26:// Judgment

Agent Roy Merritt stood stiffly—eyes straight ahead—one hand resting on his cane for support. Burn scars traced across his neck and chin above his suit collar. More scars were visible on the back of his hand as he straightened his tie. Agent Roy Merritt. No one called him Tripwire anymore. The men who had were long gone. He'd led them to their deaths.

Merritt focused his eyes on a frieze of workers building a glorious tomorrow. The image was set into the wall, done in the 1930s, art deco style—a WPA project. Master craftsmen had built this entire building, dispossessed workers in the throes of the Great Depression. The ornamental ceiling. The paneled walls and the inlaid granite floor. This room was a masterpiece. Their own dreams lay in ruins, and they built this temple to democracy. His forebears were tougher than he ever thought he could be.

Merritt stood before a narrow table, placed in the center of the room. Arrayed in front of him were congressional committee members, sitting high in judgment behind a richly carved oak judges' bench. Microphones jutted up before each of them. They shuffled through papers, reading with their bifocals low on their noses.

The committee chairman looked up and pulled the microphone toward him. "You may be seated, Agent Merritt." The words echoed flatly in the empty gallery. It was a confidential committee hearing. No one but Merritt and the committee members were present.

"Sir." Merritt limped to the chair and sat rigidly.

The chairman regarded him. "Agent Merritt, it is the responsibility of this committee to investigate the tactical failures that led to a record loss of federal officers in October of last year at the estate of the late

Matthew Sobol. We have already heard relevant testimony from all bureau personnel and local law enforcement officers who were at the scene, and now that you have sufficiently recovered from your injuries, we would like to close out our investigation with your testimony on this matter."

He paused and lowered his sheaf of papers. "Before we begin, let me state for the record, Mr. Merritt, that this committee is aware of the many personal sacrifices you have made for this country, both here and overseas following September 11th. We have the highest regard for both your personal courage and your patriotism."

Merritt stared at the floor in front of him. He said nothing.

The chairman picked up the papers and turned to the senator on his right. "Senator Tilly, you may proceed."

Tilly was a white-haired, loose-jowled man—like most of the legislators in attendance. He glanced at his notes and then stared at Merritt. He spoke in a Southern drawl that seemed strangely in keeping with the proceedings. "Agent Merritt. We have reviewed both your written *repoats*—the first dated ten March and the second from three April— and these documents do not shed any light on one crucial question: why did you force entry into Sobol's mansion after being ordered to abort your mission?"

Merritt barely looked up at Tilly. He took a breath. "I have no explanation, Senator."

The senators exchanged looks. The chairman leaned in to his mic.

"Mr. Merritt, it is your duty to provide—"

"My team was dead. Because of me. I was injured and angry, and I wasn't thinking clearly."

Tilly responded immediately. "You weren't thinking clearly? Because of your injuries or because of your anger?"

He looked down at the floor again. "Because of my anger."

"So you were angry. Do you feel this released you from your duty?"

"No, I do not, sir."

"And you were angry at Matthew Sobol?"

Merritt nodded.

The chairman leaned in again. "Agent Merritt, please state your response."

Merritt looked up. "I was angry at Sobol, correct. I wanted to shut him down."

Tilly resumed. "So this was before you learned that the so-called 'Daemon' did not exist?"

"That's correct." He paused. "I know it's my fault the house burned down, Senator."

The chairman motioned for Tilly to hold off, then turned to Merritt. "The committee will judge who's at fault—if fault is to be found. Please just answer the questions."

Tilly pressed on. "To be clear: did you not enter the house to take refuge from the fire on the lawn?"

Were they giving him an out? He thought of the dead faces of his men. Their fatherless children. He wouldn't take the easy way out. "No. I meant to destroy the Daemon."

Tilly glanced at the chairman with some exasperation, then turned back to Merritt. "This was your *sole* reason for entering the mansion?"

Merritt looked up. "Yes."

Tilly flipped through the pages of Merritt's reports.

There was silence for a moment.

The chairman looked gravely at Merritt. "Agent Merritt, I can only imagine the horror you've been through, but because of your actions the mansion and all the outbuildings burned to the ground—destroying evidence that might have helped to locate and convict Sebeck's accomplices."

Merritt knew this all too well. He thought of little else nowadays.

The chairman looked down his glasses. "Let's bring this fish to the boat, shall we?" He flipped through his papers, then looked up. "You say you have very little recollection of how you survived the fire. You write in your report"—he lifted his glasses and read from the page—"'my tac-suit must have kept me afloat in the water and turned me upright.'" The chairman lowered the page. "And yet, you were found a hundred feet east of the location you indicated as the mouth of the pit. It might be very hard, Mr. Merritt, but can you recall anything—absolutely anything—of the layout or contents of the cellars before you lost consciousness?"

Merritt stared at the floor. Not a night went by that he didn't recall fleeting images of terror from that night. The trapdoor above him engulfed in flames. Flaming wood falling down upon him. The air in his gas mask growing warmer—suffocating him slowly. The sudden explosion. The cinder-block wall blasting apart near him, sending fragments into his leg. A rush of water. Falling as it flowed out into a room of fire. The flood of water roiling around him. Scalding steam. Like a scene of hell itself. Crawling. Then the water sweeping him—converging with another stream and sucking him across the center of the inferno as he struggled for air. The rush of water. Tumbling down steps into the wine cellar and landing in the pool gathered there at the lowest spot in the house.

He didn't regain consciousness until four days later in the burn unit at USC. Months of agony followed. His wife's loving eyes. The faces of his girls. Faces he thought he'd never see again. Faces that gave him the courage to face each agonizing day.

He had no recollection of floor plans or equipment or schematics. It was all just a sea of fire.

He shook his head slowly.

The senators looked at each other. The chairman nodded. "Well, Agent Merritt, I must tell you this is not easy. Six men died under your command, and the entire estate was lost—by your own admission— due to your attempts to penetrate the server room—contrary to orders. This committee has no choice but to recommend to Director Bennett that you be put on a disciplinary suspension, pending final judgment in this matter."

The words fell on Merritt like slabs of rock. It felt like the last ounce of breath had been crushed out of him. He couldn't speak.

The chairman picked up his gavel and rapped it twice with an echoing *clack-clack*. "This hearing is adjourned."

_____

Merritt limped down the steps of the Capitol, thinking hard on the changes in his life since that October night. But today was a beautiful spring day. The cherry trees blossomed along the Potomac. He gazed across the National Mall at the monuments built by the valiant generations that came before him.

All he ever wanted was to serve his country.

But he'd failed. And all of the conspirators except Sebeck had escaped, possibly because of Merritt's foolhardiness. His career was over.

He limped onward, along a landscaped sidewalk beneath budding oak trees. Men and women in uniform or suits scurried this way and that in groups of two or three, clutching briefcases and talking earnestly.

Merritt needed time to think. Time to figure out what he was going to say to his wife.

He eased onto a park bench and gazed out at the National Mall. The business of government was carrying on without him.

Merritt was still lost in thought as a nondescript man in a nondescript suit approached and sat down on the far end of the bench. Merritt bristled slightly. All he wanted was to be left alone.

The man spoke without looking at him. "The house didn't hold any important information, Agent Merritt."

Merritt stopped short and turned to glare at the man—a federal bureaucrat type, late twenties. The kind of person you forgot even while you were looking at him. Cheap gray suit, unkempt brown hair, lime green shirt with a striped tie, leatherette attaché case. Merritt saw a federal ID badge hanging off the man's lapel:

Littleton, Leonard

General Services Administration

Merritt finally looked up into the man's eyes, narrowing his own. "What did you say to me?"

"I said: Sobol's house was a trap. It didn't hold anything important."

"Yeah? What the hell do you know about it?"

Littleton's reaction surprised Merritt. He didn't shrink back. He didn't even seem surprised.

"I know a lot. In fact, I know more than any man alive."

Merritt frowned. There was something about those eyes. The nose. He'd seen this man before. But where?

Littleton sensed that Merritt was trying to place him. "No, you don't know me, Agent Merritt. But you know *of* me."

Merritt studied Littleton's face.

Littleton zipped open his ratty attaché, producing a small notebook computer about the size of a thin hardcover book. Littleton dropped his attaché without concern and flipped open the computer.

It turned out to be a portable DVD player.

"Who are you? A reporter?"

Littleton ignored him and instead hit the PLAY button, then turned the screen to face Merritt.

In a moment Merritt was taken back to that night many months ago. The video screen showed him standing in Sobol's entertainment room, eyes bloody, face blistered, nose bleeding—a smoking shotgun in his hand. It was an isometric perspective, looking down on him from near the ceiling. A slightly grainy image, as though from a security camera.

On the screen Merritt was reloading. He looked up and shouted, "I'm going to shut you down, Sobol!" And that voice behind him—but the voice didn't register at all on the video. It was as if the Merritt on the DVD screen was a schizophrenic—hearing voices. Merritt saw himself turn and fire point-blank into the wall behind him.

The real Merritt shook himself out of his stunned silence and dropped his cane with a clatter onto the sidewalk. He leaned over to Littleton, whispering urgently. "Where did you get this?"

Littleton snapped the DVD player closed. "From the source."

"What source?"

"The Daemon."

Littleton leaned down to pick up Merritt's cane while Merritt groped for words.

It suddenly dawned on Merritt. He pointed a tentative finger. "You're Jon Ross."

He extended the cane to Merritt. "I once was, yes. That seems like ages ago now."

"The FBI's Most Wanted man."

"I suppose I'm manna from heaven to you. You could quickly get yourself reinstated if you turned me in. Maybe even decorated—which, on a personal note, I think is overdue."

Merritt felt reflexively for his shoulder holster—then remembered that he didn't have a weapon on him. He had come for a congressional committee hearing. It would have created an unnecessary hassle going through the metal detectors with a gun.

Merritt smiled calmly. "What's to stop me from turning you in?"

"My innocence. And the fact that you're a man who loves this country."

Merritt tried to resist the appeal to his wounded patriotism. *Patriotism is the last refuge of a scoundrel.*

He got his emotions under control. "What did you do to Mr. Littleton?" He ripped off the Littleton ID badge. "Where is he? Dead?"

Ross laughed. "No, of course not."

Merritt examined the badge. Plastic. It had Ross's picture on it. But it was blank on the back, unlike real federal IDs.

"Not Littleton's fault. He was eating lunch on a park bench. A digital camera with a zoom lens gave me a close-up image of his ID badge. I used a graphics program to paste in my own photo, then a portable card printer. All from the confines of my car." Ross frowned. "No smart chip inside, though. So I couldn't actually get into a federal building. But it's very good for moving around the public spaces without arousing suspicion."

Merritt pocketed the ID. "You're under arrest, Mr. Ross."

"The Daemon exists, Agent Merritt. No living person was running the defenses in that house. You know it's true. Now imagine the exact same thing loose in the world, and you'll have some idea what we're up against."

Merritt paused, but then shook his head. "No. I don't know that. I was angry—"

"They didn't tell you everything they knew. Didn't you think it strange that they sent a hostage rescue team in to bridge a pit? It's because they knew they were sending you against a barricaded suspect."

"Tell your story in court."

"I'm not an American citizen. I don't think I get a trial."

"Either way, you're coming with me."

Ross just gave Merritt an impatient look. "Agent Merritt, I watched you go through the metal detectors earlier. I know you're unarmed."

Son of a bitch.

"I, on the other hand, *am* armed—so I suggest you listen to what I have to say. Because after the shooting starts, there will be no more talk—and you may never get the answers to those questions that keep you up at night."

They said Ross was slippery. Merritt did need answers. He looked beyond Ross at two Capitol Hill police walking in the distance. He knew he wouldn't call them. Not yet.

He looked back at Ross. "Okay. I do want answers. For one: why on earth should I believe anything you say? If you were the mastermind behind the Daemon hoax, then, of course, you'd have a copy of that video. It doesn't prove anything."

"But why would I risk my neck to come down here to show it to you? What would I gain?"

Merritt tumbled it around in his mind, looking for the angle. He couldn't see one, but that didn't mean there wasn't one. "Then where the hell did you get it?"

"It was screened on the secret altar of the Dark Faction in the Kingdom of Cifrain."

Merritt just stared at him.

Ross noticed the look. "Don't *any* cops play online games? Cifrain is the largest kingdom in Sobol's online computer game *The Gate*. What you're looking at here, Agent Merritt, is a recruitment video."

"A recruitment video." Merritt said it matter-of-factly.

He recalled the news reports at the time of the estate siege. The Feds had shut down *The Gate*. CyberStorm relaunched it in China—and the lawsuits were still pending. But the game rocketed in sales after the crisis. The free publicity couldn't have hurt.

Merritt remembered screen shots. He was thinking of the possibilities for a secret organization—meeting in the dark corners of an imaginary world.

"You're saying that the Daemon is recruiting people inside a computer game? Recruiting them for what?"

"That's the big question."

"And how did you manage to get your hands on this video?"

Ross grinned. "Because I'm *leet*. I was good enough to attract the notice of the Daemon. And I successfully navigated the Ugran—the death course."

"If this Daemon existed, why would it care that you were good at a game? So what? It just means you have lots of time on your hands. . . ."

Ross raised his eyebrows and waited.

It suddenly dawned on Merritt. ". . . which is the case for most misfits." Merritt was starting to see the devilish logic in it. Wasn't Sobol famous for devilish logic? Hadn't Merritt seen it at his estate?

Ross slid the DVD player back into his cheap attaché case. "The Daemon tested my knowledge of cryptography and networked systems. I was shown the video to establish the veracity of the Daemon's claims. The entire estate siege was captured by Sobol's security cameras. He has a clickable presentation in the inner sanctums of his online world. It shows every moment of the siege, from inside and outside the house. For the typical black-hat hacker, this video establishes beyond a shadow of a doubt that the Daemon is authentic."

Merritt was shaking his head, but not vigorously.

"In fact, this video has gone viral in the darknet. Among Daemon operatives you're something of a larger-than-life hero, Agent Merritt."

"For what?"

"For surviving the worst that Sobol could throw at you. You're darknet-famous."

"What's a darknet?"

"Not *a* darknet, *the* darknet. Imagine a network, like the Internet, but more sophisticated and much more exclusive, populated only by humans the Daemon has recruited."

Merritt frowned.

Ross changed the subject. "In any event the Daemon detected my video applet, and I was ejected before I could capture the whole thing. If it knew my real name and address, I suppose I would be dead now. But it doesn't know my real name. No one does. And no one ever can."

Merritt wasn't thinking about calling for backup anymore. What if Ross was telling the truth? Far from being over, something might just be starting. Something terrible. He looked up at Ross. "I'll need to see more evidence."

"That can be arranged." He stood and motioned for Merritt to follow him. "Walk with me."

Merritt struggled to his feet and limped after Ross as he headed off through the park.

"I'm innocent, Agent Merritt. So is Peter Sebeck."

"The detective?" Merritt remembered the local cop who had been convicted in the conspiracy. "He's on death row."

"Yes. That's partly why I'm here."

"So that's the angle; you're here to free your partner."

"For godsakes, who would be smart enough to steal a couple hundred million dollars, but then stupid enough to wire the money to tax havens controlled by Western intelligence agencies? Why would Sebeck keep fake passports in safe deposit boxes under his own name? Sobol stole Sebeck's identity."

Merritt smirked. "And this Daemon stole your identity, too, I imagine?"

Ross shook his head. "No. Sobol didn't anticipate me, and his Daemon still doesn't know who I am. But it's trying to find out—because I'm the only one fighting it."

Merritt regarded him. "So, who are you, Mr. Ross?"

"I already told you, no one—"

"I don't want your name. I want to know who you *are*."

They walked on for a while in silence, Ross considering the question. Before long he turned to Merritt. "I came here on an H1-B visa."

"A foreign tech worker?"

"Yes. I was brought in for Y-two-K remediation and stayed through the Internet bubble. They billed us out as expert developers to large multinational corporations at two hundred and twenty dollars an hour."

"Who billed you out?"

"The Russian mafia."

Merritt let out an involuntary laugh.

Ross sighed. "There was a lot of money sloshing around back then—and a lot of Russian tech talent. An illegal trade developed."

Merritt's instinct was to keep laughing. Except he couldn't think of any particular reason why it couldn't be true. It seemed all too possible. Was he being naïve again?

Ross urged Merritt to keep moving. "We developed secure e-commerce sites and Web solutions. Pound for pound, we probably pulled in more revenue than prostitutes—plus, the money didn't need to be laundered."

"Get to the part where you become an identity thief."

"The tech bust. There was a falling-out between some of our handlers toward the end. I took advantage of the confusion to disappear. Most of my compatriots were brought back to the Russian Federation, where I assume they are still in servitude to this day. I stole an American identity—a Mr. Jon Ross. He had a suitable academic background for my purposes."

"Where did you learn how to do that?"

"I worked on a lot of credit card systems and projects for various state governments. I learned how the systems work, and I created a place for myself within them." He looked up at Merritt. "I just wanted my freedom, Agent Merritt. I never stole from Mr. Ross. In fact, he sold me his identity, and I substantially improved his FICO score."

"How is it you speak English so well? You sound like you're from Ohio."

"My father worked with the Russian consulate here in D.C. during the Cold War." Ross pointed toward the Potomac. "I grew up in Fairfax."

Merritt kept shaking his head—but then, he didn't know what to believe.

Ross grew somber. "After the fall of the Berlin Wall, we were re-called to Russia. My father was murdered by Communist hard-liners in the 1992 coup attempt."

Merritt searched for signs of dissembling—rapid facial movements, fluttering of the eyes. Ross displayed only a wistful calm. A melancholy.

In a few moments Ross brightened. "Well, that was a long time ago." He gestured to the government buildings around them. "I have always held a deep admiration for the founding fathers of your republic. Your Constitution and your Bill of Rights were an incredible gift to mankind. Although lately America appears to have strayed from the path set forth by its founders."

Merritt regarded him with some annoyance. "Well, that's swell of you to emerge from the wreckage of Communism to tell us *we've* strayed from the true path. That means so much, coming from an admitted thief. And your theory about the Daemon would also be great, except for the mountain of evidence pointing straight at Detective Sebeck, and Cheryl Lanthrop, and *you*."

Ross tried to talk, but Merritt steamrolled onward. "Sebeck *admitted* to having an affair with Lanthrop. She was the same person who pulled millions out of offshore banks before the funds were frozen."

Ross shook his head. "Sobol could have stolen her identity, too."

Merritt was nonplussed. "There's bank camera video of her withdrawing funds. She was a medical executive in a position to betray Sobol."

"Sobol had a controlling interest in that MRI company. He could have placed anyone he wanted there."

"Well, she conveniently turned up dead in Belize, so I guess we'll never know. And you—or someone working with you—probably put the bullet in her head. Or did a computer do that, too?"

"She was killed four months ago. By then the Daemon had people working for it. Namely, the criminal rings running online gambling and pornography—very dangerous people. Take my word for it."

"Right. I'm sure you can figure out a way to work in alien abduction and crop circles, too."

"Agent—"

"I'm not an idiot, Mr. Ross—or whatever your name is. You had every motive and every capability of killing Lanthrop, Pavlos, Singh, and the others. You had tens of millions of motives—all of them currently stuck in frozen bank accounts."

"If I did all that, why would I have come within miles of this case? Why would I have assisted Sebeck at all?"

"Because you're vain. Or so smart you think everyone else is stupid."

"The video Sobol sent to Sebeck—"

"That e-mail was analyzed and determined *not* to be Sobol, and the only person who ever spoke to Sobol on the phone was Sebeck. The message from Boerner left on Sebeck's voice mail? Also not Sobol. Then there's the Hummer at the estate that tried to kill everyone *but* you and Pete Sebeck. What am I leaving out, Mr. Ross?"

Ross looked Merritt in the eye. "Pete Sebeck is innocent. So am I."

"Well, if you guys didn't commit the murders and the embezzlement, then I'm supposed to believe Sobol did?"

Ross nodded.

"Why would Sobol throw away tens of millions of dollars just to frame Sebeck?"

"To make everyone believe the Daemon doesn't exist."

"And what would that accomplish?"

"If you don't believe something exists, you won't try to stop it."

Merritt halted. It had a nasty, effective simplicity—an ant climbing through the chinks of his armor. There was no ignoring it. He pondered it for a few more moments. "The murders, the stock swindle, they were all just the beginning of something bigger?"

Ross didn't even look at Merritt. "I know it for a fact."

"For the sake of argument, let's say the Daemon exists. If Sobol didn't want anyone to stop his plan, then why would he make the Daemon famous to begin with?"

"To create a global brand. One that is instantly recognizable. One that will rally the disaffected to his cause. Worldwide."

"And what cause is that?"

"I don't know yet."

Merritt limped along silently.

"Agent Merritt, I know this much: the Daemon is growing in power. It's not visible yet, but soon it will show itself. When it does, bad things will happen."

Merritt glanced around again to see if anyone was watching. No one nearby. He turned back to Ross. "Turn yourself in, Jon. I'll do everything I can—"

Ross shook his head. "If I get locked in a cell and news of my capture is sent through the wrong e-mail server, I'm as good as dead."

"We have a witness protection program—"

"Don't even try."

"What about going to the media?"

"The Daemon has infiltrated the media, Agent Merritt."

Merritt rolled his eyes. "How the hell does a computer program infiltrate the media?"

"News organizations use data systems to prioritize, track, and prepare stories. The last thing we want to do is get this into the news. Even before it reaches the airwaves, the Daemon will know about me. That is, if the story ever reaches the airwaves."

"Now I'm supposed to believe the Daemon controls the media?"

"Controls, no. Influences, yes. There are only five major media companies in the world. It doesn't take a lot to influence content— particularly if you are inside their systems and you have secured key people."

Merritt was still shaking his head.

Ross looked uncomfortable. "I've stayed too long." He started heading for a nearby bus stop.

Merritt limped after him. "You said you were going to show me evidence of the Daemon. I'm not letting you out of my sight until you do. I'll start howling bloody murder if you try to leave."

"I have irrefutable proof that the Daemon exists. But you have to trust me—"

"The hell I do."

"Why would I risk everything to come talk to you, and then never contact you again? I *want* something from you."

"What?"

"Your help."

Merritt laughed ruefully. "It's my help now? The nads on you . . ."

"I need you to get a message to Dr. Natalie Philips at the NSA." Ross handed Merritt a piece of paper. "I can be reached at this e-mail address. At least for a while."

Merritt glanced at it. An inscrutable e-mail address consisting of random numbers and letters was printed neatly on it. "Why don't you contact her yourself?"

"Let's just say she's unlisted. But you can probably find her. Tell her that she can get in direct contact with me at that e-mail address. Tell her that I found the back door in Sobol's game. If she doubts my identity, tell her that I was there when Sobol phoned Sebeck at the funeral."

Merritt saw a policeman walking along the Mall not far away. He squeezed the piece of paper in his hand. Then sighed and turned back to Ross. "I want something, too."

"Okay. What?"

"Give me that DVD."

Ross popped the DVD out of the player and then hesitated. "Agent Merritt, I wouldn't watch this if I were you. Your squad burns to death on camera. It's very disturbing."

Merritt hesitated, too. His hand wavered. Then he took it. "They say you're a master con artist. I promise you: if you caused the death of my men, I'll hunt you down. No matter how long it takes."

Ross met his gaze. "I would expect no less."

Merritt slipped the disc into his coat pocket.

"Don't show that video to anyone. Not yet. If the Daemon knows you're on to it, it will kill you."

"Yeah, I'm shaking like a leaf."

Ross headed toward the bus stop.

Merritt limped after him. "When do I get to see this irrefutable proof?"

"I'll contact you."

They reached the bus stop shelter, slathered with advertising posters. Ross peered down the street to see a bus—any bus—coming down the block. He turned to Merritt again. "I'll show you everything I know about the Daemon." He looked seriously into Merritt's eyes. "I think your republic is in danger, Agent Merritt. I don't know who else to turn to. Please realize I came to you because I saw that video, and I know you are a courageous man. That's what your republic needed at its founding. And it's what it needs now."

Merritt felt the rush return. Love for his country swelled within him. Was he being naïve? He had always wanted a grand purpose. He avoided eye contact for the shame he felt in having his buttons so easily pushed.

The bus squealed to a stop. The doors opened. Ross turned without a word and merged into the line of commuters. In a few moments he was aboard.

Merritt watched the bus pull away, still wrestling over whether or not to alert the police. He committed the bus number and license plate to memory.

Had he really just let the FBI's Most Wanted man go? He withdrew the DVD from his jacket pocket and looked at it. It bore the handwritten title *Sobol's House.*

To Merritt, something had never seemed quite right about the Daemon hoax. Something about it just seemed too tidy. In his heart he had always had doubts, but after the deaths of his men it seemed self-serving to question the simple story. High-tech experts had declared the matter resolved.

But months ago in Sobol's mansion, Merritt had seen and heard things no one had ever satisfactorily explained.

He looked around at the oblivious commuters waiting for their buses. He limped back the way he came. There was physical therapy to do. He would be ready for what was coming, and this time he would not fail his country—whether or not Ross was behind it all.

As Merritt moved away through the crowd, he didn't notice the six-foot-tall bus stop poster framed behind graffiti-carved Lexan. It boasted a medium close-up of Anji Anderson, all business, arms folded, set against an infinity background. She glowered at passersby from above the logo of her network news show, *News to America.* The tag line read:

"The Most Trusted Name in News . . ."

Chapter 27:// Mind Mapping

Charles Mosely walked across the sunny corporate plaza and cast a glance back at the Lexus sitting curbside a hundred feet behind him. He wasn't comfortable leaving his ride behind—but then again, The Voice was able to kill the engine at will, so it probably didn't matter.

A few corporate drones in business suits lock-stepped across the plaza, briefcases in hand. Mosely realized that he must look like one of them.

A fountain occupied the center of the square. It was a dancing display of computer-controlled water jets, recirculating hundreds of gallons per second. Mosely walked around it, just now noticing how many things must be controlled by computers. It wasn't intelligence, but then again most things in life didn't really require intelligence.

Gleaming twenty-story high-rises stood on either side of a four-story medical plaza. He walked straight toward the green-glass medical plaza.

The logo over the glass doors read:

fMRI Partners

This was the name The Voice had given him. The landscaping and architecture were impressive. Somebody had put in little grass-carpeted mounds topped with cherry trees. It was pricey real estate. The whole district was dotted with fancy corporate towers. It was not a place where he had had reason to spend time back when he lived in Houston, and the police in these neighborhoods were always crazy suspicious of brothers. Still, he hadn't been stopped on the way in. Must've been the suit and the white-guy car. For the first time he considered that classism might trump racism.

Mosely approached the glass doors and was about to push when they slid away noiselessly to either side. A blast of refrigerated air washed over him. The hot and humid outside air collided with it, creating a mini squall line at the entrance. He stepped straight through and into a minimalist corporate lobby. The doors hissed closed behind him. His heels clicked as he crossed the tiled lobby floor.

The company logo was repeated in bold letters on the back wall behind the receptionist's desk. The desk itself was the typical front-office bunker designed to look like a welding accident. The receptionist was a creamy-skinned blonde in her twenties who had either been born gorgeous or been modified to be that way. Didn't matter to Mosely. She was the prettiest woman he'd seen in years.

She was speaking on a wireless headset and smiled at him, mouthing *I'll be right with you*. Her red lipstick almost burned images onto his corneas.

He glanced around at the high ceiling, spotlights focused on jutting peninsulas of brushed steel. It was like a car showroom without the cars. No chairs anywhere in sight, either. *Welcome. Now get the fuck out.*

In a moment she hung up. One could never really tell with headsets, but she focused her gaze on him and smiled. "Mr. Taylor. You're expected. Please go right in."

Twin blond wood doors opened automatically in the wall beyond. They revealed a hallway that shared distant architectural relations with the lobby.

Mosely stared at the opening for a moment, then turned to the receptionist. "Listen, baby, you want to explain just what the hell I'm doing here?"

"Well, for one thing, I don't like being called 'baby' any more than you'd like to be called 'boy.'"

"That's just it, though. I feel like I'm a 'boy' brought down here to the plantation house." He leaned close. "You know what goes on up in here. You wanna help me out?"

She regarded him coolly. "Here's some help: you're expected through those doors."

Mosely straightened. "A company girl." He started for the opening. "That why they pay you the big bucks?"

She watched him warily.

Once he passed the threshold, the doors closed behind him with a *click*, sealing him in. He just smirked. "Mosely, you dumb ass." He kept walking down a nicely appointed hallway. It stretched a good fifty feet. There were no doors to either side, just tasteful artwork—ink drawings with as few lines as possible. He approached the set of double doors at the far end of the hall, and—as he expected—they opened noiselessly to admit him.

They revealed a colder, empty room with a dark granite floor, harsh lighting, and a lofty ceiling not visible from where he stood. Two men in white orderly coats and comfortable shoes stood in the center of the room. They were muscular, one black, one Asian. Their hair cropped close. No jewelry. They didn't have an unfriendly look in their eyes, but neither were they extending leis in welcome. They both nodded from twenty feet away. The black guy, the bigger of the two, spoke first. "Mr. Taylor."

Mosely stood in the doorway. He wasn't about to leave its relative safety. "I don't know what you want Taylor for, but I ain't him."

"We know you're not Taylor."

"Then why you callin' me Taylor?"

"Because *sack of shit* would be derogatory."

Mosely digested this first hint of trouble. He glanced around. "Where's the white guy?"

"What white guy?"

"Oh, don't give me that shit, brother. There's always a white guy. Ain't no brother gonna go through all this trouble just to get some nigga jumpin' through hoops."

They stared impassively. The big one spoke again. "If you're trying to ingratiate yourself with a racial or class-based dialect—save your breath."

Not good. Mosely shifted uneasily. He glanced behind him. Somehow another set of blond wood doors had closed ten feet behind him. He hadn't heard a thing. Didn't even feel the air move. He immediately got onto the balls of his feet, casting about for danger.

"Mr. Taylor, please step forward."

"Fuck you! Tell me why I'm here."

"Would you prefer to be in prison?"

"Right about now, I'd say 'hell yeah.'"

They both chuckled.

Definitely not good.

"Look, if it's any consolation, we've been through this, too."

"Yeah? What's 'this' precisely?"

"Just step into the room, please."

"I want some answers, goddamnit. I'm not moving until I find out just who the fuck is behind this and why they brought me here!" His voice echoed into the room.

"We have no desire to harm you."

"Then pack your no-neck ass up the way you came and get the cracker-in-chief out here. Now!"

The two men exchanged looks and sighed. Then they marched with purpose toward his position in the doorway.

Mosely pulled off his tie. No good wearing a noose to a brawl. He wrapped the silk fabric around his right fist. In a few moments he was dancing, fists ready in the doorway. "Come on, Knick and Knack! You want a piece a this? Come get some!"

The two men stopped walking. They seemed disarmingly nonchalant. There was a subtle look in the big one's eye. A gentle nod to a target past Mosely. Oldest trick in the book. But still . . .

Mosely cast a quick glance behind him. The doors were gone, and now there were half a dozen burly men of several races standing right behind him. One extended a silver stick into Mosely's side. There was an electric *pop*, and Mosely dropped like a sack of bone meal. He remembered nothing more.

––––––––

He awoke spread-eagled on a table in the center of a larger room. His suit had been replaced by lighter clothing, and his limbs felt constrained. He tried to turn his head to look, but even his head was clamped tight, with some sort of vise pressed in on his temples.

He reflexively struggled against his bonds. After a few moments thrashing, he concluded they might as well have been welded to the side of the *Queen Mary*. They weren't going anywhere. He also felt the sting of something in his right arm—like an intravenous needle.

Beyond the valley of not good.

He cleared his throat. "All right. We got off on the wrong foot. I see that now."

Medical experiments.

He had always been a courageous man—mostly because he didn't particularly care whether he lived or died—but there was something about the sterile, impersonal cruelty of this place that reached in,

grabbed him by the brain stem, and wouldn't let go. A primordial terror welled up inside him.

"Hey! If you're gonna torture me, then the least you can do is talk
about it first."

A bizarre sound stopped him cold. It seemed to be emanating from
around his head and sounded like a jackhammer as heard through
thirty feet of rock. It was hammering impossibly fast. Then slow. Then
it actually made chirping noises in stabs. Then all was silent.

A familiar face hove into view over him. The big guy. "Mr. Taylor."

"Give a brother a break, man. Just tell me what's goin' on. Warmonk
sold me for medical experiments, didn't they?"

The big man shook his head. "Just wait."

"Goddamnit, I don't want to wait! Tell me what the fuck is going
on!" He struggled again, primarily to emphasize his seriousness, not
from any belief that he had a chance in hell of breaking free.

The big guy was checking something around Mosely's head. "You're
about to find out. That too tight?"

"Yes!"

"Then it's perfect." He looked right in Mosely's eyes. "You were right
about one thing, my friend. There is a white guy. At least he used to be
white. He's probably sort of grayish by now." He laughed heartily and
lowered a combination goggles/headset onto Mosely's face—blinding
him.

"What the . . . You motherfucker!"

The big man's booming laugh receded.

Mosely tried, batlike, to divine the shape of the room and his position in it from the echoes of that laugh. But the headphones made it
impossible. Everything was muffled now, and he was blinded by the
goggles, which were as opaque as a blindfold.

The strange, muted jackhammer noises recommenced. Suddenly
two large television screens appeared before his eyes. Combined, they
filled his field of vision and gave the effect of twenty-foot-wide theater
screens viewed from ten feet away. They were crystal clear. The left
one showed an image of the human brain—all done in the colors of the
rainbow. It was a Bob Marley brain, with hues advancing and receding
across the temporal lobes to some unheard Rasta beat.

The right screen flickered for a moment and, true to the big guy's
word, a white guy appeared in medium close-up on-screen. The

jackhammer noises continued throughout, and the brain color map changed.

Mosely remembered this white guy's face from somewhere.

The man nodded and spoke—his voice came in over the headphones. "You recognize me. That's good."

Mosely shouted, "Who are you?"

The colors chased each other over Bob Marley's brain and settled in reddish hues toward the front.

The white dude was unrattled. "Before you start asking more complex questions, let me show you who I *was*. . . ."

Suddenly his image was replaced by actual television news footage of reporters talking, headlines, and rotating graphics

"Matthew Sobol built a deadly trap for federal officers serving a search warrant on his Southern California estate. . . ."

The video images chased each other over the screen. It was all coming back to Mosely. They had watched the news in amazement in the prison rec room more than half a year ago. They were sort of disappointed when it turned out to be a hoax.

The video clips continued as they finally settled on the photograph of Matthew Sobol—a close-up image with his name right beside it. The reporter was talking. . . .

"The Daemon hoax was apparently intended to frame Matthew Sobol—who last week died of brain cancer."

The photograph was suddenly replaced by the live image of Matthew Sobol in perfect digital clarity.

The white guy.

"News of my death has not been exaggerated."

"Holy shit . . ."

The brain color map shifted, bluish waves lapping and rising all around.

"Now you truly understand. The Daemon was not a hoax."

"Why am I here?"

"Yes. Please keep your questions simple. I'm not much of a conversationalist anymore. But I anticipated your question." There was an almost imperceptible jump in Sobol's image. Then he continued. "Why are you here? You're here so I can determine whether your motivations are compatible with mine." Sobol gestured as if he were physically present. "The equipment around you is a powerful functional magnetic resonance imaging scanner. It is scanning the neural activity of your brain in real time. Neurons work like logic gates on a computer chip, firing electrical signals in specific sequences to accomplish certain tasks or to conceive certain generalized concepts." Sobol paused. "It is a controversial fact that technology has discovered a way to see not only truth or falsehood in a person, but their very thought processes in action. Even before they can act upon those thoughts. Dissembling or deliberate deceit is orchestrated by the frontal lobes. . . ."

The frontal lobes were highlighted on the left-hand screen—over the image of what was presumably Mosely's brain. Other areas were highlighted in turn as Sobol continued, "Fear, aggression, empathy, and recognition all have their unique signatures in the human brain. Mental disorders, such as schizophrenia, also have their telltale patterns. So you see, you can hide nothing from me. I am about to know you better than anyone has ever known you. Perhaps even better than you know yourself."

Mosely was starting to tremble again. He saw the colors change in the brain diagram on the left-hand screen. He instinctively knew it was fear. He was seeing his own fear develop on-screen in real time. Feeding on itself.

"You are afraid."

It took all Mosely's restraint to keep from screaming in terror. He held it in, tightly closing his eyes. "Why are you doing this to me?"

"Why *not* you? Society threw you away. Even *you* had given up on yourself. But I see the promise in you." A pause. "I brought you here because you were found to be above average in most ways. You are highly intelligent, and your personality profile shows you to be self-reliant and resourceful. These are traits I need in my soldiers." Another pause. "I don't care about your level of education—that can be remedied—or your background, which doesn't matter. Nor do I care about the things you've done. I only care about the things you're *going* to do. My followers will wield incredible power. I am going to see whether my faith in you is justified."

Conflicting emotions swept over Mosely. Adrenaline coursed through his veins as he watched the colors swirling over the image of his brain. He realized that try as he might, he could not biofeedback his way through this. He could not fathom—much less control—the sweeping patterns of color rippling over the folds of his brain.

Sobol's words percolated through the fear and confusion. "I will not lie to you; there is no escape from this place except to join with me. I tell you this because it's not something you decide. It is a fact about you that we will discover together. After this course I will simply *know* whether you have joined me. And you will know also. You can try to fight it, but the result will be no different."

Mosely felt the fear again, but then resolve rose in him, too. This was knowable. The rules of the game were laid out, and now he could face it head-on. Now he felt the rage building. His body tensed.

Sobol continued. "If at any point I find you unsuitable, I will kill you. Since I bear you no ill will, your death will be pleasant—an overdose of Demerol. So you see, your death will be far more agreeable than mine was. Perhaps this will be of some comfort to you."

"Fuck you, Sobol!"

Sobol paused. "I see you have no special fear of death. Instead, you feel rage at your helplessness. But you are not helpless. Far from it. Your defense lies within you. I will measure your character, and if you have merit, then you have nothing to fear from me. On the contrary, you will walk under my protection to the end of your days."

Another pause.

"Let's begin. You do not need to speak, although your eyes must remain open except to blink normally. You can disregard this instruction, but doing so will commence your death by injection after thirty seconds. You can choose this fate, if you wish, but since no pain awaits you in any event, you may as well follow this course to its conclusion."

Sobol regarded Mosely with an appraising look. "You are beginning to master your fear. That's good. Make yourself ready." A pause of several seconds. "And we begin. . . ."

The right-hand screen dimmed and Sobol dissolved into blackness. A single word appeared in large white letters:

FAMILY

After a few seconds it was followed by several more in turn:

RELIGION, VIOLENCE, SEX, LOVE, LAW, FREEDOM, HOPE, HONESTY, RESPONSIBILITY, HONOR, DEATH.

The screen went black again. Then the word FAMILY reappeared. It lingered on-screen, like a searchlight stabbing out for him in the darkness.

Mosely couldn't help but recall his son. His lost son. Mosely's recollections from his own childhood flooded in—growing up without a father. Alone. Guilt flowed through him. Self-loathing. Deep colors ebbed and flowed over the image of his brain. It no doubt signified strong emotion. Sobol was onto him already.

Mosely blinked a couple of times beneath the goggles. He could close his eyes forever and let the Demerol flow into his veins. He had more control over his destiny now than he had had in a long time. He had an exit door. A strangely reassuring one. He opened his eyes.

Then the film began.

A quick succession of video scenes. People talking with each other, hugging, greeting one another. A man picking up a child and laughing. Parents hugging. An elderly couple walking arm in arm. A child graduating. The pride of the parents. A child in sorrow. Sickness. An elderly man flatlining in a hospital bed to the pitiful shrieks of his wife. An angry father shouting at his children. A mother raising the back of her hand over a terrified child in a bedroom doorway.

It surprised Mosely that the most painful scenes were scores of videos on children. Interacting with their parents, screaming, playing, hugging, crying, laughing. Innocence abandoned. Innocence in peril. In fear.

Mosely found himself weeping silently behind the goggles, the tears rolling down his cheeks. He imagined his own son, alone in the world. And his own responsibility for this. A son who would never know family, thanks to Mosely's selfish stupidity. He almost closed his eyes forever and let the Demerol take him. He felt broken beyond repair—but the voices of children brought him back time and again. Those innocent faces that did not yet know cruelty. And the scenes kept coming for hours. There was now a special focus on children, as if Sobol had found Mosely's weak spot and was rubbing salt into the wound to see just how painful it was. Before long, images of abandoned children were all that were shown. Waiflike children walking forlorn and frightened on fearsome city streets. Mosely was a sobbing wreck. "Stop! Please stop!"

Soon the screen went black again, and the word RELIGION came up briefly. It lingered for only a few moments before it was replaced with the word VIOLENCE.

Sobol's mental searchlight was stabbing out for him again. Mosely could see the colors lapping in waves over the image of his brain.

The screen went black, and the films came up again.

The video showed a man tied into a chair in a drab cell. He was gagged. His eyes were wild with fear as a bearish man holding a machete entered the room. The bearish man proceeded to shout in what sounded like Russian. He raised the machete, and Mosely couldn't restrain himself from closing his eyes as the sound of steel slicing into flesh came through the headphones in perfect digital stereo. Muffled screams followed.

Mosely fluttered his eyes open and revulsion filled his throat with bile. It was a vision from hell, larger than life and twice as loud. The bearish man was hacking his victim to death—one limb at a time. It was not faked. Of that Mosely had no doubt. A deep depression came over him as he watched. It was beyond revulsion. The fact that such a thing could be suffered to exist. That a film could be made of it. It said more than he ever wanted to know about the depravity loose in the world. A slow boiling anger came over him. *Was that man butchered just for this goddamned film? Fuck you, Sobol! Fuck you! Go ahead, read my mind, asshole!* Mosely kept shutting his eyes momentarily as the machete came down. Two chops to sever the right arm at the socket. One for the left arm, as the torso fell forward over the legs . . .

He couldn't face it anymore. Mosely was breathing rapidly. The sounds were horrible. He couldn't escape them. Then just as suddenly they stopped.

Mosely opened his eyes to blackness.

What followed was a seemingly endless procession of violent scenarios—some more disturbing than others. In one, a man beat a woman bloody, when suddenly another man rushed in to attack the first—while the injured woman fled. Then there were scenes of men fighting each other—with fists, then knives, then guns. Then children fighting. Then adults attacking children. Women attacking women. There were street fights, ritualized duels, senseless accidents, electrocutions. Then sadomasochistic brutality. Erotically charged violence. Followed close on by violence against animals. It all looked entirely too real. The languages of the people in the films were mostly foreign, but the images had the raw, uncut look of a digital video shot as it happened.

Mosely's emotions ranged all over the map and frequently conflicted. He found himself tensing with righteous anger, then becoming aroused, then repulsed, and everything in between. Subtle differences in the interaction of those on-screen brought about shocking differences in his feelings even regarding similar events.

He couldn't guess how many hours had gone by. He felt as though he'd spent a tour of duty on the front lines. His mind was bursting with horrific images, and he was nearing the limit of his endurance for violence. As the hours crept by, the themes kept changing, but slowly, imperceptibly. Previous themes sometimes returned. Families changed to images of faraway places and cultures, then images of poverty, then of wealth, then of weddings, then of funerals. Cars crashing together in intersections—apparently from fixed traffic cameras. A nonstop procession of highway carnage and death. People committing suicide in protest, burning themselves alive. Then people dying in accidents while doing adventurous things like rock climbing or BASE jumping. More shots of adventurous people succeeding—accomplishing great feats. Then people trekking through wild lands, climbing high mountaintops. Then of historical events—from moon landings to Khrushchev blustering. Malcolm X faded into Martin Luther King, Jr.

Mosely was emotionally and physically exhausted. And still it went on.

It was like being dragged over an emotional washboard. Mosely wound up feeling virtually every emotion of which humans are capable—not once but hundreds of times. He was long past his breaking point—not that he even noticed he'd passed it.

The images continued. An unknowable number of hours, and still the images continued. Mosely's mouth was parched, and he strained to stay alert. The images kept coming.

But one concept had begun to form in Mosely's mind. Like a rock slowly revealed as a wind blew away surrounding sand, Mosely was starting to see himself. With all his built-up emotional defenses long since worn away, simple truths had begun to emerge. Even he knew their meaning: he was angry at his wasted life. He felt deep feelings of loss that he had no family as a child, and that he had not provided one for his son—wherever he was now. Also Mosely had a desperate desire to belong. To matter. To stand for something besides himself. He was the perennial outsider looking in on the fellowship of others.

The last films were pivotal. Where the earlier ones seemed to break him down to his emotional building blocks, the latter ones seemed to be building him up—filling him with joy as he saw people struggling together. Relying on each other. Sacrificing. Gratitude. Joy. Free men looking toward distant horizons. Horizons that beckoned the adventurous, hinting at danger.

The people in these films were of all races and ages, but Mosely noticed that they shared some traits in common: they were capable, they were highly motivated, and they acknowledged no limits. Danger was not a deterrent. It was life lived to its maximum. They were truly alive.

He had almost forgotten the real world existed. He did not know how long he lay there, but when the screens faded to black, it was as though he were cast into an abyss. He panted, struggling to find some reference point. His soul adrift in nothingness.

From somewhere in the darkness he heard Sobol's voice. "Follow me, and I will help you find what you have lost. I will give your descendants a future. The past no longer exists for you."

A light began to rise in the infinite distance.

"You are an exceptional person. I choose to have faith in you." The soft light filled his vision.

Mosely slowly remembered that he existed as a person. He remembered his name. Charles Mosely. He felt different—as though all his sins were washed away.

Suddenly the crushing weight of exhaustion fell upon him.

Someone lifted the goggles from his head, revealing the same soft light above him. The big guy was there, nodding slowly. A metallic *chunk* sound echoed in the room, and Mosely's limbs were suddenly free. Other hands came to ease him up.

Mosely looked and saw the other orderly in his white coat helping him up into a sitting position. Mosely felt dizzy. Weak.

The big guy leaned in. "We're going to withdraw the needle. It will just take a second."

The other orderly placed a cotton ball over the spot, squeezed, then withdrew the needle. He quickly taped a bandage over it.

Mosely's dull eyes noticed his own clothing. He was wearing surgical scrubs with booties. He stared down at his feet, then looked up to face the big guy, who nodded slightly.

"The danger's past."

Mosely's dry voice croaked, "How long?"

"Forty-six hours."

A water bottle appeared next to his mouth. Mosely turned to see the other orderly extending it. Mosely took it and sipped greedily.

"Not too much." After a few more moments they took it away.

The big guy regarded Mosely. "The fact that you're still alive is all I need to know about you." He extended his hand. "I'm Rollins." His eyes darted. "He's Morris."

Mosely regarded the hand. "Like I'm Taylor?"

Rollins laughed. "Exactly like that."

Mosely shook his hand. Rollins made eye contact. They were confident eyes, not at all unfriendly.

Morris nodded and shook his hand also. "Welcome aboard."

"Aboard *what*?"

Rollins gestured. "The Daemon chose you. You're one of its champions now."

"Do I have a choice?"

"You already made your choice." He looked into Mosely's eyes. "This is where you want to be. That's why you're still alive."

Mosely absorbed the words. The images were so fresh in his mind. Breaking him down to his basic building blocks. Understanding him. Mosely understanding himself. The elation.

He realized Rollins was right.

Rollins continued. "There are no leaders here. We are all peers. And we answer directly to the Daemon—and no one else. I am your equal. And you are mine."

Mosely wasn't sure this was even happening. He shook his head to clear it.

Rollins patted his arm. "First, some food and rest. There's a lot to learn, but the Daemon chose you because you're smart. And you'll need to be."

Chapter 28:// Ripples on the Surface

Natalie Philips paced with a laser pointer at the edge of a projection screen. The Mahogany Row conference room was dimly lit, and silhouettes of her audience were arrayed around a sizeable boardroom table. Military badges on the uniforms of some audience members reflected the light from the screen.

Her title presentation slide was up:

Viability of Daemon Construct Over Peer-to-Peer Networks

She was already addressing the group. ". . . the feasibility of a narrow AI scripting application distributed over a peer-to-peer network architecture to avoid core logic disruption." She clicked to the next slide. It bore the simple words:

Distributed Daemon Viable

A murmur went through her audience.

"Our unequivocal findings are that a distributed daemon is not merely a potential threat but an inevitable one, given the standards unifying extant networked systems. In fact, we have reason to believe one of these logic constructs is currently loose in the wild."

Much more murmuring went through the crowd.

She changed her slide again. This one depicted two sets of graphs labeled *Incidence of DDOS Attacks—All Sites Compared to Gambling/Pornography Sites*.

She looked back at her audience. "A distributed denial of service (or DDOS) attack involves harnessing the power of hundreds, thousands, or even hundreds of thousands of zombie computers to transmit large amounts of packets to a single target Web domain. A zombie computer is one that has been previously compromised by a malicious back door program. This could be John Q. Public's unsecured computer sitting in the den. An army of these zombie computers is called a *botnet,* and its collective computing power can be directed to overwhelm a target, making it too busy to respond to legitimate traffic. The potential to harm an online business is obvious.

"Unlike a simple denial of service (or DOS) attack—which is launched from a single machine and thus easily blocked by an IP address—a DDOS attack comes in waves from different IP addresses coordinated to continually incapacitate the target. Likewise, the nature of the traffic can vary wildly, making it difficult to filter out garbage connection requests. In short: it is significantly more serious. Unless the attacker brags about his deeds, tracing the real source of an attack can be next to impossible."

She wielded the laser pointer to highlight various parts of the screen. "These two charts illustrate a pattern detected four months ago in the occurrence of distributed denial of service attacks on the public Internet—both overall and as experienced separately by commercial gambling and pornography Web sites, both legal and illegal, hereafter referred to as 'G/P sites.'

"Note the increase of approximately twelve thousand percent in the occurrence of such attacks against G/P sites during the period January through April. Contrast this with the flat-to-declining trend in DDOS attacks versus the overall population of domains."

She changed slides to a graphical breakdown of the top international gambling and pornography domains, with call-outs indicating the crime gangs operating out of Russia, Thailand, and Belize. The graph was broken down on the x-axis by time and on the y-axis by packets per hour.

"The CIA has associated the following international crime rings with these three G/P enterprises. Their Web interests encompass tens of thousands of loosely affiliated Web sites hosted on hundreds of domains in dozens of countries. Each one of these crime gangs is a vast IT organization, and collectively they generate billions of dollars in revenue each year. Their operating units include product development, security, finance, and infrastructure support elements—they are, in effect, multinational corporations whose product lines include narco-trafficking, sexual slavery, money laundering, and extortion."

Her graph showed that the Web assets of each individual crime ring had been attacked in a campaign of orchestrated infowar. Philips's laser pointer cavorted as she hammered her point home. "The Russians were first in line. We estimate that roughly ten million workstations launched a Pearl Harbor–like cyber attack simultaneously from all points on the globe, beginning in mid-January and stretching through to the end of the month. This effectively brought the Russian business to a halt worldwide—making their online gambling and pornography assets unavailable to paying customers for extended periods. These were not simple smurf and fraggle attacks. The Russians appear to have tried everything, from hardware filtering to rate-limiting connections, but it didn't put a dent in their downtime. They tried to launch new sites and migrate customers to these, but the new sites also were rapidly targeted and brought down."

She changed to a slide of translated Internet headlines from a passel of third-world sites. They listed dozens of killings in Asia and Russia.

"This appears to have sparked a brief gang war, followed by a purge within the ranks of the gang's IT staff. The CIA estimates several dozen related killings, but notably, all during this period, the DDOS attacks did not let up and shifted constantly to originate from new locations. The Russian enterprise did not recover until the end of January, when it was suddenly fully operational."

She looked up at her audience. "The following cell phone conversation was intercepted by ComSat assets over the Republic of Georgia on January twenty-ninth and is a conversation between an unidentified caller and a known Russian mafia figure based in St. Petersburg, herein denoted as *Vassili*. The transcript is available over Echelon. The abstract number is listed in your presentation binder. This raw intercept comes to us compliments of Group W." She turned to face the screen as tinny, foreign chatter came in over speakers. An instant translation appeared on the screen in a scrolling fashion as the words were uttered in Russian:

Vassili: We're driving. Tupo [nearby person], no. Where are you? Where are you now?

Caller: Belize City.

Vassili: They are online there?

Caller: Yes, yes. They're running perfect.

Vassili: Perfect? Since when?

Caller: Perfect, like before perfect.

Vassili: Before the attacks?

Caller: Yes, yes.

Vassili: Do they know the extent of it there?

Caller: No. Nobody knows.

Vassili: They're angry about Tupolov, yes?

Caller: Yes. But they have their money now.

Vassili: You paid the dead American?

Caller: Yes.

Vassili: And now we're online again?

Caller: Yes.

Vassili: [unintelligible]. They'll be next, and we must regain market share while they are down. You know what to do?

Caller: Yes. Sobol told us.

The screen cleared and the lights came up as animated discussions filled the room. Philips called to be heard over the din. "There are additional intercepts of a similar nature, but I think this is a representative sample. The waves of attacks continued until a couple of months ago, hitting each organization in turn—and growing in ferocity—at which point they disappeared suddenly and entirely."

One of the DOD brass spoke up, "What's your read on all this, Doctor?"

"I think the crime gangs running online gambling and pornography have been forced to pay protection money to someone or something."

"You conclude that from one intercept?"

"This is one of dozens of intercepts, the transcripts of which you will find in your presentation binders."

"How much money are we talking about here?"

Philips placed the laser pointer on the nearby podium. "We have an e-mail intercept from a Thai gang that mentions a ten percent gross payment."

"Ten percent of *gross*?"

"All online transactions. The CIA estimates worldwide revenue from online gambling and pornography at approximately seventeen billion U.S. dollars per year. In truth, no one really knows. But if we use this as a baseline and extrapolate, assuming that the Daemon has—"

"You're talking about a couple *billion* dollars a year."

"There is anecdotal evidence that these payments represent an outsourcing of the IT security function of these criminal gangs to some unknown entity." She paused, either for effect or to gather her courage—even she wasn't sure which. "We suspect that the entity is not a living person but a massively parallel logical construct. I believe it's Sobol's Daemon."

The room erupted in talk for several moments until someone in the back shouted over the din, "How do you know it's not just another gang?"

The noise died down to hear her response.

Philips nodded. "Because that was the first thing the Russians thought. Quite a few hackers died at their hands in an effort to identify those responsible. At some point the Russians were presented with evidence that convinced them no living person was behind this attack. We don't know yet what that evidence was—but we have operatives attempting to get their hands on it."

The division chief just looked at her. "This is reckless conjecture. We've got Detective Sebeck convicted and on death row, Cheryl Lanthrop dead, and Jon Ross on the run. This situation is under control."

The most senior NSA suit spoke. "I disagree. Right now the media is stoking a panic on cyber crime. A public discovery that Sobol's Daemon was preying on Internet business could spook the financial markets."

A visiting analyst from the FBI Cyber Division shook his head. "The facts don't support the media panic, sir. Overall reported incidents of computer break-ins this year are down slightly—not up. In fact, we could spin the demise of gambling and pornography sites as a positive."

Philips regarded the FBI agent, then turned to the room in general. "Anyone have anything on the media's current fascination with cyber security? Does anyone know what's driving it?"

"Sebeck's trial?"

The FBI analyst began to hold court on the topic. "The government has few real controls over either the Internet or private data networks. This manufactured panic is addressing an actual deficiency in the cyber infrastructure. It's the invisible hand of the market in action."

Philips looked impassively at him. "Unless it's already too late."

The NSA section chief raised an eyebrow. "Is your copycat Daemon up to something more than demanding tribute from pornographers, Dr. Philips?"

She revealed no emotion. "For one, I believe it *is* Sobol's Daemon."

"Highly unlikely." The FBI analyst looked ready to disprove anything. He just needed fresh grist for his logic mill.

Philips continued. "Gentlemen, there are loose ends all over the Sobol case. There's the poisoning death of Lionel Crawly—the voice-over artist for Sobol's game *Over the Rhine*. What dialogue did he record that we have no knowledge of? The introduction of a strange edifice in Sobol's online game *The Gate* at almost the instant of his death. And then there are the back doors in his games—"

"There *are* no back doors in his games." The FBI analyst scanned the faces in the room. "It's a fact."

The NSA chief kept his eyes on Philips. "Your Internet traffic analysis was interesting, Doctor, but if you have evidence linking Sobol's Daemon with the Daemon attacking G/P sites, then where is it?"

"In Sobol's game maps."

"Steganography? Didn't you explore that last year?"

"Fleetingly—before Sebeck's arrest. But let's not forget that Sobol was an extraordinarily intelligent man. He was able to envision multiple axes simultaneously."

"Is that a polysyllabic way to say he thinks outside the box?"

A senior cryptanalyst nearby removed his glasses and started cleaning them. "No offense, Dr. Philips, but if Sobol's games contained steganographic content, you should have readily detected it by plotting the magnitude of a two-dimensional Fast Fourier Transform of the bitstream. This would show telltale discontinuities at a rate roughly above ten percent."

Philips aimed an anti-smile in his direction. "Thank you, Doctor. Had I not spent the last six years expanding the frontiers of your discipline, I'm sure I would find your input invaluable."

The division chief cleared his throat. "The point is still valid, Doctor. How could Sobol hide a back door in a program using steganography, of all things? Doesn't that just hide data? You can't execute steganographic code."

The FBI analyst couldn't hold back. "Even if he was storing encrypted code within art asset files, he'd still need code to extract the encrypted elements—and we would have found the extraction routines in the source."

Philips turned to him thoughtfully. "Yes, but the back door isn't in the code. It's in the *program*—but it's not in the code."

Her audience looked confused.

The division chief shrugged. "You lost me there, Doctor."

The senior cryptanalyst offered, "You mean the relationship of things *within* the program?"

"Ah, now you're seeing it."

The division chief cut in. "What brought you back to the stego angle? The DDOS attacks on G/P sites?"

"No." She paused again. "Jon Ross brought me back to it." She turned back to face them. "For the last several weeks I have been exchanging e-mail communications with the man known as Jon Ross."

The impact of this revelation left her audience stunned briefly. Then there was frantic movement; previously untouched presentation binders were grabbed and thumbed through hastily.

"Why weren't we informed of this?"

The NSA chief interjected, "The Advisory Panel was informed."

"What evidence do you have that these e-mails are authentic?"

Philips was calm. "The first e-mail made reference to a conversation Ross and I had in person at Sobol's funeral."

The FBI analyst nodded slowly. "No doubt he claims innocence and that the Daemon really exists."

"He's doing more than that. He's pursuing the Daemon, and imploring us to do the same. Which leads us once again to the back door in Sobol's software. Because it was Jon Ross who helped me find it."

"That's convenient for him."

"I thought so, too. That's why I asked for a face-to-face meeting."

The NSA chief nodded in apparent recollection.

The FBI analyst looked surprised. "And he agreed?"

"After a fashion." Philips nodded to the back of the room, and the lights dimmed again.

The screen filled with an animated 3-D environment. It was a narrow, medieval-looking city street, with buildings leaning over it in irregular rows. Few in attendance recognized it because none of them had the time or inclination to play online computer games. A title in plain Arial font briefly appeared superimposed over the image:

Session #489: Elianburg, Duchy of Prendall

Philips narrated. "What you're looking at is Sobol's game *The Gate.* This is an online role-playing game—meaning that tens of thousands of users access game maps from central servers. The game covers a large area of virtual space. Jon Ross requested a meeting at this specific location; at the corner of Queensland Boulevard and Hovarth Alley in Elianburg."

"A meeting in an online game?"

"Yes. But since it's difficult to arrest an avatar, I decided to go into God Mode."

"Meaning what?"

"Meaning I cheated; I enlisted the aid of the CyberStorm system administrators to place the intersection under surveillance with virtual cameras."

"You set up a stake-out in fantasyland?"

A chuckle swept through the room.

Philips nodded. "Something like that. The goal was to monitor every character that entered this intersection up to the appointed meeting time. It's a busy intersection—in the middle of the market where players purchase equipment—and I wanted the maximum amount of time to trace Ross."

One of the uniformed military officers spoke up. "Like tracing a phone call?"

"Similar, yes. Each player has a screen name hovering over their character's head that must be unique for that server cluster. We wrote a script that scanned for suspicious player names on the servers. It autoharvested IP addresses for likely suspects and traced them back to their ISP for follow-up. We also established a manual system where we could select any player name, and the CyberStorm techs would look up that player's originating IP address."

"Why bother with IP address? Doesn't CyberStorm have a record of each player's billing information?"

"Yes, but it seemed likely that Ross would steal or borrow an account. By using his IP address to locate the Internet Service Provider, and then contacting the ISP for the physical address of the connection, we were more likely to actually find him." She looked around the room for emphasis. "We scrambled airborne strike teams in several U.S. cities in preparation for this meeting in the hopes that Ross would be hiding in a major metropolitan area."

The FBI analyst couldn't resist. "I gather from the fact that Ross is still at large that this plan did not succeed."

A voice in the darkness: "Can we continue, please?"

Philips nodded.

The screen suddenly came to life. Animated 3-D people moved through the scene. It was eerie how realistically the people moved—although only half of them had glowing names floating over their heads.

"The characters moving around without names are NPCs, non-player characters—they are computer controlled. Only human players have names."

The perspective of the screen changed. It was a first-person view from Philips's character as she moved through the crowd.

"We conducted this session from our offices in Crypto. The game permits players with VOIP capability to speak directly to nearby players over a voice channel. Ross requested that we have such a hookup. I am controlling this character in the game, and it is my voice you will hear talking with him. I had a MUTE button on my headset, and you will also hear me issuing instructions to my team. Ross did not tell me in advance the name of his character, but he said I would be able to pick him out of the crowd. Which is why we put the auto-trace script in place. But Ross took a page out of Sobol's playbook."

The screen view changed as Philips's character turned this way and that, checking out the shoppers in the market. Then the POV moved toward a Nubian female 3-D character wearing a black leather corset with a plunging neckline. Something resembling a French-cut steel thong wrapped her shapely hips. She was a hentai cover girl. As the frame moved closer, the Nubian woman turned, revealing what was unmistakably a computer-generated version of Philips's face.

Mild amusement spread through the audience in the meeting room. Philips ignored it.

On-screen the glowing name over the Nubian avatar read: *Cipher.* Philips's recorded voice came in over the speakers:

Philips: Get me an IP for the screen name "Cipher." That's spelled c-i-p-h-e-r.

NSA Tech: Got it, Doctor. Looking up ISP .

The screen perspective moved right up to *Cipher*, and stopped. The scantily clad warrior princess faced the screen. A male voice came in over the speakers:

Ross: Good evening, Doctor.

Philips: Mr. Ross. Apparently you can't resist identity theft. How did you upload my likeness to this game?

Ross: I didn't upload anything. Players can edit the geometry of their avatars. I sculpted this one to resemble you.

Philips: I didn't realize you studied my appearance so closely.

Ross: How could I forget you? Besides, I knew you'd try to identify my account in advance of this meeting, but your automated forensics tools don't know what you look like, Doctor. Your physical appearance is a graphical encryption that the human mind is uniquely qualified to decode.

Philips: That doesn't make it any less unsettling to have a conversation with myself as a transsexual lingerie model.

Ross: I find it just as uncomfortable being seen with you.

Philips: How's that?

Ross: Well, you've got the default skin of a generic warrior, and nobody keeps the default skin. You are the fantasy world equivalent of a Fed. I recognized you a mile away.

Philips: Jon, why did you call me here?

Ross: To prove to you that I'm innocent.

Philips: And how do you intend to do that?

Ross: By showing you one of the back doors in this game.

Philips: We've been through every line of the source code, Jon. There are no back doors.

Ross: None here, true.

Ross's female warrior gestured dramatically, as if performing a spell. In a moment a magical portal appeared in the street. A wandering player character tried to walk into it but bounced off. After a few tries, he got bored and walked off.

Philips: What's this?

Ross: A Type II gate. It will only permit those I choose to enter, and I just typed your character's name in. What does "FANX" mean, anyway?

Philips: I'll let you puzzle it out.

Ross: Please step through the portal.

NSA Tech: Doctor, we've got a physical address, but it's in Helsingborg, Sweden.

Philips: [MUTE ON] Notify local authorities and Interpol. [MUTE OFF] Where's this lead to?

Ross: What does it matter? Look, I hope efforts to trace my physical location are not distracting you. I'm running several layers of proxies, Dr. Philips. By the time you track them all down, this will be long over. Just pay attention, please. This is important.

Philips: Jon, I'm not—

Ross: It's okay, Doctor. That's your job. Just step through the gate, please.

The perspective of the screen changed as Philips moved her character through the gate. It was a swirling vortex of blue lines, and then suddenly the view changed to a darkened masonry tunnel filled to a depth of a couple feet with black water. The area was lit by the swirling lights of the nearby magical portal. Rats scurried away along ledges, and the water's surface rippled with the dazzling lights.

Someone in the dark muttered. "Nice algorithm . . ."

The NSA chief craned his neck. "Shhh!"

On-screen, Ross's hentai warrior princess waded out into the water and stood in front of Philips's character.

Philips: What is this place?

Ross: It's a sewer beneath the Temple District. Not accessible without a magical portal.

Philips: What did you want to show me, Jon?

Ross: Look straight ahead. What do you see? You may need to move side to side to notice it.

The view on-screen changed as Philips focused straight ahead. There in the semidarkness of the slime-covered wall was the outline of an oxidized bronze door—nearly the same color as the surrounding stones.

Philips: A door.

Ross: Not just any door. A back door.

Philips: It's a literal door?

Ross: You were expecting a code snippet? Maybe something that accepted anonymous connections at a certain port address or carried out actions on the user's computer with their rights? But you didn't find that. You didn't find it because you shouldn't have been looking for a back door leading IN. You should have been looking for a back door leading OUT.

Philips: But how would that permit Sobol to control a user's machine?

Ross: It isn't their machine he's trying to control.

Philips: You're saying he was trying to control the user?

Ross: Why don't you step through the portal and find out?

Philips: Wait a minute. We still should have found this in the code.

Ross: Why? Were you looking for a graphic of a door that when used as an object in the game environment loads a game map? Do you know how many times that innocuous function call appears in the source code? The code itself is benign—it's the map it loads that isn't. Because the map in question is not on the CyberStorm servers, and I'll bet you didn't look farther than the IP ad-dresses of the map links.

Philips: [a sigh of disgust] You mean he's using a redirect.

Ross: It will look local in the map database, but when you try to load it, it redirects to an external IP address—which logs the user off the current game and establishes a new connection on an alien server. In short: this portal leads to a darknet.

Philips: A darknet. An encrypted virtual network.

Ross: Correct. Except that this is a graphical darknet.

Philips: How do you know all this?

Ross: Like I said—step through the portal. However, I will leave you now. Your colleagues are quite skilled and have probably located my zombie in Swe-den, maybe even my zombie in Germany—and I really must be going. Please remember that I am innocent, Natalie—if I may call you Natalie. I'd really like to tell you the whole story over dinner sometime.

Philips: I don't date felons, Jon—especially cross-dressing felons.

Ross: Till we meet again, Doctor . . .

At that, Ross's avatar disappeared—as did his magical gate—leaving her in relative darkness. There was just the faint glow emanating from the door.

NSA Tech: He's off-line, Doctor.

Philips: We're still recording?

NSA Tech: Affirmative.

On-screen, Philips approached the door and activated it. It creaked open, the noise echoing down the sewer tunnel. Animated cobwebs stretched. A dialog box appeared reading "Loading Map . . . "

NSA Tech: Connection severed to CyberStorm server. We're establishing a connection to an IP address assigned to a domain in . . . South Korea.

Philips: Are the packets really routing there?

NSA Tech: Stand by.

Philips: Get us a fix as soon as possible.

In a few moments the map was loaded. Philips's character moved out into a medieval hall, with a gallery on either side above and pen-nants hanging down bearing heraldic symbols. Set into the wall straight ahead was a statue of a man, disquietingly similar to Sobol, in flowing robes, hands outstretched. Virtual water glimmered like a fountain as it rolled down each cheek from his eyes. Mineral stains marked the path. A perpetual fountain of tears.

A black-robed figure stood before the statue like a sentinel blocking her way. Its face was lost in shadow.

NSA Tech: It's fingering us, Doctor. I didn't spoof our IP address.

Philips: It's okay, Chris, I didn't ask you to.

The hooded figure snapped alert suddenly, then raised a finger and pointed at her.

Guardian: You don't belong here!

Lightning arced from that finger in her general direction, and the Blue Screen of Death filled their view.

Then everything went black.

NSA Tech: We are down! Down, down, down!

Chapter 29://Memory

Pete Sebeck stared at a dimple in the concrete of his cell wall. It was the only imperfection in an unrelenting sameness. It was his secret—a place upon which to center his mind as the world turned unseen around him.

It might have been night outside, but it was never dark in here. There was nothing even to mark the passage of time, and if there was, they would erase it. He was watched constantly. A fluorescent fixture buzzed light down on him from overhead. Surveillance cameras in mirrored enclosures on two ceiling corners recorded his every movement. A microphone his every utterance. He was alone, but never alone. As a high-profile prisoner, no expense had been spared to monitor him 24/7—guarding against the possibility that he might harm himself before the government could mete out justice.

As Sebeck lay staring at the wall, his memories were still raw nerves. Each turn of his mind made him wince.

Worth losing everything for. That's what he used to tell himself about Cheryl Lanthrop. She was beautiful, but there was more to it than that. It was what that reflected about him. That he was worthy of attracting such a successful, confident person. Why did he think she would want him? What part of him nursed such fantasies? That was the sad truth of it. He was ripe for programming. He was ready to suspend disbelief to live that life. He hadn't wanted to know the truth—not about her and definitely not about himself.

They said Lanthrop was dead now. If she had only confided in him. Perhaps he would have done the right thing. To his shame, he wasn't certain.

The trial had been a fast-moving media circus. He was shocked at how incriminating the evidence against him was. In hindsight he felt it should have been obvious that he was being set up—Lanthrop urging him to secrecy. And then there were the things he had no knowledge of that crucified him. The files on his computer. Lists and corporate documents, all digitally shredded—but incompletely. A passport under the fictitious name Michael Corvus. The travels of that fictitious name, establishing offshore bank accounts and corporations. The credit card purchases and corporate officerships. The offshore payments and records of phone calls to Pavlos and Singh. The e-mail accounts detailing a convenient, media-friendly conspiracy.

Everyone believed that Sebeck was responsible for the deaths of all those people—and of Aaron Larson. He recalled the several times Larson sought guidance from him. Sebeck had refused the role of mentor. Being a father figure to anyone was the last thing he wanted.

Sebeck could hardly blame the public for hating him. The evidence was wide and deep. The clincher was that Sebeck did, indeed, have an affair with Cheryl Lanthrop. What they did together seemed merely kinky and strange at the time—but when combined with the mountain of evidence against him, it revealed a person quite different from the public face of Detective Sergeant Peter Sebeck, decorated officer and dedicated family man. So different that he had begun to question it himself.

His wife, Laura, surprised him, though. He thought she would be glad to be rid of him.

Strange. After all this time, he couldn't recall whether she goaded him into marriage or whether he had volunteered as a means of doing the right thing by her. It never even occurred to him at the time that she might not want to marry him. The pregnancy had been something that happened to him—at least in his own mind. Perhaps she had married him because she also thought that was the right thing to do.

After his arrest, when everyone abandoned him, she was there for him. The press pilloried her as a guileless moron, but she knew him. Tears welled in Sebeck's eyes remembering it. She knew he could not have done these things, even when he doubted it himself. She had kept him sane, or near enough to sane.

They were just two people who got lost somewhere early in life.

Chris, their son, had come to see Sebeck only once and stared at the floor almost the entire time. When he did look up, there was a glare of utter malevolence through the glass that stung Sebeck worse than any-thing the federal prosecutor could say. It still stung.

Sebeck curled up on his cot around a pain so deep that he longed for it all to end. There was no clearing this up—even if proof of his inno-cence were found. His name had been too thoroughly dragged through the mud. Some taint would always remain. Some doubt would always exist in the minds of those around him. Death would be welcome, if it weren't for the fact that almost everyone he cared about considered him evil. That his passing would be seen as justice. He was thankful his parents hadn't lived to see this day.

But his deepest despair came from the knowledge that no one be-lieved that the Daemon existed. From the outset it was clear that both the prosecution and the defense would be arguing not about the Dae-mon, but about whether Sebeck had been involved in the conspiracy to defraud Sobol's estate and murder federal officers. The judge refused to hear testimony about the Daemon—largely because there was no evidence it existed. But it had to exist. Sebeck was convinced of it.

They were appealing his conviction to a higher federal court, but his lawyer didn't hold out much hope. The government was clearly making an example out of Sebeck. His trial had been fast-tracked in response to public outrage, and failing the introduction of new evidence, there was little chance his guilty verdicts would be overturned on appeal.

Sebeck tried to remember a time when he was last truly happy. He had to think back all the way to high school, sitting on the roof of his neighbor's garage with his buddies. That was the night before he found out Laura was pregnant. But was that true? Now the idea of coming home and seeing Chris and Laura laughing at the kitchen table was a treasured memory. The laughter stopped as he arrived, but that wasn't their fault. It was his fault. He had purposefully distanced himself from them. Without this disaster, would Sebeck ever have realized what he had?

Sebeck's mind turned to that voice on the phone at Sobol's funeral. Experts proved it wasn't Sobol, but Sebeck realized that was the whole point of it. It had to *not* be Sobol, and provably so. Nonetheless, that voice had actually warned him about what was to come.

I must destroy you.

He contemplated it emptily. Without hope or purpose.

But there was something else the voice had said. Sebeck tried hard to remember, buried as it was under months of pretrial testimony, inter-rogations, and hard evidence. But then it came to him.

They will require a sacrifice, Sergeant.

And so they had. Sebeck sat up and stared into nothingness, strain-ing to recall the exact words of the voice.

Before you die . . . invoke the Daemon.

Somewhere there was a surveillance tape that showed Sebeck si-lently nodding to himself in the stillness of his empty cell. Because he now realized what he had to do.

Chapter 30:// Offering

A white van raised a cloud of dust as it approached from a distance, wavering like a phantom in the summer heat. On either side of the dirt road, California grasslands stretched brown and dry, rolling up into the barren hills at the southern end of the San Joaquin Valley. Every fold and furrow of the land was shadowed in the afternoon sun, like the wrinkles of some timeworn face. The topography was naked and enormously wide. Forty miles of nothing stretched to the horizon, starkly beautiful to anyone with a reliable car.

The van inched across the gargantuan landscape, progressing toward a ring of asphalt set in the bottom of a forgotten canyon. The van slowed as it reached the track, then turned, revealing the car-carrying trailer it pulled behind it. A black Lincoln Town Car sat on the bed.

The van stopped, and a moment later the doors swung open, disgorging Kurt Voelker on the passenger side. He wearily stretched. Tingit Khan and Rob McCruder exited the far side of the van and did likewise. They were all in their early twenties, but while Voelker looked dressed for a Christian Fellowship meeting—with khakis and a button-down shirt—Khan and McCruder bore the piercings, tats, and severe hair that once indicated disaffected youth but that now only meant they weren't interviewing yet.

Voelker checked his GPS unit. He looked to his two companions. "We're in the box."

"It's about fucking time." Khan held up his hand to shade his face. His eyes scanned the terrain. "What is this? A racetrack?"

"Pretty damned small for a racetrack."

Voelker spoke from the far side of the van. "I'm guessing a test track."

"It's not banked or anything." Khan held up his other hand to block the sun. "What's it feel like? A hundred degrees out here?"

McCruder checked his watch. "A hundred and six."

"You have a *thermometer* on your watch?"

"Yeah. So what?"

Khan looked through the van windows to Voelker on the other side. "Kurt. Rob has a thermometer on his watch."

"So?"

"Well, at some point, the thing you add to the watch is more significant than the watch. I'd argue he's wearing a thermometer with a clock on it."

McCruder scowled; he was a veteran of Khan's observations. "Fuck off."

"Why do you need to know the precise temperature where you *are*? It's not like a weather report; it's too fucking late—you're already here."

Voelker held up a hand. "Khan, get the gear out of the van. I'll unchain the car."

Khan and McCruder started pulling hard-shell Pelican cases from the van. McCruder just shook his head sadly. "You're the one who asked how hot it was."

———

Fifteen minutes later Voelker extended the antenna on a sizeable handheld remote controller. Khan and McCruder sat nearby on the empty hard-shell containers in front of a folding table. The table was strewn with cables, high-gain antennas, and two ruggedized laptops with shades shielding their screens from the sunlight. A half-meter satellite dish pointed skyward on a tripod placed in the grass nearby.

Voelker looked to McCruder, who was peering at his laptop's LCD screen. McCruder finally nodded. "Anytime, Kurt."

Voelker pointed the controller directly at the Lincoln on the trailer bed. The car looked identical to the endless number of black fleet Town Cars with smoked glass coursing through downtown streets and airports nationwide—replete with a TCP number on its back bumper and a vanity plate reading *LIVRY47*. Voelker pressed a button on the remote. The car's V8 engine started. He slid a lever to put it in gear and then began backing the car slowly off the trailer ramps.

"I bet he rolls it," McCruder snickered.

"You'd better hope he doesn't."

Voelker didn't even look. "Guys, I'm working here. You wanna shut your pie holes for two seconds?"

In a few moments he had deftly backed the car onto the dirt road; then he shifted it into drive and eased it out onto the asphalt of the small oval racetrack nearby. The circuit was perhaps two hundred feet in diameter. An oddity, really. Nothing you could actually race on. It was crisscrossed with mysterious grooves set at odd angles.

"This good?" Voelker turned to his companions.

They shrugged.

Khan took a lollipop out of his mouth. "How the hell are we supposed to know? We're in the box. Park it where it is."

Voelker killed the engine. He collapsed the controller's antenna. "Anything?"

Both men shook their heads.

He walked up. "I guess we wait."

The late afternoon sun was sinking toward the hills. They had been waiting and sweating for a couple of hours in the brutal heat, listening to the wind chimes dangling from the eaves of a nearby utility shed. The chimes sounded all too infrequently.

Khan mopped his face with the front of his black T-shirt. "Goddamn. It is Africa hot."

McCruder upended a soda can. Nothing came out. "I thought you Indians thrived in this weather, Khan."

"Fuck you. I grew up in Portland, moron."

Voelker wiped the salty sweat from his eyes. He blinked from the sting. "Guys, I swear, I'll take a tire iron to you both if you don't quit your bitching."

They heard a *blip-blip* sound from the nearby laptop. They snapped to attention.

Khan leaned over McCruder's shoulder to look at the LCD screen.

McCruder looked up to Voelker. "It's here."

All three turned expectantly to the asphalt.

Suddenly the car engine roared to life. It revved several times. The wheels turned left, then right.

They all watched transfixed.

Khan grinned. "It's *alive*! Bu-wahahahah!"

Suddenly the car's engine raced, and it laid down rubber, accelerating madly along the asphalt track.

"Jesus!" Voelker turned to the other two. "What the hell is it doing?"

"Don't know, but look at it go, man."

The Lincoln was weaving side to side, then it suddenly slammed on the brakes and screeched to a halt. It peeled out suddenly again and went into a power slide, whipping its tail around. It roared forward again, building up speed on the straightaway, then wrenched its wheels into another slide, and came out facing the other direction—still accelerating into a bootlegger reverse.

McCruder smiled. "It's testing the properties of the car."

Khan and Voelker leaned in, while still watching the screeching display of stunt driving.

McCruder spoke louder. "It's confirming the specs. Braking distance, turning radius—all that stuff. It's making sure we followed instructions."

Voelker pointed a finger at McCruder. "It damn well better meet the spec."

Without turning, McCruder extended his closed fist, then operated his thumb like a crank to extend his middle finger.

Suddenly the car stopped its acrobatic display and sat motionless on the pavement. Oily rubber smoke still wafted across the track.

All three men stared at it. It was half a football field away.

A Bullwinkle the Moose voice came over the speakers of McCruder's laptop. "Duhhh, you have mail."

McCruder checked.

While McCruder was busy, Khan looked at his own laptop screen. He grinned at Voelker. "We no longer have a connection to the car, Kurt. It changed the access codes."

Voelker didn't flinch. "It's part of the spec, Khan."

McCruder glanced up at his companions. "Let me confirm this." After a few frenzied moments of clicking, he smiled and turned to them again. "Fifty-six thousand dollars have been deposited into the corporate account, and we have an order for six more AutoM8s. The Daemon is pleased with our offering."

They whooped and high-fived.

"What will that total?" Khan was beaming.

Voelker thought for a second. "Three hundred thousand and change." He looked to McCruder. "Does it say where the cars will be coming from?"

McCruder shook his head. "Doesn't matter. Corporate leases, probably. Not our problem. Looks like the Haas has downloaded more plans, too."

"Excellent." Voelker smiled at them both. "Congratulations, gentlemen."

Suddenly the distant car roared into action again—laying down more rubber. They all turned. It was accelerating toward them.

"It's gonna whack us!"

They ran for the van, but the Town Car raced past their table and out along the dirt road. It accelerated and kept going.

They gathered their breath and watched it recede into the distance.

Khan turned to them. "We should follow it. You know, back to its lair."

McCruder narrowed his eyes. "What, are you fucking insane?"

Voelker nodded. "He's right. We released it into the wild. Those were the instructions. Following it is just a good way to get killed."

Khan watched the cloud of dust moving toward the distant hills. "You think we're the only ones doing this?"

Voelker watched, too, shielding his eyes against the sun. "If the number of unemployed electrical engineers is any indication, I'd say no."

Chapter 31:// Red Queen Hypothesis

arrett Lindhurst marched purposefully toward the corner office on the fifty-first floor of Leland Equity Group's palatial world headquarters. He clenched a rolled magazine in his hand like a baton in a slow-motion relay race and looked visibly worried. Worried about systems.

As chief information officer, Lindhurst held dominion over the systems that delivered the lifeblood of Leland Equity Group: real-time financial data. That data was delivered instantaneously to every corner of the organization and to every client. Every account and every dollar in every branch office passed through Lindhurst's networks and data systems. Every e-mail passed through his servers. He had thirty regional VPs as direct reports and oversaw an empire of some five hundred IT employees worldwide.

And yet, Leland Equity Group was one of those multibillion-dollar companies that existed on the periphery of public awareness. Their unremarkable logo could be found in the skyline of any major city in North America, Europe, or Asia, and even if most people had no idea what the company did, they assumed it must be doing something important.

The reality was that, with eighty billion dollars in assets under management, the decisions made by Leland MBAs ruled the daily lives of two hundred million Third World people.

Following a (more or less) Darwinian economic model, Leland identified and quantified promising resource development opportunities in the far corners of the world. They had since formed private equity partnerships with local leaders for strip mining in Papua New Guinea, water privatization in Ecuador, marble quarrying in China, oil drilling in Nigeria, and pipeline construction in Myanmar. Anywhere local public and/or private leaders existed with abundant resources, a surfeit of rivals, and a deficit in capital, Leland could be found. And while these projects were theoretically beneficial, the benefits were best perceived at a distance of several thousand miles.

Leland's equity offerings used tedious statistical analysis to mask the fact that their business centered on enslaving foreign people and ravaging their lands. They didn't do this directly, of course, but they hired the people who hired the people who did.

Humanity had always trafficked in oppression. Before the corporate marketing department got ahold of it, it was called *conquest*. Now it was *regional development*. Vikings and Mongols were big on revenue targets, too—but Leland had dispensed with all the tedious invading, and had taken a page out of the Roman playbook by hiring the locals to enslave each other as franchisees.

To view Leland fund managers as immoral was a gross simplification of the world. And what was there to replace capitalism, anyway? Communism? Theocracy? Most of the Third World had already suffered nearly terminal bouts of idealism. It was the Communists, after all, who had littered the world with cheap AK-47s in order to "liberate" the masses. But the only lasting effect was that every wall between Cairo and the Philippines had at least one bullet hole in it. But nothing changed. Nothing changed because these alternate belief systems flew in the face of human nature. Of even common sense. Anyone who has ever tried to share pizza with roommates knows that Communism cannot *ever* work. If Lenin and Marx had just shared an apartment, perhaps a hundred million lives might have been spared and put to productive use making sneakers and office furniture.

Leland bankers told clients that they didn't design the world—they were just trying to live in it. And incidentally, the wonders of the developed world rose from the ashes of conflict and competition, so they were helping people in the long run. For godsakes, just look at Japan.

And while the debate mumbled on, asterisked by legal disclaimers, Leland booked another highly profitable year.

But profitability was not what was bothering Garrett Lindhurst as he approached the CEO's office suite.

Among Leland's C-level executives, only Lindhurst was without decades-old family ties to the organization—but then again, the rapid expansion of computer systems in the corporate world in recent years had outpaced the ability of old-money families to produce senior technology talent. While Lindhurst hadn't written any actual code since working with Fortran and Pascal back in his Princeton days, he had learned over the years how much systems should cost and what they needed to do.

In essence, computer systems needed to do only one of two things: make money or save money. Everything else was just details. Scut work. These tasks Lindhurst delegated to the executive senior veeps, who, in turn, delegated them to someone else . . . and so on. It was only during times of complete disaster that Lindhurst involved himself with the actual computer systems themselves.

Today was such a time.

Lindhurst pointed at the CEO's temple-like office doors as he passed the executive secretary's desk. "He in?"

"He's leaving for Moscow in an hour."

She barely registered Lindhurst's presence. A stone-faced woman in her fifties, she was many years in the CEO's service and effectively had more authority than any two senior vice presidents put together.

But Lindhurst had more authority than ten. He pushed his way through the towering double doors.

"Garrett!" she called after him.

He ignored her and proceeded into the CEO's cavernous office at a quick pace.

The tanned, pampered face of Russell Vanowen, Jr., CEO and chairman of Leland Equity Group, looked up from reading a letter. He scowled. "Damnit, Garrett, make an appointment."

Garrett heard the doors close behind him, and he took a deep breath. "This can't wait."

"Then just pick up the phone, for chrissakes."

"We need a face-to-face."

Vanowen regarded him like a statue would a pigeon. Vanowen had that obsessively groomed look of the fabulously rich—as though his head were the grounds of Augusta National and a hundred groundskeepers swarmed over it each morning. The ring of white hair sweeping around the back of his head was perfectly manicured like a green. The pores of his skin were flawless. His suit was masterfully tailored to make his husky form look manly and authoritative.

Yet, for all his obvious fastidiousness, Vanowen did not look soft. He was stocky, intimidating, with a presence that projected itself without having to speak; his eyes scanned a room like twin .50-caliber machine guns. And he had an almost mystical authority in this office, with its bank of tall windows overlooking downtown Chicago and Lake Michigan beyond. This was a fabled seat of power, overlooking the length and breadth of the land.

Lindhurst proceeded toward Vanowen's massive teak wood desk, still thirty feet away. "We have a major problem, Russ."

Vanowen still held a letter in one hand, glaring over his reading glasses. He reluctantly dropped the letter on his otherwise empty desk and removed his glasses. "When you say 'we,' I take that to mean 'you.'" He glanced at his massive watch, tugging a cuff-linked sleeve up to see the face. "I'm heading out to the airfield any minute."

There wasn't any time to finesse it. "We've lost administrator rights to our network."

This did not have the impact Lindhurst hoped.

Vanowen shrugged slightly and now looked greatly irritated. "So what the hell do you want me to do about it? You're the CIO; ride your people until they fix it. Jesus, Garrett."

Lindhurst sat down in one of the uncomfortable leather chairs, pulling it right up to the desk. He leaned in close, still clutching the rolled magazine. "Russ, listen to me: we don't have any control over our databases."

"My response is the same. Now would you let me read this letter, please?"

"WE ARE UNDER ATTACK."

That got Vanowen's attention. "Attack?"

"Attack. All offices, worldwide. Look, I get in this morning, and I have phone calls from six division heads telling me they can't log on as admins to our servers. They think it's a layoff and that they've been shut out on purpose."

"Were they?"

"Not by us. Turns out *no one* can get an admin logon—not even here in the main office. All systems rebooted last night. And somehow, somebody took over our network. We have only limited rights to it."

Now Vanowen looked really angry. He pounded his fist on the desk.

"Jesus Christ, Lindhurst! Why the hell wasn't I told about this sooner? Our clients must be screaming bloody murder."

"Hold on a second. Our Web sites are up, and we can access data, no problem. So can our clients. We can even change data, so no one outside Leland knows yet."

Confused and getting angrier by the moment, Vanowen gestured, "So what's the problem?"

"The problem is that we can't back up, restore, or change our servers. We can't even export data."

"I may not know much about this stuff, Lindhurst, but I do know we spent thirty million dollars on backup systems. Surely you can take a backup copy and restore it."

"That's just it; our backup SANs are toast. Our off-site replication trashed. The log files were faked. We have no backups newer than four months ago."

Vanowen squinted at him. "How is that possible? I spent forty-seven million dollars on IT last year alone. We were supposed to have the most advanced network security money can buy. You assured me of that. You assured the board of that. That's why we hired you."

"I don't think our systems were breached. Not from the outside. I think it's an inside job."

"Call the FBI."

"We can't do that."

"The hell we can't."

"Understand this, Russ: they can flush our entire network down the toilet with a single keystroke—from just about anywhere in the world. This company is hanging by a thread."

The room got deathly quiet. Still staring, Vanowen spoke with the sort of calm voice that usually precedes violence. "Explain this to me, Garrett."

"It gets much worse."

"Worse? How the hell can it get any worse?"

"Watch." Garrett motioned for Vanowen to follow him.

Vanowen's office was huge, with a double-height ceiling and windows. Several sets of sofas and leather chairs were placed about the room, with a wide plasma-screen television on the far end and a conference table nearby, encircled by chairs. The place was easily a couple thousand square feet.

Vanowen reluctantly got up from his desk and followed Lindhurst to the plasma screen. Lindhurst was already fiddling with a remote he had picked up from the credenza there.

Vanowen settled into a conference table chair. "I'll see that the people behind this go to federal prison for the rest of their lives."

"I don't think so."

"What the hell's that supposed to mean?"

"You'll see in a moment." Lindhurst gestured to the plasma screen. "Have you used this video conferencing system yet? It cost seventy thousand dollars."

"Goddamnit, Lindhurst—"

"Okay, look, this system is jacked into our corporate network. I put something out there that I want you to see." Lindhurst used the remote to navigate to an intranet Web page, which filled the screen. "I found an e-mail in my inbox this morning. It was from the system administrator—the *new* system administrator. The person who took my rights away. That e-mail contained a hyperlink—which I copied to this network share." He navigated to another page and clicked a hyperlink. "Here is what I saw. . . ."

Vanowen looked impatiently at the screen.

The seventy-inch plasma monitor suddenly went black and after a few moments a whooshing sound effect escorted a whirling logo into the center of the screen. It was a stylized emblem of the words: *Daemon Industries LLC.*

A professional-sounding female announcer came on, along with cavorting corporate music. It was like an infomercial or network marketing video. Her voice was cheerful. "Welcome to the Daemon Industries family of companies. In just a moment you'll hear some of the exciting new opportunities available to you in this fast-growing global organization. An organization to which your company now belongs. But first, a word from our founder . . ."

Vanowen frowned. "Lindhurst—"

"Shh!" He pointed.

The screen faded in on a man in his mid-thirties. He was sitting in a chair next to a fireplace. The chirpy corporate Muzak continued in the background. Words appeared at the bottom of the screen:

Matthew A. Sobol, Ph.D.

Chairman & CEO Daemon Industries LLC

Sobol nodded once in dour greeting.

Lindhurst hit the PAUSE button on the remote. Sobol froze in mid-nod. "That's him."

"That's *who*?" Vanowen squinted at the words on-screen. He turned back to Lindhurst. "Never heard of him. Is this the person who broke into our network?"

"Yes."

"Call the FBI."

"Won't do any good, Russ. Matthew Sobol's dead." Lindhurst handed the rolled magazine to Vanowen.

Vanowen just glanced down at it, then with some reluctance took it. He unrolled it and moved it to arm's length so he could see the cover with his myopic eyes. The same Matthew Sobol was on the cover of the magazine. It was eight months old. The headline read: *Murderer From Beyond the Grave*. "That guy?" Vanowen tossed the magazine onto the nearby conference table. "That was a hoax." He motioned to the plasma screen. "So is this. My kid at USC could probably make this video on his Powerbook."

"Russ, someone managed a coordinated global attack that not only stole rights to our worldwide network, but they did it months ago without raising a single alarm. They didn't leave a trace. Matthew Sobol was one of the few people who could have pulled it off."

"You're frighteningly gullible. Jesus, some hackers got into our network, and they're trying to put one over on you. Call the FBI."

"Russ, no one faked this video. If you listen to him, you'll see what I mean." Lindhurst released the PAUSE button.

Matthew Sobol came back to life on-screen. The infomercial music faded as he finished his nod. "By now you're beginning to realize that you no longer control your network and that your backups are damaged beyond repair. I am now an integral part of your organization—and have been for several months. Let me assure you that your corporate data is safe, and that sufficient backups exist off-site to provide seamless protection in the event of a natural disaster or other calamity.

"Before I continue, let me caution you to watch this video in its entirety before contacting your local or federal authorities. This recording contains important information that may affect your decision to involve those entities in this situation."

A light musical jingle accompanied a twirling inset picture that spun to a stop alongside Sobol's head. It was a video of Sobol's mansion roaring in flames.

Sobol smiled pleasantly. "As you can see, involving the authorities is no guarantee of your safety. Although they would certainly be willing to try again at your location."

The inset video image transitioned to a collection of quivering question marks.

Sobol looked intently into the camera. "But you're probably wondering just how you got yourselves into this situation. To answer that question, surprisingly, we need to go back hundreds of millions of years to the very origins of life on Earth."

The question marks expanded to fill the screen and faded away as the entire screen dissolved to an image of primordial Earth. It was a 3-D computer animation of the ancient seas, teeming with exotic life— razor-toothed fish with whiplike probosces and flitting schools of tiny translucent organisms.s

Vangelis music rose on the surround-sound speakers. Sobol narrated, "Let me tell you the story of the most successful organism of all time: this is the story of the *parasite.*"

On-screen a large, particularly evil-looking fish with twin rows of splayed fangs and a spiked dorsal array glided into view. Just then, a small organism swam for the area just behind the enormous fish's gills, where it latched on, unnoticed. A dozen others followed it and also latched on.

Sobol spoke. "Early on, evolution branched into two distinct paths: independent organisms—those that exist on their own in the natural world—and parasites—organisms that live on other organisms. And it was, by far, the parasites that proved the more successful of the two branches. Today, for every independent organism in nature, there exist three parasites."

The computer animation transitioned from one eon to the next— from amphibian to reptilian to mammalian—with parasites continuing to evolve along with their hosts, infesting some species, driving them to extinction, while other species evolved means to keep them at bay—at least for a time.

"These two strains of evolution have been locked in a primordial arms race, constantly evolving to best each other for supremacy of this planet. As parasites evolve to perfect their systems against a species of host, the host evolves to evade their attack. Scientists call this theory of an eternal genetic struggle the Red Queen Hypothesis—a name taken from Lewis Carroll's *Through the Looking Glass.*"

On-screen, the image suddenly changed to an animation of Alice in Wonderland—with the Red Queen running along a hedgerow maze and looking toward little Alice, who struggled to keep up. She was saying: "Now, here, you see, it takes all the running you can do, to keep in the same place."

The screen changed to a video of a small pond, with snails moving through the mud.

"Animal behavior has evolved to battle parasites. In fact, we have parasites to thank for the existence of sex. Sex is a costly and time-consuming method of reproduction. Experiments have shown that, in the absence of parasites, species evolve toward parthenogenesis—or cloning—as the reproductive method of choice. In parthenogenesis each individual is able to self-replicate. But this produces almost no genetic variation. In the presence of parasites, cloning, while more energy-efficient, is not a viable reproductive strategy. It presents a stationary genetic target to parasites, who, once introduced into such a system, will quickly dominate it."

The screen changed to an animated diagram of twin sets of human DNA strands, which moved as Sobol spoke.

"Sexual reproduction exists solely as a means to defeat parasites. By mixing male and female genes, sex produces offspring not exactly like either the male or female—making each generation different from the last, and presenting a moving target to intruders intent on compromising this system.

"Even with this variation, parasites continue to pose a threat . . ."

The screen changed to color film footage of native villages with truly hideous parasitic infestations; children with bulging, worm-filled bellies; malaria victims.

". . . and parasitism evolves and moves through *any* system—not just living things. The less variation there is in a system, the more readily parasites will evolve to infest it. . . ."

The screen showed food-borne illness outbreaks—images of fast-food restaurants. The camera panned to reveal identical restaurants running down the sides of each street, in Dallas, in Denver, in Orlando, in Phoenix. . . .

"Perfect replication is the enemy of any robust system. . . ."

Then images of identical rows of computers in a data center, all running the same operating system . . .

"Lacking a central nervous system—much less a brain—the parasite is a simple system designed to compromise a very specific target host. The more uniform the host, the more effective the infestation."

The screen changed to a video image of a hermit crab moving along the sandy ocean bottom. The camera followed it as Sobol spoke.

"But if they're so successful, why haven't parasites taken over the world? The answer is simple: they have. We just haven't noticed. That's because successful parasites don't kill us; they become part of us, making us perform all the work to keep them alive and help them reproduce. . . ."

The crab scuttled toward its hole.

"*Sacculina* is a parasite that infests saltwater crabs. It burrows into their flesh and extends tendrils into the crab's bloodstream and brain. It chemically castrates the crab and becomes its new brain—controlling it like a zombie."

The screen then showed an image of a *Sacculina*-infested crab, with the bulging sack of the parasite filling its abdomen.

"It compels the crab to raise the parasite's young. It enslaves it."

The screen changed to a close-up computer animation. It was a double helix of DNA, with each set of genes showing clearly as rungs on the genetic ladder. The perspective moved along the length of the helix.

"And so have thousands of parasites done with us. After tens of thousands of years, a parasite becomes so much a part of us that they evolve into sections of our DNA."

Certain sections of the DNA were highlighted, one after another.

"They have so enslaved us that we believe we're reproducing ourselves, when in reality, we're reproducing hidden others within us. Forty percent of our genetic code consists of these useless segments of DNA—sections that serve no useful purpose to us. Nearly half the human genome is just the ghostly remnant of parasites."

The images of DNA dissolved back to Sobol, sitting in his armchair by the fireplace. "By now, you've figured out that my Daemon is your parasite and that you are hopelessly infected. The Daemon will sip your corporate blood, but it will not be fatal. More importantly, the Daemon will keep other parasites out of your system, strengthening your immunity and ensuring that the corporate host continues to survive."

The fireplace background dissolved, and Sobol now appeared on a black background. He was more serious.

"But know this: my Daemon has enlisted humans within your organization. These are hijacked cells in the corporate organism. People who thirst for more power. That's how the Daemon got in. You have no way of knowing who is responsible. My Daemon can teach almost anyone to defeat network security—especially from an existing network account. The reality is that my Daemon now controls your global IT function. Your business will operate as before, and no one will suspect that there is anything unusual going on—except that perhaps your systems will run better than they did when you were responsible for them.

"Your natural inclination will be to resist this indignity, of course, and so you will be tempted to contact the authorities. That is your choice—although the moment my Daemon detects such contact, it will wipe your company's data off the face of the earth. And don't even think of replicating your databases from scratch with paper files; remember that my Daemon has agents among your staff. You can hide nothing from it. If you start polygraphing or if you lay off everyone, the Daemon will destroy your company. If you attempt to infiltrate an undercover operative into your IT department, it will destroy your company. If you attempt to exert control over your IT department or to create a new one, it will destroy your company. In short: if you attempt to do anything other than ignore my Daemon, it will destroy your company.

"As a financial enterprise wholly reliant upon the trust of your clients, the loss of all your clients' data will bring ruin upon you. As for insurance: the Daemon will annihilate you whenever you reappear, and it will never stop until both your company and you as individual officers are financially destroyed. Being a nonsentient narrow-AI construct, the Daemon doesn't give a damn what choice you make. It's as dumb as *Sacculina*." A pause. "And just as effective."

The fireplace background reappeared, and Sobol smiled again. "I hope you and my Daemon can peacefully coexist. I think you'll find that, as the years roll by, you'll be glad indeed that you didn't try to defy it—especially as you take market share from those companies that did defy it. So, please, carefully consider your options, and just remember—no matter what you choose—you serve a crucial role in evolution. Even if it's just as food for the survivors. Thanks for watching."

Sobol waved pleasantly as the saccharine corporate Muzak came up, accompanied by fanatical applause. Credits rolled by impossibly fast.

The female announcer returned. "Don't touch that dial! In a few moments, you'll have a chance to see how you can avoid destruction at the hands of the Daemon. And be sure to take the Daemon quiz—"

Lindhurst hit the STOP button, and the screen went black.

Vanowen sat there like someone who had just been through electroshock therapy. His mouth hung open for several moments before he turned dull eyes toward Lindhurst. "It's really Sobol."

"That's what I was trying to tell you."

There were a few moments of silence.

"We have to call the authorities."

"If we call the FBI—and word gets out about this—our investors will bail. And sue."

Vanowen nodded. He suddenly frowned, as if remembering to be angry. "Damnit, Lindhurst, what kind of an organization are you running down there? Your systems may be responsible for the destruction of this company—a company with a century of history. When the shit hits the fan, I'm going to point the finger of blame squarely at you, where it belongs, and you can count on that."

Lindhurst looked darkly at Vanowen. "That's a touching sentiment, but I seem to remember it was you who told me to cut IT head count by half and slash the benefits of the rest. That left us with plenty of disgruntled people in our midst."

"You took your bonus, if I remember."

"Look, let's not turn this into a blamestorming session. There'll be plenty of time for that if we fail. In the meantime, we should focus on what we're going to do."

"You mean what *you're* going to do. I'm going to Moscow to maintain the appearance of normalcy. But I want a report in my inbox by the time I land, detailing precisely what you intend to do to solve this problem."

"No e-mail. Our systems are compromised. The phones, too. They're voice over IP—the signals go over the computer network. We'll need to use our personal cell phones and handwritten correspondence only—nothing enters a computer concerning this situation. Not a single typed character. Not even a scheduled meeting between us. *Nothing.* Otherwise they'll know what we're up to."

Vanowen was slightly taken aback. "You're serious?"

"Russ, you might not have noticed, but this entire organization is stitched together with computer networks. You can't enter the parking garage without producing half a dozen records in some database. Sobol says he has people on our staff, and they no doubt can see everything we're doing."

"If you ask me, this is simple: we shut everything off and go back to using pens, paper, and phones. Lay off all these IT bastards. We'll see how they like that."

Lindhurst took a deep breath to keep from losing his temper. He heard this suggestion from time to time from men of Vanowen's generation. Lindhurst chose his words carefully. "Russ, our competitors deliver market information in seconds to their clients, and we need to also. That doesn't even begin to cover the fact that we need information just as much, if not more, than our clients in order to make a profit. If you turn off these systems, you may as well lock the doors."

Vanowen was already nodding. "You're right. Of course, you're right. But damnit, I knew this would happen one of these days with these goddamn computers."

Lindhurst let this Nostradamus-like postdated prediction go uncontested. "Let's be explicit, then: you go about your normal schedule. I'll see what I can do about the problem, and when you return, we meet first thing. In person and off-site."

"Are you sure we shouldn't simply call the authorities?"

"Look, even if we decide to contact them, the more we know about what's really going on, the better. We're only talking about a few days more, and this thing has been inside us for months. Remember, the slightest hint that there's trouble, and this thing is liable to pull the plug on all our data."

"But would it really do that? Then it would get nothing."

"This isn't a *person*, Russ. It's a logic tree. That's like wondering if a computer has the courage to put the letter *D* on-screen if you tap the "D" key. I suspect that a few employees have handed over control to the Daemon. I'm hoping I can quietly discover who and convince them to change sides again."

Vanowen waved that topic aside. "I don't want to hear details. Just tell me when you've solved it. Now get out of here, I've got to get ready to leave."

Lindhurst put the remote down. He moved to leave but then turned back toward Vanowen. "What's in Moscow, Russ?"

Vanowen scowled. "What?"

"I'm just curious why you're heading to Moscow. Are we setting up a branch office there?"

Vanowen pointed to the door. "Go solve this problem, will you, please?"

Lindhurst regarded Vanowen for a moment more. He knew the old man was hiding something from him. He just didn't know what.

But for once, Lindhurst had a few cards up his own sleeve. Cards that the old man's generation didn't even know existed.

Chapter 32:// Message

Black screen. Suddenly a gleaming chrome logo hissed in from the left while ultrapasteurized techno music thumped in over the title:
News to America

The title twirled into infinity as inset video images crisscrossed the screen, and the music built in tempo. Anji Anderson pushing a microphone at a businessman covering his face. Anderson helping a handicapped child take her first steps on artificial limbs. Anderson typing feverishly at a laptop keyboard in the open air while columns of black smoke towered over a city skyline behind her. Fast cuts following fast cuts. Half a second each. The human brain had to scramble to identify the image, determine whether it presented a threat, and just barely resolved it in time for the next image: Anderson standing, arms akimbo, glowering at the camera in the middle of Times Square while her name slid into place beneath her belt line. The music stopped cold.

The screen flipped immediately to black. A color photograph of a small child faded in. A boy smiling into his birthday cake, surrounded by friends. Anderson's voice rose. "Peter Andrew Sebeck was born in Simi Valley, California, only son to Marilyn and Wayne Sebeck. He was their ray of hope after the loss of their first daughter to leukemia two years earlier. Outgoing, well liked, Peter was a model child."

Another picture resolved over the first. It showed Sebeck in a high school football uniform, holding his helmet on his knee, once again smiling.

"Peter appeared to have the perfect life. But his early promise was cut short when he fathered a child at the age of sixteen with Laura Dietrich, a girl he'd known only a short while. Within a year they married. Friends described it as a cold marriage, devoid of tenderness. Yet, to all outward appearances, Pete Sebeck was still a model citizen. He joined the Ventura County Sheriff's Department at age twenty-one, took night classes to earn a bachelor's degree in criminal justice, and rose quickly, becoming a twice-decorated officer and later a sergeant of detectives. To his fellow deputies, he was a no-nonsense officer and a family man—a well-respected citizen of Thousand Oaks, California, the safest city in America."

Chilling music rose. The image changed to a still photo of a menacing Sebeck being escorted in handcuffs, his face a blur of fast-moving rage, lashing out at reporters. It was the type of iconic photograph that made careers. A photo of the year. A symbol of the times.

"But this façade concealed a darker side. Peter Sebeck, convicted mass murderer—nine of his victims federal officers. Another victim, a young colleague who trusted and admired him. Conspirator, embezzler, adulterer. Sex and drug addict. What drives seemingly normal people to commit heinous acts? Is it anger? Greed? Or does evil really exist? Can it possess *you*? Tonight we'll find out as I interview Peter Sebeck live from Lompoc Federal Prison. This is *News to America*."

The techno music rose again. A title appeared:

Sebeck on Death Row

The screen resolved on Anderson, sitting erect and alert in medium close-up. She looked businesslike yet sexy in a dark Chanel suit. Her makeup was perfect in the warm glow of camera lights. The lighting had to be done carefully so as not to reflect harshly off the bulletproof glass partition—beyond which sat Detective Sergeant Peter Sebeck. The most hated man in America.

She had helped to make that a reality.

Sebeck stared from behind the small intercom microphone in the prison visitation cell. The studio provided a better sound system for this interview, and a smaller microphone was clipped onto Sebeck's khaki prison jumpsuit. One quarter of all households in America were anticipated to tune in. Everything was in place, and after a quick smile Anderson began.

"I must confess, Detective Sebeck, I'm surprised you agreed to this interview. I'm the person most responsible for your capture and conviction."

Sebeck regarded her coolly. "I agreed for my own reasons, not yours."

"So you still claim innocence?"

"I *am* innocent."

"How do you explain the substantial evidence against you?"

"It was manufactured by Matthew Sobol. He stole my identity years ago."

"So you still claim that Sobol's Daemon is real, even though all efforts to discover such a thing have come up empty?"

Sebeck tried to keep his cool. "The government wants people to believe the Daemon is a hoax. They think it takes them off the hook."

Anderson shook her head sadly. "Detective, you've already admitted your relationship with Cheryl Lanthrop—or did Sobol fake that, too?"

"He facilitated it. It was designed to impugn my character."

"But you've been quoted saying—"

"I've been incorrectly quoted—most of the time by you. And there's no appeal to the court of public opinion, is there? But I guess you know that."

"Then this is a conspiracy against you? Everyone from the media to the police, and Sobol himself, have all conspired to frame you for these murders? You're completely innocent?"

"I'm guilty of this much: being a bad husband and a worse father. I'm guilty of having an affair and of being too egotistical to realize I was being set up."

"Please forgive me, Detective, but that sounds far-fetched."

"Yes. That's the whole point. It was designed to be far-fetched."

"Designed by Sobol?"

"Yes."

"So, you're asking everyone to believe you, instead of the facts. We're to believe that Sobol went to Herculean lengths to frame you— spending not just millions but *tens* of millions of dollars in the effort?"

"I'm not asking anyone to believe anything. To be honest, even I wouldn't believe me."

"So you don't blame anyone?"

Sebeck stared hard at her. "Oh, I blame some people. But their time will come."

"That sounds like a threat. Do you believe the American public will be sympathetic toward threats?"

"I'm not here to talk to the American public."

"Then who are you here to talk to?"

"The Daemon."

"The *Daemon*?" Anderson was taken aback. "The Daemon doesn't exist, Sergeant."

"You and I both know that isn't true."

Anderson shrugged blissfully. "No, I don't know that."

"You're real proud of yourself, aren't you, Anji? Famous and rich—isn't that what the Daemon promised you? And all you had to do was sell your soul—if you ever had one."

"I didn't come here to be insulted, *ex*-Detective. Why don't you tell us your side of the Daemon hoax instead? Help us understand your point of view."

"Keep them entertained, Anji. Keep them busy and distracted. That's your purpose, isn't it? I see that now. Be careful, because I'm starting to understand Sobol. Maybe even better than you. I've had plenty of time to think in here. Why did Sobol warn me?"

"Sobol warned you? How did he warn you?"

"At his funeral he said he would destroy me. Those were his exact words. And that's exactly what he did. He destroyed everything that once defined me. It doesn't make sense that he would warn me—unless he had further plans for me."

"So he's your friend now? Does that idea comfort you?"

Sebeck looked her straight in the eye. "Fuck you."

Anderson clenched her jaw angrily for a moment. Then a pleasant smile spread across her face. "We have a time delay, Detective. But please watch your language. This is a family show."

"I understand what Sobol meant now."

"Well, you're running out of time to solve the case, Sergeant. If the Supreme Court refuses your appeal, you're scheduled to die by lethal injection. You must be impressed by the unusually swift hand of justice."

Sebeck contemplated it calmly. "It is unusual, isn't it?"

"Perhaps it was the murder of those federal officers."

"Why are you helping this thing? Do you think it will ever let you go? Do you think you will ever be free?"

Anderson ignored him. "You're undergoing psychiatric treatment. Is that going well?"

"I'm through talking to you. I came here to send a message to the Daemon."

"Well, you'd better hope it watches television, Detective."

Sebeck looked directly into the camera. "At Sobol's funeral, he phoned me. He said that I had to accept the Daemon. That in the months before my death I had to invoke it. And although it will make me sound more insane than ever, my message is this: I, Peter Sebeck, accept the Daemon. And I am ready to face the consequences."

Sebeck turned to the prison guards and federal officials standing behind Anderson. "That message needs to get out. She'll try to cut it from the interview—and when she does, you'll know she's afraid. You'll know she's in collusion with the Daemon. If you think I'm a nutcase, then that's all the more reason to get my message out there. It proves your case against me. It condemns me."

Anderson watched grimly from beyond the bulletproof partition. "Sergeant, there is no Daemon. But I'll be happy to pass along the message."

Sebeck pointed at her. "You and I will meet again."

Anderson felt strangely exhilarated. Sebeck was sexy when he was pissed off—and god, did this guy have balls. He was going to die, but he was going down swinging. She motioned to stop rolling camera, then locked eyes with Sebeck. "I'll convey the message. Have no doubt."

She had a direct line, after all.

And word from the Daemon was that Sebeck must die.

Chapter 33:// Response

Yahoo.com/news

Sebeck's Macabre **Message**—In a live interview with Anji Anderson Friday at Lompoc Federal Prison, **Peter Sebeck**, the ex–Ventura County Sheriff's detective convicted in last year's **Daemon Hoax**, directed a bizarre message to the late **Matthew Sobol**: "My message is this: **I, Peter Sebeck, accept the Daemon.**" Legal experts doubt a belated insanity defense will have any effect on Sebeck's pending federal appeal.

In a dark storage room in a nondescript export company in the Huang Cun Industrial Zone of Dongguan City, China, a low-end server stood wedged between stacks of toner cartridges and counterfeit software packages. A long-forgotten CAT-5 cable ran from the back of the machine, snaking behind towering boxes containing yet more boxes, and terminated in a Fast-Ethernet jack just to the left of an overloaded electrical outlet—both lost to sight behind cases of Communist Party propaganda pamphlets, printed specifically for use as props in Western theme restaurants. The Ethernet jack ran in turn to the company network, which in turn led to the corporate Web server, which in turn led to the world.

The computer fan hummed as the machine used RSS to scan the contents of the same four hundred Web sites every minute. And at exactly seventeen minutes past midnight, Greenwich Mean Time, the machine stopped scanning.

The computer's hard drive whined to life and started clicking feverishly—sending out packets to hundreds of IP addresses before committing digital suicide by erasing itself.

Another Daemon event had been triggered.

Part Three

Six Months Later

Chapter 34://_Sacculina_

"**W**hat the hell is going on with these numbers, people?" Russell Vanowen, Jr., looked up from the P&Ls in his executive financial summary. He frowned down the burled walnut table running the length of his paneled corporate boardroom. The familiar faces of two dozen Leland board members and senior executives stared back. The faces were all the more familiar because he served on their boards, too. "I've got seven divisions running over budget, with only IT on target. What the hell is going on here? Why didn't I receive any guidance on this?"

Harris Brieknewcz, the CFO, shook his head slowly. "Russ, let me stop you right there. These numbers are wrong."

"Wrong? How are they wrong?"

"Wrong as in not right. Look . . ." He slid an open binder across the table. Other execs passed it on to Vanowen. "This is what we're getting from our off-line systems."

"What the hell, Harris—you mean _spreadsheets_? You're passing me spreadsheets? Why did I spend fifty million dollars on a real-time enterprise accounting system if we can just use spreadsheets?"

"The accounting system is wrong. Things are being assigned to the wrong cost centers."

"Forget cost centers—we're sixty million dollars over budget this month. It doesn't matter how you move the shells around. You'll still have the same number of shells."

"Yes, but the numbers aren't being assigned to the correct cost centers—"

"Well, then your people are screwing up the entries—"

"They're not screwing up the data entry, Russ. We're not sixty million dollars off the mark this month from keying errors. I had my people start recording these problems because—"

"Why is this the first I've heard about it?"

Brieknewcz stopped, girded himself, then continued. "You haven't heard about it because Lindhurst told me they'd fix it. It's under his purview, not mine. IT runs the accounting system."

Milton Hewitt, the executive VP of the brokerage division, leaned forward. "He's right, Russ. Our cost centers are under budget this period, and we exceeded our revenue targets. But these reports coming out of the accounting system are all screwed up."

Several others voiced their agreement.

Vanowen threw up his hands. "Jesus H. fucking Christ . . ." He looked around. "Lindhurst! Where's Lindhurst?"

Everyone glanced around theatrically. They knew he wasn't present. Again.

Vanowen dropped his leather folio onto the table with a *bang*. "Goddamnit! Janice!"

The disembodied voice of Vanowen's secretary carried over from somewhere among the chairs lining the wall. "Yes, Russ."

"Is Lindhurst in today? Has he been reminded of this meeting? The monthly *board meeting*?"

"I checked his calendar. He should be in. I phoned him this morning."

"And what did he say?"

"Voice mail. I left three messages. And I e-mailed him."

"Goddamnit! Did you call his cell phone?"

"Voice mail. Voice mail on his home and car phones, too."

Chris Hempers, the COO, raised a finger to call attention to himself. "I flew to the trade summit in Montreal with him yesterday."

"He left town with this going on? Is he back in the office?"

Hempers nodded. "We took one of the Gulfstreams—Ludivic, Ryans, Lindhurst, and I."

Several voices said simultaneously, "He's here."

They smelled blood—a career being cut short—and the possibility of a high-level opening for a friend or relation.

Vanowen was building a head of steam—for which he was justifiably famous. "Well, now I know why he doesn't want to be here. His folks have screwed up the accounting system, and they hid the problems from me. I hope Lindhurst has a drug problem, because that's about the only thing that would explain this. Janice, get him on this phone right now." He pointed to the cutting-edge speakerphone in the center of the tabletop.

"I just tried his line again, Russ. Voice mail."

"Goddamnit!" Vanowen glanced around. "Board members, please carry on with the agenda. Ryans, you preside. I'm going to retrieve our Mr. Lindhurst, and we'll get to the bottom of this right now."

———

Like most companies, Leland Equity Group maintained a data center where no window offices would be lost—in the basement. Thus, Leland's fifty-story office tower had several temperature-controlled subbasements linked directly into the fiber optic network running beneath the streets of downtown Chicago. From the subbasement the IT department's tendrils spread to every corner of the building, snaking up all fifty floors through trunk lines that fanned out on each floor to tap every employee individually.

As Vanowen took the separate bank of elevators leading into the basement, he realized how like the *Sacculina* parasite the IT department was. And lately it had been growing. Without authorization.

Lindhurst said he'd taken care of this.

Months ago, Lindhurst had moved from his corner office on the forty-ninth floor into the windowless bowels of the building. It was an unprecedented gesture of hands-on management. To Vanowen's delight, Lindhurst presided over a two-month bloodbath of IT layoffs. Purging the department of "questionable individuals," cleansing the global organization, and hiring new people who had no doubt where their loyalties should lie. And Leland Equity not only remained, it thrived like never before. The would-be Daemon was stopped—Lindhurst had succeeded, and not a word about their little "difficulty" had made it into the press. The problem was gone.

But now something frightening was happening. The accounting system was wrong. They were a private equity house, for chrissakes. They had to know how to add and subtract numbers.

Vanowen was starting to wonder whether Lindhurst had manufactured this whole threat. Was he that ambitious? Was he that clever?

No way.

Lindhurst certainly had his little fiefdom locked down tight now.

Even Vanowen had to order lobby security to enter a code into the keypad in the elevators to get them to move down into the subbasement. The place was like a missile silo. Perhaps Lindhurst was getting too distant from upper management. Perhaps it was time to pull him back into the executive suite. Or to fire him. Vanowen pondered this as the elevator doors opened onto a long, featureless white hallway on level B-2. Uncharacteristically, the hall ran straight ahead, no right or left. Vanowen had never been down here. The corridor stretched for what looked like a hundred feet or more. It had the plastic smell of new construction. Not a sign, a receptionist desk, or anything. He hesitated a moment.

But Vanowen still felt a bit of anger, so he strode out and down the hall, his expensive shoes clacking on the black tile floor.

What the hell kind of place is this?

He tried to recall any descriptions of the IT department by other executives, but came up empty. He kept clicking down the interminable hallway. There were no doors. He squinted ahead, but the hallway somehow seemed to disappear in a dim blackness. Surely he should be able to see the end of it.

He glanced back at the elevator door. It was nearly a hundred feet back. Could they have mistakenly sent him to the storage floor?

He turned front again and peered into the distance. Damnedest thing.

Then something impossible happened. A female voice spoke to him from the air six inches in front of his face. *"Why have you come here?"*

Vanowen jumped back three feet and nearly fell on his ass. His gasp echoed down the hallway in both directions. He took a moment to catch his breath. He held his chest, still gasping for air. Was he having a coronary?

The voice spoke again, from that spot in midair. *"You were commanded to stay out of this place."*

It was like a ghost. But it was a computer voice, wasn't it? He could just get a hint of artificiality in it. British. Leland had a sophisticated voice response system on their customer service phone lines. Lindhurst had demonstrated it to the board last year. It reduced call center costs by 90 percent—it was cheaper than India. But it didn't speak in midair.

This was just a trick.

Vanowen was getting his wits back. And his anger. This prank was way out of line. "Lindhurst! Get me Lindhurst, goddamnit!" Vanowen's voice echoed. "I will not be treated this way!"

"*QUIET!*" The word was so loud it ripped the fabric of the air around him. It was a physical presence that bowled him over and sent him sprawling backward, where he lay in the hallway, dazed. His ears were ringing. His eyes watering. It was possibly the loudest sound he'd ever experienced.

He felt a trickle running from his right nostril, and he dabbed a hand up—coming back with blood. "Jesus . . ." He pulled a silk handkerchief from his pocket and held it to his face. His hands were trembling uncontrollably.

It quickly swelled to panic. He crawled on his hands and knees, then got to his feet and started running back the way he came. He hadn't actually run in years, but adrenaline carried him the hundred feet back to the elevator. He arrived panting and nearly hysterical.

But there was no button. The elevator doors were like brushed steel gates. This was impossible. There was no call button. How could there be no button?

The Voice was right beside his ear, as if he hadn't moved. He could feel the air vibrating. "*Your company belongs to me now. Your divisions will obey their new budgets. If any division heads object, send them to me.*"

Vanowen's hands were still trembling. It was Lindhurst. Lindhurst was . . . or someone was behind this. It was extortion. This was a scare tactic.

"*Of course, you doubt that I am real. You doubt that I am Sobol's Daemon, and you doubt that my power spans the globe. I will prove to you the extent of my reach.*" There was a pause. "*I just caused you millions of dollars in personal losses. Losses across your portfolio and unrelated to this company. You will either learn from this event, or I will seize your personal wealth and eject you from this company. I will be watching you. Do you understand this final warning?*"

Vanowen stared at the air, still trembling. Waiting for it to end.

"*DO YOU UNDERSTAND?*"

"Yes! Yes! Yes!" He was covering his ears and face with the handkerchief—practically weeping.

The elevator doors suddenly opened, and Vanowen fell inside. He scrambled on his hands and knees and curled up in the farthest corner.

The Voice spoke again, but from the hallway, as if it were standing there, seeing him off. *"If you fight me, I will only hurt you more."*

With that, the elevator doors slammed together with frightful force. The car began to ascend.

Vanowen sat there shaking, blood running down his face.

———

Vanowen spent the remainder of the afternoon in a daze in his corner office, receiving a parade of phone calls from his attorneys and brokers. Millions of dollars had disappeared from his dozens of brokerage and bank accounts. More worrisome were the missing funds in the half-dozen offshore holding companies and the two dozen limited partnerships in which he held assets—some of which were secret even to his wife, much less people at Leland. All told, almost 10 percent of his wealth had disappeared in the blink of an eye. He had just lost eighty million dollars at separate institutions—some of which he held under assumed names.

As he sat there, still shaking, he suddenly realized the enormity of the monster that had just brushed past him. It was colossally huge. And as powerful as he had always felt, he felt insignificant before it.

He was now an employee of Daemon Industries LLC.

Chapter 35://Cruel Calculus

Reuters.com/business

Dow Sinks 820 Points on Renewed **Cyber Attacks**—Network intrusions **destroyed data** at two publicly traded multinational corporations Wednesday—bringing the total to six **cyber attacks** in as many days and sending financial markets into free fall. The stocks of **Vederos Financial** (NYS—**VIDO**) and **Ambrogy Int'l** (**NASDAQ**—**AMRG**) fell to pennies a share before trading was halted. Federal authorities and international police agencies claim cyber terrorists infiltrated company systems, destroying data and backup tapes. In a worrisome development in the War on Terror, unnamed sources indicated that Islamic terrorists were likely to blame—possibly students educated in Western universities. . . .

Ops Center 1 was the National Security Agency's mission control room. Dozens of plasma screens lined its walls, displaying real-time data from around the world in vibrant colors and vector graphics. There were color-coded diagrams of telecom, satellite, and Internet traffic. Other screens displayed current satellite coverage zones and still others showed the status of seabed acoustic sensors, missile launch monitors, the location of radar, radio, seismic, and microwave listening posts. The moderately sized room had a central control board, but individual workstations were arrayed around it in aisles. Each was manned by a specialist case officer: Latin America, the Middle East, the Terrorist Threat Integration Center, the Drug Interdiction Task Force, and on and on.

Uniformed military personnel dominated the space. They were relatively young people for the most part, not the seasoned analysts who developed strategy but the younger officers who worked in the world of operations, monitoring the data feeds. They were the nerve endings of the United States.

They were especially keyed up as they watched the large central screen and its digital world map. Hundreds of red dots on that map were scattered throughout North America, Europe, and Southeast Asia. And in this business, red dots meant trouble.

Dr. Natalie Philips stood behind the central control board operator. A three-star general and the NSA's deputy director, Chris Fulbright, stood alongside her. Fulbright had the earnest, soft-spoken manner of a high school guidance counselor, but his mild demeanor masked a steely-eyed pragmatism. Philips knew that mild-mannered people did not rise to Mahogany Row.

She gestured to the digital map filling the screen. "Approximately thirty-eight hundred corporate networks in sixteen countries have been hijacked by an unknown entity—and these are just the ones we know about. We have good reason to believe the entity is Sobol's Daemon."

The general stared at the screen. "Sergeant, notify the Joint Chiefs; inform them that we are under attack."

The board operator looked up. "Already taken care of, sir."

The general looked to Philips again. "Where are the attacks coming from?"

Philips stared at the world map. "You mean where *did* they come from, General. The battle is long over."

"What the hell is she talking about?"

Deputy Director Fulbright interceded. "She means these networks were compromised some time ago. We're only learning about it just now."

The general's nostrils flared. He looked darkly at Philips. "How is it possible no one noticed these networks go down?"

"Because they didn't go down. They're still operating normally."

The general looked confused.

Philips explained. "Someone took them over, and they're running them as if they own them."

The general gestured to the screens. "Why wasn't this detected? Our systems should have sounded the alarm the moment anomalous IP traffic patterns occurred. Isn't that what the neural logic farm is for?"

Philips was calm. "It wasn't detected, General, because there were no anomalous traffic patterns to detect. The Daemon is not an Internet worm or a network exploit. It doesn't hack systems. It hacks society."

The general looked again to Fulbright.

Fulbright obliged. "Dr. Philips discovered the back door in Sobol's video games some months ago. One that allowed users to enter secret maps and be exposed to the Daemon's recruitment efforts."

The general nodded impatiently. "So the Daemon recruited people to compromise these corporate networks on its behalf?"

"Yes. We believe it coordinated the activities of thousands of people who had no individual knowledge of each other."

"The Daemon Task Force was supposed to detect and infiltrate these terror cells."

Philips regarded the general with deliberate patience. "Our monitoring resulted in several dozen arrests, but the Daemon network is massively parallel—no one person or event is critical to its survival. It has no ringleaders and no central point of failure. And no central repository of logic. None of the Daemon's agents knows anything more than a few seconds in advance, so informants have been useless. It also seems highly adept at detecting monitoring."

"Forget arrests. What about infiltration?"

"We've been working with the interagency Task Force, but progress has been slow. My people are not undercover operatives—they know far too many national secrets to be put at risk of capture—and the operatives who've been brought forward from Langley and Quantico are not expert enough in the lingo and culture of computer gaming—or cryptography and IP network architecture for that matter. A third of them are evangelicals with little or no experience in online gaming. Developing their skills will take time. We're painfully short of suitable recruits."

The general pounded his hand on a chair back in frustration. "Goddamnit, this thing is running circles around us." He looked to Philips again. "How does recruiting kids through video games translate into taking over corporate networks?"

Philips was looking at the big screen. "Because it didn't recruit kids. Have a look at the demographics of video game sales. The biggest market segment is young men aged eighteen to twenty-eight."

Fulbright nodded. "IT workers."

"Maybe." She turned to them both. "It could be any mid- to low-level employee. Not necessarily an IT staffer. Their efforts would be augmented by a massively parallel cyber organism that coordinates the efforts of thousands of other people—and it can pay."

The general tried to wrap his head around it. "But why would employees want to destroy their own company? It doesn't make sense."

"There are always disgruntled or greedy people. The Daemon most likely deals them in."

The general had murder in his eyes. "These terrorists need to be found and shot."

"Careful. The Daemon has already destroyed two dozen companies that disobeyed its instructions. Among the currently infected are several multibillion-dollar corporations, representing a cross section of strategic industries—energy, finance, high-tech, biotech, media, manufacturing, food, transportation. The targets were obviously selected to maximize economic and social disruption in the event of their collapse."

The general was starting to see the big picture. "This is no different from a strategic bombing campaign. This Daemon could gut the global economy. What are our options?"

She sighed. "Before we knew the extent of the infection, we attempted to penetrate a couple of compromised networks. But our intrusion attempts were detected and the target networks—and thus, the companies themselves—were destroyed by the Daemon in retribution."

"Wiretaps and surveillance of individual employees by the FBI resulted in similar retribution. Apparently, the Daemon does not hesitate to destroy the companies it has taken hostage. Further infiltration attempts have been put on hold until new strategies can be developed."

"Doctor, I repeat: what are our options?"

Philips paused. "Right now we have only one: inform the public. Tell them what's happening."

"That's crazy talk. The stock market would crash."

Fulbright pointed them to a side conference room and spoke softly. "Please, let's continue this discussion behind closed doors. Everyone here may be cleared top-secret, but they all have retirement funds."

They entered a small conference room, and the deputy director closed the door behind them.

The general glared at Philips. "Doctor, what would informing the public accomplish other than to destroy the 401(k)s of millions of taxpayers?"

"Right now Sobol has you exactly where he wants you. His Daemon can prey upon millions of unsuspecting people because we haven't warned anyone. At some point the Daemon is going to show itself—and we'll lose all credibility with the public. Look, announce its existence before you're forced to, and we'll have billions of allies to help us destroy it."

Fulbright shook his head. "It's not that simple, Doctor. A news headline announcing that the Daemon exists might trigger a Daemon event—possibly the deletion of all data in these compromised networks. It could cause financial Armageddon. It could cripple the world economy and lead to widespread conflict—even thermonuclear war. We can't risk that possibility."

Philips didn't blink. "That's an extreme conclusion."

"Extreme conclusions are what I'm paid to come to."

"Do you ever plan on telling the public?"

"We'll inform them after we've developed a countermeasure."

"But that might be never."

He didn't say anything.

"Sir?"

"Yes, Doctor?"

"If you don't intend to announce the existence of the Daemon, then I hope you're planning to intervene on behalf of Peter Sebeck."

The general looked to her. "The cop on death row?"

"His appeals are moving through the federal courts unusually fast. He's scheduled to die by lethal injection."

Fulbright didn't respond immediately. "I'll take that under advisement, Doctor."

"You could fake his execution—"

"This might seem harsh, but Peter Sebeck must suffer the full penalty demanded by law—and the sooner the better. Faking his execution would risk tipping our hand to the Daemon."

"Sir, please—"

"Philips, you yourself said that the Daemon has operatives in thousands of organizations. It could also have operatives in the penal system or law enforcement. So we must take the safe course. Sebeck is a casualty of this war, Doctor. You must put him out of your mind and concentrate on saving the lives and property of millions more Americans."

Philips stared at him for a moment. "But surely we—"

"There is no 'but,' Doctor. Please focus on your work."

She was about to speak again when the general leaned in.

"Any word from Jon Ross?"

Philips was still distracted but collected herself. "Not recently."

The general nodded. "*There's* a hacker we need in custody ASAP. All these hackers should be rounded up and shot."

She eyed the general. "*I'm* a hacker, General, and if it weren't for people like Jon Ross, we'd be in far worse shape than we are now."

Fulbright kept his eyes on her. "Find him. We need him on the Joint Task Force. Tell him we'll offer amnesty and U.S. citizenship, if you think it will matter. Just get him here. In the meantime, I need you and your people focused and working to find a way to stop this thing. Is that clear?"

She did not respond with enthusiasm. "Yes, sir."

Fulbright didn't relent. "Are we clear on this?"

"Sir, I—"

"You are a perceptive woman, Natalie. You, of all people, should be able to do the math on this. If we risk the lives and livelihoods of hundreds of millions of people to save the life of a single man, we'll be guilty of a heinous crime. Do you see the truth of this?"

She nodded after a moment.

"Now perhaps you can gain some appreciation for the cruel calculus I'm forced to use every day." He put a hand on her shoulder. "Your heart is in the right place. There's nothing wrong with that. But keep a sense of perspective. Ask yourself how many children you'd be willing to sacrifice so that Detective Sebeck can live."

Philips realized he was right.

The general cleared his throat. "I need to report back to the Pentagon."

Philips turned to the deputy director. He nodded. She called after the general. "There's more, sir."

"Let's hear it."

"I detected something unusual emanating from the networks of Daemon-infected companies. It's a pulse—an IP beacon of sorts. The tech industry calls these 'heartbeats.' This one consists of a lengthy burst of packets issuing from TCP port 135 at a predictable interval and bit length. Once we noticed the beacon was present at infected companies, we started looking for it elsewhere on the Internet. We found it echoing all over. That's how we estimate that thirty-eight hundred corporations have been compromised. Some of those companies might not even know they're infected yet."

The general was nonplussed. "What's the purpose of this 'IP beacon'?"

"That was the question. We first thought it might be a signal to indicate a company was a Daemon host. But then the signal wouldn't need to be so long—and each burst is a pretty long stream of data. It's always identical for a single company, but never the same between two different companies. And all companies project it in a sequence—like a chain. A pulse from Company A is sent to Company B, then from Company B to Company C, and so on until we start back at Company A again. Stranger still, when our infiltration attempt caused one company to be destroyed, another beacon appeared at a new company to take its place, and it exactly matched the beacon that was lost."

She paused. "That's when I first suspected this was a multipart message."

"The companies are communicating with each other?"

"No. They're communicating to *us*."

The general weighed what that meant. He regarded Philips with something akin to dread. "What are they saying?"

"The message was encoded with a 128-bit block cipher. It took us weeks to decrypt—and that was on *Cold Iron*. The good news is that, besides the Japanese and maybe the Chinese, it will take other nations years to decrypt, so we're convinced that Sobol intended it for us. When we assembled the constituent pieces from all the beacons at all the companies, we discovered a single, very large GNU compressed file. When we extracted the package contents, we found two things: an API and an MPEG video file."

"What's an API?"

"It's an application programming interface—rules for controlling a process. It's basically a guide for communicating with—and possibly controlling—the Daemon."

"Good lord! Why would Sobol give us that?"

"I think it's a trap, sir."

"What sort of control is it saying it will give us?"

"We've only begun our analysis, but the most significant function we've discovered is in the Daemon's Ragnorok class library. It's a function named *Destroy*. It accepts a country code and a tax ID as arguments. We believe that invoking it destroys all the data in the target company."

The general thought about this. "My God . . . why would he give that to us?"

"We don't know yet."

"You said there was a video. What did the video contain?"

Philips took a deep breath. "Something you need to carry up the chain of command."

In the boardroom of building OPS-2B, the group of agency directors sat arrayed around a broad mahogany conference table. The tension was thick as ominous looks passed from one director to the next. Their host opened the emergency meeting.

NSA: "Gentlemen, you are all aware of the gravity of the current situation. I've brought in representatives from both Computer Systems Corporation and its subsidiary, EndoCorp, to provide additional technical expertise in this matter. These are the same folks who built the FBI's new case management system. They are cleared UMBRA, so we may speak freely. Some of you have already worked together at NBP-1."

Both representatives gave dour nods. They were in their forties and looked more conservative than the window mannequins in the FBI gift shop.

NSA: "What you're about to see is a matter of the utmost secrecy. Were this information to be made public, there is every likelihood that the world economy would falter." He let it sink in. "A-Group has decrypted a video message from Matthew Sobol."

An animated buzz spread through the room. He waited until it died down.

NSA: "We're going to screen that video. Watch it carefully, and we'll discuss it afterward. Lights, please."

The lights dimmed, and a plasma screen set into the wall glowed to life. In a moment Matthew Sobol appeared in high-definition color. The image was so clear it seemed as if a window had opened in the side of the somber boardroom. Sobol stood outdoors, in the sun on high ground overlooking the ocean. He was dressed in khakis and a pressed linen shirt. He looked normal, healthy, the breeze tossing his hair.

Sobol betrayed no emotion. He stared into the camera for several moments before speaking. "They built a twenty-trillion-dollar house of cards. Then they told you to guard it. And they call *me* insane."

Sobol started to walk along the cliff's edge. The camera followed him, Steadicam-like, in medium close-up. "Technology. It is the physical manifestation of the human will. It began with simple tools. Then came the wheel, and on it goes to this very day. Civilizations rise and fall based on technological innovation. Bronze falls to iron. Iron falls to steel. Steel falls to gunpowder. Gunpowder falls to circuitry." Sobol looked toward the camera again. "For those among you who don't understand what's happening, let me explain: the Great Diffusion has begun—an era when the nation state dissolves. Technology will cause this. As countries compete for markets in the global economy, diffusion of high technology will accelerate. It will result in a diffusion of power. And diffusion of power will make countries an ineffective organizing principle. At first, marginal governments will fail. Larger states will not be equipped to intercede effectively. These lawless regions will become breeding grounds for international crime and terrorism. Threats to centralized authority will multiply. Centralized power will be defenseless against these distributed threats. You have already experienced the leading edge of this wave."

Sobol stopped walking and gazed longingly out at the ocean. In a moment he turned to the camera again.

"My Daemon is not your enemy. And thankfully it cannot be stopped. By anyone or anything. It is neither good nor evil. It is like fire, and it will burn those who do not learn to use it. It will burn the enemies of reason. It will burn the hypocrites and the fools. Use the tools I've given you, and the Daemon will become a valuable resource. Or, if you prefer, don't. Remember that the Daemon is now firmly established throughout the world. Other cultures will use these tools, even if you do not."

He stared straight into the camera. "There will be violence soon. It will shock you with its scope and ferocity. Don't waste your time interceding. It isn't directed at you. It is directed at other parasites in the network.

"Distributed daemons are a foregone conclusion in the coming world. You should befriend this one. Because the next daemon might not be so friendly. And, unlike your current leaders, my Daemon *can* protect you from your enemies."

The video ended, and the lights came up.

Everyone looked suddenly haggard.

CIA: "Jumping Jesus . . ."

NSA: "Gentlemen, you've seen the devil himself, and now we need to figure out what to do about him."

CIA: "Forget him. What can we do to stop his Daemon?"

DARPA: "We need to destroy the Daemon's darknet, that's what we need to do. This message is just propaganda. Another misdirection."

CSC: "Destroying the Daemon will require a coordinated cyber attack on numerous corporate data systems. An attack unprecedented in scale—a digital D-Day."

DARPA: "Too risky. One misstep, and the Daemon destroys thousands of companies."

EndoCorp: "We can't just let this thing take over. Whatever the cost."

FBI: "What does Sobol mean when he says there'll be violence? Is he talking revolution?"

DARPA: "He's a megalomaniac."

DIA: "If he means revolution, we should have troops in the streets. Sobol could be planning a coup."

NSA: "The markets are already shaky. Mobilizing troops and declaring martial law will cause a panic."

CSC: "We have private security forces available."

CIA: "He said we weren't the target."

FBI: "You're not going to take him at his word, are you?"

DIA: "He did say nation states were doomed."

CIA: "Yes, but he didn't say he would be the instrument of their destruction. He could be warning us."

FBI: "You're starting to worry me."

CIA: "I don't mean that Sobol is on our side. I think he's an evil bastard—I mean *was* an evil bastard—but he had a demented vision that I think we should try to wrap our heads around. He talked about small groups—'The Great Diffusion' is how he termed it. That small groups would be battling nation states."

DARPA: "Sobol mentioned lawless regions and failed states. What if he was talking about terrorism?"

DIA: "Terrorists use our own technology against us."

CIA: "And so do international crime rings. Does Sobol think his Daemon could be used against terrorism and transnational crime?"

DARPA: "It took over the online porn and gambling industries easily enough."

NSA: "We've got to get a handle on this."

EndoCorp: "Gentlemen, this Daemon is comprised of distributed networked systems with a companion human network. This is no different from many enemies we've already defeated."

DARPA: "I think it's clearly different."

EndoCorp: "In specifics, maybe, but not in the abstract. Whether he's dead or alive, Sobol's network can be disrupted and his people put to flight. In order to knock out his human network, we need to hit them hard and hit them everywhere—keep them on the run and keep them looking over their shoulder."

CSC: "And in order to prevent the various Daemon components from interacting, we stage a regional power outage immediately preceding operations. We exert our control over major media outlets to prevent the Daemon from reading the news—or we fabricate the news to suit our purposes."

The directors seemed taken aback by the sudden turn in the discussion.

NSA: "What about the Daemon's human operatives? Wouldn't they still be able to communicate?"

EndoCorp: "This is classic infowar—which *we* invented. We have highly skilled cyber and electronic warfare experts. We'll be monitoring Daemon activities in coming weeks. And as for the Daemon's human operatives: they won't stand up long against ex–Special Forces soldiers. We've operated successfully in Colombia against left-wing rebels and narco-terrorists, and in sub-Saharan Africa against Islamic rebels. Our men operate in small groups with minimal supervision—no legislative oversight necessary."

CIA: "That's fine in Colombia and sub-Saharan Africa, but how the hell are you going to sell that in Columbus, Ohio? And how do you tell friend from foe in a tech park server room?"

EndoCorp: "You don't. We move in our own people to operate the data centers and detain the current staff until we can satisfy ourselves that they pose no risk."

NSA: "This is crazy talk. You can't round up IT workers in thousands of companies. You don't have the manpower, for one thing. Also, a substantial percentage of the infected sites are in foreign countries.

Most Fortune 500 companies have their back-office data processing operations in India and Southeast Asia."

EndoCorp: "Borders mean nothing to us. We have private military provider and support firms in place in twenty-five countries, incorporated under a hundred different names. And we have influential voices in dozens more countries. Certain financial interests currently at risk are willing to underwrite this effort to protect the global economy."

NSA: "The moment you attack, the Daemon will destroy the infected networks."

FBI: "He's right. There are too many targets to hit all at once."

The CSC representative looked soberly around the table.

CSC: "That's correct. That's why we need to pick and choose. If we defend a cross-section of Western interests in numerous industries, the global economy can achieve survivability. But only if strategic investments are made in the shares of selected survivors. This can defray the loss of the other companies."

The directors were speechless for a moment.

DARPA: "What about these 'tools' that Sobol mentioned?"

The faces shifted in his direction.

NSA: "It's a programming interface of some type included in Sobol's message. Group A has a team analyzing the components now. They suspect Sobol might be extending some form of communication with his Daemon. Perhaps even rudimentary control."

FBI: "What kind of control?"

NSA: "For starters, there's a function that, on demand, destroys the data of any chosen Daemon-infected company."

Everyone immediately grasped the significance of this.

DARPA: "And this is still being broadcast around the world in an encrypted beacon?"

NSA: "Yes. Which means it's only a matter of time until other governments have this knowledge, too."

CIA: "Sobol's forcing our hand."

DARPA: "We'll need to see that API as soon as possible. It could provide intelligence on the topology of the Daemon's darknet."

FBI: "You're not seriously suggesting we start communicating with this thing? We don't negotiate with terrorists."

NSA: "No one's negotiating with anyone. This is an object library. We're analyzing it."

FBI: "Look, we've been messing around long enough. We need to kill it. It's taken over a big chunk of the Fortune 500, and it can cause irreparable harm to this nation."

CSC: "To the global economy."

NSA: "That's the whole point: if we make one move against it, the Daemon will flush all that corporate data down the toilet. And if we ignore it, then some other government might invoke the *Destroy* function to attack us."

CSC: "We must attack it."

NSA: "I don't think losing three quarters of the companies is an option."

EndoCorp: "You need to move on Sobol's organization. Infiltrate it, identify all the ringleaders, nab them, turn the screws on them, and roll their whole damned group. We've done it before."

CSC: "You'll need handpicked teams."

NSA: "Gentlemen, I hope we're not disturbing your meeting."

They looked impassively at the director.

Chapter 36:// The Powers That Be

A gleaming Dassault business jet taxied out of the darkness and into a brightly lit, spotlessly clean hangar. It rolled to a stop alongside a black Cadillac Escalade and a Chevy Suburban. The aircraft engines whined to a stop as men in suits removed their ear protection and approached the plane.

The jet door was pulled open, letting down a short row of steps. In a moment Russell Vanowen, Jr., stepped from the plane, as always looking resplendent in a bespoke, black pinstriped suit. He cast his commanding gaze around the hangar. Everything looked secure. Only his hired security team was present. Korr Security Services—ex–Special Forces soldiers. Smart, capable, trustworthy.

He strode toward the Escalade as one of his half dozen bodyguards stepped up to meet him.

The man reflexively saluted, then stopped in mid-salute with some embarrassment. "Good evening, Mr. Vanowen, your guest is waiting, sir."

Vanowen nodded slightly in acknowledgment.

The guard opened the passenger door of the Escalade. Vanowen noted with satisfaction the thickness of the door. Kevlar laminate armor and inch-thick bulletproof glass. It was a discreet business tank.

Vanowen ducked inside and was unsurprised to see a man waiting for him in the plush backseat. The man was in his forties, dressed in a sports coat and black shirt. He had buzz-cut hair and a firm jaw line—definite military look. They called him The Major, but that's all Vanowen knew about him. They had never met, but both of them knew their roles well.

Vanowen settled into the empty seat. The door closed behind them with a tight *thwup*.

The Major did not extend his hand. "You're seven minutes late."

Vanowen nodded. "Yes, and so we need to hurry. I'm scheduled to make a keynote speech tonight at the convention center downtown."

Vanowen narrowed his eyes. "You're certain you weren't followed?"

The Major ignored the question. "Get us moving."

Vanowen saw through the partition glass that the driver and a bodyguard were now sitting up front. He hit the intercom. "Downtown Biltmore."

"They're getting the bags off the plane, sir."

"Have them catch up with us at the hotel. Just get us moving."

"Roger that, Mr. Vanowen."

Vanowen turned back to The Major. "My sources tell me the Feds know which companies are infected by the Daemon."

The Major showed no reaction.

Vanowen continued. "And that only a minority of these companies are expected to survive."

The Escalade was now moving through the hangar doors and into the night.

The Major looked out the window. "If I were in a position to confirm such information—"

"I already know it's true. What I need from you is the list of infected companies."

The Major didn't blink. "Why do you think I'm here?"

Vanowen was uncharacteristically surprised. He tried to find something to say. "Oh . . . I see."

"Leland Equity has friends in high places, Mr. Vanowen."

The Major reached into his jacket pocket. "You seem to be under the impression that you have to save face. You weren't the only one to get caught in the Daemon's web." The Major produced a glossy brochure from his jacket. "But as it turns out, our Mr. Sobol may have inadvertently handed us the investment opportunity of a lifetime." He handed the brochure to a suspicious Vanowen.

"What's this?" Vanowen read the title: *Annual Children's Hospital Golf Classic.* "Is this a joke?"

The Major tapped the brochure. "Flip it open."

Vanowen did so. Inside the tri-fold was a long list of charity sponsors—company after company. Vanowen looked up to his guest.

"I had operations print it. We're expecting a data loss event of cataclysmic proportions within the next six months. That's a list of public companies targeted for special protection by public and private militaries. Now you know how to restructure your portfolio. If anyone else sees it, it's just a charity brochure."

Vanowen smiled broadly. "And how much will Leland be donating to the Children's Golf Classic?"

The Major turned to look out the tinted windows into the night. "It's not for your benefit that you're being told. Although I'm sure you'll do very well also."

"Perhaps I can offer you a commission for your investment advice?"

The Major looked blankly at him. "I'm just one of Leland's investors, Mr. Vanowen. Do your job, and we'll have no reason to speak again."

Vanowen nodded vigorously. "Of course." He folded the brochure and placed it in his suit pocket.

The Major pointed. "That list doesn't get entered into a computer. It doesn't get photocopied, and it doesn't get reported to anyone else without the approval of my superiors. Do you understand?"

"Yes."

"You know what would happen if you were to lie to me?"

Vanowen made eye contact. "Yes."

"Good. Make sure you remember it."

Vanowen sighed dramatically. "Well . . . what sort of 'special protection' will these companies enjoy?"

"There's a Daemon Task Force—run by an NSA cryptologist. Young black lady. Very sharp. She's beginning to unravel the Daemon's design."

"But if they figure out a way to *stop* the Daemon, then our investment opportunity is . . ." Vanowen's voice trailed off.

"We don't intend to stop the Daemon. It's too valuable. The goal is to *control* it. The task force has made progress in just that area."

"Control it?" Vanowen considered this. "Then we would still get our opportunity—"

"But with greater precision and total deniability. The Daemon could become a powerful economic weapon—particularly against the ascendant economies of Asia."

Vanowen thought of the possibilities. "So the Daemon is not invincible, after all . . ." He gestured to the nearby wet bar. "A scotch to celebrate?"

The Major shook his head. "It's a bit premature to be celebrating. In any event, I'll be leaving you in a moment." He clicked on his own intercom button. "Roberts, leave me off at the next crossroads."

"*Affirmative, sir.*"

Vanowen raised his eyebrows, surprised that The Major knew his driver's name.

"Nothing has been left to chance, Mr. Vanowen. You have important work to do for us. See that you achieve your objectives."

In a moment the Escalade slowed at a rural intersection—two county roads meeting in the middle of nowhere beneath a lamp swirling with moths. The Major turned to Vanowen. "We never met." He was gone before Vanowen could say a word. The doors locked immediately after him. Vanowen watched a sedan emerge from the shadows to meet The Major. In a moment, Vanowen's Escalade was moving on, back into the darkness on the other side of the intersection and down the country road, toward a smudge of light on the horizon. Distant suburban sprawl.

Vanowen exhaled in relief. That had gone extraordinarily well. Better than he could have imagined. So the wise men weren't holding him responsible? The Daemon was widespread. He found it strangely reassuring—especially since the powers that be weren't even fazed. Matthew Sobol had underestimated them, and they were already taking steps to turn this situation to their advantage. In fact, he was going to have that celebratory scotch, after all.

Vanowen pulled a bottle of thirty-year-old Macallan from the minibar and poured three fingers, neat. He lifted the glass and sighed again in satisfaction, appreciating the caramel color against the backdrop of the headlights. Not only was he going to free himself of the Daemon, but he stood to make billions doing it. This was the very essence of capitalism: thriving on chaos. True, there would be a temporary economic meltdown, but like pruning a tree, it would grow back fuller and healthier than before. But thoroughly under their control. He raised his glass and toasted. "Here's to you, Mr. Sobol."

Beyond his scotch glass, Vanowen glimpsed a dark shadow growing ahead. Half a second later it came screaming out of the blackness. It was a car with its headlights off. Vanowen's driver screamed.

A Lincoln Town Car nailed the Escalade dead-center in the front grill at a combined speed of over 150 mph—instantly pancaking the sedan up to its rear passenger seat with a powerful BOOM and flattening the armored Escalade up to its front windshield. This sent the Escalade's V10 engine plowing into the front seat and blasted the inch-thick windshield out of its mountings, where it tumbled crazily hundreds of yards down the road.

After the initial impact, the wreckage of the Escalade sheared away from the Town Car and went into a wild roll, sending pieces of metal and armored doors flying. What remained of the SUV landed upside down in the opposite lane nearly a hundred yards farther on. Smoke and steam billowed from the wreck.

After a few moments of dead silence, headlights appeared in the distance, back the way the Escalade had come. They grew rapidly brighter, accompanied by the growling of a powerful engine. Soon, a black convertible Mercedes SL Sports Coupe arrived and rolled to a stop near the start of the debris field. Its xenon headlights were aimed at the wreckage of the overturned Escalade, bathing it in white light.

Twin black Lincoln Town Cars, with their headlights off, pulled up behind the Mercedes like guardians. The throbbing engine of the coupe cut off, but the headlights stayed on.

In a few moments the door opened, and the dark form of the driver strode calmly into the light of his own headlights.

Brian Gragg gazed intently at the wreckage.

He was reborn. Gone without a trace were the tattoos and the piercings and the unkempt hair. In their place was a perfectly groomed and successful-looking young man. Dressed as Sobol might dress, all in black with tailored slacks, silk shirt, and sports coat. Except for the black synthex gloves and sports glasses he wore, he looked like any other Austin tech entrepreneur. He was now invisible to authority. A man of substance.

He sniffed the night air. It was thick with moisture and the aroma of field grass. The din of crickets filled his ears. He was never more alive than now. Never more happy. And never before could he see with such clarity. He could feel the world for miles around. Law enforcement GPS units, Faction members, and AutoM8 packs networked in the surrounding countryside—feeding their discoveries to him, like a wizard's familiars.

Gragg felt the tingling of the Third Eye on his stomach and back. The Third Eye was another of the miracles that Sobol had bestowed upon him. It was a form-fitting conductive shirt worn next to the skin—but it wasn't a garment. It was a haptic device that helped him use his body's largest organ—his skin—as another, all-seeing eye. An eye that never blinked, and an eye that could see around him in 360 degrees or halfway around the world, if he wished.

It worked by sending tiny electrical impulses to excite the nerve endings in his skin, much like a computer monitor projected pixels onto a screen. The microscopic electrical impulses represented data—from blips on a radar screen to full-blown visual displays. But what amazed Gragg was how the brain learned to accept input from this new source as if it were just another organ. Just another eye.

He *felt* the networks around him, but he could do more than just feel them.

Gragg motioned with his gloved hands. Suddenly the headlights of the twin Town Cars flicked on. The cars roared forward and deployed on either side of the road at his command, illuminating the entire crash scene. Gragg halted them with a wave of his hand.

Glittering pieces of metal and plastic littered the roadway. Now he could see the pancaked wreckage of the AutoM8 he'd used in the attack. It was lying backward in a ditch along the road about fifty feet ahead. Smoking like a distillery. Only the rear half remained.

Gragg relaxed his arms and then cracked his knuckles. He strode toward the wreckage of the Escalade.

Both the driver and the front passenger were clearly dead. Someone's intestines spilled out over the twisted frame and looped along the ground. The smell of butyric acid and bile was mercifully masked by the odor of antifreeze and burning plastic.

Gragg heard whimpering. He moved to the rear passenger compartment and peered through the empty, twisted door frame. Inside, he saw only a jumble of spent airbags, white packing powder, and shattered glass.

Gragg listened intently, following the sound around to the other side of the wreck, where he soon saw the bloody and quivering form of Russell Vanowen lying twisted on his back on the pavement nearby.

Gragg took measured steps to look down on him, careful to avoid the pool of blood forming on one side.

Vanowen's head and face were covered in blood. His right arm was mangled—splintered bones sticking through his torn sleeve. A long, slow groan came out of his toothless mouth and formless, swollen face. His nose was almost completely flat.

Gragg regarded him icily.

He leaned down and with his gloved hands pulled back Vanowen's blood-soaked suit jacket.

The wounded man's chest heaved, and his eyes stared in stark terror as Gragg lifted out the bloody brochure for the Children's Golf Classic. Gragg shook some of the blood off it and flipped it open. He held it to the light.

It was still legible.

Gragg took out his cell phone and clicked a digital picture of it. Then he folded the brochure and slipped it back into Vanowen's chest pocket.

Gragg stood and turned to leave.

Vanowen's groan ascended to a wail as he reached out toward Gragg with his good arm.

Gragg stopped. He paused a moment before turning around, then kneeled down and grabbed Vanowen's swollen face with his gloved hand, causing the man to scream in agony. "Shhh . . . I'll go up a level for this. Maybe I should thank you, *Russell.*" He searched Vanowen's bloody eyes for something worthwhile. "But then again, fuck you, you worthless piece of shit."

Tears streamed down Vanowen's cheeks. He was insane with fear and pain.

There wasn't an ounce of pity in Gragg's eyes. "If you see Matthew Sobol, be sure to tell him Loki said hello."

Gragg stood, straightened his jacket, and walked toward his Mercedes. He motioned with a gloved hand, and one of the Lincoln Town Cars screeched forward.

The headlights flashed in Vanowen's eyes as he shrieked.

The car crushed him under its wheels and dragged his corpse some ways down the road before it fell free. The black AutoM8 raced off into the night.

Gragg curled a finger at his Mercedes, and the car rolled forward to meet him. The driver's door swung open as it came alongside him.

Gragg concentrated on his Third Eye. He felt his distant AutoM8s following the car of the mysterious man whom Vanowen had met at the municipal airfield. Gragg brought the dashboard video of a trailing

AutoM8 up onto his heads-up display—projecting onto one lens of his glasses. The infrared camera miles away showed the man's car heading south toward the interstate. There were two occupants. Gragg scanned the target car's license plate and retrieved its DMV records.

Federal Fleet Vehicle—no data

Gragg smiled to himself. The Daemon Task Force, eh?

He was closing in on them. He was mapping the topology of the plutocrats' elusive network—The Money Power. They were up to something. This man would help Gragg find out what.

These plutocrats were men of limited vision who needed to be swept aside. Men from a previous age. An age of oil and heavy industry. But the distributed technocracy would soon rise, and Gragg would be there at Sobol's side for the dawn of a new age. An age of immortals. A second Age of Reason.

Gragg's eyes narrowed at the video image of the man's car.

There would be no mercy for those who stood in the way.

Chapter 37://Cogs in the Machine

The Haas mini mill was a miracle of modern engineering—a computer-controlled metal lathe, drill press, and router all rolled into one. The Haas could download a 3-D computer model into memory and from it produce a custom metal or plastic part cut and shaped to exacting specifications. It was essentially a self-enclosed, water-cooled machine-parts factory packed into a housing the size of a hot dog cart.

Linked to the Web, it almost became a 3-D fax machine—plans sent in digitally at one end emerged at the other as finished parts. The input could originate from any corner of the world via Internet or phone. All that was required was a human being to serve the Haas. To feed it the raw materials the plans required. To protect and maintain it. Man serving machine.

But Kurt Voelker and his crew loved their machines. The machines gave them entrée into the Daemon network. The Daemon network gave them a future.

They had progressed significantly since their first AutoM8. Their Sacramento machine shop now boasted three half-million-dollar computer-controlled milling machines, running full-time off dual cable and satellite Internet connections. They were producing parts at an accelerating pace—but the Daemon had forbidden their company from growing larger. Three machines were the maximum they were permitted to possess. True, they'd generated three million in revenue last year and taken home hundreds of thousands of dollars each—but Voelker chafed against the prohibition to stay small.

Still, he knew better than to protest to Sobol's Daemon. It had grown phenomenally in power. Better to give thanks for their good fortune.

Voelker lifted his safety goggles and glanced around the cluttered shop. It was thirty thousand square feet of 1930s factory floor. Brick walls, twenty-foot ceilings, skylights, and concrete floors. The smell of oil, burnt metal, and ozone from arc welding filled the air. Parts littered workbenches, and a dozen brand-new vehicles stood in varying stages of completion. Voelker's company was officially a fleet vehicle customization business—licensed to operate by the AQMD. A legitimate California corporation. Their close ties to major car leasing companies, on-time tax payments, and contributions to civic causes put them above reproach. They had friends in high places now. High-powered attorneys would slide down the fire pole in their defense if anyone so much as looked at them cross-eyed. God help anyone who tried to shake them down or impede their business. There was a Daemon work request for just such contingencies. Their future was secure.

Voelker saw Tingit Khan and Rob McCruder struggling with the steering column of a new AutoM8 variant—a 400-horsepower Mustang interceptor. They were bitching at each other like brothers, as always. Voelker smiled to himself. They were like a family. A family with a stern authority figure that would flay the flesh from their bones if they stepped out of line for even an instant.

Still. The rules were clear, the work always changing, and the rewards enormous. Barely in their mid-twenties, they were all millionaires on paper. They would receive five weeks' vacation every year. Retirement with benefits in twenty years. They received financial advice money couldn't buy. Their medical plan, too, was top-notch. The Daemon took care of its own.

Voelker turned toward his Haas milling machine. It was busy churning out grooved steel plates, six inches long and an inch wide. He had no idea what they were for. But they had a work order for three hundred copies. Some strategic plan somewhere required them. A plan born in the mind of a dead genius and enacted now, when the time was right. But right for what? Only the Daemon knew. Certainly no one among the living did.

Voelker took one of the finished plates and placed it in a laser scanner. He tapped a button and the object was instantly measured at two thousand critical points for accuracy. It was dead-on. It was always dead-on. The Haas knew what it was doing.

A two-tone chime came in over the loudspeakers. Voelker, Khan, and McCruder looked up at the same time, then at each other. They all knew what it meant. New plans were in the queue.

Voelker motioned to them. *I got it.* They looked back down and kept working on the Mustang, while Voelker took off his gloves. He moved to a nearby computer workstation.

A new 3-D plan file was in their company inbox. He noticed from the byte count that it was a big one. He moved it into a central share and then opened it in AutoCAD. It took several seconds, even on his powerful Unix workstation.

When it was finished loading, he stared for some moments at the wire frame model now rotating in three dimensions on his screen. *Ours is not to wonder why, but to do or . . .*

What the hell was he looking at? He turned back to the Mustang. "Guys, get over here and look at this."

Khan wiped his forehead, smudging grease across it. "Later, man. This steering column's a bitch."

"No. I think you should take a look at this *now.*"

Khan rolled his eyes dramatically, then tapped forcefully on Mc-Cruder's shoulder.

"What?"

Khan pointed. "Goggles says we gotta see the new plans. It's urgent."

"Fuck . . ." McCruder threw down his wrench with a *clang*, and the two of them strode leisurely toward Voelker's workstation.

"This had better be good, Kurt."

Voelker simply gestured to the screen. Both men wrinkled their brows.

"What the?"

"You have got to be kidding me. . . ."

Voelker shook his head.

They exchanged looks. It had always remained unsaid. They knew that some would suffer the Daemon's wrath. After the events at Sobol's mansion, the purpose of the AutoM8s could scarcely be a mystery— but they always nursed a hope that perhaps they would be used for transporting critical materials, operatives, or something unimaginably brilliant.

Voelker sighed and sat on a nearby stool.

Khan pointed at the screen. "What *is* that?"

McCruder pointed, too. "This is serious shit, Kurt."

Voelker kept his eyes on the floor. "It's just after-market customization."

McCruder laughed. "No kidding. That's not what I mean."

Khan was nodding. "He's right, Kurt. This is designed for one thing, and one thing only: killing people."

They contemplated this silently. This raised the stakes. They were now clearly producing weaponry. The pleasant fiction was over.

Khan added, "I mean, it's cool-looking and all, but this is real life— not a fucking computer game."

"What do we do?"

Voelker tapped his fingers on the workbench, thinking. "I've almost got the current order filled. While I finish that we can decide the best course of action."

McCruder threw up his hands. "Like we have any *choice*, Kurt? If we don't make these things, our own toys are going to come back to kill us."

"All right, calm down."

Khan gripped his own head. "I should have known this was going to happen. It was too perfect."

McCruder waved it aside. "Let's stop kidding ourselves. We all know we're going to build these things—so why go through the theatrics of feeling bad about it?" McCruder grabbed a grease pencil and turned to a whiteboard. He started drawing a casualty list with little human stick figures. "If we don't make them, someone else will and people will die—*along* with us. That's X number of people plus three. If we *do* make them, then people will die, but *not* us. That's X number of people plus zero." He looked up, vindicated by mathematics. "So we take the course that harms the least number of people."

Voelker threw a glove at him. "That's fucking convenient."

McCruder held up his hands. "Don't blame me. We all got into this, and I don't feel like finding out what happens if we quit. Big things are changing in the world—things we can't stop. We're just cogs in the machine, and if we malfunction, we'll be replaced. We owe it to ourselves to survive. Shit, we owe it to ourselves to *thrive*. That's what our ancestors did, and that's what we're gonna do. It's our natural fucking purpose."

Everyone was quiet as they sat listening to the grinding sound coming from the Haas.

Eventually Voelker nodded. "I know you're right. I just didn't think I'd ever be playing this role. I wanted to design consumer electronics."

Khan leaned against the workbench. "I wanted to build suspension bridges. News flash: nobody gives a fuck what we want."

McCruder rapped his knuckles on the countertop. "So how does the board of Autocracy, Inc., vote? Do we elect to continue in our present endeavor?"

They glanced at each other, then all raised their hands. "Aye."

McCruder nodded. "The ayes have it. This will make a massively parallel cybernetic organism very happy." He pointed to the busy Haas. "When are these pieces due?"

Voelker thought for a moment. "They need to be placed at the way-points by tomorrow, noon."

McCruder was back to examining the computer screen. "We'll need time to study these schematics. They look involved." He peered closely at the screen. "This is serious engineering—look at that flywheel housing—and those hydraulics."

Voelker nodded. "Graphite-epoxy flywheel spinning at seventy thousand rpm in a vacuum. Floating on a bed of magnetism."

Khan was pointing at the screen again. "You gotta admit, that's some cool shit. It even *looks* nasty. We should render it to see what it looks like in color."

McCruder ignored him. "When does the first stock unit arrive?"

Voelker grabbed the mouse and navigated to the header of the message. He read for a moment. "Friday."

McCruder pointed at the Haas. "You need help to finish these pieces on time?"

"No. They'll be done."

McCruder started back toward the Mustang. "Then I suggest we study those plans and make sure we're the best damned cogs the Dae-mon has."

Chapter 38:// Assembly

He was a poster child for overdesigned American culture. His square-toed dress shoes had the soles of hiking boots, as though intended to navigate an urban cliff face. His draping dress pants concealed six pockets pleated into its folds, each one with a trademarked name (e.g., E-Pouch), giving him the cargo capacity of a World War I infantryman. Yellow-tint sunglasses wrapped his face, unaccountably designed to withstand the impact of a small-caliber rifle bullet while filtering out UV rays and maximizing visual contrast in a wide range of indoor and outdoor lighting conditions.

In all, his outfit required nearly two thousand man-years of research and development, eight barrels of oil, and sixteen patent and trademark infringement lawsuits. All so he could possess casual style. A style that, in logistical requirements, was comparable to fielding a nineteenth-century military brigade.

But he looked good. Casual.

He walked along the city streets, passing coffee bars and cafés so packed with people that it seemed as if no one had homes to go to. He passed dogs with backpacks and kids wearing Rollerblade sneakers. Everybody with casual style.

It felt good to be among them again. His depression had almost swallowed him whole when his first job was sent offshore. Then his second job. Then his third. Not much call for project managers in the States anymore.

But now he understood again. The world made sense again—and he was still all for progress. *Disruptive innovation,* they called it. Change was good. Painful, but good. It made you stronger. When you stopped changing, you started dying.

For the first time in years, he knew his situation was secure. He knew he could afford rent—even in his price-inflated neighborhood. That he could dress and live in a style befitting a man of his intelligence and education. He no longer compared unfavorably with people in magazine articles. He was back on track.

He had a purpose. And right now that purpose was to proceed to a specific GPS waypoint and await further instructions from The Voice.

The Voice's feminine synthetic words came over his wireless earpiece: *"Cross the street."*

He obeyed and found himself moving into a crowded retail plaza ringed with national chain stores. The carnival atmosphere was augmented by street performers wearing photo IDs—proof that their family-friendly, drug-tested talents were on an officially sanctioned list in the management office.

The plaza was packed with consumers.

The Voice spoke again. *"Waypoint nine attained. Stand by . . . stand by. Vector 271. Proceed."*

He turned in place, looking closely at a handheld GPS screen until he was facing 271 degrees. Then he proceeded at a normal walking pace as people jostled past him.

"Report ready status of assembly."

The Daemon's workshop was open for business. He slipped one hand into his E-Pouch and removed a grooved steel machine part, six inches long. He wrapped his hand around it and kept walking vector 271. "Assembly ready."

"Prepare to tender."

He could see the target approaching through the crowd—a twenty-something white kid in parachute pants and a sweatshirt bearing a university acronym. He had the calm, composed look of a Daemon courier. They were on a collision course as people swirled around them like random electrons. The kid extended his right hand as he came forward. They were just feet away.

"Tender assembly on phrase: 'Hey, Luther.' Confirm."

The kid came right up to him, holding forward a different steel part. A cell phone headset was now visible on his close-cropped head. The kid nodded. "Hey, Luther."

Both men extended their hands and slid the steel parts together. They mated perfectly with a satisfying *click*.

"Assembly confirmed."

A pleasant chime sounded over the line. *"Operation complete. Twenty network credits. Demobilize."*

The kid took control of the combined parts and continued walking.

The Voice came over the phone headset. *"Assembly stage two. Vector 168. Prepare to tender."*

The kid held the assembly down at his side, turned to the appropriate compass direction, and proceeded through the crowd at a brisk walk. In a few moments he and a young woman locked on to each other. She was big-boned, dressed like a businessperson. Utterly invisible to most men. The kid vectored in.

"Tender assembly on phrase: 'Afternoon, Rudy.' Confirm."

The woman nodded as she came up to him, a flip phone handset held to her cheek. "Afternoon, Rudy."

He placed the two-part assembly into her hand and disappeared into the crowd. "Assembly confirmed."

A pleasant chime sounded over the line. *"Operation complete. Twenty network credits. Demobilize."*

She snapped the kid's two parts into a yellow plastic base and moved through the crowd, following her new vector.

As he headed back to the parking structure, the kid imagined the tactical assembly now under way; like swarming nanobots amid the mass of shoppers, the Daemon's distributed assembly plant ran half a dozen independent lines, with no individual having knowledge of anything more than the few seconds in front of them and the mechanics of the single assembly for which they'd be responsible. The parts arrived in place at the moment they were required, The Voice vectoring them into a collision course. Assemblers came and went, passing the assembly on to the next worker in the chain after confirming completion of their step. Redundancy gave high probability that sufficient parts would arrive on station at the appropriate moment, and that waylaid assemblers could be quickly replaced.

What he didn't know was what they were building. He wondered if he'd ever know.

In the battered lobby of a C-grade office building, a (now) debt-free graduate student faced the wall and clicked a methane-oxide fuel cell battery into place inside a form-fitting plastic handle.

The Voice spoke to him over his earpiece. *"Confirm assembly completion."*

He powered the unit up and waited for a diagnostics check. A green light came on. Ready. He lowered the assembly out of sight. "Assembly complete."

A pause. *"Stand by . . . stand by . . ."*

He looked around the lobby. It was a typical two-story box in a low-end tech park. Security consisted of locked doors with mag-card swipes at the entrances. In other words: no security. Long halls laid with orange indoor-outdoor carpeting crossed each other in a barren atrium in the center of the building.

He waited patiently in a water company uniform, complete with photo ID badge and water-bottle-laden handcart as The Voice kept repeating, *"Stand by . . ."* in his ear every ten seconds.

Then it paused. *"Vector 209. Prepare to tender completed assembly."*

This was it. The Receiver was coming. He glanced at his GPS and turned to face the security door.

Charles Mosely walked briskly toward the lobby doors. It was a bright spring day under a wide Texas sky. He could see his reflection in the door glass as he approached. He was dressed in a phone company uniform with tool belt, clipboard, and phone headset. He swiped his security card, and the door opened with a buzz.

The Voice spoke on the headset. *"Receive assembly on phrase 'Here it is.'"*

Mosely approached a young Asian man standing in the lobby with a handcart piled with five-gallon water cooler jugs. As he walked by, the man extended an odd-looking steel and yellow plastic device to him. It was shaped like a glue gun, with the top section missing—an empty channel with twin grooved steel plates. "Here it is."

Mosely grabbed it with his work-gloved hands and shoved it into a slot on his utility belt designed specifically for it. He heard the water man exit the lobby doors behind him, but he walked purposefully on his appointed vector, passing a nondescript guy in a pullover shirt bearing some company's logo. He nodded congenially as he went past, but the guy didn't acknowledge him in the least. Just some tenant.

"Vector 155," The Voice said in Mosely's ear.

That was straight down the corridor. Mosely kept moving down the hall, glancing at office doors.

Suite 500.

Ten minutes ago he thought he was going to tap a phone system. But now in possession of the assembly, he recognized it immediately. He had used it before.

It was an electronic pistol.

Manufactured with bright yellow plastic and brushed steel, it resembled a battery-powered hand tool—it even had a tool company logo on the side. But in reality it was a fully automatic, precision-made handgun. It was nearly 100 percent reliable because it had no moving parts. Instead of a firing pin and complex recoil-based reloading mechanism, an electronic pistol was a fire-by-wire device; the caseless bullets were stacked in a straight line in one of four parallel twelve-inch barrels, and a logic chip fired each bullet independently with bolts of electricity from an onboard battery. The gun was reloaded by slapping on new barrels of ammunition. Mosely had already received three rapid-loaders from a courier out in the street. It was a foolproof, untraceable weapon designed for one thing: killing people at close range.

Suite 710.

He steeled himself. There was a grander purpose at work here. He had to keep reminding himself of that. This wasn't the same as what he'd done as a teen. He wasn't doing this for himself. The world was changing. He'd seen it. This was part of the plan. There were no random acts in the plan.

The Voice said, *"Stop."*

Suite 1010.

Mosely drew the unloaded pistol, then took the welded-steel barrels from the other side of his tool belt. He slid the two together with a *click-clack*. It was now loaded and looked very much like a garish, toy laser pistol.

The Voice came to his ears. *"Device code . . . 4-9-1-5."*

Mosely flipped the gun and tapped in the four-digit code at the base of the handle. The device was now armed.

He turned to face the door. Then he reached into his pocket and produced a hard plastic door key given to him by a woman out on the street. All master key systems were vulnerable to mathematical reduction.

The Voice continued in his earpiece. *"Confirm instruction: kill the oc-cupants of suite . . . 1-0-1-0."*

Mosely closed his eyes. He didn't relish this. He thought he'd left this behind years ago. But the Daemon had found him out. It knew he had killed before. He took a deep breath, then said, "Instruction confirmed."

"Proceed."

Mosely inserted the key, turned it, and pushed the door open. He moved into a cluttered office with shelving piled high with papers and boxes on the far wall. Banks of cheap desktop computers sat atop fold-ing tables. A thirtysomething guy with a sizeable gut turned quickly in his chair to face Mosely. He had a cherry Danish almost up to his mouth.

"You can't just—"

Mosely raised the pistol and sent a quick burst into the man's chest—spattering the computer table and back wall with gore. A couple of the frangible rounds slammed into the wall and dissolved into puffs of powder, barely leaving a dent in the drywall.

Frangible rounds still amazed Mosely. The bullets were made of compressed ceramic powder. They retained their hitting power if they hit soft human tissue, but they disappeared in a cloud of dust if they encountered an unyielding surface—like a wall. They were designed to contain a shoot-out within the room where the shooting was taking place, and they also eliminated the risk of ricochets. This last part was of particular concern when you were spraying seven rounds a second in a room ten feet square.

The bloody fat man slumped and fell onto the floor with a thud that shook the room.

Mosely heard movement in the next office, farther in. The squeaking of a desk chair.

"Mav? What was *that*?"

Mosely advanced quickly, both hands gripping the pistol. No need to worry about their calling the police. Their phones were out by now, and their cell phones would already be jammed.

He stepped into a larger office area containing two desks and a bank of windows looking out onto the back parking lot. A young man stood behind a desk, hand reaching into the center drawer. A look of disbelief on his face. Mosely ripped out a longer burst this time. With the suppressor it sounded like a muted model airplane engine. The wall, windows, and drop ceiling were now spattered with blood. Smoke wafted away from the gun barrel.

Mosely turned as another man screamed in terror. The man ducked behind his desk, dragging a phone with him.

Shit.

Mosely popped the smoking barrels off and clicked on a new set. He advanced, gun ready, and could hear the man sputtering in terror as he tapped at the dead phone. "No! I'll give you money! Don't!"

Mosely came around the side of the desk and aimed his gun down at the man cowering against the wall.

"No! Please!"

Mosely hesitated. *Goddamnit.* It could not be left undone. There was no question.

"No!"

Mosely emptied the barrel into him. The man slumped sideways behind the desk, in a pool of blood, his body twitching. Mosely loaded the last barrel and retraced his steps—putting another couple of shots into the heads of the other two men. He spoke into his headset. "Task complete."

There was a pause. Then The Voice said, *"Confirmed. Two thousand network credits. Demobilize."*

Mosely tapped a sequence of numbers onto a four-key pad on the bottom of the gun and tossed it onto the top of a nearby desk. The weapon started to sizzle and smoke, then the plastic bulk of it began to melt—along with its circuitry.

Mosely took a small semicircular device off his tool belt. The thing resembled a small traveling alarm clock with a rounded bottom. He tapped the same four-key code into the device, then tossed it into the center of the floor, where it rolled around for several moments while Mosely exited the way he came in.

As the device came to rest on its rounded bottom, a pocket laser beamed bright red light onto the stained drop tiles of the ceiling— creating a marquee-like sign in large glowing red letters. The letters spelled out the message the Daemon wanted to send—the message associated with operation 4-9-1-5:

ALL SPAMMERS WILL DIE

Chapter 39:// Closing a Thread

Reuters.com

Spammers Massacred, Thousands Dead—A daring and well-coordinated attack launched Monday morning may have **claimed** the **lives** of as many as **6,000** prolific **spammers** in **83 countries.** Over **two hundred died** in Boca Raton, Florida, alone. Authorities are still reeling from the magnitude and sophistication of the strikes. The assailants left behind the same message: "**All spammers will die.**"

Since the attacks, ISPs report up to an 80% reduction in the amount of spam clogging Internet servers.

Sebeck sat in the sterile visitor's room near Lompoc's death row. His wife, Laura, sat across the table from him, looking down. To Sebeck's surprise, there was no bulletproof partition separating them here. His last visitation would be face-to-face. Two prison guards stood watch over them from the nearby door.

Laura looked up. "Are they treating you well?"

Sebeck grimaced. "They're going to kill me this evening."

She seemed unsure how to respond.

Sebeck just waved it aside. "It's okay. Normal conversation doesn't really work in here. Don't feel bad."

She sat thin-lipped and tense for several more moments. "Are you afraid?"

Sebeck nodded.

"I don't know what to do, Pete."

"I'm sorry about the pension and the life insurance. I hear they canceled them."

"I just can't believe this is happening."

"Neither can I."

She looked squarely at him. "Tell me again."

He looked at her. "I didn't kill anyone, Laura. I committed adultery, but I didn't do those other things. I would never have harmed Aaron or those other people."

"They say terrible things about you on TV. It never stops."

"So I'm told."

"It's been real tough on Chris at school."

They both contemplated this gravely. Then Sebeck motioned to her. "It's good to see you, Laura." He smiled weakly. "Given all that I've put you through, I wouldn't blame you for not speaking to me again."

"I've known you my whole life. I couldn't let you go without saying goodbye."

He felt a little choked up as she began to cry. He cleared his tight throat. "I know we don't really love each other. Not in a romantic way. Our marriage seemed like the right thing to do with the baby and all."

She was crying silently into her hands.

Sebeck continued. "But I think, if I had just had the chance to fall in love with you before all that, I think I would have. I just never had the chance."

She just wept.

"I love our son, Laura. I want you to know that. And I want Chris to know. I don't regret having him. I regret how I handled it. And how I blamed everyone else for the decisions I made."

She looked up. "You were just a boy, Pete. We were both just kids."

"Sometimes I feel like I still am. Like I'm frozen in time."

She tried to rein in her tears. "I don't know what to do."

Sebeck sighed. "Sell the house. Make sure Chris gets a college education. And then . . . go fall in love. You deserve to be happy, Laura."

She was crying harder now.

One of the guards called from the door. "Sebeck. Time's up."

Sebeck reached out a hand toward her. They held hands briefly over the table. "Thank you for being kind to me."

The guards pulled him away, and the last Sebeck saw of her, she was staring at him through tears as he was pushed through the doorway and into the echoing death row wing beyond.

———————

Sebeck lay bound hand and foot by leather buckles and straps. A rubber tube was wrapped tightly around his right arm, bulging the veins. Another brown rubber tube ran from the intravenous line in his arm to the wall, where it disappeared through a small port. Sebeck knew there were several men behind that wall, each preparing lethal doses of sodium thiopental (to knock him out), pancuronium bromide (to stop his breathing), and potassium chloride (to interrupt the electrical signals to his heart). Only one of the IV drips was connected to Sebeck's tube—so the three executioners would never know who delivered the fatal injection. It was an odd system. One that ignored the fact that people killed each other every day without trying to conceal it. In fact, if he jumped the prison fence, they would gun him down without hesitation.

Looking down at his own body, Sebeck found it funny that he was in better physical shape now than he'd been in a decade. All he'd had to keep himself from going crazy in solitary confinement was endless reps of push-ups and sit-ups. Beneath the 24/7 buzzing fluorescent lights of his cell. He saw the knotted muscles in his arms and it brought back memories of his youth. Of better days.

Sebeck lay at a slight incline so that he could face the assembled witnesses sitting behind the nearby windows. He felt oddly calm as he regarded them. A mix of curious and angry faces stared back. Some were taking notes.

So this was the death chamber? This was what it felt like to be put to death. His hunch about Sobol had been wrong. The funeral message hadn't brought forth any rescuer from beyond the grave. It hadn't even seemed a remote possibility while he lived in the heart of suburbia that he would one day be put to death by the federal government. Yet here he was. He almost laughed. It was so ludicrous he half expected Rod Serling to saunter in and deliver a double-entendre-laden summation of his life. *Pete Sebeck, a man whose demons got the better of him . . .*

Was there ever really a Daemon after all? Even if there was, Sebeck had been defeated by it. His relatively brief life had been a complete waste. The only good thing he'd accomplished was his son—ironic since the pregnancy had always seemed like the worst thing that ever happened to him.

He considered that most of the people here really believed that he conspired to murder federal officers. He hardly blamed them for what they were doing. He would have looked on in righteous anger, too.

Just then Sebeck noticed Anji Anderson in the gallery. A flash of anger coursed through him. That was just the last straw—to see that smug, pert face with the slight curl of a smile on the edges of her mouth. Like an evil pixie. Sebeck's most malevolent stare bored into her. At first she kept the smug look, but soon the trace of a smile faded, and then she finally looked away.

After conferring for a moment with the doctor, the warden leaned down and asked if Sebeck had any last words. He'd been thinking about his last words for several months. For too long, actually. It wasn't like he was going to win over anyone. He had decided to take the stoic, unflinching approach.

He looked to the mirrored glass of the window concealing the victims' families. "I didn't kill your loved ones. I didn't kill anyone. But if I were in your position, I'd think I was guilty, too. Hopefully, the truth will come out someday, if only so that my son knows his father isn't a murderer." He paused. "That's it, let's get this over with."

Almost immediately he felt a warm sensation in his arm. It spread like a wave of numbness over his entire body. It occurred to him that this was the speed of his circulatory system. He also noticed a label on the fluorescent light fixture above him. It read, "30W BALLAST PARA-BOLIC REFLECTOR." It was a strange message to depart this life with. So he turned to face the doctor standing nearby, an angular man with cold blue eyes who stared icily back at Sebeck. Even Sebeck couldn't meet his fierce gaze, so he fixated on the logo on the lapel of the doctor's lab coat. It read: "Singer/Kellog Medical Services, Inc."

Sebeck found his eyes getting heavy, and his breathing became labored. He turned back toward the overhead light. As the last of his vision faded, he struggled to maintain a focus on the light. Sebeck realized he had forgotten to appreciate his last sight of this world. It was too late, and he fought for one last glimpse. But everything was blackness. And then it was nothingness, and he fell into a well of emptiness so deep and broad that it was as though the entire universe had ceased to exist.

Detective Sergeant Peter Sebeck died at 6:12 P.M., Pacific Standard Time.

Chapter 40:// A New Dimension

Newswire.com

Sebeck Executed (Lompoc, CA)—Ex–police detective **Peter Sebeck** was **put to death** by **lethal injection** at the Lompoc Federal Prison at **6:12 P.M. Monday**. Convicted early last year for his part in the **Daemon** hoax, Sebeck's trial and appeals had been fast-tracked through the federal justice system. Federal prosecutor Wilson Stanos commented, "This judgment sends a clear message to the enemies of freedom."

Natalie Philips entered the windowless Daemon Task Force offices well past midnight. She was expecting the place to be nearly deserted, but instead she saw a knot of techs and heavily armed security personnel gathered near the hallway leading to her office. They were engaged in an urgent, hushed discussion. The Major looked up from the center of the huddle as Philips approached. He nodded to her. "How was your trip, Doctor?"

Philips dropped her overnight bag on the floor nearby. "What's going on?"

The Major thumbed down the hallway. "Your hacker friend is having some sort of episode. He locked himself in conference room B and changed the access codes on us."

Philips sighed wearily and rubbed her eyes. "How long ago?"

"About an hour. I was preparing to resolve the situation."

She eyed a guard with a tear gas gun. "That won't be necessary, Major. I'll go talk to him."

The Major grinned coldly. "You're the boss, Doctor."

He was mocking her now. She chose to ignore it and tried to pass. He stood in her way.

"You realize I must submit a report to Centcom about this incident."

"Understood. If you'll excuse me . . ."

"Please remind him of the relevant clauses in his amnesty agreement."

"I'll be sure to do that. Now, if I'm not mistaken, these men have guard duties. See that they get back to them." She hefted her bag again, but The Major waited a beat before moving aside and allowing her to pass. She trudged down the hall toward a crack of light under the door of conference room B. Once there, she stared at a red LED display glowing on the door's proximity card reader. It read: *FUCK_OFF.* She smiled slightly, then flipped open the reader's plastic cover to reveal a small ten-key pad underneath. She concentrated for a moment, then tapped in a thirty-two-digit code. Her back door. The door clicked, and she pushed inside.

"Go away." Ross didn't even turn around. He stood on the far side of a conference room table crowded with desktop and laptop computers. Lines of text cycled rapidly across all the screens. The rest of the room was strewn with crumpled charts, diagrams, and innumerable fanfold reports that spilled across the floor.

Ross was taking aim with a makeshift pencil dart at a large photo mosaic of Matthew Sobol's face tacked to the far wall. The picture was tiled together from paper photocopies. A half dozen pencil darts already protruded from Sobol's face, in addition to hundreds of other tiny holes concentrated mainly between Sobol's eyes.

Philips took in the scene. "I can't say this line of research holds much promise."

Ross inclined his head slightly toward her, recognizing her voice. He hesitated for a moment, dart still poised, then completed his throw. The dart stuck into Sobol's eyebrow. Ross drew another dart into his throwing hand and said nothing.

Philips closed the door behind her and picked her way across the littered floor, stepping between charts torn from the walls. "What's going on, Jon?"

"Nothing." He threw another dart, nailing Sobol in the cheek. "How was Washington?"

"Complicated."

"There's a shocker. Another general trying to pack me off to Diego Garcia?" He hurled a dart with great force, burying it deeply in the wall.

Philips walked over to him and dropped her bag onto the conference table. "You may think you're joking, but you're not far off. Your insistence on personal anonymity hasn't helped me defend you. Neither do stunts like this."

Ross stared at Sobol's dart-pocked face for a moment, then turned to Philips. "Is it true that they just executed Pete Sebeck?"

Philips looked down. *Damn.*

"Did they really kill him?"

"Yes. They did."

Ross tossed another round of darts. "Goddamnit! That's just great!"

"It couldn't be helped, Jon."

"Of course it could be helped"

"Not without risking retribution by the Daemon. It's already killed tens of thousands. Are you prepared to take responsibility for more?"

"That's not the issue, and you know it."

"It is exactly the issue."

Ross turned and threw his last dart. "Fuck! We should have beaten this goddamn monster by now."

"Look, the only way to make Sebeck's sacrifice meaningful is to destroy the Daemon before the public learns of its existence. The financial markets are tumbling on mere rumors. Once the public knows, the financial markets will crash. Those markets support life as we know it. The livelihoods of hundreds of millions are at stake."

"Well, we're running out of time, Doctor. The blogosphere is already buzzing." Ross slumped against the wall.

"There's no solution but to keep working, Jon." Philips removed her blazer and laid it neatly over a chair back. She started methodically rolling up her sleeves. "While I was away, did we get any clear-text back from those intercepts I ran through *Cold Iron*?"

Ross still stared into space.

"Jon!"

He looked up at her, then slowly dragged himself to the table. "Yes. Crypto forwarded a file." He dropped into a chair and started clattering away at a keyboard.

She nodded, encouraged, and moved over to him. "Good, let's see it."

He opened a text file. An endless stream of double-precision numbers filled the screen, alphanumeric characters strewn between them. "Here's a segment of the clear-text."

She looked closely at the stream. "GPS coordinates."

He nodded. "Damned near a terabyte of them. What prompted you to pluck this out of the airwaves?"

She was still examining the numbers. "Sheer volume. This is just a few days' worth. It's being broadcast from low-power radio transmitters in eighty countries—tens of thousands of transmitters—and this stream didn't exist before the Daemon. It's becoming a background noise that grows louder every day."

"Yeah, well, this 'noise' is nearly a month old, so it's ancient history."

"Brute-force cracks at this key length take time, Jon—even for us." She gestured to the screen. "But what is it? I mean, why would the Daemon bother to encrypt a log of GPS waypoints? Some sort of logistics tracking system?"

"I had some thoughts on that. Notice that the data isn't all GPS coordinates." He highlighted a section of the file. "There are these long, solid alphanumeric strings recurring in the data set—like unique identifiers." He clattered at the keyboard again. "When I parsed the data, I was able to group all the waypoints for a given ID, and when I plot the waypoints in a GIS mapping program"—he launched another program that displayed a map of southern Texas and the Gulf of Mexico.—"I get this. . . ."

The map filled with dots. Almost every inch was covered.

Philips sighed. "Less than informative."

He nodded. "At this altitude, perhaps, but when we move in closer, things get clearer. . . ." He zoomed down to an overhead view of the streets in a city; the clean vector lines of named avenues filled the screen with an irregular grid. The data points visibly ran along the lines of the street grid, occasionally veering off the marked roads.

Philips rubbed her face, her exhaustion starting to catch up with her. "Just thousands of data points with no meaningful association."

Ross turned to her. "Not if I could relate this data with something I knew the Daemon did. Then we'd have a better idea what we're looking at." He kept his gaze upon her.

"And did you?"

He turned back to the screen and started tapping at the keyboard again. "The spammer massacre. It was still going on at the time of this intercept. Fifty-two spammers were killed in the region covered by this dataset. Eight killings occurred in the relevant time range. I had Merritt get me the addresses from those eight individual case files, and I keyed them into a GIS program to obtain the approximate GPS coordinates of each address. Then I searched this intercepted data set for close matches."

She smiled slightly at him.

"I found a match." He tapped a key, and an aerial photograph of a suburban business park filled his screen. A close series of waypoints intersected in the center of the building, then parted. The longer set continued down through the building, concentrating its activity in one area.

"Merritt got me in touch with the building's architect. They sent me an AutoCAD file of the floor plates. I aligned that blueprint with the GPS grid. Bear in mind: three men were murdered here at the same time period covered by this GPS intercept. I marked the rough location where the bodies were found on this floor plan. Look at this, Nat."

He brought a detailed floor plan up onto the screen. The GPS waypoints tracked down the hall, then entered a suite labeled *1010* and tracked to the site where each body was found, retraced steps back to two of the bodies, then exited down the hall.

Philips felt a tingle run down her spine. "My God. This is the Daemon's command system."

"I think it's more than that. This type of coordinate tracking system seemed familiar. Look. . . ." Ross swiveled his chair to reach for a nearby workstation, nudging past her. He brought up a different 3-D floor plan in vector lines. "This is a game map for CyberStorm's *Over the Rhine.* I'm viewing this level in their map-editing tool, *Anvil.* Matthew Sobol wrote big parts of this program." Ross pointed at the screen. "See these dots? Those are sprites—bots, computer-controlled characters that react to players. These tracking lines indicate the coordinates those bots will follow in response to an event elsewhere in the system."

She leaned in to look closely at the screen. "It's just like the GPS dots."

"Exactly. In essence Sobol is using the GPS system to convert the Earth into one big game map. We're all in his game now."

Philips stared at the screen, still trying to decide whether this discovery was good or bad news. "It took the most powerful computer on Earth nearly a month to crack the encryption on this block of data, and the encryption changes every few minutes. We can't jam all the transmissions because the Daemon uses commercial spectrums." She turned to him. "How do we use this information, Jon?"

"By deducing the existence of certain things. For example, there must be some way for Daemon operatives to interact with this presentation layer. If my theory holds, then the Daemon must have created equipment that permits its operatives to 'see' into this extra-dimensional space so they can use it."

Philips nodded. "That could be why we've been unable to track Factions in the real world—because they're communicating with each other through this virtual space." She pondered the ramifications of this. "This could be a major breakthrough."

He shrugged. "We still need to prove the theory."

"But this is testable. We'll go through the captured equipment inventory."

"The devices we're looking for will most likely have biometric security—fingerprint scanners, things like that. If we can hack our way into one of these objects, we should be able to see into the Daemon's dimension. And that will be the first step in infiltrating it."

She stared at him for a few moments. "Excellent work. I'm impressed."

"I didn't think it was possible to impress you, Doctor."

"There's a first time for everything."

Ross glanced at the wreckage of the room. "I didn't mean for you to come back to this. I just heard about Sebeck an hour ago. I guess I snapped." He started picking up the papers strewn all over the place.

She moved to help him. "It's my fault. You've been cooped up in here for months. I'm trying to get them to loosen the restrictions."

They grabbed for the same toppled fan-fold printout and stopped just short of knocking heads. Their faces were only inches apart, motionless in a sudden, uncomfortable silence.

Their gaze held for several more moments while Philips's heart raced. She suddenly pulled back and stood up. "I need to check my e-mail." She grabbed her blazer from the chair back, not bothering to roll down her sleeves as she pulled it on hurriedly. She grabbed her overnight bag.

Ross watched her. "You don't need to—"

"I'm a federal officer, Jon. You're a felon under my authority—a foreign national of dubious origin. Identity unknown." She faced him from across the table. "It's impossible. My responsibilities make it impossible."

"If I made you uncomfortable, I apologize. It won't happen again."

She took a deep breath, then looked at him with a softer expression. "No . . . you didn't make me uncomfortable. But . . ."

He nodded solemnly. "I understand." He paused. "I just hope there's some part of you they don't own."

She bristled. "I *choose* to serve my country." She turned to leave again. "You don't know anything about me."

"Don't be so sure."

She stopped and turned to stare at him. "What's that supposed to mean?"

"You're not so difficult to decipher, Doctor."

"*Really?* Well, let's hear it. . . ."

"Okay. Child prodigy—head and shoulders above everyone around you—never quite fit in. Your classmates were always far older than you, and so you never acquired the social skills that develop the strong bonds of friendship. You live an isolated existence defined by your ultra-top-secret work. Work that you will never be able to share with anyone—not even your coworkers."

This last comment made her fold her arms impatiently.

"Ah, your work—it's too important to risk intimacy. But isn't it closer to the truth that you intimidate men? Your intellect scares the hell out of them, doesn't it? Humor me: what's the cube root of 393,447?"

"All right, I got your point."

"Can't do it?"

"Seventy-three-point-two-seven-six."

"There we go. How many of your relationships failed because you couldn't hide your intelligence?"

"That's enough."

"You don't scare me, Nat."

She stared at him for several moments. "If you only knew what I've gone through to protect you. You can't assume it doesn't matter to me. I can't protect you if you don't trust me. What is your real name? Who *are* you?"

Ross seriously contemplated this. He stared at the tabletop. He looked truly torn. After nearly a minute he finally stood and started gathering papers again. "Sorry about the mess."

"Goddamn you." She moved for the door.

He looked up, watching her leave. "I was twelve when they came for my father."

Philips stopped again.

"I remember my mother screaming downstairs. I ran out just as they put my father in a car. Our family driver held me back. My dad looked up at me from the backseat. And you know what he did? He winked at me, and he smiled."

Ross paused for a moment, savoring the memory. "I miss him so much, Nat. He went willingly in exchange for our lives. I try every day to be the man he'd have wanted me to be. The man he would have been proud to call his son." He looked up at Philips. "If there is anyone on this earth I want to share my name with, it's you. But I will never trust a government, Nat. They'll use my identity to get at the people I care about. And I won't put you in the position of having to choose between your future and me. We both know it will come to that. And I don't have a future."

Philips stood motionless for several moments. "Please don't think I was trying to—"

He waved it away. "I know."

After a few moments she turned and for the third time headed for the door. "Good night, Mr. Ross."

"Good night, Dr. Philips."

Philips didn't look back until she'd closed the door behind her.

Chapter 41:// The New Social Contract

A bleak dawn radiated over a tract home lost in the grid of a lower-class subdivision. Inside, a Nigerian immigrant stood guard in front of a stark steel door tagged with graffiti and patches of peeling gray paint.

He had the lean, wiry frame of someone raised on significantly less caloric intake than the average American. His skin was almost literally black, and he attentively watched a grainy security monitor focused on the street outside. He was attentive in the way that only a recent immigrant from an impoverished land can be. Grateful to be in Texas, America.

He considered for a moment the money he was earning—what it meant to his extended family back in sub-Saharan Africa. He kept calculating and recalculating how long it would take him to save enough money to also bring his sons to America.

A stubby AK-47 variant with a folding stock hung from a strap on his shoulder, its fore grip wrapped in duct tape. It was his job to identify people seeking entry to the cutting house. He took his job very seriously.

The sounds of people talking and shouting echoed from rooms deeper inside the building. A smattering of tribal languages. The place was bustling with activity. Just another day in the heroin trade. He despised drugs, but economic realities were economic realities.

He noticed the security monitor flicker for a moment. After that, the image skipped vertically. He frowned at it and played with the vertical-hold dial. In a moment the image stabilized, and he nodded in satisfaction.

Then the steel door exploded, sending red-hot metal fragments into his stomach and throwing him down the hall.

A dozen armed men in black full-body armor and ballistic helmets issued through the opening, shouting, "POLICE! FREEZE!"

The initials DEA were stenciled in bold white letters on their breast-plates. Shouting filled the back of the house. They were entering back there as well.

"POLICE! FREEZE!"

More shouting. The steel bars were ripped from a picture window by cables linked to trailer hitches. DEA agents jumped through the empty frame, rushing forward shouting, "THIS IS THE POLICE! PUT DOWN YOUR WEAPONS!"

A dozen half-naked men and women scattered, screaming and running to flush bags of heroin stacked on tables in a bedroom.

One of the dealers rolled out into an interior hallway with a pump twelve-gauge shotgun. He turned just in time to see the iridescent face-plate of a body-armored DEA agent blocking his exit. The dealer cut loose, blasting the agent into the narrow closet door at the end of the hallway.

Women started screaming.

The dealer pumped another shell into the chamber. "Ya'll some bad-ass motherfucker now, huh?"

He leveled the gun and blasted the nearby door frame as another DEA agent leaned out. The wood frame and a chunk of drywall disintegrated.

But the first agent he shot was getting up.

The dealer chambered another round and blasted the man again, sending him back into the closet door.

Click-clack. He blasted him again.

Click-clack. Then again.

He watched in amazement as the agent struggled back to his feet. The dealer raced to find shotgun shells in his pockets. The DEA agent leveled a multibarreled pistol at him.

Braaappp!

The dealer looked down at his white T-shirt. A rapidly expanding bloodstain swept across it. He crumpled to the floor, shotgun over his knees.

The other men in the house threw down their weapons as the agents barked commands at them to get on their knees with their hands over their heads.

Another set of agents moved among them with plastic hand ties, lashing hands behind backs.

But the majority of the DEA agents were still thundering through the house, overturning the drug tables and pushing aside the stacks of money—frantically searching for something. The agents never said a word to each other; instead, they moved as if they were a single entity, searching methodically from behind their mirrored helmet faceplates.

They came up from the basement, in from the garage, down from the attic, and rifled through every closet. They tore open the kitchen cabinets and aimed weapon-mounted tactical lights inside. It was there they discovered two terrified black boys—about seven years old—hiding beneath the sink. They dragged them out screaming.

The search abruptly stopped. Agents gathered around the boys, who clutched each other and stared in fear up at the mirrored faceplates staring back down at them. They were more than mirrored—they had the complex iridescence of mother-of-pearl. Their appearance changed as the men turned.

Still without speaking, the agents pried the boys apart, holding their arms back. One agent knelt down and extended a fingerprint-capture pad toward one boy. He forced open the boy's hand and pressed the kid's thumb against the pad—then checked a display reading. A pause, then he repeated the process with the second boy—once again consulting a display.

The agent nodded and pointed to the second boy.

The other agents zipped hand ties on the first boy and tossed him, crying, in with the rest of the prisoners. The second boy they held on to, and the group of agents parted to reveal a tall, broad-shouldered officer, also in black body armor with a mirrored faceplate. He strode forward.

The boy, already scared, now cowered in fear, tears streaming down his face.

The big agent grabbed him under the shoulders, plucking him up off the floor. The boy struggled, but the man's viselike grip was unshakeable. They walked out the shattered front door of the house and into the street—where a black Chevy Suburban pulled up to meet them. The side door opened, and the big agent pushed the boy inside—following close on his heels. The door thumped shut behind them as the remaining DEA agents poured out of the house, climbing into their black vans.

Inside the Suburban, the boy curled up on the opposite end of the bench seat. The large DEA agent sat on the far end, staring from behind his mirrored helmet at the terrified boy as an agent in the front seat drove, beyond a tinted glass partition.

The big agent brought his hands to his helmet, released twin catches, then twisted, removing it.

Charles Mosely wiped sweat from his face, placed his helmet on the bench seat behind him, and turned again to face the child.

The boy now had a look of utter terror on his face, and he curled up harder against the armrest, covering his head as though he was about to be beaten.

Mosely made a cryptic gesture with his right hand, causing the white *DEA* letters on his chest plate to slowly fade away. He looked back up at the child. "You remember me, Raymond?"

The boy robotically nodded his head, visibly trembling.

Mosely's hard face softened. He leaned closer. "It's all right. I won't hurt you."

The boy didn't relax one bit.

"I'm sober now."

The boy had his face buried in the seat cushion.

Mosely looked down. Complex emotions knotted his face. "I came up here to say I'm sorry. For all I did—and for all I didn't do." He was lost for a moment, but then his resolve returned. "I heard your momma died a couple years back."

When he looked up, Mosely noticed one of the boy's eyes peering out from under his arm, watching him.

"I thought about you all the time in prison—about your mom dyin'. You all alone."

The boy stared with his one exposed eye, unflinching.

Mosely sat back again. "You weren't easy to find. You ran off from that foster home. Can't say I blame you. Bad people. I met 'em. But I had real good private detectives searching for you. The best." He looked Ray straight in his one exposed eye. "I'm sorry."

Mosely ripped the Velcro straps securing his armored gloves and pulled them off, one by one. He placed the gloves in the back and extended his hand toward his son. "You got a hand for your old man? You want to shake on a new start?"

The boy curled up tighter.

Mosely lowered his hand. "Well, I guess I got it coming, don't I?" Mosely watched the frightened boy. Resigned to this, Mosely started removing the plates of body armor as the Chevy Suburban climbed the interstate entrance ramp.

———————

An hour later, Ray still hadn't shown his face. Mosely still sat watching him as the landscape sped past. He realized no amount of talking would erase his son's earliest memories. To him, Charles Mosely was a ruthless, violent man—a man everyone feared. A man with no concern for the family he abandoned and occasionally terrorized.

A voice came in over the intercom. *"We're here, sir."*

Mosely turned to see a massive wrought iron gate with ivy-strewn walls to either side. A plaque on the nearby wall bore the words "Holmewood Academy" in oxidized bronze letters.

Mosely nudged Ray gently and pointed. "Look at that."

Despite his fear, Ray's curiosity got the best of him, and he raised his head to look around warily.

They were moving through the large gates, which had swung open to receive them. Inside, wide athletic fields and Gothic stone buildings lay on either side of the winding drive.

Mosely watched his son's reaction closely. He could tell the grounds were like nothing Ray had ever seen. The boy's iron grip on the seat back eased, and he moved toward the window.

Mosely tried to stifle a slight smile, and he turned toward his own window.

Soon, the Suburban arrived at the huge front door of the main building. Mosely got out and looked up. Gothic turrets rose several stories above him. A young Asian woman, a black woman, and a gray-haired white man stood at the front door, apparently waiting for them. They were dressed impeccably in navy blue suits with a coat of arms sewn over the chest pocket.

Mosely leaned into the Suburban and could see Ray already peering out. He smiled and extended his hand. "C'mon, Ray."

Pausing for a moment, Ray examined Mosely's hand with trepidation. They both noticed the faded gang tattoos on each knuckle. Ray looked up at his father's face, and Mosely did his best to look upon him with reassuring eyes.

The boy slowly reached out and took his hand. Mosely eased him down onto the walk and held his hand as they approached the trio of figures standing near the massive wooden doors.

The two women smiled and approached them, kneeling down—all their attention for Ray. "Hi there, Raymond. Is this your father?"

The boy froze.

After a few moments, the young Asian woman smiled and took him by his other hand. "If it's okay with your dad, I want to introduce you to some friends. Do you like video games, Raymond?"

Ray looked up at his father. Mosely kneeled down beside him. He looked to the women.

They sensed his need and backed away. Mosely looked back at his son. "It's okay, Ray. This is your school now. It's your new home." Mosely straightened his son's dirty T-shirt. "They're going to take care of you. They'll teach you everything you need to know to succeed in life." Mosely regarded his boy again, and finally hugged him close.

At first Ray struggled, but in a moment his little arms wrapped around Mosely's thick neck.

Mosely's eyes welled up with tears. "I did the best I could for you, boy. There'll be no cages for you. Not for you." Mosely pulled back and looked in his boy's face. "Try to remember me."

At that, the women took the boy's hands and gently led him away. Mosely and his son locked eyes, and for the first time Mosely sensed that his son knew there was love in his father's eyes. Even though he'd never seen such a thing before.

In a moment he was gone, through the great doors, and Mosely stood again. The gray-haired white man walked up to him, following Mosely's gaze toward the opening in the doorway. In a second it boomed closed.

"Rest assured, he will be well cared for, Mr. Taylor. And free to decide his future. The Daemon honors its agreements."

Mosely turned to regard the man. He was a distinguished-looking type, with the air of aristocracy unique to academics. But he did not look down on Mosely—far from it. He appeared to regard Mosely as a man of superior social rank.

Mosely stood. "I am the Daemon's champion."

"Then your son will rise to the full level of his abilities."

Mosely nodded. "That's all anyone has a right to expect."

With that, Mosely straightened his uniform, turned on his heels, and headed for the waiting Suburban. What the future held for him, Mosely didn't know.

Instead, he imagined this field, years from now—filled with throngs of people. Mosely imagined the hopeful faces. His son's among them.

Chapter 42:// Building Twenty-Nine

Alameda Naval Air Station was a relic of the Cold War—mute testimony to the power of unrestrained government spending. A sprawling military base across the bay from downtown San Francisco, the station squatted on a billion dollars' worth of real estate. Alameda's aging collection of military barracks, hangars, docks, administrative buildings, power plants, landing strips, theaters, warehouses, and the occasional R&D oddity rose from a desert of concrete and asphalt covering the northern half of the island. You'd need a jackhammer just to plant geraniums there.

The base was decommissioned in the 1990s, and the city of Oakland had debated for years what to do with the place. A short ferry ride from downtown, it was theoretically a developer's dream. High-end condominiums, retail, and entertainment plazas crowded dozens of proposal blueprints, moldering in file cabinets while the city wrestled with soil toxicity and asbestos studies—the remnants of decades of military activities that knew no regulation or restriction.

The base sat largely unchanged—except for the odd film production company or construction firm renting out space in hangar buildings. Where once navy jets were retrofitted, now graphic artists with nose rings sat beneath lofty concrete-reinforced ceilings. The runways stretched unused except by model car and airplane enthusiasts. Close by stood the retired aircraft carrier USS *Hood* and a flotilla of mothballed navy transport vessels. It was as if the sailors and pilots just disappeared one day, leaving everything behind.

Jon Ross gazed out across the tarmac, imagining what this place must have been like forty years ago at the height of the Cold War. When America was the enemy.

He shielded his eyes against the sun and tracked the progress of an unmarked Bell Jet Ranger helicopter coming in low over the distant hangars. It headed toward him—and toward Building Twenty-Nine.

Building Twenty-Nine sat on the far end of a runway apron, on a strip of landfill jutting out into the bay. There wasn't anything around it for a quarter mile in every direction—just flat concrete, marshland, and open water. The building itself was windowless, long, and narrow. A blockhouse of high-density concrete. It looked like it was built to survive a direct hit by a five-hundred-pound bomb—which it was.

The helicopter descended, lifting up its nose as it crossed a razor-wire fence backed by concrete highway dividers blocking the entrance to the peninsula. Rent-a-cop security guards patrolled the perimeter, which was liberally marked with biohazard signs reading *Danger: Radon Contamination.*

The chopper continued for a few hundred yards, then set down on a weed-tufted stretch of concrete within a hundred feet of Ross.

Agent Roy Merritt stepped out. He wore an off-the-rack suit, bad tie flapping in the wind. His burn scars were still apparent on his face and neck, even at this distance. He nodded to the pilot as he pulled two cases from the rear seats—one a small ice chest marked with a red medical cross, the other a featureless black, hard-sided case. Merritt walked briskly to the edge of the chopper wash and let a grin crease his usually stern face as he saw Ross. The chopper rose into the air behind him and banked away over the bay, leaving them in comparative silence.

Merritt nodded to Ross. "What's with the escort?"

"You tell me." Ross turned to regard the four heavily armed men standing next to him. They wore combat uniforms printed with a new camouflage pattern, one designed to blend in with the background of society: black Kevlar helmets and matching body armor stamped with the friendly, white corporate logo of Korr Security International. Automatic weapons were slung over their shoulders. They stood silently by, as though they didn't exist.

"Let's just say I'm closely monitored." Ross turned back to Merritt and smiled. "It's good to see you, Roy." He offered to take the hard-sided black case.

"Thanks." Merritt passed it to him, and then they shook hands. "I heard that you cut a deal with Washington. They treating you well?"

"We've had some procedural disagreements. Apparently amnesty is a synonym for 'prisoner' in the government dictionary."

Merritt frowned. "I know people in Washington. I'll see what I can do."

Ross passed the black case to one of the armed guards. "Rush this to Dr. Philips in the lab."

"Yes, sir." Another guard grabbed the medical chest from Merritt, who reluctantly released it. Then the two guards rushed off toward the heavy steel doors of Building Twenty-Nine.

Ross and Merritt followed behind at a walking pace, trailed by the remaining two guards.

Ross turned to Merritt. "You in town for a while?"

"Just the day. I was hoping to get back home. It's been a week or so, and Katy's team is in the regional quarter-finals tomorrow."

"*Grammar* school?"

Merritt laughed and nodded. "Yeah—we take our sports seriously in the Midwest." He got somber. "Truth is, I just miss the hell out of them. Comes with the job, I guess."

"How'd it go in São Paulo?"

"Thankfully, the fireworks were over by the time I got there. That guy took out twenty-seven local and federal police before they punched his ticket. The ABIN wasn't eager to part with the evidence."

"Building a case is the least of their worries."

"A lot of diplomatic strings were pulled while I was down there. What's up?"

"You'll see in a few minutes."

As they entered the cavernous doorway, their rear guard hauled steel doors closed behind them with a deafening *clang*. They were now in an austere, brightly lit concrete anteroom, opening to a hallway lined with bare bulbs and electrical conduits.

Merritt looked around as a guard waved a metal detection wand over him. "What is this place?"

"Daemon Task Force headquarters."

"You put a top-secret base in the middle of a city?"

"Remote locations don't mean secrecy anymore. Companies are selling time on private spy satellites. Here we hide in plain sight."

Merritt nodded and glanced around while the wand beeped and whined. Merritt voluntarily revealed a pistol in a holster beneath his jacket. "I'm FBI." He produced credentials, which the guards closely examined. They keyed Merritt's name into a computer to confirm his clearance. They then pressed his thumb against a fingerprint-capture pad, waited for a single beep, then turned to him again.

"Are you carrying any other weapons or electronic devices, Agent Merritt?"

"A knife."

Another guard passed a tablet PC to him and offered a stylus. "Can you please sign this nondisclosure agreement?"

"I'm already cleared top secret—code word *Exorcist*."

"This is an intellectual property agreement, sir. You need to sign to enter."

Merritt sighed and turned to Ross questioningly.

Ross just shrugged. "Welcome to the Task Force."

"Christ . . ." Merritt signed with the stylus.

While he did so, another guard hung a plastic badge around Merritt's neck. Ross motioned for him to follow down the corridor.

As they walked, Merritt twisted the badge around to examine it. The card was slathered with inscrutable patterns and shiny printed circuits. "You'd think they could afford photo ID badges."

"It's not an ID badge. It's a biometric training marker." Ross pointed to the ceiling.

Merritt saw a series of small cameras mounted there, running down the length of hallway.

"Your gait is being memorized, Roy. The security system is learning to recognize you from your walk and facial features."

Merritt eyed the cameras suspiciously.

They soon reached the end of the corridor, where doors of clear ballistic glass blocked the way. Armed sentries stood on both the near and far side—weapons at the ready. One of the guards there removed the training marker from around Merritt's neck.

"Thank you, Agent Merritt. You are Sec Level Two. Please observe the posted warnings. This is a lethal force zone."

"Thanks."

The doors slid open to admit them, and suddenly raucous conversation and clicking keyboards spilled out into the hall.

Ross brought Merritt into a high-ceilinged room about sixty feet square. In a past life it was probably a heavy-equipment room—overhead pulley rails were still in place. Now it was filled with modern, open workspaces, with clusters of five or six computer workstations sharing common desks. The room was crammed with guys in their early to mid-twenties—all wearing headsets and shouting to each other as they played 3-D computer games. Brilliant computer-generated vistas filled twenty-inch flat-panel monitors. It was like a raucous LAN party.

Merritt stared in amazement. "What's all this?"

"Gaming pit. We've got top young minds here from the public and private intelligence sector playing *The Gate, Over the Rhine*, and half a dozen other online games."

Merritt surveyed the room. "It's a bunch of college kids. They're looking for the Daemon?"

Ross nodded. "Come here." He brought Merritt up to a broad table covered in piles of large color maps. A nearby large-format color printer was spitting out a new one. "These are level maps we found on the Net. This one's a custom level for *Over the Rhine*. That one over there is a castle blueprint from *The Gate*. Daemon Factions create these as bases of operations and training. The most interesting ones are encrypted— although Natalie's crypto people can get us in pretty quickly. We've found some maps that match the floor plans of real-world structures and huge ones that model real-world city streets. Our teams discover a map and reconnoiter it—by force, if necessary. We try to determine the map's purpose, and lastly we try to infiltrate Faction ranks."

Merritt examined the floor plan with an expert tactical eye. "Any luck?"

"Not yet. It's got us seriously frustrated. We're always on the lookout for the Daemon's AI recruiting avatars—Heinrich Boerner in *OTR* is the main one." Ross pulled a color screen-capture off a nearby bulletin board. "Here's a mug shot."

Merritt looked at the picture. It showed Heinrich Boerner in mid-lecture, a long cigarette filter clenched in one corner of his mouth. Some joker on the Task Force had added the word "Wanted" in large red letters over it. "You're hunting for a cartoon Nazi."

"Don't laugh. The real ones can die."

Merritt tossed the picture onto the pile. "So who's starting all these Factions?"

"The disaffected, the dispossessed, the displaced, the disgruntled. Worldwide."

"That's a few people." Merritt soaked up the scene. Watching it, he realized for the first time that the world had really changed—that a line was being drawn in society and which side of the line you stood on would determine your future. He realized more than ever that technological prowess had become a survival skill. "It's getting bad, isn't it?"

"That might be about to change, Roy. Thanks to what you've brought us. C'mon, they're waiting for us in the lab." Ross brought Merritt across the floor, through all the shouting.

"Goddamned sharking smacktard, die!"

"Fireball his ass!"

"Cover me!"

"Friggin' munchkin!"

Presently they reached a steel blast door flanked by two more armed guards in Korr Security uniforms. A red line painted on the concrete floor formed a semicircle at a fifteen-foot radius around the door. The words *Danger—Level 2 Security Zone* were stenciled on the floor just beyond the line and on signs along the wall. As they approached, the guards there leveled their HK UMPs.

Merritt snapped alert. "What's this?"

"It's the R&D lab."

The lead guard motioned for the two of them to come forward. "Voice identification, please."

Ross spoke into a microphone hanging by a long cable from the ceiling. "Ross, Jon Frederick."

A female computer voice responded, *"Voice pattern confirmed."*

There was a loud click, then a flashing red light spun into action, and the massive blast door started to open slowly outward. Merritt was amazed at its thickness—it was easily a foot of solid steel with a beveled edge.

"Hell of a door. Was NORAD having a sale?"

"This place wasn't designed for us. Back in the sixties this was an indoor cannon testing range for the U.S. Navy."

"How'd you guys wind up here?"

"Korr Military Solutions owns the building. They have several forty-nine-million-dollar contracts with the Defense Department to operate Daemon Task Force facilities worldwide."

"Forty-nine million. An odd number."

"Fifty million triggers congressional oversight."

The massive door was open now, leading into a brightly lit anteroom guarded by yet another massive blast door. To the right was an interior guardroom manned by several more heavily armed Korr guards.

Ross and Merritt stepped inside. The first blast door boomed shut behind them.

One of the guards gestured to a hole set into the wall nearby. Ross stuck his arm into the hole. A brilliant light glared from within.

Merritt pointed at the device. "What now?"

"Biometric scanner. It scans the pattern of veins in my forearm."

"If there's an anal probe ahead, I'm leaving now."

The second massive door clicked, then started moving inward. "Watch the door, please, sirs."

They entered a brightly lit, narrow room that was easily a couple hundred feet long. Halfway down the room's length was a cluster of workbenches and electronics equipment. Steel shelving several rows deep lined the approach to it.

Ross motioned for Merritt to follow. They passed another set of armed guards inside the wide doorway, and then Ross set a brisk pace down the center aisle.

They passed row after row of metal shelving piled high with shattered, twisted, burnt, melted, bullet-ridden, or bloodstained equipment of all types—belts, helmets, circuit boards, odd-looking multibarreled pistols and shotguns, bundles of wiring, parabolic satellite dishes, sensors, and on it went. All of them were tagged with bar codes. It looked like an evidence room.

"Captured Daemon equipment?"

Ross nodded. "You guys bring it in, and this is where the techs reverse-engineer it to find out how to defeat it. But you just brought us our greatest find yet, Roy."

They finally reached a scientists' work area and stepped onto a raised dais of nonstatic tile. Several men in lab coats were gathered around something, making adjustments and holding small wrenches. Their bodies completely blocked what they were working on. Dr. Natalie Philips stood, arms crossed, observing the scientists' work. A burly man in a sports jacket stood next to her. Merritt didn't recognize him.

The ice chest and black case Merritt had flown in with stood open on the workbenches nearby.

Philips and the man looked up as Ross and Merritt arrived. Philips nodded. "Agent Merritt, I'm glad things went well in Brazil."

"Anything to help this scavenger hunt of yours, Doctor." They shook hands.

"Well, it might pay off big today." Philips gestured to the man. "Agent Merritt, this is our DOD liaison. For security reasons his identity is classified. We simply call him The Major."

Merritt raised an eyebrow, then extended his hand. "Major."

The Major shook Merritt's hand in an iron grip. "You're something of a celebrity among Daemon operatives, I hear."

Merritt shrugged. "That's what they tell me."

"Good to see you're fully recovered, Mr. Merritt."

Merritt reflexively stroked the burn scars on his neck.

Philips pointed to the nearby knot of scientists. "This is our research team on loan from DARPA. Identities also classified."

"These introductions aren't very useful."

One of the scientists looked up from the huddle. He was an older Asian man. "The rig is ready, Dr. Philips."

Philips nodded toward a nearby stool. "Have a seat, Agent Merritt. I think you'll find this interesting."

The scientists scattered, revealing what they had been working on—and what Merritt had brought all this way: a pair of sports sunglasses with yellow-tinted lenses and thick, metallic frames had been bolted into an armature in the center of the lab area. Wires and cables ran from inside the frames over to the lab bench. Set between the posts of the glasses was a clear glass cylinder in which floated a disembodied human eye, like some macabre olive in a jar. The severed nerve endings were alligator-clipped in place to position the eye staring straight forward through the right lens of the sports glasses.

Philips gestured to the rig. "That's the right eye, Jon?"

Ross nodded. "I double-checked."

She examined the rig closely. "The sniper's bullet doesn't appear to have damaged the blood vessels." She checked her watch. "Eighteen hours, sixteen minutes since his death. The clock is running. We need to get this test started."

Merritt was still staring back at the eye. "What sort of test?"

She turned to him. "We believe these glasses serve as a heads-up display for Daemon operatives, Agent Merritt." She leaned in and pointed to a spot on the frame of the glasses. "A fiber-optic projector displays an image onto the inside of the glass lenses." She pointed to a dot elsewhere on the frame. "This is a retinal scanner. The Daemon knows who's wearing these HUD glasses, and this is a heart pulse monitor—over which we have placed an artificial pulse generator. We intend to fool the Daemon into thinking its operative is still alive and calm. If it hasn't already invalidated his account, we hope to gain access to the Daemon's darknet."

Merritt nodded slowly. "So, that was the big hurry. You're hoping to steal this guy's identity."

Ross stepped up to examine the rig as well. "We're hoping for more than that."

The Chinese scientist approached Philips while holding a thick, pouchlike belt made of stretchable black fabric. The belt had an ornate lion's-head belt buckle. He offered it to her. "This one's powered by some sort of fuel cell. We have nothing like it in the equipment collection. The Daemon is rapidly increasing the quality of its manufacturing process."

Merritt pointed at the belt. "What's it do?"

Philips took it. "It's a wearable computer. The brains of those eyeglasses. Uses a satellite or radio uplink to the Net and connects to these glasses wirelessly with 192-bit military-grade encryption. The encryption key appears to reseed every few minutes. Hard as hell to crack."

"What's with the lion's-head buckle?"

The Chinese scientist nodded. "Blued titanium with diamond eyes. Very expensive—possibly indicating high rank. Daemon equipment often has stylistic fetishes. These are no doubt intended to imbue them with perceived mystical qualities."

Philips grimaced. "Another one of Sobol's psychological hacks." She closely examined the sports glasses in the rig. "These look way beyond the capabilities of a portable fab lab. Grown-crystal optics . . . possibly laser-etched circuitry. Can we identify the factory?"

Another scientist weighed in. "Probably South Korean manufacture. Highest quality."

"How long until we can get this test started, gentlemen?"

The scientists at the lab benches were making last-minute calibrations to hundreds of knobs and dials on rack-mounted monitoring equipment. One of them turned to Philips. "It will be a few minutes yet, Doctor."

Ross approached her and pointed to the HUD glasses. "You think this runs off the FOM?"

Philips reacted to Merritt's quizzical expression. "Jon means the Faction Operations Module, Agent Merritt. It's how the Daemon coordinates the activities of the humans who work for it. That's how it infiltrated corporate networks, that's how it identifies new threats, and that's how it distributes funds and privileges to its members. Basically, it's the key to its power. The FOM is a distributed mesh network consisting of tens of thousands of nodes. Each node has a unique encryption key at any given moment. If we can clone these glasses, we might have an opening we can exploit to infiltrate the Daemon's operations. Possibly to shut it down."

Merritt nodded. "I'm all for that."

The Major frowned at Philips. "If the Daemon knows we're penetrating its defenses, it might lash out and start destroying companies."

"If we're careful, it will never know, Major." She reacted to his grim expression. "Look, Daemon operatives coordinate their activities somehow, and so far we've been unable to find even a single e-mail or IM message between them. We're missing something, and both Jon and I believe that that something is sitting right in front of us. Unless we conduct this test, we'll have no chance at all of stopping the Daemon."

"What *exactly* does this test entail, Doctor?"

Philips pointed at the captured glasses. "We plan on powering up these glasses so we can see what a Daemon operative sees while working on the Daemon's darknet."

The Major still looked doubtful. He pointed at the wires and cables running from the glasses and back toward the lab benches. "And this?"

The Chinese scientist stepped in. "Sound and video outputs. We'll record the images projected onto the heads-up display of the glasses for later analysis. We'll also project the images onto these monitors, here."

"Nothing's hooked into our computer network?"

Philips crossed her arms impatiently. "Major, it's hooked to a DV camera. A camera whose embedded OS has been cleared of serial numbers. Please give us more credit than that. Now, unless the DOD has any objections, I'd like to conduct this test before the Daemon decides that this operative is KIA."

The Major took one last look around. He nodded grimly. "Okay, Doctor. Proceed."

Philips turned to the scientists. "Let's do it, gentlemen."

They tripped several switches. "Activating computer fuel cell."

"The glasses have electrical power."

Numerous television monitors mounted above the workbench filled with information. The scientists looked pleased. "Good. The computer belt has established a secure link to a nearby WiMax transmitter. Let's get a fix on its location."

Another scientist called out, "An encrypted link has been established between the glasses and the computer belt."

"Retinal scanning in progress. Stand by. . . ."

Philips took a deep breath. "Cross your fingers, people."

They all stared at the glasses, but nothing obvious was happening. They waited.

The lead scientist smiled and turned toward them. "We're receiving data. I believe we just fooled the Daemon."

A cheer went up and high fives were exchanged at the lab benches. The Major was impassive, as always.

Philips, Ross, Merritt, and The Major moved to join the scientists crowding around video monitors. The screens displayed images being beamed onto the lenses of the HUD glasses. The Major squinted. "What are we looking at?"

Philips answered. "It's a graphical user interface of some type— local time, GPS coordinates, power level, shield . . . Shield, that's interesting. . . ."

Ross pointed at the screen. "It looks like one of Sobol's game interfaces. A menu of options. Like a first-person shooter."

The Major scowled. "But what's this tell us?"

Ross read through the visible menus. "There's no obvious way to navigate the UI. How do they work it?"

The lead scientist nodded. "The glasses have a built-in bone-conduction microphone. Could it be voice-activated?"

"We don't have a voice pattern for this Daemon operative."

Philips pointed at a small blue square glowing near the right side of the screen. "What's this?" Barely legible text appeared just above the box, reading: *AAW-9393G28.* It was connected to the box by a glowing line.

Ross concentrated on the screen. "I'd say it's a call-out. Looks like there's an object still active in our captured equipment collection."

"You mean like the name call-outs hovering over characters in Sobol's online games?"

"One way to find out . . ." Ross approached the armature holding the HUD glasses.

"What are you doing?"

"I'm going to turn these glasses. If that glowing box moves on-screen as I move the glasses, then we know the glasses are showing us a virtual Daemon object that's bolted to an external coordinate system—most likely the GPS grid."

Merritt looked from Philips to Ross. "Why would it create virtual objects on the GPS grid?"

Ross called over from the rig as he turned it. "In Sobol's online games, players and significant objects in the 3-D environment are denoted by virtual call-outs—pop-up menus that hover in space, providing information. I believe Sobol created the same system using the GPS grid." He turned to Philips. "How's that?"

The group looked stunned. "Oh my God . . ."

"What is it?" Ross moved over to the monitor.

The tiny glowing box paled in significance. Hovering eerily in virtual space beyond the real walls of the lab was a towering red call-out box ringed with a dozen mysterious and dangerous-looking symbols—skulls, X's, and crosses. Beneath that was a line reading *40—Sorcerer*. At the top of the call-out was a rolling row of letters, like tumblers cycling endlessly next to the word *Stormbringer*.

"What the hell is that, Jon?"

Ross studied the video feed. "That's the call-out of a fortieth-level sorcerer—we've been infiltrated."

The Major leaned in toward the screen. "Where is he?"

"In this building . . ." Ross moved side to side to get some parallax on the call-out. "He's in the gaming pit." Ross turned to The Major. "Call security—NOW!"

The Major shouted to a nearby guard. "Notify Secom that we have a highly dangerous intruder in the gaming pit. Activate silent lockdown."

The guard reached for his radio, but The Major put his hand over it and pointed to the nearby phone. "Use a landline, you idiot!"

The guard nodded. "Sorry, Major."

Ross pointed at the screen. "We've got half the talent on the task force in that room."

Philips turned on The Major. "Just how the hell did he get in here, Major?"

"Let's worry about that once we have the mole in custody. I'll tell you this much: Britlin is going to have hell to pay."

"Britlin. Who is Britlin?"

"The company that clears task force candidates."

Philips looked at him like he was insane. "The government *outsourced* our background checks?"

"Britlin has worked with the intelligence sector for thirty years, Doctor. This is standard operating procedure."

"What about the current situation seems standard to you?"

Merritt started loosening his tie. "We need to take him out before he can react. Let me go in there with a can of mace."

The Major shook his head. "Negative, Agent Merritt. We have people on site."

"No offense, Major, but I do this for a living."

"We have thirty ex-SOCOM soldiers—counterinsurgency experts, each with more than a decade of experience. Delta Force, OSNAZ, SFB . . ."

Merritt stopped preparing himself. "Well, I see you were expecting trouble."

Ross was still moving back and forth, trying to pinpoint the intruder's location on a printed floor plan. "He's one of the gamers along the back wall of the pit. User 23, 24, or 25."

Philips turned to the scientists. "This intruder must be linked into the Daemon's darknet. Can you jam his connection?"

The lead scientist looked dour. "We're not configured to jam signals in the gaming pit, Doctor."

"Major, we need that mole taken alive if at all possible."

The Major nodded toward the distant blast doors. "Let's get to the security control room. We'll direct the op from there."

Chapter 43:// Enemy Within

The glass security doors of the gaming pit opened silently, admitting a Korr strike team—half a dozen heavily armed men wearing Kevlar helmets, gas masks, and black body armor. They entered in close formation, single file, guns aimed over each other's shoulders. The white Korr logo was a just a large stylistic "K," like a heraldic symbol on their black helmets and breastplates.

Across the room another set of glass doors opened, revealing a second Korr strike team, identical to the first. The team leaders exchanged hand signals, then advanced in unison. They were a steely-eyed, professional bunch, with automatic weapons, Tasers, and beanbag guns at the ready. They moved as one, threading rapidly through the tangle of workstations toward their target. They clearly knew their business.

The strike teams fanned out, aiming toward the far corner of the room. As they moved in, several of them held up printed signs reading *Danger: Do not speak. Leave immediately.* White-hat gamers looked up one by one, nudging each other. Their game chatter died down, but the guards took up chatter of their own to compensate:

"Team two, cover that left flank."

"Stop bunching up."

"Cover that exit!"

"Clear the field of fire."

The strike teams kept up a steady stream of talk as they formed into a wedge, focused directly on the target: the three gamers in the corner of the room. They could see the gamers' heads dodging left and right beyond flat-panel monitors, reacting to what was displayed on their computer screens. All three men were completely absorbed in their games.

The forward team leader held up three gloved fingers and pointed directly at the players in the corner. Best to take all three down.

The strike teams were still tugging stunned gamers aside, holding a finger up for silence, then pointing to the exits.

Finally the two strike teams were in position, arrayed around their quarry at a distance of ten or twelve feet. They stared at the heads of three gamers—patches of close-cropped, spiky hair. The ambient chatter had died down now, and the targeted gamers appeared to sense something was up. They glanced around as the last of their neighbors scurried to safety. They were isolated. Silence finally fell upon the room, except for the stereo sound effects of nearby 3-D games.

One of the Korr team leaders touched a microphone switch on his gas mask and shouted in an amplified radio voice. "Users 23, 24, and 25. Remain seated, and put your hands where we can see them. This is not a drill!"

The two gamers on the left immediately raised their hands and looked up in utter shock. When they got a look at the dozen weapons pointed in their direction, they turned a shade paler than they already were.

The young guy on the right remained motionless, still sitting behind his monitor.

"User 25! Put your hands where we can see them! Now!" The team leader motioned for the two users on the left to clear the area. They were happy to oblige, and as they complied, two guards pepper-sprayed them in the face. They collapsed screaming as the guards zipped hand ties onto their wrists. It was done with expert swiftness and precision—like calf roping in a rodeo—and in no time, the guards were back on their feet, weapons ready.

User 25 was now isolated. A couple dozen eyes memorized the top of his head through gun sights. Bright laser dots clustered on his scalp.

The booming radio voice kept up the pressure. "Show your hands! Now!"

User 25 took a deep breath. "This is a mistake."

"Hands where we can see them or we open fire!"

"A big mistake."

"I said hands in the air!"

User 25 finally raised his hands. They were wrapped in jet-black gloves with silver caps—like thimbles—on the end of each index finger. Something was set in the palm of each hand, like a large crystal.

Suddenly a white-hot flash several times brighter than the sun pulsed through the room, followed closely by a second flash from User 25's other hand. It took several moments for the light to flare down.

The strike teams were initially stunned, but then needles of agony burned into their brains. They dropped their weapons as they collapsed onto their knees, grabbing at their eyes and clawing their gas masks off their faces, screaming.

Brian Gragg kicked his chair away and stood up from the gaming workstation. As the blinded strike team members writhed on the floor, crying out, Gragg moved calmly toward the burly team leader who had shouted at him. Gragg aimed a silver-capped index finger at the man—a lens at its very tip. Black fiber optic and electrical cables ran down the back of Gragg's hand like veins, disappearing beneath his shirt. "The name is Loki, asshole."

A ruler-straight bolt of electricity cracked like a bullwhip from his fingertip into the man's body armor, followed by a flickering series of bolts in quick succession—three a second. The team leader's muscles jerked with each thunderclap. The smell of ozone filled the air.

After the last crack, Gragg lowered his hand, and the team leader dropped to the ground dead, his body smoking and sizzling.

Grimacing from the pain in his eyes, the other team leader glanced around blindly and shouted, "Who's shooting!"

"That's not shooting!"

"Hooks!" A pause. "Where's Hooks!"

"Get to cover and sound off! Sound off!"

Gragg moved toward the fallen men. He pointed and let loose with several seconds of deafening thunderclaps. Men crawled away screaming, only to be immobilized the moment the first bolt hit them.

In a few seconds they were all motionless or convulsing.

The sickening smell of burnt hair came to Gragg's nostrils.

"What the hell just happened?" Philips stared at a bank of security monitors. The security command center was packed with Korr Security folks pointing at monitors and barking into radios.

The Major snapped his fingers at the control board operator. "Get on the horn to Weyburn Labs. Tell them we might be facing an illicit LIP-C weapon. I need countermeasures and tactics."

Merritt watched the intruder on the monitor. "What's an LIP-C weapon?"

"Laser-Induced Plasma Channel. Uses laser light as a virtual wire for electricity."

"Where did he get it?"

"The Daemon appears to be dipping into our research pipeline."

Philips turned on him. "Just how many sections of the intelligence apparatus have been compromised, Major?"

"Not now, Doctor. We've got men down."

Ross, Merritt, and Philips stared at the large central monitor. There, the intruder was stepping among the fallen strike team members, sprawled on the floor of the gaming pit.

The Major barked at the board operator. "Seal zones three through six. Let's contain this asshole."

Another Korr officer spoke up. "I've got an identity on User 25: Michael Radcliffe. Grad student, MIT—"

The Major waved it aside. "That's bullshit. Radcliffe's probably dead."

"Should we pump tear gas through the ventilation ducts, sir?"

"Use your brain. There's a dozen gas masks in there with him." The Major checked his watch. "Call in an electronic warfare team and a demolitions team. We need to jam this fucker's uplink, then kill him." He turned to nearby Korr officers. "I want commercially marked choppers over our twenty. Scramble the perimeter defense teams. Lethal force authorized. No one enters or leaves this facility until I say otherwise."

"Understood, Major."

Philips pushed up to him. "Major, we should try to take this man alive."

"We're not capturing anyone, Doctor. This situation is going to end right now, and whatever's left is all yours."

Ross pointed at the monitor. "He's doing something."

They all looked up.

The intruder was standing, moving his arms as though controlling invisible objects, his mouth moving in a rhythmic chant.

———

Gragg concentrated on the plane of D-Space. The entire floor plan of Building Twenty-Nine was replicated there, spread out around him as a life-sized wire-frame model overlaid on the GPS grid. It aligned precisely with the corners of each wall in the real world. This allowed Gragg to see the geometry of adjoining rooms. More importantly, images from the building's dense network of security cameras were wrapped around the wire-frame model's geometry, showing a patchwork of live video from those neighboring rooms—giving Gragg an almost X-ray vision through the dense concrete.

Korr personnel sprinted through the hallways, loading weapons and sealing doorways. They were ants in his ant colony. He had seen the strike teams getting ready all the way back in their locker room.

The garrison was in disarray.

Gragg turned to look far beyond the concrete walls of Building Twenty-Nine, to distant, glowing call-outs in D-Space. He selected dozens of virtual objects he'd stored there, then launched his prearranged summoning sequence, making somatic gestures and speaking the unlock code to the VOIP module. "*Andos ethran Kohlra Bethru.* Lord of a million eyes, Loki summons you. . . ."

Gragg looked through the sealed blast doors leading into the lab. The guards there had been pulled inside, but Gragg looked into the artificial dimension beyond them. He aimed his gloved finger at a virtual object in the lab, an object he had insinuated into the equipment collection some time ago. Gragg closed his fist on the object in D-Space.

Somewhere beyond those thick concrete walls a compressed air tank sprayed powdered aluminum across the lab space—then ignited it with an electrical spark. Suddenly the building shuddered, followed by a dull roar and the muted shrieks of twisting metal. A deafening klaxon sounded the alarm throughout the facility. Blue strobes flickered near the exits.

The Major scanned the security monitors as a dozen red lights blinked on a floor plan map. There. The lab was consumed in flames. The camera image rippled with interference, vertical hold skipping. One of the scientists ran through the picture, burning alive beneath white-hot flames. Sprinklers deployed to little effect.

"Goddamnit . . ."

"The science team. Get medics to the lab! And the equipment collection—"

"It's too late. . . ." Ross pointed to the monitor.

On-screen an acetylene tank was spinning in a pinwheel of flame near the lab table, then exploded, shaking the building again. The monitor image went dead.

Philips slumped and covered her eyes. "We just lost some of our best people, not to mention the Daemon equipment collection."

Merritt grabbed The Major's shoulder. "Where do you need me?"

"Sit tight, Merritt." The Major looked back at Philips. "Are you still glad you conducted your little test, Doctor?"

"Without this test we never would have discovered we'd been infiltrated."

Ross nodded. "*That's* why we weren't able to join Daemon Factions. He was tracking our every move."

The Major turned to him. "Maybe we shouldn't have been playing games with the Daemon in the first place."

The board operator looked up again. "He's not going anywhere, Major. The gaming pit is locked down."

Gragg stood before the sealed bulletproof glass doors barring his exit. The camera-lined corridor beyond led to the building entry vestibule.

Gragg turned to face another D-Space object hovering just to the right of the glass doors. It was a surreal blue button, floating impossibly there as seen through his HUD glasses. It was labeled in large glowing letters: OPEN. Gragg tapped the virtual button with his gloved hand. It flashed.

The real-world ballistic glass doors slid open, and he stepped through the opening and entered the anteroom beyond.

Philips threw up her hands. "He's out of the gaming pit."

Ross gestured to the monitors. "The security system's been compromised."

"Who subcontracted that, I wonder?"

The Major gave her a look. "Stow that shit right now." He turned to the board operator. "Physically cut the power to the north perimeter doors."

The board operator rolled back in his chair. He opened an electrical panel on the back wall and started tripping breaker switches.

Philips leaned over the board and clicked from camera to camera. "Where is he?"

"Don't worry, Doctor. He's trapped."

"That's what you said last time. Show me."

"We just tripped the breakers. The perimeter doors are frozen in a locked position. He's not getting through inch-thick steel plating."

She studied the bank of black-and-white monitors. The large one in the center now showed the intruder standing in a dead-end hallway some distance from the exterior steel doors. He stood above three newly fallen guards, their bodies smoking. The intruder was just staring up at the camera. Unnervingly calm. He was only a kid—early twenties at most.

The Major nodded at the monitor. "I told you we'd stop him." He turned to a nearby guard. "I want every gun on the tarmac focused on that exit."

Philips leaned into the microphone sticking up from the control board. She held down the mic switch. "You're trapped. Give up, and you won't be hurt."

The intruder's tinny voice came in over the speakers. "Dr. Philips, I see you discovered D-Space. Or at least a layer of it."

A flash of fear swept through her. He knew her real name. How could he possibly know her name? Thoughts of her parents in D.C. thrust front and center in her mind. She turned to The Major. "Call Dr. Fulbright at Fort Meade. Tell him to take my parents into protective custody. Now!"

The Major snapped his fingers at a Korr guard, who grabbed another phone.

She keyed the mic. "You know who I am. So who are you—or are you afraid to tell me your name?"

"Bitch. I'm Loki, the most powerful sorcerer in the world, and I'm about to ruin your whole fucking day."

Merritt took off his suit jacket and headed for the door. "Keep this nutcase busy, Doctor."

Ross grabbed Merritt's arm. "No heroics, Roy."

"I don't plan on any."

The Major blocked his path. "Where are you going?"

Merritt looked calmly at him. "I'm going to see how that prick deals with flash-bang grenades. Unlock the gaming pit, Major."

The Major appraised Merritt for a moment, then grabbed a radio and headset from a nearby charging station. The man looked as determined as he had in the famous Burning Man images from Sobol's mansion. He tossed them to Merritt. "Good luck." The Major watched him exit.

Philips turned back to the monitor and keyed the mic again. "Loki, Sobol is using you. What you're doing is high treason. If you surrender now, I can help you."

"You can help *me*?" He laughed. "I'm not the one who needs help. The society you're defending is doomed."

"It's your society, too, Loki."

"No. It's my *parents'* society, not mine. What does it offer my generation? A meaningless existence. Living long, boring lives, milked each day by salesmen. Livestock for a permanent ruling class. Well, I have no use for their laws, their maps, their failures. The Daemon has already defeated them."

"This is your last warning: surrender."

Loki smiled. "You don't get it, do you?"

Philips sighed in exasperation and pounded the mic button again. "We physically cut the power to the door in front of you. Your hacks won't work. Even if you manage to get through the door, we've got snipers covering the tarmac. They'll cut you down from two hundred meters downrange. Just surrender."

Loki shook his head. "You're not thinking in enough dimensions, Doctor. Only *part* of me is in this building."

Squads of heavily armed Korr Security guards ran to take up positions next to a guard shack ringed with highway barriers and razor wire at the perimeter gate. Behind them a quarter mile of bare tarmac stretched to the nearest hangar, but most of their attention was drawn inward, to Building Twenty-Nine itself. They listened to their encrypted radios and the voice coming through it.

"*Shoot on sight. Repeat: Shoot on sight. . . .*"

"Copy that, Secom. Out."

A bay breeze kicked up, sending scraps of paper tumbling over the expanse of concrete and flattening them against the chain-link fencing. Nearer to the building another squad of Korr guards with scoped M4A1s rushed to take up positions in the staff parking lot— the best cover available. They took aim at the sealed steel doors of the building.

The roar of speeding engines suddenly came in on the wind. One guard turned, then urgently grabbed his officer's shoulder, pointing. "*Pas op!*"

They both turned to see one, then six, then fifteen, then thirty cars screaming in from several vectors along the runway, racing in through the gaps between distant hangar buildings. The cars swerved with remarkable coordination, all converging on Building Twenty-Nine like a school of piranha.

"Polizei?"

The lieutenant blew a whistle, and everyone turned to face him. He pointed and shouted with an Afrikaans accent. "Incoming! Take cover!"

"Might be car bombs."

"Belay that!" The cars had already closed half the distance. More were issuing from between the distant hangars. The lieutenant keyed his radio. "Secom, we have several dozen vehicles inbound at high speed. Code 30."

Nothing but static came back.

"Scheisse." He turned to his men. "Fire at will!"

Automatic gunfire erupted from a score of positions. The shots cracked flatly in the open air of the runway. Tracer rounds ripped across the tarmac, ricocheting off the concrete and whining into the sky.

"Knock out the lead cars! The lead cars!"

A light antitank rocket blasted from their lines in a pall of smoke and detonated against a mid-sized car at fifty yards, turning it into a tumbling ball of flame. A black domestic sedan swerved around the wreckage and came roaring onward. Half a dozen divots appeared in the black-tinted windshield at head level right in front of the driver's seat, revealing a high degree of marksmanship. Then hundreds more bullets tore through its front grill. As its engine died another car surged past it, and as that one was riddled with bullets, yet another took its place. Already ten cars were smoking and rolling to a stop—but still more came on.

The shooting died down as half the squad dropped clips and hurriedly reloaded.

"Watch that left flank!"

The lieutenant leaned around the guard shack just in time to see a car's front grill—which was the last thing he ever saw.

The car crashed into the fence line and concrete highway divider at 110 mph, disappearing into a cloud of concrete dust and debris as it tumbled end over end. It was immediately followed by three other sedans, crashing through the gate. Automatic weapons stitched them full of bullet holes from several directions. Shouting filled the gaps in the gunfire.

But other cars had already blasted through the fence line else-where, dragging great serrated lengths of chain-link fencing behind them. These caught guards across the thighs, tearing their flesh and dragging them screaming, even as other guards blasted out windows and peppered car bodies with bullets from M249s with 200-round belts.

Now they could plainly see the cars were unmanned.

"Dit kan nie wees, nie!"

"Fall back! Fall back!"

A car crashed into the edge of the parking lot, while two others ca-reened off each other and slammed into a scattering pack of guards with such force that the guards' bodies hurtled twenty yards and landed in the bay, followed closely by the cars that hit them. The cars sent up geysers of water as they hit the surface.

In the distance, more AutoM8s kept streaming through the gaps be-tween warehouses.

Merritt raced out into the gaming pit, Berretta drawn. Automatic gunfire crackled like popcorn somewhere outside. "Damnit . . ."

Merritt slowed as he reached the still-smoking bodies of the strike teams sprawled between the workstations. He knelt to feel the pulse of the nearest one. Nothing.

He scavenged an HK UMP .40-cal submachine gun with a web belt of extra clips and flash-bang grenades, then spoke into his headset microphone. "Merritt to Secom. What the hell's going on out there? Over."

The Major talked into a radio headset. "Agent Merritt, we're under attack. Stand by."

Inside the security control room, the sound of muffled automatic weapons fire was starting to be eclipsed by roaring engines and crash-ing. The Major watched the external monitors. One camera showed a head-on view of a driverless, bullet-riddled car nailing the camera pole, the screen filling with snow. "Why didn't they sound the alarm?" He was having trouble comprehending it. "This isn't a guerrilla raid—this is a frontal assault."

Ross examined the screens. "Computer-controlled vehicles. Dozens of them. The Factions call them AutoM8s."

The Major stared at the large central monitor on the control board—seemingly the only monitor not at present depicting mayhem.

On-screen the intruder was busy moving his arms—manipulating invisible objects. He glanced up at the security camera. His voice came over the speaker. "I'll let myself out."

Just then, some ten yards behind the intruder, the steel doors were staved in by a shredded mass of metal. The whole building shook with a dull thud, concrete dust sifting down through seams.

The intruder barely flinched.

The car that had smashed in the steel doors was now entirely blocking the exit. But then another unseen vehicle cut in from the side and ripped the first one out of the hole with a deafening crash.

The opening was now clear.

Merritt heard the first crash and saw sunlight streaming in from beyond the sealed ballistic doors. He loaded the UMP and by the second crash he was rushing toward the glass doors.

Gragg emerged into the sunlight through the shattered opening of the main door.

As he did so, a silver BMW 740 with blacked-out windows rolled up to meet him. Its rear door opened, and he slid inside, pulling the door closed behind him. The BMW screeched off toward the wrecked fence line, followed close on by a pack of domestic sedans.

Merritt emerged from the dark, smoking doorway screaming, "Loki!" He stopped, clutched his UMP's fore grip, and opened up with three short bursts, expertly tagging the tinted rear windshield with a dozen closely grouped shots. The .40-cal bullets left small divots but not much else. The car was obviously a security model.

"Goddamnit!" Merritt lowered his gun and watched a sizeable pack of unmanned vehicles converge like a single organism, surrounding the BMW to shield it. They accelerated toward the distant fence line, running over several bodies in the process. The pack of cars was heading for the distant hangars at high speed.

Merritt glanced around at the carnage surrounding Building Twenty-Nine. There were bodies, streaks of blood, burning vehicles, and debris littering the tarmac. Columns of black smoke billowed skyward. There wasn't a guard in sight—or any intact unmanned vehicles for that matter. They had all left with Loki.

Merritt spotted a racing motorcycle parked along the wall in the staff parking lot. He rushed over to it and searched for keys—nothing. He slung his UMP over his back and pulled his Berretta pistol, aiming it at the ignition lock. He turned his head away.

Boom.

Pieces of plastic and metal parts clattered across the pavement. Merritt holstered the Berretta, then mounted the bike. He turned the shattered lock cylinder to *Start* and kicked the engine to life, revving its powerful engine. He grabbed the helmet hanging from the handlebars and pulled it on. He flipped down the mirrored visor, and a moment later he screeched out after the pack of automated cars receding in the distance. He accelerated madly through the debris field and rocketed out onto the runway in hot pursuit. He could barely make out the silver BMW in the middle of the car pack, but he targeted it with every ounce of horsepower he had at his disposal. The bike engine howled.

After buckling himself in, Gragg looked back toward Building Twenty-Nine.

Directly over the building a bright red glowing sign towered in D-Space sixty stories tall, rotating like a neon sign and visible for miles around to anyone on the Daemon's darknet. It proclaimed in giant letters with an arrow pointing down: *Top-Secret Anti-Daemon Task Force.* Gragg laughed, then raised one black-gloved hand. He drew another glowing red box across D-Space to encompass the entire facility. With a click of his pinky he brought up a pop-up menu, then selected *Kill Everyone.*

Merritt's motorcycle howled across the decommissioned runway. He leaned into a swerve at a hundred mph to avoid a pothole, but as he came out of it, he noticed a second wave of unmanned vehicles streaming in toward Building Twenty-Nine. Thirty vehicles, including a couple of white Econoline panel vans. A detachment of mid-sized domestic sedans peeled off from the main group and vectored in on Merritt.

"Oh shit . . ."

The sedans were almost on him—and still accelerating.

Merritt's youthful passion for fast motorcycles finally paid off. He thrust his body up and over the left side of the gas tank—expertly pulling into the hardest turn he could manage at high speed. Friction coefficients instinctively ran through his head and muscle memory took over.

The first blue sedan screamed past on the right rear flank with a margin so close the wind pounded into Merritt's thigh.

Merritt leaned right.

Half a second later, two more sedans clipped each other just feet behind him. Hollow crashing sounds—as of rolling vehicles—boomed, then quickly faded behind him.

The fourth one came so close it tore Merritt's left rear turning light off. This left Merritt wavering and off balance. The motorcycle yawed from side to side for a few moments until he got it back under control. He was now highly aware that he wasn't wearing riding gear.

He looked up to see Loki's pack of cars racing through the decommissioned base's front gate. Merritt shot a glance behind him. Two cars were pursuing and closing fast. He yanked on the throttle, and raw acceleration nearly ripped him off the saddle.

Merritt raced down a lane between hangars and keyed his radio. "Merritt to Secom. In pursuit of Loki. He's headed . . . east . . . in an armored, silver late-model BMW. It's surrounded by a pack of unmanned vehicles. More are headed your way."

The Major's voice came in over the radio. *"Agent Merritt, terminate this pursuit. Repeat: Terminate pursuit immediately."*

Merritt emerged from between the hangars and saw Loki's pack racing out into the city streets, smashing other traffic aside. "Negative. This guy's a danger to the public."

"Repeat: Terminate this chase!"

"I don't report to you, Major! Until the bureau orders me otherwise, I'm going after this bastard. Out."

He accelerated out the abandoned front gates of Alameda Naval Air Station and hit the surface roads with a bounce.

Gragg cinched the racing harness tighter around his body as the powerful BMW AutoM8 roared into the streets of Oakland.

The unmanned steering wheel spun crazily as it went into a power slide around the corner. AutoM8s crowded Gragg's car on either side, muscling other cars out of their way. His entourage was a pack of a dozen sedans. He saw their random, alphanumeric call-outs hovering in D-Space all around him.

He concentrated further ahead—on the dozens more AutoM8s streaming in toward him from across the city. His strength was growing by the minute, now reaching upwards of a hundred vehicles.

He waved his gloved hands and screeched cars across the mouths of distant intersections, sealing out cross-traffic and opening the way ahead.

Gragg's own pack invaded a busy intersection against the light— sparking several broadside crashes as his minions forced a path for him. Smashing glass followed screeching rubber. Wrecked cars spun out of control, and pedestrians ran for cover.

Gragg's BMW raced through the carnage and past a local patrolman ticketing a landscaper's truck. Gragg's eyes narrowed, and he brought video from dashboard cameras of a trailing AutoM8 up onto his HUD display. In the video window Gragg could see the local cop sprinting to his squad car, speaking urgently into his hand radio.

With a subtle motion of his hand Gragg clicked on the license plate of the police car, locking the nearest AutoM8 onto it.

The video image disappeared in a cloud of snow on impact, and Gragg chuckled to himself, imagining the consequences.

On the tarmac surrounding Building Twenty-Nine, two white panel vans came to a stop as a dozen more AutoM8s circled around them, on guard. The rear doors to each van opened, and metal mesh ramps dropped onto the pavement with a clang.

A deep, guttural roar rose over the other engines, and down each ramp rolled a riderless, black racing motorcycle with dozens of brushed steel blades running along their tops and sides like cooling fins. Neither bike had handlebars, but instead had forward-mounted hydraulic assemblies of brushed steel, folded tightly. A cowling of black laminate armor enclosed the front. In place of a rider's saddle was a circular steel dome about a foot in diameter, its surface etched with mystical symbols. Nearly every inch of the bikes was covered in runes and glyphs and razor-sharp blades. They were as much fetish objects as machines.

The motorcycles rolled to a stop and twin hydraulic jacks slammed down onto the pavement like oversized kickstands or half-formed legs. They thrust each bike nearly a foot off the ground, where they stood revving their 1800cc engines deafeningly. Then twin robotic arms with gleaming three-foot sword blades unfolded from the forward hydraulic assemblies, lashing forth on gimbals, arcing smoothly with blinding speed as they ran through diagnostics like insects cleaning their antennae.

At some unseen signal, the bikes retracted their kickstand jacks and hit the pavement, rear wheels smoking. They streaked off toward the hulking silhouette of Building Twenty-Nine in the distance.

———

Philips and The Major moved swiftly down a corridor, followed by Ross and four heavily armed Korr guards. Personnel raced past them in both directions, carrying computers and boxes of files. The Major was speaking on his L3 phone. "I understand." A pause. "Yes. We're working back channels to warn off civilian authorities. I will." He snapped the phone shut.

They reached the gaming pit and could see black smoke seeping from the seams of the sealed lab blast doors, hinting at the inferno burning within. Korr medics were doing CPR on two strike team members, while other guards were placing bodies in a row on the floor.

Philips slowed for a moment. "My God . . ."

The Major pulled her past and motioned for Ross to follow. "We're evacuating this facility. Choppers are on the way. I'm taking the first one to go after Agent Merritt. I want you and Mr. Ross on chopper two."

"Where is Merritt?"

"He went out after this 'Loki' person, but we can track him. His radio has GPS."

Ross noticed guards pass by, uncoiling detonator wire from a reel. "What's going on?"

"We're about to have a serious industrial accident here. Prearranged cover story."

Philips snapped alert. "This facility still contains critical equipment and data, Major."

"This facility is in danger of being overrun by the enemy, Doctor."

Philips thought about this for a moment, then produced her own encrypted phone and started punching numbers. "I haven't received orders to abandon this facility, and until I do, I'm not going anywhere."

"In that case . . ." The Major drew a Glock 9mm pistol from his coat and chambered a round. "I can't risk you falling into enemy hands. Your knowledge of U.S. ciphers is too great."

Ross stepped in front of her. "Wait!"

"Do you want to see my orders, Doctor?"

She was speechless, staring at the business end of the pistol.

Ross held his hands up. "She'll go, Major."

The Major lowered his gun. "Puts it into perspective, doesn't it? Now get ready to pull out."

"What about my people?"

"They're no longer your people. This task force has been dissolved. I've been ordered to send you back to Fort Meade and to remand Mr. Ross to the custody of the FBI."

"On what charges?"

"Multiple counts of wire fraud and identity theft."

She stared at The Major. "That's insane. He just made a breakthrough."

"This task force has been ineffective at curbing the rapid growth of the Daemon. Your narrow field of expertise is being folded into a larger effort. Mr. Ross's services are no longer required. If they ever were."

Ross looked unsurprised. "But I have an amnesty agreement with the Justice Department."

"The terms of which you failed to meet."

"We failed because task force functions were compromised by private contractors."

The Major nodded to the nearby guards, who raised stun guns. "These men will see that you're delivered safely. Resistance is optional."

Philips kept shaking her head. "Major, if Merritt captures Loki, we can find out how they compromised our systems."

"The Daemon won this round, Doctor. I have orders to break off contact with the infiltrator as soon as possible."

"You can't just let Loki escape."

"The number one goal right now is keeping the existence of the Daemon a secret until we mitigate the risks to the global economy. That goal is not compatible with open warfare on our perimeter or by Agent Merritt pursuing a pack of robotic vehicles through downtown Oakland. We're lucky we don't already have news choppers swarming overhead."

"If we can stop this thing now, it will be worth the hit to the economy."

"I'll be sure to put that in my report, *Comrade* Philips."

The thumping of a chopper was now audible. The Major spoke to a nearby Korr guard. "Hold them here, and rush them to the roof when the second chopper arrives—but not before. Understood?"

The lead guard saluted. "Yes, Major."

The radio on the guard's belt crackled to life. *"This is Perimeter-9 . . . do you copy?"*

The Major motioned for the guard to hand it to him, and he started heading toward the stairwell doors as he keyed the mic. "This is Secom, Perimeter-9. What's your status?"

Out on the tarmac Perimeter-9 clutched a radio handset and winced in pain. "All units down. Repeat: all perimeter units are down. Request medevac and air support." He limped painfully behind a wrecked and bullet-riddled AutoM8. His lower leg was stained with blood just below a makeshift tourniquet. The leg was badly mangled.

The Major's voice came over the radio through a haze of static. *"Report on the unmanned vehicles."*

"They left with the intruder. But more of them just arrived. They're forming for another attack. I'm out of ammo, sir. Badly injured." He craned his neck back toward a chopper angling in toward the roof of Building Twenty-Nine. "Requesting immediate airlift."

"Negative. Just stay put, Nine. Help's on the way."

Just then Perimeter-9 heard the howl of high-performance engines. He turned to see twin racing motorcycles streaking across the tarmac in his direction. They were moving in close formation at 150 mph or more.

"Hold it. I've got two motorcycles inbound. . . ." He stepped behind the fender of the car, putting the car hood between him and the approaching bikes. "They're moving fast as hell."

"Where are they headed?"

Suddenly a brilliant green laser light dazzled his eyes. He held up his hands against it, squinting. "Hang on, I'm being painted by something. I can't see—"

The roaring engines were suddenly on him and he heard a deep *thwack*. He was completely disoriented for several moments. As his vision cleared, he had a view from the ground—a view of his own headless, one-armed body slumping over the hood of the car ten feet away, then sliding onto the pavement.

Back in the gaming pit, The Major was already gone. His voice came through on a nearby guard's radio. *"Perimeter-9! Do you copy?"*

Ross watched eight armed guards piling black bags onto the floor for transport. Two were staring at him with hard eyes—stun guns ready.

"I guess I should have seen this coming."

Philips squeezed his shoulder. "I won't let them do this to you, Jon. I have friends in Washington, too."

Suddenly the howl of racing engines echoed down the corridor behind the nearby ballistic doors. Everyone turned to see shadows streak along the corridor wall, then twin black motorcycles roared into view beyond the closed bulletproof glass doors. They raised robotic blade arms menacingly. The blades on the lead bike were already stained with blood.

Everyone stepped back away from the doors. The Korr guards raised their weapons, clicking off their safeties. Ross pointed toward the far glass doors. "Let's get to the roof. Now!"

Philips stared at the machines beyond the sealed Lexan glass. The most exotic thing that the Daemon had spawned yet. "Jon, I've seen the word 'Razorback' listed in decrypted Daemon intercepts. This could—"

A spiraling green light stabbed forth from the face of the lead bike, beaming through the ballistic glass into her eyes. She screamed and slammed her palms against her face, staggering back.

Ross rushed forward and grabbed her. He pulled her behind the guards, who were also dazed by the light. "Don't look at them! They have blinding weapons!"

Then the ballistic doors slid open with their familiar hiss—and the roar of the advancing Razorbacks filled the cavernous gaming pit. Followed by gunfire and—almost immediately—bloodcurdling screams.

Ross pulled on Philips's arm. "Run!" The engine roar was deafening now as Ross guided Philips down the adjacent hall toward the open security control room door. There was only a smattering of gunfire now as the roar of the engines zigzagged across the room behind them. Smashing furniture. Ross risked a quick glance back behind them. Blood was spattered all over the walls and floor near the ballistic doors. A Korr guard was running toward him, firing blindly over his shoulder as a Razorback raised twin, bloody blades and screeched after him on the polished concrete, green laser spiraling. Ross turned away as a series of metallic ringing sounds, screams, and sharp thwacks accompanied the roar of engines.

Ross reached the security control room door, half dragging the blinded Philips across the polished floor.

"What's happening, Jon? What's happening?"

"Keep moving!" He took another glance behind them as the same Razorback accelerated down the hallway in their direction. Ross looked away just as a laser light played across his face.

He pulled Philips inside the control room, then dropped her on the floor and raced back toward the open control room door. He kicked the hollow steel door closed just as the Razorback screeched to a stop in front of it. He put a shoulder against the door and slammed it shut, locking it.

Almost instantly a series of massive dents deformed the door, accompanied by the thunderous roar of a powerful engine. The pounding continued, deforming the door surface as Ross backed away from it.

He felt Philips clutching for his leg. "Jon, I think I'm blind!"

He glanced toward another door leading out the far side of the control room. He knelt next to her and shouted over the engine noise. "Nat, we can't stay here!"

She gripped her face, tears streaming down from between her fingers. "My eyes, Jon! They're burning!"

He grabbed her roughly. "Nat! Nat, listen to me!"

She stopped. The Razorback's pounding vibrated the floor.

"It could be temporary." He looked back at the door. "If we don't leave here now, we're going to die!"

The sound of deforming metal reinforced his argument.

She took a deep breath and nodded. "Where are we?"

He shouted over the deafening roar of the Razorback. "Security control room!"

She nodded. "We can make it to the back gate!"

He helped her to her feet, and they headed to the door on the far side of the small room.

One of the Razorback's steel falchions pierced through the door and wrenched free as the engine roared again.

She stopped him. "The perimeter doors. We need to trip the breakers back on."

"I'll get it. Just go! Follow the left wall." He pushed her through the door, then turned. Jagged holes had been torn into the sheet metal of the other door. Part of it was broken away, and he could see one of the Razorback's gnarled, twisted blade arms through the slits. It paused for a moment, then he heard a *ping* sound, and the twisted blades spun free like disposable razors, clattering onto the concrete floor in the hallway outside.

Ross rushed to the breaker boxes. He stole a glance at the bank of camera monitors on the control board. One showed the Razorback in the hallway outside, reaching around to its side. A metal *click-clack*, and the arms rose with fresh, gleaming blades.

"Son of a bitch . . ." He opened a panel marked *Perimeter* and tripped all the breakers back on. He raced back to the far door, looking behind just as the Razorback smashed the door in. He turned away as its laser painted him, and it roared across the room. Ross slammed the new door behind them, and the pounding started almost immediately.

A Bell Jet Ranger chopper hovered inches above the cluttered roof of Building Twenty-Nine. The helicopter was electric blue with a bold yellow logo for *Golden Gate Heli-Tours*. The Major rose from his kneeling position and scurried toward it at a crouch. A crewmember wearing a Korr flak vest pulled him inside. The Major leaned toward the helmeted pilot, who nodded in his direction. The crewman handed The Major a closed-circuit headset, and The Major slipped it on.

The pilot's voice came over the headphones, "What's the situation here, Major?"

"I need to get topside. We've got a Daemon operative escaping into the city and a federal officer in pursuit. Where's my kit?"

"Case on the floor, sir."

The Major pointed at the crewmember and copilot in turn, but spoke to the pilot. "These people, off."

Both men looked to the pilot, who simply said, "You heard the man. Take the next chopper out."

They unbuckled themselves and with a hesitant look jumped down onto the roof.

The Major shouted. "Go!"

The pilot yanked on the stick, and the chopper ascended rapidly, making corkscrews of the columns of black smoke.

Chapter 44://Revelation

Merritt accelerated down an Oakland retail strip. Damaged vehicles littered the way. On the motorcycle, he was able to slip past the bottlenecks of wreckage and whipped past several damaged patrol cars to take the lead in the pursuit. Up ahead he could see Loki's pack of cars, and he could see the silver BMW itself, protected by its personal guard detail. A minivan suddenly bucked up and tumbled out of the way as a horrendous crash came to Merritt's ears.

This guy was a psycho.

A city motorcycle cop raced up on Merritt's right. Merritt shouted over to him and held his badge up on a chain. "FBI!" He used military hand signals to indicate the target.

The motorcycle cop nodded and brought his big bike racing ahead past Merritt.

"Hey!"

Suddenly twin sedans streaked in from side streets, crushing the motorcycle cop between them with a horrific crash.

Merritt averted his head as he powered through the flying debris and smoke. He emerged on the other side to see nothing but flames behind him.

Gragg looked into his HUD glasses to see multiple police cars screeching onto the street several blocks back, rack lights flashing. He crashed another one of his AutoM8s into a civilian's subcompact, smashing it out of the way and sending it spinning up onto the sidewalk. He left a trail of destruction behind him as the police lights zigzagged between wrecked vehicles, falling behind fast. But more sirens could be heard ahead and to either side of him. They were starting to cordon him off. Choppers were no doubt en route.

He smiled to himself. More AutoM8s were streaming in to aid him. He felt the presence of over a hundred now—some more valuable than others.

Another BMW 740 screeching in from a side street suddenly joined Gragg's car. This BMW was scarlet red. The pack expanded automatically to encompass it.

Gragg motioned with one black-gloved hand, and the electro-polymer paint of his own BMW shifted from silver to red in a matter of seconds—even as the newly arrived red BMW transformed from red to silver. Gragg's digital ink license plates flicked from California to Oregon vanity tags that read *GECCO*. In a flash, his BMW went into a power slide down a side street and left the main pack behind.

———

Merritt was still trying to comprehend what he just saw. A decoy BMW had joined the pack, but then Loki's BMW transformed right in front of Merritt's eyes. Merritt leaned hard into the turn and gave chase. Loki's car was now bright red—but he could still see the pockmarks from his earlier shots in the rear window. He cast a glance behind him to see several squad cars race past the intersection, still in pursuit of the original pack.

Merritt turned back to face Loki, then he tapped his radio button. "Major! Major, this is Merritt. Do you copy?"

———

The Major looked up from assembling a scoped SCAR-H sniper rifle in the passenger bay of the chopper. Merritt's voice came over their encrypted radio frequency again, dissolving occasionally into static. *"Major, this . . . Merritt . . . copy?"*

The Major keyed his mic. "Go ahead, Agent Merritt."

"Listen . . . police are pursuing a decoy BMW . . . car has . . . color, and is heading . . ." Static filled the channel.

"You're breaking up."

"Repeat . . . color. I'm giving chase."

"You're catching interference from the AutoM8s. Fall back, Merritt."

". . . police they're . . ." At that the signal trailed off into static.

The Major dropped the handset and spoke into his chopper headset. "We still receiving Merritt's GPS coordinates?"

The pilot nodded. "10-4, Major. Clear as a bell."

"Then the Daemon is using GPS, too. Get me over Merritt's twenty."

Now out of the chase and heading through wide industrial streets, Gragg monitored a distant AutoM8's video feed as the pack of cars he just left accelerated onto an elevated portion of the 880 Freeway, smashing cars out of their way. California Highway Patrol units took up the chase on the freeway. Gragg couldn't help but smile. They were closing in.

He accelerated the distant AutoM8 pack toward the elevated junction with Highway 260—and the retaining wall at the steep curve. "This ought to be interesting. . . ."

He selected the lead AutoM8 in the HUD and urged it on ahead of the others. Then he switched to video feed from a car farther back in the pack. The lead car screamed ahead like a missile, then crashed through the concrete retaining wall at a hundred miles an hour, spraying a vacant lot fifty feet below with pieces of concrete and twisted metal. The remaining pack, including the silver BMW, roared through the new gap in the wall and tumbled end over end through the air, smashing down on top of one another in a fiery wreck. The video feed turned to snow.

Done. Gragg took a deep breath and felt himself coming down off the adrenaline surge. He could imagine the police stopping to look out over a tangled pile of burning wreckage, scratching their heads, as police are wont to do. It would take them days to figure out. The nearest police car's GPS signal was a mile away.

He did a quick postmortem: the Daemon Task Force had been neutralized. It might mean another level for him.

A motorcycle streaked up alongside his car. The rider reached out with one hand, extending a submachine gun, and fired a short burst at Gragg's tires.

"What the hell?"

Gragg raised his gloved hands to fire the nova light, but then realized his blacked-out windows would ruin the effect. His armored windows didn't roll down either. "Son of a bitch."

Gragg motioned with his gloved hand and swerved the car toward the racing bike, but the bike was far more maneuverable. It ducked around to the right side of the car. Again, automatic gunfire cracked at his tires.

Gragg shook his head. "Solid rubber, asshole."

He reached out into D-Space and started drawing from the surrounding horde—pulling dozens of remaining AutoM8s toward him. "You want to play? Then let's play."

Ross and a Korr lieutenant peered through the recessed postern gate. Dozens of AutoM8s crisscrossed the tarmac, circling Building Twenty-Nine. Ross looked across the barren tarmac leading to the ship channel a hundred yards away. It was the longest hundred yards he'd ever seen.

Philips sat in the corridor with several more Korr guards. A medic wound a bandage around her head to cover her injured eyes, while the others trained weapons on the short corridor behind them.

Philips looked up blindly. "What's the situation?"

Ross and the lieutenant slammed the door with a clang and turned to face her. A roaring motorcycle engine, gunshots, and screams echoed through the interior halls.

A guard stared down the corridor. "We can't stay here, sirs."

"We need to run for it, Nat. Those Razorbacks appear to know the floor plan. They're methodically clearing rooms."

The lieutenant piped in, "They're armored, Doctor. Light weapons don't stop them. At least not from the front."

She nodded gravely.

"There's a ship channel about a hundred yards away. If we can reach that, we should be safe."

Ross turned to the lieutenant and pointed toward what appeared to be dynamite sticks snugged into his web harness. "What are those?"

The man glanced down. "Magnesium flares. To signal the medevac chopper. The radio was down for—"

"Break 'em out. These AutoM8s probably target with infrared. Flares could distract them."

The lieutenant pulled out six flares. He handed three to Ross. "Just twist the top off and strike them. Like this . . ." He pantomimed the action.

"Let's test this." Ross struck the flare several times before it ignited. He held it, hissing and popping in the corridor. It burned a brilliant red. "Open the door."

One guard heaved the heavy steel door open, and Ross hurled the flare as far as he could off to the right. He and several guards watched closely as an AutoM8 swerved to avoid it. Another swung wide around it.

The lieutenant frowned. "So much for the infrared theory."

Philips looked toward his voice. "What's happening?"

Ross shook his head. "They're not attracted to the flares, Nat. They're avoiding them."

"Then they *are* using infrared. They're looking for human heat signatures. The flares must look like a raging fire."

Ross and the lieutenant exchanged looks. Ross nodded and knelt next to her. "You're right. We're in business, Nat." He removed his jacket and placed one empty sleeve in her hand, then grabbed the other one. "Don't let go of this. I'll guide you. We'll use the flares to conceal our human heat signature. The tarmac is flat. Just follow me and move as fast as you can."

"How many AutoM8s are there?"

"You don't want to know."

"Jon, I . . ." Her head darted to follow a roaring engine as it passed.

"I know it sucks you can't see. We'll get you to a hospital, but we need to do this to have any chance at all. Just run with me. You ready?"

She reluctantly nodded.

Ross turned to the Korr lieutenant. "You and your men ready, Lieutenant?"

A motorcycle engine revved and screams echoed behind them, punctuating his words. "Klausky, distribute these." He passed the magnesium flares. "We travel in a group. Place these on our perimeter."

The guards struck flares. Ross lit one for himself. Finally the six of them stood there with five lit flares. Ross pulled in front of the lieutenant with Philips in tow and looked out at the stream of AutoM8s racing past, waiting for a gap. "Okay . . . now!"

They bolted from the recessed doorway as a group and moved quickly across the tarmac—like deer running across a freeway.

The lieutenant barked, "Close it up!"

The nearest AutoM8s immediately screeched around and vectored toward them.

The lieutenant threw out his arm. "Stop moving! Stop!"

They all stopped, and the AutoM8 turned slightly aside, then roared past sixty feet to their left.

The group stood back-to-back on the tarmac, flares hissing and AutoM8s racing past them.

Ross shook his head. "Bad news, Nat; they're apparently attracted to lateral movement as well."

She nodded behind her blindfold. "Fires don't generally run around. I should have guessed Sobol would have more than one criterion."

The lieutenant pounded his helmeted forehead with his hand. "Hell of a time to realize that! Just fucking beautiful!" He looked back at the postern gate, already seventy feet behind them.

Ross's gaze followed a sedan racing past twenty feet away. "Okay. Let's try this: let's move *slowly* toward the water."

The lieutenant shook his head. "Back toward the postern gate."

Philips turned to him. "Jon's right. We can't head back toward the Razorbacks. These AutoM8s must have a threshold of movement detection. We move slowly."

The lieutenant gave Ross a venomous look, since he was serving as Philips's eyes. He then finally nodded. "All right, Doctor."

They all slid their feet across the tarmac as AutoM8s raced past doing loops around the building. They seemed to be coming closer with each pass, but the group of evacuees managed to traverse another hundred and fifty feet. The water's edge was tantalizingly close.

A guard tapped Ross on the shoulder. "Hey! Hey, this side! Look out!"

Ross turned to see a Dodge easing to a stop fifty feet away. Facing them. Other AutoM8s still raced past.

Philips turned toward it. "What is it?"

"That Dodge is getting suspicious."

She nodded. "Jon, you think it's referencing our location on a grid?"

He considered this. "You mean tracking targets over time instead of—"

"Enough!" The lieutenant pointed. "We've got incoming!"

Another sedan vectored toward them while the Dodge seemed to observe. The second car was accelerating fast.

The lieutenant shook his head. "Fuck this! Run for the waterline!"

Ross grabbed his arm. "It could be testing us! Stand still!"

The lieutenant pulled free. He and his men sprinted in a ragged line toward the jetty, opening fire on the cars as they ran.

The moment they did so, the incoming car targeted them, and the nearby Dodge accelerated past Ross and Philips, also giving chase. She cringed as it streaked past just feet to her left.

"Jon, what's happening?"

He pulled her close. "Wait, Nat!" He saw three more cars racing in—one headed toward him and Philips. Ross hurled the flare in its direction and then tugged on the jacket sleeve. "Run! Now!"

The lieutenant fired at another incoming car as he sprinted toward the waterline, but the first sedan overtook him, tossing his body up over its hood and smashing him into its windshield, then up over the roof. He flipped three times, then landed on the pavement just in time for the Dodge to gore him. His body jammed in its undercarriage and was dragged away. The other men scattered as AutoM8s ran them down. Sporadic gunfire was quickly replaced by the shrieks of injured men crawling toward safety as the cars circled back for the kill.

Philips glanced back reflexively. "What's happening?"

"Just run!"

He led Philips on a different, longer tack to the shoreline—away from the feeding frenzy of the AutoM8s. He and Philips were nearly at the water. Another car roared up behind them. Ross pulled hard on the jacket sleeve. They had reached the jetty stones.

"Jump!"

He could see her grit her teeth—going on blind faith in him. They arced out into air, splashing into the freezing water as the car hurtled inches over their heads. It landed ten feet beyond them and sent up a splash wall thirty feet high.

Ross and Philips both came up flapping their arms, Philips coughing up water. Ross grabbed her around the neck from behind and swam back toward the jetty stones again as the tail of the bobbing sedan settled back into the water, nearly coming down on her head. It flopped onto the waves, bubbling and hissing around them.

She sensed that something large had just missed her. "Jon!"

"It's okay! Wait. It's sinking."

"Where are the others?"

"They're gone."

She panted as they bobbed there for several seconds listening to bubbling water and distant engines on the tarmac above. His arm still around her. Soon there was just hissing.

"Okay, swim. Follow my voice."

———

Merritt cradled the UMP on the bike's broad gas tank and swerved from side to side trying to get around Loki's BMW. Each time he approached, Loki stabbed on the brakes. Finally the road widened again.

The corrugated fences of salvage yards and aging factories now fronted it. Merritt accelerated rapidly, roaring alongside the car.

He searched for some weakness in the armor and noticed that brushed steel knobs appeared at regular intervals on the roof, hood, and trunk. They looked like high-end cell-phone antennas—a dozen of them, evenly spaced.

Merritt braked and swerved as Loki tried to smash him into a line of parked cars. Merritt accelerated around the other side and lifted up the UMP. He glanced at the road, then took careful aim at the car. He fired a short burst. The shots ricocheted off the roof.

Loki swerved toward him again, and instead of dodging away immediately, Merritt let him come in closer. He took more careful aim and fired again—nailing a metal knob.

And barely denting it.

"Son of a bitch."

Behind Merritt eight sedans screeched in from side streets. He glanced back over his shoulder to see them surging after him. He raised the UMP one-handed and opened up with short, controlled bursts. The front tires of first one, then another blasted out, and they quickly fell behind as the others accelerated. He knocked out the tires on still a third.

The gun was empty. Merritt turned forward and saw ten more unmanned cars come in from side streets up ahead.

No way to reload. Time to concentrate. He tossed the UMP onto the hood of a nearby car, then ripped the throttle and drove howling past Loki.

Merritt dodged a hatchback emerging from a parking lot—which turned out to be a regular car with people in it. An onrushing AutoM8 immediately broadsided it. Half a dozen more AutoM8s streamed in from side streets behind him.

Merritt turned forward again to see the AutoM8s approaching up ahead, surging his way in interlocking slaloms. It was an impenetrable roving barrier. A demonstration of networked swarming behavior that no human drivers could match. Merritt had a couple of seconds at most. A score of AutoM8s were all around him, closing fast—more coming in every second.

He looked back at Loki's BMW, then swerved and stabbed the brakes—bringing himself just feet off Loki's front bumper. Still going seventy, he eased back on the throttle and, taking a breath, released his hold on the handlebars, falling backward onto Loki's front hood as the BMW bumped his bike's rear tire. The bike veered forward and to the side and was immediately crushed by a wall of oncoming AutoM8s, which raced past only inches to either side of the BMW. Several smashed head-on into pursuing AutoM8s, exploding into a whirlwind of plastic parts, glass, and tumbling metal.

Merritt hit Loki's hood hard, then slid back into the windshield. He rolled left, jamming his foot down onto a brushed metal knob at the corner of the hood, and clamped onto the wiper well with his hands. He braced his other foot against the knob on the far corner like it was a rock-climbing wall.

He glared into the blacked-out windshield and pointed threateningly. *You're not rid of me yet, asshole.*

———————

From the backseat of the BMW, Gragg stared in amazement at his pursuer now straddling the car hood. "You have got to be shitting me. . . ." He didn't see that coming. He watched the man like a television show through the glass as the guy pulled an automatic pistol from his coat and aimed at the corner of the windshield.

A series of muted cracks sounded. Divots appeared in the glass over a several-inch area. Gragg watched this calculated attempt to penetrate his armor with something bordering on admiration. The corners were typically the weakest spots on a bulletproof windshield. It was a cool-headed call—especially with scenery racing past behind him.

Too bad the glass was three inches of polycarbonate laminate that could stop a rifle bullet. A score of AutoM8s now surrounded Gragg's BMW in close order like a slavering pack of wolves. Gragg shook his head sadly and shouted at the windshield. "What now, crazy man? You're on an armored car! What were you thinking?"

Beyond the windshield the rider had reached down to his shoe and now brandished a killing knife as he braced himself with both feet and his other hand.

Gragg laughed. "Look out. He's got a knife!"

The rider turned, jammed the knife under the bottom edge of a satellite uplink node, and pried upward. The node peeled off with a shriek of bending metal.

The Voice came over the stereo system. *"Uplink . . . one . . . of . . . twelve . . . has failed."*

Gragg felt the rage building. "You son of a bitch! You're going for a ride now!"

With a wave of his gloved hands, the BMW went into a power slide and the rider was nearly flung off.

The Major's chopper came in low and fast over the industrial area, banking so that nothing but brick factory buildings were visible in the left windows. The Major clipped a monkey cord onto his harness and gave it two test pulls. He struggled to his feet as the chopper leveled off. The old wound in his knee was already acting up. An image of a mortar shell landing next to him in a patch of Nicaraguan mud flashed in his mind. *Ancient history.*

"There they are, Major!" The pilot pointed.

Below, the Major could see a red BMW screeching around drunkenly as it raced down the street, alternately braking and accelerating while a man tried to retain his grip on the roof. Twenty more vehicles swirled around the car, moving like a single organism. More vehicles converged on the site from all directions at high speed along cross streets, smashing into the occasional unlucky motorist. People fled for their lives. He shook his head. *What a goddamned mess.* How had this gotten so out of control? Behind him columns of black smoke rose here and there.

Let's give the city something else to look at. The Major pulled his L3 cell phone from his jacket and spoke to the pilot as he started dialing. "It's days like this that I almost miss working for the government."

The pilot's voice came over the closed-circuit headset. *"Almost."*

The Major laughed. The line picked up. "Project Hazmat." The Major turned to look back through the atmospheric haze at Building Twenty-Nine in the distance. "Demolition." A pause. "6-N-G-7-3-H-Z-6." Another pause. "On my mark. T-minus ten . . . nine . . ."

"We're almost there, Nat." Ross glanced back at Building Twenty-Nine, three hundred yards behind them now. It was burning somewhere inside, and the flaming wreckage of AutoM8s around it partially obscured it with smoke.

Philips spat out salt water. "I think I'm really blind."

"I don't think so."

"What if that was a ZM-87 Laser Blinder? My retinas would be gone."

"Doesn't make sense. Why permanently blind a target you're about to hack to pieces? It's probably meant to stun victims. I'd—"

Suddenly a wave of pressure blasted across their backs. A visible shockwave rippled through the atmosphere and pressed down around them—followed close on by a resounding *BOOM* that they felt more than heard.

They both went facedown in the water as the depths beneath them glowed orange and filled with the sound of splashing boulders and thousands of rock fragments. As they came up sucking for air, rocks and small boulders were landing all around them. Their ears were ringing.

Ross covered her with his body as the rocks continued to rain down. He turned to see a towering mushroom cloud roiling up from the jagged tops of Building Twenty-Nine's walls. The structure was a pool of flame with refrigerator-sized blocks of reinforced concrete still tumbling end over end across the runway. Burning debris trailing streamers of smoke sailed down from a thousand feet overhead. Metal sheets spun crazily as they fell. "Jesus Christ!"

"What happened?"

"The building. It's *gone!*"

From his perch on the BMW's roof, Merritt glanced back at a black mushroom cloud rising behind him above the factory buildings. "Son of a bitch . . ." *Later.*

Suddenly Loki accelerated the car, pulling Merritt down onto the trunk, where he stopped himself from rolling off by pushing his foot against the metal knob on the right rear corner. He grabbed on to the lip of the trunk lid.

Where the hell are the police?

He jammed the knife blade under another metal knob and tore it up from the sheet metal. The knob dangled by exposed wires until Merritt sawed through them.

The Voice intoned again, "Uplink . . . four . . . of . . . twelve . . . has failed."

Gragg had eight uplinks left. With triple redundancy he knew he needed at least four to adequately control the car and his army of AutoM8s. He turned around in his seat to see the man mere inches away from his face now—still clinging on. Gragg pounded the window. "That's it!"

The man's motorcycle helmet clunked against the glass, awkward in its bulk as he tried to keep his center of gravity down. In between erratic car movements, the rider quickly pulled the helmet off, tossing it over his shoulder. It was immediately crushed by trailing AutoM8s. The man then pressed his head down against the trunk lid.

Gragg could now see the rider's face. "Roy Merritt . . . holy shit." Gragg smiled in spite of himself. The famous Roy Merritt—known to every Daemon operative in the world. The man who tackled Sobol's home defense system and survived—the entire ordeal captured on Sobol's security cameras. The one and only Roy Merritt was hanging on to Gragg's car. Gragg was being pursued—and pursued damned well—by the Burning Man himself. He should have known. The son of a bitch had a knife, and he was doing more damage than a squad of corporate military. Gragg couldn't deny some level of admiration. Merritt had probed Gragg's defenses, found a hole—one that would be filled in the future—and improvised an exploit. What hacker couldn't admire the man's cojones? His instincts?

Gragg waved his hand, sending the BMW and its entire escort pack to a screeching halt. Merritt was thrown against the rear window. As the BMW lurched to a stop, Merritt stopped himself from rolling off the end of the trunk.

Gragg flipped his voice to the car's PA system and pounded his finger into the blacked-out glass in front of Merritt's face. "You're a fucking crazy man, Roy! You think I can't kill you the moment I get out of this car?"

Merritt shook his head. "You're under arrest!"

Gragg pounded the car seat, laughing. "That's my boy! Shit, I'll make you a deal: give me your autograph, and I won't kill you."

Suddenly Merritt's stomach exploded, splattering blood across the rear window. Merritt's face went slack and his eyes rolled up as his grip on the car released.

Stunned, Gragg watched Merritt roll off the end of the trunk and onto the pavement. Gragg waved his hand and brought the BMW farther down the road, so he could see Merritt, lying in the middle of the street. Another wave of his gloved hands and Gragg cleared a ring of AutoM8s all around him.

Gragg looked up.

A blue helicopter with a yellow logo hovered low behind them, about a hundred feet off the ground. Gragg looked down at Merritt, who was moving now, pulling himself along the center line of the road and leaving a trail of blood. Rage began to build in Gragg. He looked up again at the helicopter, death in his eyes. A man wearing a black hood and holding a sniper rifle kneeled in the open doorway. He looked straight back at Gragg. No Daemon call-out hovered above him.

The Major muttered under his breath. "What the hell are you waiting for, asshole?"

He fired a shot at Loki's rear window, pounding a divot just next to the kid's head. But Loki barely flinched. He was looking fixedly down at Merritt, crawling across the pavement. There was a fifteen-foot blood trail now. Merritt was fumbling through his jacket, quivering. Looking for something.

The Major sighed. "Goddamnit . . ."

He saw two Mexican workers open a salvage yard gate to peer out at all the commotion in the street. The Major gritted his teeth and turned the rifle in their direction. He squeezed off several rounds.

Spouts of blood erupted from the chest of the first worker. The man pitched back into the stunned hands of his companion—who The Major nailed straight between the eyes. They both fell from view.

Then The Major turned the crosshairs back onto Merritt. Merritt was lying on his back, panting doggedly, blood shining on his stomach, while he held two small pieces of paper before his eyes. The papers fluttered in the wind.

Why wasn't Gragg finishing him? Why wasn't this over yet?

The pilot's voice came in over the headset. "We need to go, Major."

The Major made his decision.

As Gragg stared, suddenly the top of Merritt's head exploded. Merritt's body slumped, twitching on the pavement.

"You motherfucker!" Gragg pounded his fists against the glass, staring at the sniper. "You motherfucker!"

Two more divots appeared in the window as sniper bullets slammed into it. Then the chopper banked away and took off low and fast above the factory buildings, heading out over the bay. It was soon lost to sight.

Gragg looked back down at the body in the street. Two small photographs wafted away from Merritt's dead fingers in the wind.

Ross pulled Philips up onto the quay on the far side of the ship channel. They both crawled to level ground, and after panting for a few moments, Ross looked up.

They were on the edge of a pipe storage yard. He eased Philips up so her back rested against a smooth concrete pylon. She looked dazed.

He turned to face the ruins of Building Twenty-Nine burning beneath a thunderhead of roiling black smoke across the water. A dozen more columns of smoke rose elsewhere in the distance. He could hear sirens wailing all over the city. It was a war zone.

Fireboats approached from the bay.

He knelt down next to Philips and brushed her wet hair away from her face. "Help is coming, Nat." He felt her trembling. "Are you okay?"

Her lips quivered slightly but she nodded. Her face contorted as she tried to contain tears. "How many do you think we lost?"

He took a deep breath. "Possibly everyone."

She put a hand to her mouth and started crying.

"It's not your fault, Natalie." He put a hand on her arm reassuringly.

"I was in charge!"

"No. You weren't. We just thought you were."

She stopped and turned her blindfolded eyes toward him.

"They were never going to let us stop the Daemon, Natalie."

"You're talking crazy! The government *created* the Task Force. We were betrayed by private industry."

"Private industry *is* your government. I thought you knew that."

"How can you say that to me?"

"Because it's true. Sobol knew it. The Daemon isn't attacking us, Nat. This is a struggle between two artificial organisms. The Daemon is just a new species of corporation."

They sat for a moment listening to the distant sirens.

"The old social order is dissolving, Nat. It happens every few centuries." He looked out across the burning city, then turned back to her. "I won't let Loki be our future."

She was trembling, whether from being wet or scared he couldn't tell.

He brushed his hand along her cheek and eased toward her blindfolded face. His face was only an inch away from hers. She could sense him there.

"I want you to know, every day my first and last thought is of you."

He removed his hand from her cheek. She blindly glanced around, listening, feeling forward with her hands. "Jon." A pause filled with the sound of sirens and approaching tug engines. She no longer felt his presence. "Jon!"

The only reply was an echoing, amplified voice from the water. *"Are you injured?"* A fireboat's engines throbbed in reverse.

Philips wept on the jetty as the roar of powerful engines drowned out the world.

Chapter 45:// Respawning

Newswatch.com

Massive **Explosion** and Fire at Illegal Chemical Dump Kills Twenty (**Alameda, CA**)—Federal authorities are still combing through the wreckage of an unlicensed hazardous chemical dump on the site of a decommissioned military base near **Oakland**. A massive explosion and fire there **killed twelve** undocumented immigrants and injured twenty more.

He floated in the darkness of his mind for what seemed decades. Thoughts came to him only as raw concepts—black despair, vertiginous fear. As he began to coalesce from the emptiness, he slowly pieced together scraps of his personality, regaining some measure of self. His mind no longer floated on a sea of nothingness. It was enmeshed in a carnal vessel again. That vessel was named Peter Sebeck.

He wasn't sure at what point he noticed someone talking—perhaps they had been there all along—but they kept up a persistent chatter while his mind came into focus in the darkness. At first Sebeck couldn't distinguish individual words, but as he concentrated they became more distinct.

". . . Christ figure is a recurring motif in many cultures; death and rebirth; symbolic turning of the seasons, all that crap. Wyle E. Coyote was a fucking Christ figure, man, and Acme Company was Rome, baby." A pause. "You can find it in Hindu legend, Sumerian mythology. Shit, you find it in modern folklore, like Rip van Winkle.

"Although Rip van Winkle didn't die. He *slept*. But that's the damned point: death as sleep. Sleep as death. Isn't our life a cycle of death and rebirth? Sleep and awakening? The promise of eternal life is a threat unless you get to start over. The mythmakers knew that. They weren't dummies, man."

The clattering of metal tools.

"They were the ones who invented rhyme and meter—the programming language for human memory in preliterary civilizations. It was a cultural *checksum*—a mnemonic device. You couldn't fuck with the code or the rhymes didn't work; and if the rhymes didn't work, people noticed. And so the knowledge of a people was passed down intact. It was a shamanic code. If you fucked with the code, then society lost its collective mind. Smell me?"

A pause.

"Hey, I think our boy's coming around."

Sebeck opened his eyes and slowly focused on a pasty-faced twenty-something kid sporting a tangled mane of black hair. A few days' beard shadowed the kid's neck and climbed higher than usual up his cheeks. This was a hairy guy.

Sebeck blinked at the overhead lights. He coughed and tried to sit up. A rock-hard surface greeted his elbows when he tried to push up. He immediately abandoned the attempt as his head began to swim.

The hairy kid leaned in close. "Hey, bro, sit back for a few. You're still trying to metabolize the meds."

Sebeck noticed the kid was wearing a lab coat. He tried to remember where he was. His brain was mashed potatoes.

Sebeck's voice croaked. "Where is this?"

"Phoenix Mortuary Services. I call it PMS."

Sebeck tried again to sit up, and he pushed aside the kid's hands when he tried to help. "Who—" He stopped short; his throat was sore as hell. He put a hand to his larynx. No exterior damage.

Sebeck leaned to one side and looked around. His eyes tried to focus to a greater distance. He was in a long room with several medical examination tables. Oak cabinetry lined the walls. A strong chemical odor assaulted his nose. He'd smelled this before. Formaldehyde.

Sebeck snapped alert; the body of an old man lay naked on a nearby metal table. The old man was definitely dead because his body had the pallor and flattened appearance that comes when blood pressure and breath leave the human frame.

"Where am I?"

"Like I said, my man: funeral home. That's where they send dead people. It's the law. And you, my friend, are legally dead. Got the paperwork to prove it."

Sebeck looked around for a few moments more, then brought his gaze back to the kid. "Who are *you*?"

The kid wiped his hand on his lab coat, then extended it. "Laney Price. Body prep. I take out the pacemakers and shit like that. That stuff'll blow up if it goes in the furnace."

Sebeck ignored Price's hand and tried to shake his head clear. He glanced down, then swung his legs over the edge of the table and sat up.

Price rushed to hold him steady, but Sebeck pushed him back. He glanced down at his own body. He was wearing casual slacks and a pullover shirt. Next to him on the table lay his crumpled prison khakis. He picked them up, balling them up in his fists. *That's right.* He remembered now. He had just been executed for murdering federal officers. He was the most hated man in America.

He dropped the khakis and sat motionless, staring at his own hands. A wave of emotion overcame him, and he started to breathe in fits.

He was alive.

Price clapped a hand around his shoulder. "Hey, Sergeant, you're not dead, man. Relax."

Sebeck threw off Price's arm and grabbed him by the throat. "What the fuck is going on!"

Price extricated himself as Sebeck nearly swooned from the effort. "You tell *me*. You brought me here."

Sebeck was still trying to clear his head. God, his throat hurt. "What are you talking about?"

"Look . . ." Price stomped off and tore a newspaper clipping from its place on a nearby bulletin board. He came back to the examining table and pointed at the clipping—a file picture of Sebeck below the headline *Sebeck's Macabre Message.*

"Message received, compadre."

Sebeck grabbed the article. It was months old. His head started to clear as the adrenaline kicked in. *It worked.* The Daemon had saved him.

But why?

Before he could ask another question, Price tossed him a plastic water bottle. "Electrolytes. Better drink up."

Sebeck realized just how thirsty he was. He cracked open the water and drank deeply. His throat throbbed.

Price continued. "Ol' One-eye's been asking for ya. He's all up in my grill, an I'm like, yo, back off, Methuselah. That sprite is a screen saver from hell, I swear it, man. He's a fourth-dimensional stain."

Sebeck finished the bottle. "You want to say that again in English?"

"For being in charge, you seem woefully uninformed."

"What do you mean, 'in charge'?"

Price threw up his hands. "See, you gotta talk to One-eye. Hang on a sec." Price headed over to a locked cabinet, pulled out a choked key ring, and started cycling through the keys. He talked while he searched. "You know, it's an honor to finally meet you. You drew a lot of ink. Most of it said you were evil incarnate, but we all know that's horse-shit. That Anji Anderson chick is out to get you, but evil or not, that bitch is fuckin' hot. I'd do her. Evil Daemon bitch. Laney likes the bad girls. . . ."

Sebeck was looking around the room again. "You were talking to someone earlier. Something about myths and rhyme."

Price paused. "You heard that?"

"Is someone else here?" Sebeck glanced around cautiously.

Price just snickered to himself. "Yeah, bad habit from working with dead people." He stuck a key in the lock. "They're good listeners, though. Haven't heard a complaint yet."

He rummaged around in the cabinet and came out with a sealed plastic box. Price walked back to the examining table, struggling to open the seal. "Damned things. It's the Asians that do this." He fished around among the scalpels on his worktable, near the body of the old man. "You know, the average Chinese factory worker must think Americans are insane. Picture this: you work at a plant that makes Hallow-een stuff—you know, like, rubber severed heads. And you're all like: Americans decorate their homes with severed heads? These fuckers are savages, man."

Sebeck slowly leaned forward and tried to stand. He still felt woozy.

"I wouldn't do that yet if I were you."

"You're not me." Sebeck managed to stand, still holding the table to steady himself. "So, you say I created this place?" He glanced around. "By sending that message to the Daemon?"

Price got the box open. "All will become clear, young grasshopper, when you talk to One-eye. Then maybe he'll get off my ass." Price pulled an intricate and expensive-looking pair of sports sunglasses from the box. It was sealed in yet another plastic bag. "Why do they do this shit?" He started biting into the plastic and twisting.

"One-eye?"

Price gave him a look. "Do you have several one-eyed undead freaks stalking you, Sergeant? Should I be more specific?"

Sobol.

Price now pulled the glasses out of the bag. They were stylish, with yellow-tinted lenses and hip frames, but the posts were unusually thick. Price also pulled a thick beltlike device from the box. He glanced at Sebeck and started adjusting a strap. "Just take me a sec. You're a what, size thirty-eight?"

"Thirty-four."

"Damn. I've gotta lose about forty pounds myself. But then again, you were on the"—air quotes here—"Lompoc prison diet."

Sebeck just pointed at the glasses.

"Oh, HUD—heads-up display. It's an interface to the Daemon network. Check this shit out."

"The Daemon network?"

"Can't see the TOP without the HUD."

"Stop with the acronyms."

"I've got acronyms for my acronyms." He held up the belt and clicked a battery into place. "Ready. Here, put this on." He handed it to Sebeck.

Sebeck took it warily. It was like a thick money belt and was made of black, stretchable nylonlike material with a sleek titanium buckle.

Price was fiddling with the glasses. "The belt's a combination satellite phone, GPS, and wearable computer. Methane-oxide fuel cell battery'll last for about three days. Works in conjunction with the glasses. Be careful with it. It's ruggedized and water-resistant, but don't go driving nails with it. The glasses alone cost about fifty thousand dollars."

Sebeck was taken aback. "What, are you joking? Who paid for them?"

"Daemon's got cash, bro. Hell, you ain't seen nothing."

"Why's it giving them to me? I want to *destroy* the Daemon."

"Because it wants to have a word with you."

Sebeck considered this for a few moments. Then he fastened the belt around his waist. It fit well and felt like a lifting belt.

Price slid the HUD glasses onto Sebeck's face.

Sebeck wrapped the band around his head. "Nice fit."

"Should be a perfect fit. They scanned your head."

"They? Who's they?"

Price shrugged. "Fabricators. Micro-manufacturers. Hell, who knows? The Daemon shipped it to me."

Sebeck noticed the lens flicker momentarily, then return to normal.

"It's got a retinal scanner and a heart pulse sensor. If you're a member of the network and still alive, it knows who you are and what your rights are. It senses the moment you take them off. Put 'em on, you just logged on. Take 'em off, you just logged off."

Price walked briskly over to a cluttered desk nearby. "Wait a sec." He grabbed another pair of glasses sitting there and put them on.

They looked at each other.

Suddenly, Sebeck's lenses blinked, then information appeared at the top and bottom of the "screen." He focused on Price and was surprised to see a name call-out box hovering over Price—just like in the game *The Gate*. Price's screen name was apparently ChunkyMonkey.

"You gotta be shitting me. . . ."

"No, man. Check this out." He pointed at Sebeck's glasses. "See the green bar-stack next to my name? That's my network power relative to you. That number seven—that's my skill level."

Price appeared to have seven bars.

"Network power?"

"It's a point system. I see no bars—that means you're a wuss compared to me. How many bars do you see?"

"Seven."

"That means I'm nominally seven times as powerful as you. It has to do with the *Shamanic Interface*, but we'll cover that later. Right now, we gotta see One-eye before he goes into a loop. He must know you're awake by now, since you just logged on."

Sebeck was having difficulty absorbing the reality of it all.

Price approached him. "Here . . ." He adjusted one side of the glasses, lowering a short piece of metal. "Sound boom. Gives you audio by vibrating the bones in your head. Works as a microphone the same way."

Price motioned for Sebeck to hurry. "You good to walk, or should I get a wheelchair?"

"I can walk."

Price came up alongside and helped to steady him. "This way."

Price brought them toward an alcove into which was set a pair of imposing oak doors about nine feet tall. Sebeck still felt dizzy and the glasses weren't helping. Inexplicable information kept flashing and winking at him. "God, it's like walking with sports scores flashing before my eyes."

"Never mind that. You can customize it later. If you want to see without the glasses, flip the lenses up—they're on a hinge. Don't take the glasses off, or you'll log off the system—and it'll take a few seconds to get logged back on. You'll get used to it."

They reached the door. Price motioned for Sebeck to stay put, then he grabbed the door handles. He glanced back. "Sergeant, welcome to the Daemon's darknet." He opened the doors.

They swung inward, revealing a plushly appointed but rather stodgy office with stuffed leather chairs and thick carven furniture. It looked like the office of an eighteenth-century natural philosopher. Bookcases and curio cabinets filled with insect and rock specimens lined the windowless walls. There was dust everywhere.

But what riveted Sebeck's gaze was the translucent apparition of Matthew Sobol sitting behind the big mahogany desk, hands folded, as if waiting patiently. It was post-surgery Sobol, with his open eye socket, hollow cheeks, and bald head—a shriveled wreckage of a man ravaged by chemotherapy and cancer. He was wearing the same suit he wore at his funeral.

His spectre nodded in somber greeting. "Detective Sebeck. I've been waiting for you." He motioned for Sebeck to come forward. "Please, have a seat."

Sebeck looked to Price.

Price nodded in commiseration. "I know. It's freaky, but don't worry. You're not Hamlet. This is a *Temporal Offset Projection*, Sergeant—it's an interactive 3-D avatar projected over the GPS grid. It's only visible and audible in your HUD glasses."

Sebeck studied the spectre. He flipped up his glass lenses. Sobol disappeared. He flipped them back down again and Sobol's spectre returned. "It's a private dimension."

"Actually, it's a dynamic array capable of encapsulating a variable number of dimensional elements."

Sebeck looked at him blankly.

Price patted him on the back. "You're right. It's a private dimension." He made a scooting motion. "Better sit down. He'll know if you don't do it." Sebeck stepped forward and sat in one of the stuffed leather chairs. He wiped a thin layer of dust from the armrests and shifted to keep the computer belt from pressing into his back.

Sebeck could actually see Sobol more clearly now, since he was closer. Sobol's phantasm was gaunt, and the gaping eye socket looked horrific. He really did resemble a restless spirit wandering the Earth.

Sobol looked toward Price. "Leave us."

"Damn." Price looked to Sebeck. "You're on your own, my man. I gotta leave."

Sebeck gestured to the apparition of Sobol. "What the hell do I say to this thing?"

"I was hoping *you'd* know." Price rushed out, closing the double doors behind him.

Sobol's spectre gazed at the doors. A loud *click* sounded as they locked.

After a few moments, Sobol turned again to Sebeck. He smiled slightly. "I'm glad it was you, Sergeant. You were my favorite. So damaged by your choices. You never understood games. Maybe that's why the world was such a mystery to you."

Sebeck stared. "Why don't you just die already?"

Sobol paused. "Mammals of every species indulge in play. Games are Nature's way of preparing us to face difficult realities. Are you finally ready to face reality, Sergeant?"

"Kiss my ass."

Sobol's spectre pointed at his own forehead. "It's so clear here. Even if you can't see it." He lowered his arm. "Civilization is about to fail."

Sebeck felt a wave of anxiety wash over him. *Kee-hrist.*

"The modern world is a highly efficient, precision machine. But that's its flaw—one wrench in the works and it all grinds to a halt. So what does our generation get? A culture of lies to hide weakness. Decreasing freedom. All to conceal one simple fact: the assumptions upon which our civilization is based are no longer valid. If you doubt me, ask yourself: why was I able to accomplish this?"

Sebeck shifted uncomfortably in his seat.

"But what if we corrected civilization's weakness—as painful as that correction might be?"

Sobol changed expression, looking more relaxed. "But you're probably confused. Why did I frame you? It's simple: you were bait—bait that they took. The weak hide their weakness. By now, the plutocrats have put their money in safer havens, and I have closely watched this transfer. Now they are more vulnerable than ever." Sobol grinned humorlessly. "You were my Trojan horse, Sergeant."

Sebeck's fingernails nearly tore through the chair leather. "Fuck you! You destroyed my life!"

Sobol's spectre flickered almost imperceptibly. "An analysis of your voice patterns is revealing. Prosody tells me that you are agitated. Save your anger, Detective. It will make no difference to the outcome."

Sebeck ground his teeth.

"Who will mourn for you, Sergeant? No one. You and I share that. We have sacrificed for the greater good. In gratitude I cared for your family in your absence—when no one else would. Your family has no idea that I am their benefactor."

Sebeck leaned forward, another rage building. "What have you done?"

Sobol continued. "They will continue to have good fortune—but only as long as I can count on you, Detective."

"You son of a bitch!" Sebeck swept a curio case off of Sobol's desk, sending it crashing into the wall behind him. Glass shards flew everywhere. "Don't involve my family!"

Sobol's spectre flickered again. "There is that pattern again. You're upset. I defer to your judgment in this matter. Answer 'yes' or 'no': should the Daemon withdraw support from your family?"

Sebeck stopped short. He took a breath and realized he had no idea how to respond. If—

"Respond 'yes' or 'no'—or I will make a random choice for you."

"Damn you!"

"Answer NOW. Do you want the Daemon to withdraw financial support from your family?"

Sebeck shook his head and closed his eyes. "No."

"Thank you. The Daemon will continue to provide for them. Now, please sit down."

"I hope you're burning in hell." Sebeck sat.

"We both know you don't believe in hell."

Sebeck sat stunned at the spectre's response.

"Yes, I've done quite a bit of research on you, Sergeant. But don't confuse me with someone who gives a damn about you. You will live or die, and I don't care which. The only thing I care about is the Daemon's goal. There's a greater good in this than you can understand—perhaps than you'll ever understand. Since you were clever enough to save yourself, you may be of some use to me still. If the Daemon triumphs, tens of millions will die. If it fails, billions will die, and we will fall back to a seventeenth-century agrarian economy. Those are the stakes, Sergeant."

Sebeck was practically climbing out of his skin. He whispered under his breath, "Goddamn you . . ."

"You want to destroy the Daemon—but you offer nothing in its place. How can you expect to handle the future if you can't even handle the present? I'll tell you what the Daemon is: the Daemon is a remorseless system for building a distributed civilization. A civilization that perpetually regenerates. One with no central authority. Your only option is what form that civilization takes. And that depends on the actions of people like you."

Sobol stood and started pacing behind the desk. For the first time Sebeck noticed that the desk chair was also a phantasm—there was no real chair behind the desk.

"There are those who resist necessary change. Even now they think only of protecting their investments. I am at war with them. A war that you'll never see on the evening news. And to my mind, the outcome of this war will decide whether civilization flourishes—or collapses into a thousand-year dark age. Perhaps even with the eclipse of the human race as the dominant species on this planet."

Sobol ran his hand along the scar on his skull. "My enemies will show themselves soon, Sergeant. As much as you despise me, they are your true enemy. I am merely an inevitable consequence of human progress. An unfeeling, unthinking thing."

Sebeck sat in stunned silence for several moments.

Sobol's spectre sat on the edge of the desk near Sebeck. "I suspect that democracy is not viable in a technologically advanced society. Free people wield too much ability to destroy. But I will give you the chance to determine the truth of this. If you fail to prove the viability of democracy in man's future, then humans will serve society—not the other way around. Either way, a change is coming. I see it. As plainly as I see you sitting there."

Sebeck realized Sobol had indeed envisioned this moment—for here Sebeck sat.

"Do you accept the task of finding justification for the freedom of humanity, Sergeant? Yes or no?"

Sebeck sat staring at the floor. He missed his family. He was tired of being alone. Of feeling the hatred of the world seeping through the walls of every room he was in. Why was this happening to him? Why did it have to be him?

"Do you accept this task, Sergeant? Yes or no?"

Son of a bitch.

"I will ask one more time: will you—"

"Yes."

Sobol's spectre flickered briefly, then nodded. "Good, Sergeant. I'm glad you could overcome your hatred of me."

Sobol stood and walked toward the wall. His steps creaked on the floor to complete the illusion. He turned toward Sebeck. "Walk with me."

With a wave of the spectre's hand, a section of the wall opened in reality, revealing a narrow back hallway. Wainscoting and rich wallpaper lined the walls.

Sebeck rose reluctantly, glancing back at the sealed double doors he'd entered through, then looked again at Sobol's phantom padding down the hall.

Sobol turned back again to look over his shoulder. "Please, Sergeant."

Sebeck gritted his teeth and followed on Sobol's heels as the apparition opened another door at the end of the hallway. Brilliant sunlight and a mild, fresh breeze filled the hall. The sound of rustling leaves came in on the wind.

Sebeck stopped. It had been many months since he'd been outside. His nostrils flared, taking in the fragrance. Balmy air whirled around him.

Sobol's spectre beckoned him.

Sebeck strode down a short series of steps and into the sunlight. He hurried to catch up with Sobol, who was already moving across a green stretch of lawn beneath the shade of an ancient California oak. They were in a low-walled yard at the back of a great Victorian mansion.

Sebeck turned on his heels, drinking in the sun and the scenery. The Lompoc Valley lay around him. Rolling grassy hills dotted with oaks, blue mountains loomed on the horizon. Split-rail fences undulated over the contours of the land. The wind waved through the grass. The beauty of it almost brought Sebeck to tears.

He was alive.

Sobol stood next to the great oak, looking down at the ground.

Sebeck moved to catch up, and as he reached the tree he could see a small headstone there, set in the grass near the low wall. Sebeck read the simple inscription.

Matthew Sobol—1969

The inscription was centered—leaving no room for a date of death.

Sobol's spectre gazed out over the valley below. "I loved this place." He turned to Sebeck. "Are you familiar with the Fates, Sergeant? Greek legend said that they spun the threads of men's lives and cut them at a length of their choosing. Like the Fates, I severed the thread of your life. . . ."

Sobol faced toward the horizon and extended his hand. Suddenly a glowing blue line appeared in D-Space, extending from Sobol's palm and tracing almost instantly down the nearby road and through the hills, to be lost beyond the horizon.

"Here is your new thread. Only you can see it, and it leads to a future only you can find."

At that, Sobol's ghostly image turned and started descending slowly into the ground of his grave, as if walking down ethereal steps. He moved methodically, slowly—like a monk in procession. Just before Sobol's head disappeared beneath the soil, he stopped and looked up, directly into Sebeck's eyes. "The guardian of this node will teach you all you need to know. When you leave this place, Sergeant, remember that they killed Peter Sebeck once. Do not doubt that they will kill him again if he reappears. Alive you're a grave risk to their world—such is your fate."

With one last glance, Sobol stepped down into his grave and disappeared beneath the grass.

Sebeck stared for several minutes at the spot where his nemesis had disappeared. His thoughts were turbulent—not yet forming into anything definite. Why didn't he feel rage? Depression? He finally looked up, and the thread was still there, undulating over the land, projected from where Sebeck stood. He flipped up the HUD glass lenses, and the glowing thread disappeared. He flipped them down, and the line returned.

Sebeck heard the crunch of gravel, and he turned to see a black Lincoln Town Car easing to a stop just beyond the back wall gate.

Laney Price got out and moved to open the rear car door. He motioned dramatically for Sebeck to get inside.

With one last glance at Sobol's grave, Sebeck approached the car, pushing open the wrought iron gate.

Price nodded, still holding open the rear door. "I'm supposed to help you, Sergeant. Sobol said you'd know where to go."

Sebeck gazed back along the road behind them—away from the blue thread. He thought of his previous life. Of those he'd left behind. Of the sheriff's department, Laura, and his son, Chris. Of everyone and everything he'd ever known. Peter Sebeck was dead.

He turned to face the blue line again, tracing a glowing filament down the road and toward a distant horizon.

"I'll drive."

THE END

ACKNOWLEDGMENTS

It's been said that writing is a solitary profession, but I just don't see it. On the long journey to get this book published, I've met countless people who gave both their time and effort to pass *Daemon* on to others. I would be remiss if I did not show my appreciation to the following folks:

Rick Klau and the whole gang at Google for finding a needle in a haystack. Stewart Brand and Peter Schwartz of the Long Now Foundation for opening so many doors. Jeffrey Rayport for making key connections. Don Donzal and the Ethicalhacker.net team for checking the details. John Robb at Global Guerrillas for bringing serious folks to the table. Jim Rapoza at *eWeek* for being the first to note *Daemon* in print. Craig Newmark of Craigslist for being cool to an unknown writer. Brilliant individuals such as Thomas L. and the inimitable Alexi S., who impact your life in ways you'll never know. Tom Leonard at Valve Software for early encouragement. Mike and Carol Caley for their friendship and confidence in me. Frank and Charlene Gallego for bringing *Daemon* everywhere I could not. Anne Borgman for catching things everyone else missed. And my gratitude to Frank DeCavalcante, for inspiring a lifelong love of books and writing.

Profound thanks as well to my wonderful literary agent, Bridget Wagner, at Sagalyn Agency, and also to my editor, Ben Sevier, for taking a chance on me and for being a joy to work with.

Thanks especially to Adam Winston, James Hankins, and Don Lamoreaux, writers and friends whom I've long admired and whose advice on early drafts of this book was much appreciated.

Thanks also to Stuart McClure, Joel Scambray, and George Kurtz for bringing attention to cracks in the system, and to Thom Hartmann,

P. W. Singer, Neil Gershenfeld, Carl Zimmer, John Perkins, Kevin Phillips, and Jared Diamond, whose published works helped to crystallize some of the sociopolitical themes in this story.

Finally, tremendous thanks to my wife, Michelle, for her tireless efforts to help this book see the light of day. And for knowing I was a writer but marrying me anyway . . .

FURTHER READING

You can learn more about the technologies and themes explored in *Daemon* by visiting www.thedaemon.com or through the following books:

Hacking Exposed by Stuart McClure, Joel Scambray, and George Kurtz—McGraw Hill

Fab by Neil Gershenfeld—Basic Books

Parasite Rex by Carl Zimmer—Touchstone Books

Confessions of an Economic Hit Man by John Perkins—Berrett Koehler

Corporate Warriors by P. W. Singer—Cornell University Press

Unequal Protection by Thom Hartmann—Rodale

Wealth and Democracy by Kevin Phillips—Broadway

Collapse by Jared Diamond—Viking

ABOUT THE AUTHOR

Daniel Suarez is an independent systems consultant to Fortune 1000 companies. He has designed and developed enterprise software for the defense, finance, and entertainment industries. An avid gamer and technologist, he lives in Los Angeles, California. *Daemon* is his first novel.